Unfortunately Yours

Unfortunately Yours

a novel

TESSA BAILEY

AVON

An Imprint of HarperCollinsPublishers

HarperCollins books may be purchased for educational, business, or sales promotional use. For information, please email the Special Markets Department at SPsales@harpercollins.com.

FIRST EDITION

Designed by Diahann Sturge

Cat with bow tie illustration © lexlinx / Shutterstock

Library of Congress Cataloging-in-Publication Data has been applied for.

ISBN 978-0-06-323903-6 (paperback)
ISBN 978-0-06-323907-4 (library hardcover)

23 24 25 26 27 LBC 5 4 3 2 1

Acknowledgments

When I sat down to write this enemies-to-lovers book, I asked myself, "What is the one thing I need to feel satisfied after a book about two people feuding? What is going to make me feel better after the harshly spoken words?" The answer came to me right away. I need irrefutable proof that the hero has loved the heroine all along. I hope you'll agree that is exactly what we have here. August and Natalie are some of my favorite characters I've ever written—please enjoy them and their stubborn with a side of vulnerable ways.

Thank you so much to everyone who worked on this beloved book of mine, with a special thanks to my incredible editor, Nicole Fischer, who never fails to help a story sparkle. Thank you, as well, to Daniel H. who let me ask him questions about finance. I still can't do math.

And as always, thank you to the best READERS on earth. Your tits look insane.

Love,
Tessa

Unfortunately Yours

Chapter One

$\mathcal{F}$or as long as August Cates could remember, his dick had ruined everything.

In seventh grade, he'd gotten a hard-on during a pep rally while standing in front of the entire school in football pants. Since his classmates couldn't openly call him Woody in the presence of their teachers, they'd called him Tom Hanks, instead. It stuck all through high school. To this day, he cringed at the very mention of *Toy Story*.

Trust your gut, son.

His navy commander father had always said that to him. In fact, that was pretty much all he'd *ever* said, by way of advice. Everything else constituted a direct order. Problem was, August tended to need a little more instruction. A diagram, if possible. He wasn't a get-it-right-on-the-first-try type of man. Which was probably why he'd mistaken his "gut" for his dick.

Meaning, he'd translated his father's advice into . . .

Trust your dick, son.

August straightened the wineglass in front of him in order to forgo adjusting the appendage in question. The glass sat on a silver tray, seconds from being carried to the panel of judges.

Currently, the three smug elitists were sipping a Cabernet offering that had been entered into the Bouquets and Beginners competition by another local vintner. The crowd of Napa Valley wine snobs leaned forward in their folding chairs to hear the critique from one judge in particular.

Natalie Vos.

The daughter of a legendary winemaker.

Vos Vineyard heiress and all-around plague on his fucking sanity.

August watched her full lips perch on the edge of the glass. They were painted a kind of lush plum color today. They matched the silk blouse she wore tucked into a leather skirt and he swore to God, he could feel the crush of that leather in his palms. Could feel his fingertips raking down her bare legs to remove those high heels with spikes on the toes. Not for the first time—no, incredibly far from the first time—he mentally kicked himself in the ass for sabotaging his chances of taking Natalie Vos to bed. She wouldn't touch him through a hazmat suit now, and she'd told him as much umpteen times.

His chances of winning this contest didn't bode well.

Not only because he and Natalie Vos were enemies, but because his wine sucked big sweaty donkey balls. Everyone knew it. Hell, August knew it. The only one to call him out on it, however, was preparing to deliver her verdict to the audience.

"Color is rich, if a bit light. Notes of tobacco in front. Citrus aftertaste. Veering toward acidic, but . . ." She held the wine up to the sun and studied it through the glass. "Overall very enjoyable. Admirable for a two-year-old winery."

Murmurs and golf claps all around from the audience.

The winemaker thanked the judges. He actually bowed to Natalie while retrieving his glass and August couldn't stifle an eye roll to save his life. Unfortunately, Natalie caught the action and raised a perfect black brow, signaling August forward for his turn at the judging table, like a princess summoning a commoner— and didn't that fit their roles to a T?

August didn't belong in this sunny five-star resort and spa courtyard on a Saturday afternoon ferrying wine on a silver tray to these wealthy birdbrains who overinflated the importance of wine so much it felt like satire. He didn't belong in sophisticated St. Helena. Wasn't cut out to select the best bunch of grapes at the grocery store, let alone cultivate soil and grow them from scratch to make his very own brand of wine.

I tried, Sammy.

He'd really fucking tried. This contest had a grand prize of ten thousand dollars and that money was August's last hope to keep the operation alive. If given another chance, he would be more hands-on during the fermentation process. He'd learned the hard way that "set it and forget it" didn't work for shit with wine. It required constant tasting, correcting, and rebalancing to prevent spoilage. He might do better if given another season to prove himself.

For that, he needed money. And he had a better chance of getting Natalie in the sack than winning this competition, which was to say, he had no chance whatsoever—because, yeah. His wine blew chunks. He'd be lucky if they managed to let it rest on their taste buds for three seconds, let alone declare him the winner. But August would try to the bitter end, so he would never look back and wonder if he could have done more to bring this secondhand dream to life.

August strode to the judge's table and set the glasses of wine in front of Natalie with a lot less ceremony than his competitors had, sniffed, and stepped back, crossing his arms. Disdain stared back at him in the form of the two most annoyingly beautiful eyes he'd ever seen. Sort of a whiskey gold, ringed in a darker brown. He could still remember the moment the expression in those eyes had gone from *take-me-to-bed-daddy* to *please-drink-poison*.

Witch.

This was her domain, however. Not his. At six-foot-three and with a body still honed for the battles of his past life as a Navy SEAL, he fit into this panorama about as well as Rambo at a bake sale. The shirt the entrants had been asked to wear for the competition didn't fit, so he'd hung it from the back pocket of his jeans. Maybe he could use it to clean up the wine when the judges spit it out.

"August Cates of Zelnick Cellar," Natalie said smoothly, handing glasses of wine to her fellow judges. Outwardly, she appeared cool as ever, her unflappable New York demeanor on full display, but he could see her breath coming faster as she geared herself up to drink what amounted to sludge in a glass. Of the three judges, Natalie was the only one who knew what was coming, because she'd tasted his wine once before—and had promptly compared it to demon piss. That occasion was also known as the night he'd blown his one and only chance to sweat up the sheets with Princess Vos herself.

Since that ill-fated evening, their relationship had been nothing short of contentious. If they happened to see each other on Grapevine Way or at a local wine event, she liked to discreetly scratch her eyebrow with a middle finger, while August usually inquired how many glasses of wine she'd plowed through since nine A.M.

In theory, he hated her. They hated each other.

Dammit, though, he couldn't seem to *actually* do it. Not all the way.

And it all went back to August's mistaking his gut for his dick as a youngster.

As in, *Trust your dick, son.*

And that part of his anatomy might as well be married to Natalie Vos. Married with six kids and living in the Viennese countryside wearing matching playclothes fashioned out of curtains, à la *The Sound of Music.* If all of August's decisions were up to his downstairs brain, he would have apologized the night of their first argument and asked for another shot to supply her with wall-to-wall orgasms. But it was too late now. He had no choice but to return the loathing she radiated at him, because his upstairs brain knew all too well why their relationship would never have gone past a single night.

Natalie Vos had privilege and polish—not to mention money—coming out of her ears.

At thirty-five, August was broker than a fingerless mime.

He'd dumped all of his life savings into opening a winery, with no experience or guidance, and losing this contest would be the death blow to Zelnick Cellar.

August's chest tightened like he was being strapped to a gurney, but he refused to break eye contact with the heiress. The growing ache below his throat must have been visible on his face because, slowly, Natalie's smug expression melted away and she frowned at him. Leaned in and whispered for his ears alone, "What's going on with you? Are you missing WrestleMania to be here or something?"

"I wouldn't miss WrestleMania for my own funeral." He snorted. "Just taste the wine, compare it to moldy garbage, and get it over with, princess."

"Actually, I was going to ordain it as something like . . . rat bathwater." She gestured at him with fluttery fingers. "Seriously, what's up? You have more asshole energy than usual."

He sighed, looking out at the rows of expectant spectators who were either in tennis whites or leisure wear that probably cost more than his truck. "Maybe because I'm trapped in an episode of *Succession*." Time to change the channel. Not that he had a choice. "Do your worst, Natalie."

She wrinkled her nose at his wine. "But you're already so good at being the worst."

August huffed a laugh. "Too bad they're not giving out a prize for sharpest fangs. You'd be unmatched."

"Are you comparing me to a vampire? Because your *wine* is what sucks."

"Just down the whole glass without tasting it, like you usually do."

Was that hurt that flashed in her eyes before she hid it?

Certainly not. "You are an—" she started.

"Ready to begin, Miss Vos?" asked one of the other judges, a silver-haired man in his fifties who wrote for *Wine Enthusiast* magazine.

"Y-yes. Ready." She shook herself and pulled back, regaining her poise and sliding her fingers around the stem of the wineglass containing August's most recent Cabernet. A groove remained between her brows as she swirled the glass clockwise and lifted it to her nose to inhale the bouquet. The other judges were already coughing, looking at each other in confusion. Had they accidentally been served vinegar?

They spat it out into the provided silver buckets almost in tandem.

Natalie, however, seemed determined to hold off as long as possible.

Her face turned red, tears forming in her eyes.

But to his shock, the swallow went down her throat, followed by a gasp for air.

"I'm afraid . . ." began one of the judges, visibly flustered. The crowd whispered behind August. "I'm afraid something must have gone terribly wrong during your process."

"Yes . . ." The other judge laughed behind his wrist. "Or a step was left out entirely."

The rows of people behind him chuckled, and Natalie's attention strayed in that direction. She opened her mouth to say something and closed it again. Normally, she wouldn't hesitate to cut him off at the knees, so what was this? Pity? She'd chosen *this* moment? This moment, when he needed to walk out of here with some semblance of pride, to go easy on him?

Nah. Not having it.

He didn't need this spoiled, trust-fund brat to pull her punches. He'd seen shit during combat that people on this well-manicured lawn couldn't even fathom in their wildest dreams. He'd jumped out of planes into pitch-black skies. Existed on pure stubbornness for weeks on end in the desert. Suffered losses that still felt as though they'd happened yesterday.

And yet you couldn't even make decent wine.

He'd failed Sam.

Again.

A fact that hurt a damn sight more than this rich girl judging him harshly in front of these people he'd probably never see again after today. In fact, he needed Natalie to just drop the hammer already, so he could show her how little he cared about her opinion. It was his friend's dream never being realized that should hurt. Not her verdict.

August propped his hands on the judging table and leaned forward, seeing nothing but the beautiful, black-haired dream haunter and watching her golden eyes go wide at his audacity. "You're not waiting for a bribe, are you? Not with a last name like Vos." He winked at her and leaned down until only Natalie could hear the way he dropped his voice. "Unless you're hoping for a different kind of bribe, princess, because that can be arranged."

She threw wine in his face.

For the second time.

Honestly, he couldn't even blame her.

He was lashing out over his failure and Natalie was a convenient target. But he wasn't going to apologize. What good would it do? She already hated him and he'd just found a way to strengthen that feeling. The best thing he could do to make up for the insult to Natalie was to leave town—and that's exactly what he planned to do. He'd been given no choice.

With wine dripping from his five-o'clock shadow, August pushed off the table, swiped a sleeve over his damp face, and stormed across the lawn to the parking lot, failure like a thorn stuck dead in the center of his chest. He was almost to his truck when a familiar voice called out behind him. Natalie. Was she actually *following* him after the shit he'd said?

"Wait!"

Fully expecting to turn around and find a twelve-gauge shotgun leveled at his head, August turned on a booted heel and watched warily as the gorgeous witch approached. Why did he have the ridiculous urge to move in a fast clip back in her direction and catch her up in a kiss? She'd break his fucking jaw if he tried, but God help him, his dick/gut insisted it was the right thing to do. "Yeah? You got something else you want to throw in my face?"

"My fist. Among other, sharper objects. But . . ." She jerked a shoulder, appearing to search for the right words. "Look, we're not friends, August. I get that. I insulted your wine the night we were going to hook up and you've resented me ever since, but what you said back there? Implying my last name makes me superior? You're wrong." She took a step closer, her heels leaving the grass and finding the asphalt of the parking lot. "You don't know *anything* about me."

He chuckled. "Go ahead, tell me all about your pain and suffering, rich girl."

She threw him a withering sigh. "I didn't say I've suffered. But I haven't exactly coasted along on my last name, as you seem to believe. I've been back in St. Helena for only a few months. The last name Vos means nothing in New York."

August leaned against the hood of his truck and crossed his arms. "I bet the money that comes with it does."

She gave August a look. One that suggested he was truly in the dark—and he didn't like that. Didn't like the possibility that he was wrong about this woman. Mainly because it was too late to change his actions now. He'd always have to wonder what the hell he could have done differently with Natalie Vos. But at least he could walk away from this phase of his life knowing he'd done his best for Sam. That's all he had.

"Did you ever want to get to know me? Or was it just . . ." Her attention dropped fleetingly to his zipper, then away, but it was enough to make him feel like he was back in that middle school pep rally trying not to get excited. "Just about sex?"

What the hell was he supposed to say?

That he'd seen her across the room at that stupid Wine Down Napa event and felt like he'd had an arrow shot into his chest by a flying baby? That his palms had sweat because of a woman for the first time ever that night? He'd already been in that Viennese countryside holding a picnic basket in one hand and an acoustic guitar in the other. God, she was so beautiful and interesting and fucking hilarious. Where had she been all his life?

Oh, but then somehow it all went to shit. He'd let his pride get in the way of . . . what? What would have happened if he'd just taken her verbal disapproval of his wine on the chin and moved forward? What if he hadn't equated it to disapproval of his best friend's aspirations? Was there any use wondering about any of this shit now?

No.

He'd run out of capital. The winery was an unmitigated disaster. He was the laughingstock of St. Helena, and he'd dragged his best friend's name with him into the mud.

Time to go, man.

"Oh, Natalie." He slapped a hand over his chest. "Obviously I wanted to twirl you around on a mountaintop in Vienna while our children frolicked and harmonized in curtain clothes. Didn't you know?"

She blinked a few times and her expression flattened as she stepped back into the grass. August had to fist his hands to prevent himself from reaching for her.

"Well," she said, her voice sounding a little rusty. *Dammit.* "Have a lovely evening at home with your *Sound of Music* references and cozy nest of wine rats. I hope you're paying them a living wage."

"It won't be my home much longer." He threw a hand toward the event that was still in full swing behind them, the judges taking pictures with the audience members, more wine being served on silver trays. "This contest was it for me. I'm moving on."

She laughed as if he was joking, sobering slightly when he just stared back. "Wow. You really can't take a little constructive criticism, can you?"

August scoffed. "Is that what it was? Constructive?"

"I thought SEALs were supposed to be tough. You're letting winemaking take you down?"

"I don't have a bottomless bank account like some people in this town. In case it wasn't clear, I'm talking about you."

For some reason, that made her laugh. A beat of silence passed, then she said, "You've got me all figured out, August. Congratulations." She turned on the toe of her high heel and breezed away, moving that leather skirt side to side in the world's cruelest parting shot. "My sincere condolences to the town where you end up next," she called back over her shoulder. "Especially to the women."

"You wouldn't be saying that if you dropped the disgusted act and came home with me." For some reason, every step she took in the opposite direction made his stomach lurch with more and more severity. "It's not too late, Natalie."

She stopped walking and he held his breath, not fully aware until this very moment how badly he actually wanted her. Maybe even needed. The continued flow of his blood seemed to hinge on her response. "You're right, it's not too late," she said, turning, chewing her lip, eyes vulnerable in a manner that stuck a swallow in his throat. *I'll never be mean to her again.* "It's *way* too late," she concluded with a pinkie wave, her expression going from defenseless to venomous. "Go to hell, August Cates."

His stomach bottomed out, leaving him almost too winded for a reply. "Hell, huh? Your old stomping grounds, right?"

"Yup!" She didn't even bother turning around. "That's where I met your mom. She said she'd rather live in hell than drink your wine."

A crank turned in his rib cage as she moved out of earshot. Too far to hear him over the event music that had started up. Definitely too far to touch, so why were his fingers itching for her skin? His chances with Natalie were subzero now. Just like his chance at succeeding as a vintner. With a final long look at the one who got away, August cursed, climbed into his truck, and tore out of the parking lot, ignoring the strong sense of leaving something undone.

Chapter Two

$\mathcal{N}$atalie searched blindly in the dark for the button on her sound machine, cranking the symphony of rain and bullfrogs to the maximum level. Julian and Hallie tried to be quiet. They really did. But bedsprings creak at four o'clock in the morning for only one reason—and creak they did. Natalie covered her face with a pillow for good measure and rolled back into the sheets, employing what she called the State Capitals Method. On the occasions her brother and his new girlfriend decided to make love down the hallway in the guest house they all shared, Natalie avoided that troubling imagery by naming state capitals.

Montgomery, Juneau, Phoenix . . .

Squeak squeak squeak.

That was it.

Natalie sat up in bed and pushed off her sleep mask, giving the wine dizziness a moment to dissipate. No more excuses. It was time to bite the bullet and go talk to her mother. It was time to get the hell out of Napa. She'd been licking her wounds far too long, and while she was happy beyond words for Julian to have found the love of his life, she didn't need to witness it in surround sound.

She threw off the covers and stood, her hip bumping into

the nightstand and knocking over an empty wineglass. One of *four*—as if she needed another sign that she'd turned into a lush in the name of avoiding her problems.

Life had ground to a standstill.

Looking out the window of the back bedroom, she could see the main house where she'd grown up and Corinne, her mother, currently lived. That was her destination in the morning. Asking her mother for money was going to sting like a thousand wasps, but what choice did she have? If she was going to return to New York and open her own investment firm, she needed capital.

Her mother wasn't going to make it easy. No, she was probably waiting right now in front of a roaring fire, dressed in all her finery, having sensed that Natalie was on the verge of humbling herself. Sure, they'd had a few softer moments since Natalie's return to St. Helena, but just under the surface, she'd always be the Embarrassment to Corinne.

Natalie tossed her eye mask in the direction of the sad, empty wineglass quartet and plodded into the en suite bathroom. Might as well get the talk over with early, right? That way if Corinne said no to Natalie's proposal, at least she'd have the whole day to wallow. And this was Napa, so wallowing could be made very fashionable. She'd find a wine tasting and charm everyone in attendance. People who had no idea she'd been asked to step down as a partner of her finance firm for a wildly massive trade blunder that cost, oh, a cool billion.

Nor would they know she'd been kicked to the curb by her fiancé, who had been too embarrassed to meet her at the altar.

Back in New York? Persona non grata.

In St. Helena? Royalty.

Snort. Natalie shed her sleepshirt and stepped beneath the

hot shower spray. And if she thought her brother doing the deed constituted an unwanted image, it had nothing on the memory of August Cates yesterday afternoon in all his beefcake glory.

I don't have a bottomless bank account like some people in this town.

If only.

Natalie didn't have anything to complain about. She was living in a beautiful guest house on the grounds of a vineyard, for god's sake. But she'd been living off her savings for more than a month now and she could barely open a lemonade stand, let alone launch a firm, with the amount left over. She had privilege, but financial freedom presented a challenge. One she could hopefully overcome this morning. All it would cost was her pride.

The fact that August Cates planned to leave St. Helena imminently had nothing to do with her sudden urgency to leave, too. Nothing whatsoever. That big, incompetent buffoon and his decisions had no bearing on her life. So why the pit in her stomach? It had been there since he approached the table to have his wine judged yesterday. The man had a chip the size of Denver on his shoulder, but he always had kind of a . . . softness in his eyes. A relaxed, observant quality that said *I've seen everything. I can handle anything.*

But it was missing yesterday.

And it caught Natalie off guard how much it threw her.

He'd looked resigned. Closed off.

Now, drying her hair in front of the foggy bathroom mirror, she couldn't pretend that hole in her belly wasn't yawning wider. Where would August go? What would he do now that winemaking was off the table?

Who *was* August Cates?

Part of her—a part she would never admit to out loud—had wondered if she would find out eventually. In a weak moment. Or by accident.

Had she been looking forward to that?

Natalie turned off the dryer with a snappy movement, ran the brush one final time through her long, black hair, and left the bathroom, crossing to her closet. She put on a sleeveless black sweaterdress and leather loafers, added a swipe of nude lipstick and some gold earrings. By the time she was finished, she could see through the guest room window that lights were on in the main house and she took a long breath, banishing the jitters.

The worst Corinne could say was no, Natalie reminded herself on the way up the path that ran alongside the fragrant vineyard. The sun hadn't risen yet, but the barest rim of gold outlined Mount St. Helena. She could almost feel the grapes waking up and turning toward the promise of warmth from above. Part of her truly loved this place. It was impossible not to. The smell of fertile earth, the tradition, the magic, the intricate process. Thousands of years ago, some industrious—and probably bored—people had buried bottles of grape juice underground for the winter and invented wine, which proved Natalie's theory: where there is a will to get drunk, dammit, there is a way.

She paused at the bottom of the porch steps leading to the main house. Old-world charm oozed from every inch of her childhood home. Greenery spilled over flower boxes beneath every window, rocking chairs urged people to sit and relax, and the trickle of the pool's water fixture could be heard from the front of the house, even though it was located behind it. A gorgeous manor that never failed to make winery visitors swoon. The place was incredible. But she had more affection for the guest house than the manor where she'd lived from birth to college. And right now, all it represented was the obstacle ahead.

A moment later, she knocked on the door and heard the sound of footsteps approaching on the other side. The peephole darkened, the lock turned—and then she was looking at Corinne.

"Seriously?" Natalie sighed, giving her stately mother a once-over, taking in the smoothed black-gray hair and perfect posture. Even her wrinkles were artful, allowed onto her face by invitation only. "You're fully dressed at five o'clock in the morning?"

"I could say the same about you," Corinne replied without missing a beat.

"True," Natalie said, sliding into the house without an invitation. "But I don't live here. Do you even own a bathrobe?"

"Did you come here to discuss sleepwear?"

"Nope. Humor me."

Corinne closed the door firmly, then locked it. "Of course I own a robe. Normally, I would be wearing it until at least seven, but I have virtual meetings this morning." In an uncharacteristic move, her mother let a smile peek through before it was quickly quelled. "Your brother has negotiated a deal making us the official wine of several wedding venues down the California coast. He is really helping turn things around for us."

"Yeah, he is." Natalie couldn't help but feel a spark of pride in her brother. After all, he'd overcome his own baggage pertaining to this place and landed on the other side much better off. At the same time, however, Natalie couldn't ignore the wistfulness drifting through her breast. God, just once, she'd love someone to talk about her like Corinne spoke about Julian. Like she was vital. Valued. Wanted *and* needed. "It's hard to tell him no when he's speaking in his stern professor voice. Takes people right back to seventh grade."

"Whatever he's doing, it's working." Corinne squared her shoulders and moved farther into the foyer, gesturing for Natalie to precede her into the living space and to the right, overlooking the rambling vineyard and the mountains beyond. They took seats on opposite ends of the hard couch that had been there since Natalie's childhood and was almost never used. Voses didn't *gather*.

They kept moving.

So in the interest of family tradition, Natalie turned toward Corinne and folded her hands on one knee. "Mother." If she'd learned anything from phase one in the finance industry, it was to look a person in the eye when asking for money, and she did so now. "I know you will agree—it's time for me to go back to New York. I've been in contact with Claudia, one of my previous analysts, and she's agreed to come on board with my new company. We're going to be small, more of a boutique firm, but both of us have enough connections to facilitate steady growth. With a couple of smart plays—"

"Wow." Corinne framed her jaw with a thumb and index finger. "You've been making important phone calls in between wine binges. I had no idea."

Clang. A ding in the armor.

Okay.

She'd expected that and was prepared for it. *Just keep going.*

Natalie kept her features composed in an attempt to disguise how fast her heart was now beating. Why was it that she could make million-dollar trades without her pulse skipping, but one barb from Corinne and she might as well be dangling from the side of a skyscraper by a pinkie, cold sweat breaking out beneath her dress?

Parents. *Man*, they truly messed up their kids.

"Yes, I have been making calls," Natalie replied calmly. She didn't deny the wine binges, because, yeah. She'd definitely done that. "Claudia is working on lining up an investor right now, but before anyone in their right mind gives us money, we'll need to register a new business name. We need an office and some skin in the investment game, however light." She tried not to be obvious about taking a bracing breath. "Bottom line, I need capital."

Not even the slightest reaction from her mother. She'd seen this coming and it burned, even though they'd both been aware this talk was on the horizon.

"Surely you've saved *some* money," Corinne said smoothly, a gray-black eyebrow lifting gracefully toward her hairline. "You were a partner in a very lucrative investment fund."

"Yes. I was. Unfortunately, there is a certain lifestyle that has to be maintained for people to trust financiers with their money."

"That is a fancy way of saying you lived above your means."

"Perhaps. Yes." Oh boy, keeping her irritation at bay was going to be even harder than she thought. Corinne had come locked and loaded for this conversation. "The excess is necessary, however. Parties and designer clothing and vacations and expensive rounds of golf with clients. Morrison and I had an apartment on Park Avenue. Not to mention, we'd put down a nonrefundable deposit on our wedding venue."

That last part burned. Of course it did.

She'd been offloaded by a man who'd claimed to love her.

But for some reason, Morrison's face didn't materialize. No, instead she saw August. Wondered what he would say about a six-figure deposit on Tribeca Rooftop. He would look so out of place among the wedding guests. He'd probably show up in jeans, a ballcap, and that faded gray navy T-shirt. He would crush her ex in an arm-wrestling match, too. Why did that make her feel better enough to continue?

"In short, yes, I do have some money. If I was simply going back to New York, I could afford to find an apartment and live comfortably for a few months. But that is not what I want to do." The kick of adrenaline in her bloodstream felt good. It had been a long time. Or maybe while getting lit to mourn the loss of everything she'd worked for, she'd accidentally numbed her ambition, too. Right now, in this moment, she had it back. She was the woman who used to look down at rows of analysts from her glass office and demand they eat their competition's balls for breakfast. "I want to return better than ever. I want my former colleagues to realize they made a mistake . . ."

"You want to rub it in their faces," Corinne supplied.

"Maybe a little," Natalie admitted. "I might have made one huge mistake, but I know if Morrison Talbot the Third had made that bad call instead of me, excuses would have been made. He probably would have been given a promotion for being a risk-taker. They met in secret and voted to oust me. My partners. My *fiancé*." She closed her eyes briefly to beat back the memory of her shock. Betrayal. "If you were me, Mother, you would want a shot to go back and prove yourself."

Corinne stared at her for several beats. "Perhaps I would."

Natalie released a breath.

"Unfortunately, I don't have the money to loan you," Corinne continued, her face deepening ever so slightly with color. "As you are aware, the vineyard has been declining in profitability. With your brother's unexpected help, we're turning it around, but it could be years before we're back in the black. All I have is this house, Natalie."

"My trust fund," Natalie said firmly, forcing it out into the open. "I'm asking for my trust fund to be released."

"My, times have changed," Corinne said with a laugh. "When you graduated from Cornell, what was it that you said at your postceremony dinner? You would never take a dime from us as long as you lived?"

"I'm thirty years old now. Please don't throw something in my face that I said when I was twenty-two."

Corinne sighed and refolded her hands in her lap. "You are well aware of the terms of your trust fund, Natalie. Your father might be racing cars in Italy and parading around with women half his age like a fool, but he set forth the language of the trust and as far as the bank is concerned, he's still in control."

Natalie lunged to her feet. "The language in that contract is archaic. How can it even be legal in this day and age? There has to be something you can do."

Her mother let a breath seep out. "Naturally, I agree with you. But your father would have to sign off on the change."

"I am *not* going groveling to that man. Not after he just blew us off and pretends like we don't exist. Not when he left you to do damage control after the fire four years ago."

Corinne's attention shot to the vineyard, which was lightening in the path of the sun. "I wasn't aware you cared."

"Of course I care. *You* asked *me* to leave."

"Oh please. You couldn't have made it more clear you wanted to get back to the almighty rat race of New York," her mother scoffed.

They obviously remembered that period after the fire very differently. Getting into the semantics of the last time she'd been in St. Helena wouldn't do her cause any good now. "We'll have to agree to disagree on that."

Corinne appeared poised to argue, but visibly changed course. "My hands are tied, Natalie. The terms of the trust are set in stone. The recipient must be gainfully employed *and* married for the money to be released. I realize that sounds like something out of Regency England, not modern-day California, but your father is old-school Italian. His parents' marriage was arranged. It's glamorous to him. It's tradition."

"It's sexist."

"Normally I would agree, but the terms of Julian's trust are the same. When the contract was set forth, your father had some grand vision in his mind. You and Julian with your flourishing families taking over the winery. Grandchildren everywhere. Success." She made an absent gesture. "When you both left without any intention of joining the family business, it broke something inside of him. The fire was the final straw. I'm not making excuses for him, I'm just trying to give you a different perspective."

Natalie lowered herself back down to the couch and implored her mother with a look. "Please, there has to be something we can do. I can't stay here forever."

"Oh, I'm so sorry that staying in your family home feels like exile."

"You try waking up every morning to the sound of Julian and Hallie trying and failing to stifle their sex noises down the hall."

"Jesus Christ."

"Yes. They call for the son of God, too, sometimes when they think I'm not home."

With a withering eye roll, Corinne pushed to her feet and strode to the front window. "You would think your father's hasty departure would bruise the loyalty of his local friends and associates, but I assure you, it has not. They still have him up on a pedestal—and that includes Ingram Meyer."

"Who?"

"Ingram Meyer, an old friend of your father's. He's the loan officer at the St. Helena Credit Union, but more importantly, he's the trustee of yours and Julian's trust funds. Believe me, he will follow your father's instructions to the letter."

Natalie's jaw had to be touching the floor. "Some man I've never heard of—or met—holds my future in his hands?"

"I'm sorry, Natalie. The bottom line is that . . . short of convincing your father to amend the terms, there is nothing I can do."

"I wouldn't ask you to do that." Natalie sighed. "Not after how he left."

Corinne was silent a moment. "Thank you."

That was it. The end of the conversation. There was nothing more to be said. Currently, Natalie was the furthest thing from gainfully employed. And even further from being married. The patriarchy wins again. She'd have to return to New York with her tail between her legs and ask for a low-level position at one of the firms she'd once called rivals. They would eat up her humility with a spoon and she'd . . . grin and bear it. Pulling together enough money to open her own business would probably take a decade, but she would do it. She'd do it on her own.

"Okay." Resigned, hollow, Natalie stood on shaky legs and

smoothed the skirt of her dress. "Good luck with your meetings this morning."

Corinne said nothing as Natalie left the house, closing the door behind her and descending the steps with her chin up. This morning, she would head into town, get her hair and nails done. At the very least, she could look good when she landed back in New York, right?

But everything changed on the way back from getting that balayage—and like some weird nursery rhyme from hell, it involved a cat, a rat . . . and a SEAL.

Chapter Three

*H*e should have closed the front door.

Now the goddamn cat was gone. She'd flown the coop in protest of his preliminary stages of packing. *Very* preliminary. He'd only taken the suitcase out of the closet and opened it on his bed. After sniffing it, climbing inside, and taking a few laps around his luggage, Menace had slunk off to the kitchen. August assumed she couldn't care less about his packing activities, but he forgot the cardinal rule about cats.

Change equaled assault. And they were casual in their revenge.

Now here he was, jogging along the path between his disastrous winery and the road, calling out for a deaf cat. How had it come to this?

Menace *never* left the house. August knew that firsthand because after she'd shown up one day out of the blue and declared him her new caretaker, he'd spent two weeks trying to coax her furry ass back outside. Apparently he should have tried packing.

"Menace," he boomed, hands cupped around his mouth. Maybe she could hear the vibrations of his voice in the air? "Do you think because I'm packing that I'm going to leave you here? Do you need to be reminded that I spent eight *hundred* dollars at the vet last week? That's long-term shit. I didn't even know cats could get gingivitis."

Silence.

Obviously.

His unlikely companion meowed on occasion, but it usually happened in the middle of the night for absolutely no reason that he could figure out. He'd always considered himself a dog person. No, he *was* a dog person. He just liked this *one* cat.

Famous last words.

Up ahead near the road, there was a flash of orange. *There she is.*

August picked up the pace of his jog, starting to get a little nervous upon realizing how close they were to the road. And when he noticed the distinct rumble of an approaching vehicle, he started to sprint, sweat breaking out along his spine.

"Menace," he barked, cursing himself for taking out the suitcase. A few months back, he'd moved her litter box down to the laundry room and she'd stopped eating for three days. Apparently he hadn't learned his lesson. Dogs didn't behave in nonsensical ways like this, but he didn't have a dog. He had a deaf cat who was two seconds from being flattened by a car. She was moving at too fast a clip and he wouldn't make it in time. Maybe the driver would see her and slow down? Menace was bright fucking orange for crying out loud.

August's mouth went dry at the screech of tires on the road and a moment later, he broke through the trees . . .

Only to find his temperamental feline rolled over onto her back, preening, two inches from the front bumper of a blue hatchback. Totally unconcerned about her brush with death. Just another day wrecking the lives of humans and getting away with it because of her pink nose and toe beans. Unbelievable.

August started to step onto the road so he could scoop up the cat and thank the driver for being extra vigilant, but a husky cry stopped him in his tracks.

Natalie?

He'd never heard her make that sound before—no, his dreams didn't count—but August knew instantly that she was the driver of the car. As a result, his body went on high alert. The kind of alert that came from tossing and turning last night, cursing himself for not being able to stop thinking about this woman he disliked, while also oddly conflicted about simply leaving her in the rearview. He hadn't expected to see her again, but there she was.

Picking up his cat and cradling the animal to her chest in a flurry of apologies and nuzzling and chin scratching. As he watched dumbfounded, the cat leaned all the way back in Natalie's arms and locked eyes with him from her upside-down position. Telling him in no uncertain terms with her bland expression that she had other options. And those options would be pursued if he made another false move, like brushing his teeth at the wrong time of day.

He should let Natalie know he was standing there. Right.

But it wouldn't hurt to take a few seconds to admire the woman from behind. Hell, it was his favorite pastime. Noticing those legs, especially in the dress she was wearing. The pointy shoes that had just enough elevation to keep her calves flexed. Sweet Lord, those legs went on forever. On his deathbed, his final regret would be missing his chance to feel them glued to his hips. Thrashing around when she got close, then wrapping him back up again for the finale.

"Poor baby," Natalie crooned to the cat, rocking her like an infant. "I didn't mean to scare you. Where is your owner?" she murmured.

"Right here, princess," August called. Natalie spun around and he gulped. *Damn.* She always looked hot, but there was something extra special about her today. "You've got a bunch of black shit on your eyes."

Her whole body sort of deflated at the sight of him. Complete exasperation in human form. "It's eyeliner, caveman."

"Why are you wearing so much of it?"

Her shoulder bounced up and down. "Maybe I had a date."

Rudely, his esophagus tied itself into a knot. "With who?"

God, he hated the idea of her on a date more than he hated . . . anything. Just because *they* weren't dating didn't mean she could just date anyone else, willy-nilly. Because *that* wasn't irrational or anything, right?

She swayed with the cat, as if trying to lull the animal to sleep. "I wasn't out with anyone," she muttered. "I went to buy foundation and ended up in a chair getting made over."

He hid his relief. "They saw that high-limit credit card coming a mile away."

A bright smile. "Shouldn't you be out clubbing a wooly mammoth or something?"

August smirked. "I *should* be packing, but my cat ran off."

Natalie adjusted her stance to jut that shapely hip out. "You expect me to believe this is your cat? She's your *pet*?"

"More accurately, I'm *her* pet."

She scrutinized the animal, lifting it up and leaning in closer. "Why isn't she wearing a collar?"

"Look, I don't know what cats allow collars around their necks, but Menace"—he jabbed a finger in the animal's direction—"isn't one of them. She'd probably pretend to like it for an hour and then I'd wake up to find a death threat written in blood on my bathroom mirror, signed with a paw print."

Did Natalie's lips jump a little or was that wishful thinking?

Because yeah, the woman had a gorgeous smile. He'd seen a lot of it up close. He'd *tasted* it. Months had passed since that night and the knowledge that he'd never taste it again wasn't getting any easier. At least not as long as he continued to run into her in St. Helena. This attraction he'd been burdened with for Natalie was a motherfucker. Once again, his dick ruined everything—and it was ruining his getaway right now. He *should* be packing, starting the journey to forgetting about what might have been if he'd just been less of an asshole. Or if she was less of a spoiled brat.

"Awww. You were just trying to escape the smell of farts and stale beer, weren't you, precious?" Natalie crooned to the cat, laying the baby talk on thick.

"If you're trying to turn my cat against me, I'm pretty sure that ship has sailed."

"She hates you?" For a moment, Natalie seemed surprised, but she quickly backpedaled. "I mean . . . she hates you. Obviously."

"It's minute to minute. I never know what's coming."

"What pissed her off this time?"

Why did he hesitate before answering? No clue. "Packing. I took out my suitcase and she lit out on a death mission."

Her expression seemed to freeze itself on. She was probably restraining herself from calling him a quitter again. "Oh." A few seconds ticked by, then she started toward him, obviously intending to hand over the cat. "Well, the last thing I want to do is delay your long overdue exit from Napa. I'll let you get back to it."

August's smile was brittle. "Can't wait to never look back."

"The wine gods are certainly rejoicing this day."

"You would know, since the wine gods are your parents."

"Please. They're not wine gods." Natalie started to hand the cat into his outstretched arms, but the feline's claws were dug into the black sweater material of her dress. She tried again. No luck. Menace wasn't letting go. "Oh! I don't want to hurt her claws."

He pushed a hand through his hair. "She's punishing me."

"She's showing favoritism to your least favorite person. I'm beginning to think you're not exaggerating about this cat's diabolical side."

Natalie Vos was far from his least favorite person, but he kept that to himself. In fact, up close like this, her smoky floral scent was taking jabs at his brain, making him forget what he ever had against her in the first place. Who could hold a grudge against a woman this beautiful and soft looking, and so much shorter than him that he started to feel like an ogre? At least until she said, "Are you going to help me? Or just stand there with your hairy knuckles on the ground?"

"My apologies, princess. You're used to people snapping to attention to assist you."

"Oh shut *up*, August. Not today."

Worry snuck in and took hold. "Why? What happened today?"

Before she could answer, a car approached on the road, maneuvering its way around Natalie's vehicle, which was still idling in the lane headed toward Vos Vineyard. Of course, Menace didn't hear the approach of the oncoming traffic, so when she caught the unexpected movement from the corner of her eye, she tensed, digging her claws into Natalie's chest.

Natalie cried out in pain.

August experienced panic the likes of which he hadn't seen since combat, his throat dropping down into his stomach so he couldn't swallow.

"Jesus, princess. Okay." His hands were useless objects, reaching for the cat's paws and tugging, but somehow making it worse. "I'm a dog person. I don't know what to do about this."

"Soothe her." Natalie gasped when the cat clung harder. "Calm her down."

"She's hard of hearing. And petting her is really a mood-based activity. Sometimes she likes it, sometimes she becomes possessed by Satan. I don't want to make it worse."

"Oh, come on, you're loving this."

"I'm *not* loving this, Natalie." No longer able to stand the sight of the claws digging into Natalie's body, he pulled the cat off her, unfortunately tearing her dress in the process—and revealing several bleeding scratches below her collarbone. "Christ."

She looked down at the injuries and winced. "It's fine."

"It's not fine." He stormed toward her car, seeing the claw marks every time he blinked. "Don't move."

"Don't order me around."

August ignored that while throwing open the door of Natalie's car, a growling—yes, growling—Menace wedged beneath one arm. Thanks to the height difference, he was jammed up against the steering wheel until he slid the seat all the way back. He threw the vehicle into drive and pulled it onto the shoulder, trying and failing not to notice the way her scent laced the air. What was in those shopping bags? The contents were wrapped in tissue paper, meaning her purchases had to be fancy. Of course they were.

So why was her car the most basic of rentals?

Couldn't she afford a Mercedes or something equally high-end?

Telling himself to mind his own business and focus on the task at hand, August removed the keys from the ignition, took one last whiff of the air, and climbed out.

"What are you doing?" Natalie demanded to know, her arms crossed over her ripped dress. "I need to get home."

"Not until I put something on those wounds." He walked past her with the hissing feline. "Let's go."

"No way. Give me my keys back."

"Not happening."

"You expect me to go through the woods and into your home with you? Alone with a man who would have nominated me for the Salem witch trials in a heartbeat?"

That drew August up short. Frowning, he turned to face Natalie where she still hesitated at the top of the path. "Are you afraid to be alone with me?"

She didn't answer. In fact, she didn't seem to *know* the answer.

Whatever vitriol lay between them, August was not okay with that indecision. "Natalie, the sight of those scratches on you is absolutely killing me. I'd just as soon put a mark on you myself than I would pursue a ballet career."

Her mouth snapped shut. She blinked several times and flounced forward, moving past him on the path. "I didn't know cat people were so dramatic," she muttered.

"Only when their integrity is in question," he countered, following her.

"Sorry. I'll stick to questioning your intelligence."

"Thank you."

Her shoulders shook a little bit. With laughter? Why now,

when he couldn't even see her face? "My only hope is that you are better at repairing wounds than you are at making wine."

"Considering I've given myself stitches in a dust storm without painkillers—twice—I'd say I'm up for patching your kitty cat scratches."

It wasn't that he was satisfied when her step faltered, it was that . . . well, he was sick and tired of this woman seeing him as incapable and hapless because he didn't know how to ferment some fucking grapes. Was it important at this stage for Natalie to perceive him as capable? No. He was on the verge of leaving. And yet he couldn't help wanting that approval from her. More than he had a right to.

They walked in silence to the house. It was a small, California-style two-bedroom with a red tile roof and beige stucco exterior. His temporary home sat on the edge of the property, two barns in the near distance. One he'd been using for poorly attended tastings, the other for production and barrel storage. Spread out on all sides were rows of fragrant grapes stretching up toward the sun. He could still remember the feeling of stepping onto the property for the first time, hearing Sam whisper in his ear that it was perfect. And it was. A vibrant slice of heaven that he never would have been able to imagine during those countless days in the desert. But he wasn't cut out for the process it took to make the vineyard run correctly.

The woman waiting to be let into his house knew it better than anyone.

He slid his key into the lock and their gazes met, held, the weight of a tire iron dropping low in his belly. This was what it would have been like, taking her home. Getting his hands on her. They would have shook this fucking town.

"I'm just here for medical intervention," she said, a suspicious scratch in her voice.

"I'm well aware that's all you want from me."

"Good."

"But you're looking at my mouth pretty closely for someone who just needs a Band-Aid." He pushed open the door. "No harm in pointing it out."

Chapter Four

Natalie expected a mess. Pizza boxes and dirty gym clothes and beer bottles. Maybe a couple of suspicious tissues. But she could have eaten off the floor of August's little house. It was that clean. Spices were lined up on the kitchen counter in front of a cutting board. The kitchen and living area were connected and the space was small, so a king-sized easy chair was his only piece of furniture, angled toward the television. He'd managed to make the scene inviting with a rug and a basket holding a blanket. It was . . . nice.

Actually, it beat her wineglass graveyard of a guest room by a million miles.

"Disappointed that I don't have centerfolds taped to my wall?"

"I'm sure they're hidden in the closets, along with the rats," she said breezily, watching the cat prance off with an air of superiority toward the rear of the house.

August circled around to look at her face and let out a booming laugh. "Look at you. You're shocked. You really expected me to live in a frat house, didn't you?" He entered the bathroom, which was behind the sole door in the short hallway leading to the bedrooms, she guessed. Flipping on the light, he gestured for her to follow him into the tiny room. She started in that direction but paused on the threshold, unsure about being crowded into such a small amount of square footage with a man that large. A man she couldn't seem to stop being attracted to, despite the fact that he was judgmental and rude and seemed to see the absolute worst in her. "Did you really give yourself stitches in a dust storm twice?"

August paused in the act of rooting through his medicine cabinet. His hand, holding a bottle of rubbing alcohol, dropped to the vanity. "Yeah."

"Where?"

He turned slightly, propping a hip on the sink. "Why? You want to judge my handiwork before you deem me suitable to fix your royal boo-boo?"

No. She was trying to delay the moment when they would be standing close enough to touch, because he scrambled her brain to the point where she started to debate the merits of sleeping with him even after over a month of insults and teasing. "It's a good practice to ask for credentials."

"Even if those credentials are high on my inner thigh?"

"Both of them?"

"One of them." He turned away and hoisted up his T-shirt, baring a profusely muscled back, devoid of ink, unlike his arms, one of which proudly bore the navy insignia. Not that she would have *noticed* a tattoo when his right shoulder was split in half by a puckered, painful-looking scar. "Here's the other. Not my best work, but I didn't have a mirror at the time."

"Yes." She tried to swallow. Couldn't. God, he was a human bull-dozer. She'd have to hold on for dear life in bed with him. Sounded terrible. Just awful. "Best for you to stay away from mirrors."

He dropped his shirt with a snort. "Don't act like you weren't ready to climb me like a ladder, princess."

No lies detected. That was then, however. This was now. "Shame you had to open your mouth, isn't it?"

August dragged his tongue along his full bottom lip. "You would have loved my mouth."

Her skin was the temperature of the sun. "Can we get this over with or are you hoping I bleed to death?"

In the space of a heartbeat, his expression went from arrogant to concerned. "Sorry. Come here."

The apology caught her off guard. So much so that she kind of lurched into the bathroom, too stunned to do anything but release the ripped edges of her dress and watch him apply rubbing alcohol to a cotton ball, trying not to notice his fresh, fruity scent while he did so. "Why do you smell like grapefruit?"

"It's this handmade soap I use," he said absently, brow furrowed while he dabbed at her claw marks, his slow, warm breath stirring her hairline. "The one and only person who ever liked my wine is too broke to buy it, so she trades me soap for a bottle here and there."

"How did she lose her sense of taste? Hot sauce accident?"

"Funny."

"Who is she?" The question was out before she could wrangle it back in her throat. She sounded like a jealous girlfriend, kind of like August had earlier when she'd lied about being on her way to a date. Good thing this man was leaving town, because their dynamic grew more confusing by the day. "Never mind. It's none of my business."

"No. It's not," he drawled, ripping open the wrappers of two

Band-Aids at once. "But I'm going to tell you anyway, so you don't snap off the countertop."

Natalie's gaze flew down to where her hands were death-gripping the ledge of the vanity, releasing the white marble as quickly as possible. "The rubbing alcohol stung."

"Uh-huh." Bottom lip fixed between his teeth to trap an obvious laugh, he laid the first Band-Aid on her chest. Slowly. Smoothing it ever so gently from top to bottom with his thumb. And her stupid, duplicitous hormones perked up like a houseplant after being watered. Natalie had to resist arching her back while he applied the second Band-Aid, taking his sweet time, almost like he was enjoying her confusing distress. "She's a mother of triplets—the one who trades me soap. I'm pretty sure anything that gets her buzzed after bedtime tastes good."

"Oh. Teri Frasier? I saw her in town last week pushing them in a stroller as big as a tank. She and I went to school together."

"I know."

Her nose wrinkled. "How do you know?"

August appeared to be silently kicking himself. "You two seemed about the same age, so I asked her."

"Why?"

He hesitated. Did his face deepen with color slightly? "Just making small talk."

At some point during the thrust and parry of their conversation, he'd moved in closer. The sink dug into the small of her back. That part of her that he'd excited months ago, but never fulfilled, was requesting payment in full. His jeans would feel so good on her naked inner thighs. He'd pull her hair in those big fists and she could finally, finally, get this oaf out of her system. What harm could it do? He was leaving, wasn't he?

Natalie looked up at August through her eyelashes, her right hand lifting with the intention of exploring those hard muscles through his shirt. "I was thinking—"

"She mentioned you spent most of your time drunk back then, too." He chuckled.

Ice crystallized on her skin, her hand dropping like a stone.

He caught it, frowning. Searching her expression. "Wait. Whoa. What were you going to say? You were thinking what?"

"Nothing."

"Tell me."

Disguising the uncomfortable weight in her chest with a saccharine-sweet smile, she scooted out from between his huge body and the vanity, fleeing the bathroom. But not before throwing a parting shot over her shoulder. "Don't let the door hit you in the ass on the way out of town, August."

"Natalie," he growled, stomping after her. "Wait."

"Can't. I need fresh air. Your stupidity is obviously contagious."

"I have your car keys."

She halted with one hand on the doorknob, turned, and held out her hand. "Give them to me."

He made no move to take them out of his pocket. Instead, he jerked his chin in the direction of the bathroom. "You *were* going to touch me in there."

"As you pointed out, my life has been a series of bad decisions." If that look on his face was regret, she didn't want to know. Didn't want to explore why he was regretful, because there was already a notch in her throat and pressure between her shoulder blades. "Look, I've had a pretty rough day, so if I was pondering a move on you, it would have been purely out of the need for a distraction."

She expected him to pounce on that last part. To try and persuade her to spend the next few hours distracted in one of those back bedrooms. To her surprise, he didn't. "Why did you have a rough day?"

"I'm not giving you that kind of ammunition."

"What does it matter if I'm leaving?"

He had her there.

And damn, Natalie was suddenly desperate to get the weight off her chest. She refused to interrupt Julian and Hallie's freakish happiness with her problems. All of her friends were in New York—mostly surface-level acquaintances who also worked in finance. To their credit, when she'd made the bad trade and the firm requested that she step down, they hadn't abandoned her. But their emails and texts had thinned over the last few weeks, a gradual ghosting that left them with a clear conscience and her with no one to call.

Could she vent to August?

Despite the acerbic nature of their relationship, she couldn't help but feel like . . . they knew each other. He was not a stranger.

She shook off the comfort it gave her to acknowledge that.

No. Whatever. She'd talk to him because it was a free chance to unload. He was leaving and wouldn't be able to use any of the information to make fun of her.

"I, um . . ." She crossed her arms protectively over her middle, wondering why he watched the action so closely. "You'll be gleeful to know that I humbled myself this morning by asking my mother for money. I asked her to release my trust fund and I was denied."

His brows knit together as he processed that. "Trust fund. Shouldn't that be released when you become a legal adult?"

"In most cases, yes, but my father made certain . . . requirements."

"Such as?"

Was she really going to tell him this? Yeah. Why not? Nothing could make today any worse. Not even his ridicule. "Not only am I obligated to be gainfully employed, I am required to be married in order for the trustee to release the assets. Julian, too."

A full five seconds ticked by. "You're lying."

It wasn't an accusation. He was . . . satisfyingly shocked. "Nope," she said slowly, hoping she was reading him right. "My father lives in Italy now. Basically, he's inflicting his will on me all the way from the motherland and his rules are circa 1930 old-school. Both my mother and I would rather stick our feet in a lake full of piranhas than reach out and ask him for a favor after a four-year silence. Imagine if he said no and we sacrificed that final shred of pride for nothing?" She shrugged. "Also, I think there is a part of my mother that enjoys Napa being my only option for a while longer."

"Your only option for what?" He reared back a little. "You're not . . . broke."

"Not *broke* broke. But not flush enough to . . ." She paused to wet her dry lips. "I'm starting my own hedge fund in New York along with a colleague of mine, and we need capital to appear appealing to investors."

"That's what you were doing before. Wall Street shit?"

She rolled her eyes. "Yes. You know, the *shit* that powers the economy."

He snorted, waved that off. "You'd rather be in an overcrowded city than your family's vineyard in Napa?"

"It's complicated."

"Sounds like *you're* complicated."

"I'll take complicated over simple." She held her hands out for the keys, wiggling her fingers, but he ignored the gesture. "*August.*"

"One second." He folded his arms over his powerful chest, cleared his throat. "You don't have any marriage prospects, right? You wouldn't marry just to get that money, would you?"

"I might," she said, even though it wasn't really an option she'd considered. Her prospects were nil. What was the point?

Was it her imagination or did lightning strike in the depths of his eyes? "I don't like it."

"I want the firm. I . . . *need* the firm. Otherwise I'm going to be known forever as a disappointment. A screw-up. A story they tell at cocktail hour."

She was saying too much now. That last part didn't need to be aired. It was hers. But she couldn't deny that the pressure in her chest eased on the tail end of the confession.

"Can I please have my keys?" she said quietly. "I need to go."

August seemed to shake himself, but his attention never strayed from her face. "Sure. Yeah." He handed them over, but when she turned to leave, he caught her wrist in a loose grip. "Hey, for whatever it's worth, I know what it's like to fail. Sank every last dime I had into this place and the bank laughed me out the door when I applied for a loan."

That gave her pause. "Was his name Ingram Meyer?"

He appeared to search his memory bank. "Yeah. That's the guy."

"What a coincidence. He's my father's trustee," Natalie murmured, peering up at the ex-SEAL, seeing him through fresh eyes. Or maybe she was simply looking at him the original way, as she'd done the night they'd met. When he was a perfect gentleman. When they'd gravitated toward each other like magnets.

No. More like the bow of the *Titanic* speeding toward the iceberg.

He's the same man who has been an insufferable jerk for months. Finding all of her weak spots and poking them relentlessly. Most likely, he'd softened his demeanor now only because he sensed a chance to get laid. No way was she giving him that satisfaction. Even if it would mean satisfaction for her, too. Somehow she just knew it would. But their obvious chemistry was neither here nor there. This was the end of the road.

"Good luck wherever you land, August," she murmured, pulling her wrist out of his grip, trying not to show her reaction to his swiping his thumb over her pulse. "If you feel a strong wind behind you on your way out of town, that's wine country sighing in relief."

He winked, then sauntered back a few steps with a smirk that never quite reached his eyes. "Maybe. But you were definitely going to kiss me in the bathroom, princess."

"If I was, it would have been purely to shut you up."

Not wanting August to get in another jab, Natalie turned and stalked out the door, sidestepping the cat, who'd apparently witnessed the whole conversation and didn't appear to be the least bit apologetic about assaulting her. She'd almost reached the path leading to the road when August's voice rang out from across the front yard.

"It's not too late, Natalie," he called, echoing his words from the contest a day earlier.

She turned to find August in the doorway of his house, forearms braced on the top of the frame, expression cocky, a swath of stomach muscles on display, biceps popping right, then left, then right. Then left again. Definitely not turning her on.

"Bonehead," she muttered in the wake of his laughter.

Laughter that died out almost as fast as it started.

Why did her legs feel more and more like rubber as she hiked to the car?

Leaving this man's company should make her feel free as a bird. It did.

Right.

With a hard swallow, she slid the keys into the ignition. And after a long pause wherein the most insane idea occurred to her, she started the car with a snort and drove away.

LATER THAT NIGHT, Natalie left the house without really knowing why.

She wasn't the type to take an evening stroll.

Back in New York, her modus operandi had been to work hard all day and collapse on the couch with a glass of wine at the end of it. Tonight, however, she had an unexplained case of jitters. Hallie and Julian were out on a double date with Hallie's friends Jerome and Lavinia, meaning she had the entire guest house to herself. She should be ordering an obscene amount of takeout and watching *Below Deck* reruns, but instead she found herself walking straight out the front door into the fragrant evening in the direction of downtown St. Helena.

Maybe she was in the mood for some atmosphere. People.

A mood lift.

Upon returning home a few months ago, she'd gone on several dates, hoping to find that perfect rebound to occupy her while she wallowed in Napa. But shortly thereafter, dating had totally lost its appeal and she refused to examine why. Refused. She'd swiped left so many times without a good reason that she'd gotten disgusted and deleted Tinder altogether. Man, her phone was a silent, desolate place these days. She should just use it as a paperweight or a doorstop.

The lights of Grapevine Way beckoned as she walked along the dirt path, live jazz music from one of the many cafés winding toward her on the breeze. August was right to question why she preferred the city over this lush valley of grapes and sunshine and merriment. People came from all over to experience the exquisite bliss of St. Helena. But as Natalie stepped onto Grapevine Way and hooked a right, still with no idea of her destination, she couldn't muster any affection for the town. It was beautiful, classy, inviting. A jewel at the foot of the mountain.

But to her, it would always be the place she wasn't wanted.

Natalie stopped at the window of a confection shop that had been there since she was a child. It had already closed for the day, but as she peered in through the darkened glass, she remembered one of the times she and Julian had been brought there as children.

Julian couldn't walk through the shop without a classmate flagging her older brother down, asking him to come sit at their table. Even though the future history professor spoke only in breadcrumbs, those monosyllables were either funny or thought provoking. And, more importantly, never unkind. As a track star and academic wonder, he'd been nothing short of revered. Popularity had come easily—and uninvited—to Julian.

But Natalie could also see herself through the glass, working overtime to be noticed by anyone. Her parents, her classmates, the cool teenagers behind the counter. For some reason, the same wealth that added to Julian's popularity seemed to reflect negatively on her. She wasn't a gifted genius. She was an average student. Didn't have a lot of athletic ability. All that money at her disposal and she'd probably just coast her whole life, thanks to being a Vos.

Around the time Natalie realized everyone thought of her as someone who'd merely won the last name lottery, she'd started acting out. Playing pranks on her friends. Always accepting the dare. And when she got older, she'd been the one to supply the booze and throw the raging parties that got everyone in trouble. It just seemed to be the only way anyone noticed or acknowledged her. If she was loud. If she was *crazy*. Softly approaching her parents for affection never worked. They were either busy or their meager amount of free parent time had to be spent on Julian, who achieved honors and medals and scholarships.

She stepped back from the glass and kept walking, at a faster clip this time. She wasn't that attention-starved kid anymore. After an embarrassing stay in rehab after high school, she'd accepted her mother's help getting into Cornell. But she'd graduated at the top of her class on her own merit. She'd made partner without any intervention from her parents. She'd proven to herself that she was capable and driven.

Being back in St. Helena, however—and flat on her face—she could sense that old itch under her skin. To come back bigger and better and louder. To do something that would get her the positive reinforcement she'd always craved but could never seem to earn. That was what this firm would be for her. A way back to the top. A way to respect herself again.

A familiar voice reached Natalie's ears then and she stopped in the middle of the sidewalk, a group of tipsy tourists winding around her in their mules and summer scarves. Up ahead, parked at the curb, was August. As she watched, he unloaded boxes of wine into the trunk of her old classmate—and mother of triplets—Teri Frasier.

"Are you sure about this?" Teri laughed, visibly overwhelmed. "Couldn't you sell it, instead of giving it away for free?"

"We've been over this, Teri. I couldn't even give this wine away to a man dying of thirst in the desert. It's all yours." He gestured to the back of her car where, Natalie assumed, Teri's triplets were sitting in their car seats. "Besides, I think you deserve it more than anyone."

"Let me give you some soap, at least."

"Nah, thanks, but you keep it. I've got enough of a supply to hold me over for a year." He patted her on the shoulder and stepped back. "You tell your husband I said hello, all right?"

"Will do."

Natalie's pulse was just about jumping out of her skin. This was it. Really it.

Clearly, August was on his way out of St. Helena. Giving away his final supply of wine, as if it had no value. And it didn't. To be clear. It was like drinking gasoline that had been marinating with dog shit for a week. But hearing him acknowledge it in such a self-deprecating way made her stomach drop.

Her fingertips started to buzz, the way they did before a hefty trade.

Oh God, she could almost hear the bad idea coming toward her on a conveyor belt of doom. Just bumping along, getting closer and closer even as she tried to talk herself out of acknowledging the possibility of . . . helping August and herself in the process. She should let him drive out of town, never to darken the doorway of St. Helena ever again. They were oil and water. He had a chip on his buffalo-sized shoulder about her status and privilege in this town that he would never shed. And Natalie . . .

Well, offering to help this man and being rejected was just about the scariest thing she could imagine. All her life, she'd offered herself as a friend, a fiancée, a coworker, a sister, and a daughter, and at some point her presence—and even love—was rejected. *She* was rejected. Fired, dumped, asked to go home. Still, she didn't even like this man. So why was her heart beating at the pace of a hummingbird's wings at the thought of *him* saying no?

Why did she care so much?

Don't do it.

Not worth the sting.

Natalie started to back up into the shadows to wait out August's departure, but in the wake of Teri driving away, he rounded the back bumper of his truck and spied her, doing a double take. "Natalie?" He paused mid-stride, frowning. "What are you doing lurking over there in the dark?" He snapped his fingers. "Let me guess. Sucking the souls from children caught outdoors after eight P.M.?"

"That's right. I wait until they've been stuffed full of chicken fingers and ice cream all day. That's when I strike." She shrugged. "But you have the IQ of a child, so I guess you'll do."

"You sucked the soul out of me months ago, princess."

"You must have retained some of it if you made a point to give Teri your wine supply on the way out of town." He reared back a little at the rare—and accidental—compliment. "I mean . . . a broken clock is correct twice a day, right?"

He was still giving her that narrow-eyed look.

Nerves jumped in her belly.

Turn around and go.

She sauntered forward instead and watched his chest muscles tighten, his spine straighten. Did he do that every time she approached? Why was she only recognizing it now? That proof of his awareness pushed Natalie over the border into bad-idea town. Because at least she wasn't an afterthought to him. Even if he couldn't stand her, at least her presence had an effect on him. "So I was thinking . . ."

"You wish you'd kissed me in the bathroom earlier."

"I'd sooner kiss an active lawnmower." She realized her hands were gesticulating wildly and folded them at her waist. "Actually, I was thinking you could use my help."

He snorted. Leaned back against the truck and crossed his thick arms. "What now?"

Natalie kept her features serene, even as the harbinger of rejection hung over her head like a freshly sharpened machete. "You mentioned the bank refusing you a small business loan. For Zelnick Cellar. But if, um . . ." All at once, the ludicrous nature of her idea registered, but she'd said too much to stop now. "If I was an official employee. And attached to . . . you . . . in some way, well, you would almost be guaranteed an approval. As you've pointed out on numerous occasions, my last name does carry a lot of weight in this industry."

For several moments, he stared at her in silence. "I'm waiting for the punch line."

"There is no punch line, you baboon. I'm suggesting . . ." She felt like she'd swallowed a fistful of dirt, her stomach beginning to churn. "I'm suggesting that—"

"Holy shit." August pushed off the truck, his arms dropping slowly to his sides. "Earlier. You told me Mommy and Daddy wouldn't release your trust fund unless you're married." His mouth opened and closed. A hand raked through his hair. "You're not suggesting . . ." Something she couldn't quite define flickered in his eyes. "You're not suggesting we get *married*, are you?"

The way he said it, like she'd proposed a stroll through a minefield, had Natalie backing up a pace. A marriage between them *would* be a minefield. Even though they would be . . .

"*Fake* married," she enunciated. "For financial purposes. Obviously this wouldn't be a romantic union. We would simply need to convince Ingram Meyer, the man who has the ability to solve both of our problems. We would just be in it for the monetary advantages."

His jaw was slack at this point.

The silence stretched, so she filled it out of nerves.

"The wine train event is tomorrow afternoon. Its inaugural ride after the interior was redesigned. We're cutting the ribbon—"

"See, it's shit like that—wine trains and ribbon cutting and redesigned interiors being a big-ass deal that had me looking forward to seeing the back of this town."

"You've made it clear that wine culture is trivial to you, August. Also, the way it tastes. Lest we forget." She crossed herself. "Anyway. If you are interested in my offer, we could . . ." Her courage was beginning to wane in the face of his visible astonishment. "We could meet with my family in a neutral setting and discuss how to proceed."

"You're actually serious," he mused with a slow, incredulous headshake. "You just *proposed* to me, Natalie?"

Speaking of souls being sucked out, hers exited her body in that moment and observed the scene from above. There she was, asking this man she hated to be her husband. "Desperate" was the only word she could use to describe herself. Out of options, with nowhere to turn. And this man had to be enjoying every single second of it. Any moment now, he would tell her she was even crazier than he'd originally thought and he'd burn rubber to escape her.

The possibility of that pressed down on her chest.

God, she was weary of being dismissed. She couldn't let it happen again, especially from August. It would cut especially deep from this Neanderthal. Giving him leverage over her burned like a cattle brand to the throat.

"Forget it," she managed to push past dry lips. "I don't want to be married to someone who doesn't know to seize a good opportunity."

Laughter burst out of him. "Marrying *you* is a good opportunity?"

Natalie turned and stalked away, ignoring the twist in her breast.

An arm wrapped around her waist before she made it three steps.

"Don't get pissed," he said a few inches above her head. "I only meant you'd skin me alive in my sleep."

"We wouldn't *sleep* together, ding dong. It would be in name only."

"I fail to see the advantage for me."

Natalie resisted the urge to relax back against his chest. He was so *warm*. And that stupid, tatted-up arm could probably lift a station wagon. Why wasn't she pulling away? Any second now. She would. Facing the opposite direction was just . . . easier. She couldn't see his scorn and disbelief this way. "Let me lay it out for you, August. We have the same man standing in the way of our success—Ingram Meyer. Loan officer at the bank, trustee of my money, and one of my father's many fanboys. If I'm married, he'll release my start-up capital from his clutches. As for you? Marrying and employing a Vos will help you secure a small business loan." She threw an absent gesture in the general direction of his vineyard. "You could continue making wine. Maybe even wine people can stand to swallow, with my help. Don't you want the winery to be a success?"

"I did." Her brows drew together over the gruff note in his voice. "I did. But I resigned myself to the fact that this is the one thing I'm terrible at."

"You're forgetting basic human hygiene."

"I must not smell that bad," he said against the side of her neck, his lips brushing that sensitive patch beneath her ear, warm breath coasting down the collar of her shirt—and that arm. It flexed where it banded across her belly, making hidden parts of her tense, too, in the process. "You know. Since you're melting on me like an M&M on the dashboard of a hot car."

Natalie twisted out of his hold like a shot, ordering her skin to cool down as she turned. It wouldn't. Was his chest rising and falling faster than before? "Look, if you want to leave St. Helena, I'm not going to stop you."

A line snapped in his cheek. "That was the plan."

"Plans can change."

A sound left him. "You must really want that trust fund."

"I *want* a new start." Momentarily, she let herself be vulnerable. Maybe because she was already halfway there after making the proposal to August. Or maybe she'd already been sawed open after humbling herself this morning to Corinne. Whatever the reason, she spoke without censure. "I need a new start. I can't just stay here, living in the shadow of my family. My brother. I might as well still be that seventeen-year-old screwup that everyone just . . . tolerates. I'm better elsewhere. I'm something. I'm someone when I'm not here."

The sound of his hard swallow reached her through the cool night air.

Damn. Too much.

She'd given him the motherload of ammunition—and since he was obviously not into the idea, she needed to get out of there before he could use it.

"Good luck, August," she said, backing away and eventually turning, picking up her pace. "It would have been fun making your life hell."

"*Natalie.*"

She didn't stop. Didn't want this man, of all people, to let her down gently. Her pride was all but dismantled, but she could hold on to a scrap. Speed walking down the pathway back to the guest house, however, she wondered how much longer she could maintain her grip.

Chapter Five

August adjusted his tie in the rearview mirror of his truck, grimacing at the sound of a marching band butchering "America the Beautiful." Across the street, the parking lot of the train station had been transformed by two high-ceilinged tents, royal blue carpet laid down over the asphalt. Waiters in tuxedos carried around trays holding glasses of red wine, others ferried hors d'oeuvres among guests dressed to the nines.

Unbelievable. All of these people had gathered to celebrate a train that served wine. Technically, any train in the world could serve wine, but these snoots in suits looked for any excuse to rub elbows in their loafers and comment on the orange-peel aftertaste of their drink. He'd been looking forward to never hearing the word "bouquet" ever again in his fucking life, but here he was. About to join this stuffed-shirt soiree in his monkey suit.

All because of a woman.

Not just any woman, though. Natalie Vos.

Jesus Christ. I must be out of my mind.

He'd been worrying about the state of his sanity since last night. She'd walked away and he'd gotten in his truck without starting the engine. And then he'd sat there for an hour. Two.

With a curse that was vile even by navy standards, he'd started the truck and gone back to the vineyard he'd never expected to lay eyes on again. He'd planned to conduct the sale with a real estate agent virtually while he spent some time back in Kansas near his parents and regrouped.

He'd made his peace with the fact that he'd never make wine decent enough to honor the memory of Sam. He'd been good with the truth—that he'd given this town his best damn shot and grapes simply weren't his area of expertise. All efforts to be successful were exhausted. He'd left nothing on the battlefield.

Until last night, when Natalie slid a new opportunity across the table.

Now? August could no longer walk away secure in the knowledge that he'd done everything in his power to bring Sam's dream to life. There was one more try available—so he had to take it or guilt and loose ends would haunt him for the rest of his life.

And the woman. She would haunt him, too.

Natalie needed something—her trust fund. He could help give it to her.

August liked to think he would help any woman who was up against some ancient bullshit contract designed to force her into marriage, but deep down he knew it was just this one. Natalie. Damn it to hell, what was it about her? Every time they were together, a needle sewed itself in and out of his gut. His palms sweat. His dick pleaded with him to be nicer so it might have a chance of seeing the light of day at some point. Or, better yet, the dark of her bedroom. They fought like they hated each other, but somehow, Lord, he'd been ready to drop to his knees in front of her on that sidewalk last night.

I'm better elsewhere. I'm something. I'm someone when I'm not here.

After the shock of hearing that breathy confession had worn off, he'd just gotten *mad*.

Who the fuck made her feel like that?

How long had she been feeling like crap without his knowing about it?

That second concern happened to be ridiculous, by the way. There were probably endless things he didn't know about Natalie Vos. Their relationship didn't exactly lend itself to a lot of quiet heart-to-hearts in front of a fire. Still, he should have known about her insecurity. That she was better off gone. He should have picked up on it. He should have shut his stupid mouth and paid better attention.

As she'd made abundantly clear, it was too late for August to romance her in any way. Attraction might be an undeniable crackle between them, but she wouldn't touch him with industrial rubber gloves, let alone her bare hands. Still, he couldn't walk away from Natalie if she needed him. Not when she'd sucked it up and asked for assistance when it clearly had been very difficult to set aside her pride. No, he'd dwell on it forever.

So he crossed the stupid street in his hot, restrictive suit with his molars grinding together, scanning the crowd for the black-haired goddess he would never get to sleep with but would apparently be marrying, because he'd lost his fucking mind. It was so hot under the tent that he immediately started to sweat. Why did these people insist on gathering to celebrate fermented grape juice? Had none of them heard of baseball? Now *that* was a reason to gather outside in the sun—

Natalie.

Up ahead.

Hot. Damn. As usual, when August laid eyes on the woman,

he had to squeeze his thumbs hard in the palms of his hands. She had these incredibly smart eyes and a soft mouth. He'd never felt the need to categorize another woman's features before. He sort of stopped at registering the color of someone's eyes and hair. Brown. Blue. Blond. Green.

Easy.

There was nothing easy about looking at Natalie. All sorts of shit was happening on her features at once and for some reason, he wanted to keep up with all of it. Sometimes she might look bored, but she'd rub her lips together over and over, letting him know she was actually anxious and hiding it. Other times, two little lines formed between her eyebrows like she might be concerned about something, but she'd hoist her chin up in the air like she didn't have a care in the world. Bottom line, Natalie wasn't a simple combination of colors, she was an ever-changing kaleidoscope he couldn't seem to stop peering into.

Although today the color purple was front and center, because in a sea of muted colors, her short lilac dress stood out. Cut high around her throat with a low back and a soft, fluttery skirt. Those long, lithe legs had his Adam's apple bobbing up and down against the starched collar of his shirt. He could see them all tangled up in his sheets. Could see them bending, locking, being pressed open onto the mattress by his hands.

Those images would never become a reality, and yet he'd love someone to try to stop him from fake marrying this kaleidoscopic woman.

On his way across the tent, he finally noticed Natalie was standing with her mother, her brother, Julian, and the blonde whom August assumed was Julian's girlfriend. They were speaking in low tones over glasses of wine, seemingly unaware that, as the legendary Vos family, they were of interest to every guest in the tent. Classy, sophisticated. A quiet dynasty that had perhaps seen better days but remained legendary.

Maybe it would be fun to mess that image up for a while.

Fun or not, this was happening.

Because if Natalie was desperate enough to ask August to marry her, then she would eventually find someone else—and the very idea of *that* made his head want to explode. Maybe that ugly thought bubble was what spurred him into acting rash. She'd suggested they have a civilized conversation about their potential marriage while in neutral territory, right? Unfortunately, there was nothing civilized about August and it was going to be fun reminding her. Catching her off guard.

When August was approximately ten yards away, Natalie's wineglass paused halfway to her mouth, her attention swiveling in his direction. She blinked back surprise and shifted in her white high heels, started to sip her wine, stopped, then glared at him. He would have laughed if he wasn't about to finally, *finally* kiss her again.

"Hey, babe. Sorry I'm late," August said smoothly, cupping her cheek and drawing her in, as though kissing her were second nature. As if he'd made a practice of it, when in reality, her smoke-and-flowers scent had his tongue seconds from rolling out of his mouth. He let himself feel the distinct pleasure of watching her golden eyes widen in shock—and then he couldn't feel anything at all but relief. Yeah, relief. There was her mouth.

Perfect as ever. Touching his. Jolting, then softening.

Thank God.

He was only going to catch her off guard a little, needle her, maybe even punish her for doubting that he'd come through—

but she inhaled quickly against his lips and he watched up close as her eyelashes fluttered and a dumbfounding one-two punch of lust and satisfaction caught him in the stomach. Their eyes closed simultaneously and they sank in, just for a second, a twisting feast of lips and a rough exhale that said *this is far from enough*. But here wasn't the place for more, so he intertwined their fingers, winking at her when no one else could see—and did his damnedest to remember this wasn't real. It was just one enemy helping out another.

Yeah.

"I . . . um." Natalie shook herself, briefly shot a glance to her mother, whose eyebrows were nearly buried in her hairline. "August. I-I thought you said you couldn't make it."

"August? So formal." He gave her a playful nudge in the hip. "What happened to 'my Adonis'?"

Temper snapped in Natalie's expression, but at least the irritation helped her focus, which had been his intention. "That's something I call you only when we're alone," she said with a toothy smile. "You know, kind of like 'shit for brains.' And 'rat king.'"

August laughed. "I love her sense of humor," he said to the group, absently plucking a glass of wine off a passing tray and taking a long guzzle. Silence had descended like a heavy drape, not only among their fivesome, but across the tent. Until now, this very second, August hadn't exactly *planned* on outright embarrassing Natalie. It was sort of a last-minute spin on his plan, born of sexual frustration and the fact that she truly believed he was a simpleton. He might not have a last name that people whispered in reverence on the streets of St. Helena, but he wasn't a moron. Holding up his end of their battle of wits seemed to be his only way of making sure she knew it.

A full fifteen seconds had ticked past and still no one had commented on his arrival.

"I think I speak for the group when I say . . ." the dumbstruck blonde—Hallie, was it?—finally ventured in a stage whisper. "H'whaaaa is happening here?"

August feigned surprise, shaking stiff-shouldered Natalie a little. "You didn't tell them, hon?" He drained the remainder of his wine, handing it off to a man who only looked confused by the empty glass. Oops, not a waiter. "Natalie and I have been seeing each other for a while now. Just like a fine Cabernet, we wanted to give ourselves room to breathe, so we've kept it quiet, but I was under the impression we were stepping out into the open today." He smiled down at Natalie, who was very clearly three seconds from ripping his throat out with her teeth. "You said you didn't want to hide anymore. You said, 'Let's shout it from the rooftops, my Adonis.'"

A sound halfway between a laugh and growl burst out of her. "I don't think I used those exact words—"

"Nope, that's what you said. Verbatim."

"I must have been sleep talking." Golden eyes crackled up at August and hell if that temper wasn't turning him on. "People are known to talk in their sleep," she continued. "In rare cases, people are even known to *murder* loved ones in their sleep. Did you know that? You might want to keep it in mind."

August dropped his head back and laughed. "There's that sense of humor again. One of the million reasons I can't wait to call you my wife."

You could hear a pin drop in the tent.

"What was that?" Corinne inquired in a smooth whisper, though her color had lightened by several shades. "Did he say 'wife'?"

"That's definitely what I heard," Julian responded, those studious eyes traveling between his sister and August. "What about you, Hallie?"

"Don't drag me into this." Then, out of the corner of her mouth, "But if that is what you said, there's a family discount on floral wedding arrangements."

Apart from the brief, appreciative smile Julian sent his girlfriend, the tension in the tent remained thicker than a porterhouse steak. All right, August had gone too far. He'd been having his fun with Natalie, but now her temper had faded into something close to regret and panic.

Thank God he'd run that errand last night.

Struck with panic-induced amnesia, he started slapping at his pockets, trying to locate the ring box—

Corinne distracted him by stepping between him and Natalie, her fingers digging into both of their forearms. "Listen to me very carefully. You've just set something very delicate in motion. Do you understand?" She drilled August with a look. "You obviously think this is some sidesplitting joke, but a sham marriage could do lasting damage to our family name." Her attention transferred to Natalie, sharpening so much that August almost dragged Natalie behind his back to shield her. Would have, if he didn't suspect the matriarch had something important to say. Something he needed to hear. "Ingram Meyer is in attendance today. He is always in attendance. At *everything*. He has eyes and ears all over St. Helena and takes his responsibilities at the bank very seriously. If he suspects this relationship is all for show, he will deny the release of your trust fund faster than you made this idiotic plan, Natalie."

Pulse rippling, August did a quick scan of the crowd, and sure enough, there was the loan officer from the bank—tall, slender, and pasty in a straw hat. This guy had barely glanced at August's application before dismissing him completely. The same man who held Natalie's fate in his grip.

"Either drop the act now," Corinne continued in a low hiss, "or understand that this needs to be a serious endeavor. You're not just convincing the bank, you're convincing the whole town of St. Helena because it's all one giant, plugged-in pipeline. You'll need to share a residence, be seen together in public. Have a proper wedding. If that's the direction of your choosing, then act accordingly. Now. Before you two make this family out to be nothing more than a bunch of cheap con artists."

Was it too late to leave and try his entrance again?

Natalie's features were carefully schooled, as usual, but the blood had drained from her face—and August loathed himself for causing that reaction.

Why do you do things like this?

No time to explore the mysteries of his universe now, because he had a feeling Natalie was seconds from backing out. Dropping the act. Of course she was. Who would trust him with something so delicate after he'd entered like a bull walking into a china shop?

He could not let this chance slip away. His dick/gut told him he'd regret it forever.

As fast as humanly possible, August drew the ring box out of his pants pocket and got down on one knee.

Natalie swayed backward a little and August's free hand shot out automatically to steady her. She looked down at him without breathing, her gaze tripping between him and the ring box, then . . . just on him. For a moment, there was no one else in the tent. Only them. And he was slightly alarmed by the rough grind in his chest, even as he was secretly grateful for the rise of nerves. She deserved to have a nervous man down on one knee, didn't she?

Hell yes, she did.

"What I meant to say, Natalie, is . . . I would like to call you my wife." He thumbed open the black velvet box without taking his attention off her. Couldn't have pried it off with a crowbar. Jesus, was there even a chance she'd say yes now? His heart lifted and wedged itself behind his jugular. "I'm asking you to spend the rest of your life trying not to murder me in your sleep. Please."

Did the corner of her mouth jump?

Had he salvaged this?

Time stood still while she peered down at the ring, those lines popping into existence between her brows. Considering the proposal? *Jesus, come on, Natalie.* Sweat was beginning to dribble down his spine. He'd been on life-and-death missions less stressful than this.

Finally, she wet her lips and held out her left hand, whispering, "No promises about the murder thing."

August's heart dropped back into place and his hearing turned normal again. When had it grown so distorted? No amount of mental orders could keep his fingers from shaking as he took out the small diamond ring and slipped it onto her finger. *Not real,* he reminded himself again after standing, looking down into her stunned face. Instinct had August pulling Natalie up against his chest, surprise crashing into him when she wrapped her arms around him and held on tight.

People were applauding. Even Natalie's family. When did that start?

Well. Everyone but Ingram Meyer was clapping.

The man regarded them through narrowed eyes over the rim of his wineglass.

Do better for her.

"Thanks," she whispered into his shoulder. "You just had to act like a mega asshole, didn't you? But I guess . . . thanks."

"Can we negotiate my conjugal rights now?"

Great. Way to do better. His dick truly ruined everything.

"Nope," Natalie said.

"Worth a shot."

She smiled up at him sweetly. "I'll give you a shot. Right in the junk—"

A voice filled the tent, cutting off the rest of her sentence, though August was pretty sure he'd gotten the gist of her threat. Natalie wiggled a little and he dropped his arms, but she let him hold her hand as they turned to face the man now speaking into a microphone toward the sunny edge of the tent. He wore an old-timey bowler hat and a carnation on his lapel, and August's eyes nearly rolled out of his head.

"Welcome to the grand reopening of the Napa Valley Wine Train, established in 1864. We are pleased to have you aboard as our first passengers in our new, elegant setting. Many of the vintage fixtures and the Honduran wood paneling are the very same—"

Several people lost their minds over this.

People in St. Helena got flustered at the very utterance of the word "vintage."

". . . but these features have been restored to a more sophisticated level of their old glory." The man with the microphone craned his neck and searched the crowd. Why did he seem to be looking directly at August and Natalie? "I hear we have an unexpected proposal in the house? Well, let me tell you, the happy couple is in luck. There isn't a more romantic setting than Napa at twilight aboard our luxurious train and"—he paused for effect—"this is the perfect time to announce the addition of our special honeymoon seating on the second level. A little corner of glass-domed opulence all to themselves called the Lovers' Nest. We have our perfect test subjects, have we not?"

"Oh . . ." Natalie called politely. "We don't need any special treatment—"

"We'll take it," August said, cutting her off to a smattering of laughs.

He squeezed her hand.

She buried her nails in the meat of his palm until he choked.

Someone snapped a picture.

Chapter Six

Everyone filed onto the train, shuffling one by one up the carpeted steps.

Natalie's neck burned. For good reason, too. Corinne watched her like a hawk from several passengers back, as did her brother and Hallie. Ingram Meyer and his Tommy Bahama hat took up the rear of the line, making no pretense about being zeroed in on August and Natalie. His brows looked so skeptical, they'd almost reached the center of his forehead, and he was obviously unconvinced that Natalie and August were a happily engaged couple.

Maybe such a feat was impossible.

Maybe this was all a huge waste of time.

"This is insane," Natalie whispered. "I'm insane."

August leaned down, bringing them nearly eye level. *Don't look at his mouth.* Natalie refused to think about the sweep of exhilaration she'd felt when their lips locked together. Her body's unwise response to this man needed to be the furthest thing from her mind. Pushed way out into the ether, because it didn't matter. This plan was meant to be a business arrangement—and already it was on shaky ground. Might not even be viable at all.

"What's insane?" August prompted.

"This. Me. Asking for your help. You just want to make a fool out of me."

Momentarily, he cast his gaze downward. "I'll admit I came on a little strong back there. I'm just . . . I'm never comfortable at these things."

"So you have to make everyone else uncomfortable to compensate?"

"Correct."

"At least you're an honest dickhead."

"The wedding vows practically write themselves," he muttered, rubbing at the back of his neck with his free hand. "Look, it's out of my system now. I'll do better."

Natalie closed her eyes, acutely aware of Corinne watching them from her position in line. Of course Corinne had spotted the subterfuge right away. Even if the trust fund wasn't hanging in the balance, giving Natalie a big fat motive for a hasty marriage, never in Natalie's life had she gotten away with a lie to her mother. Corinne was a human polygraph test that she'd been taking and failing since birth.

That's not my weed, Mom.

Our test determined that was a lie.

Natalie attempted a small smile at her mother over her shoulder and was given an impassive look in return. Ingram Meyer watched the whole exchange happen, visibly taking mental notes behind shrewd eyes. He really did see everything, didn't he? Who in this crowd and the town beyond could be considered his eyes and ears? Anyone at any time? Faking this union was going to be a lot more complicated than she'd imagined. "I'm pretty sure it's too late, Adonis," she muttered, her gaze straying back to Ingram. "I think we've been made."

August shook his head. "We'll salvage it."

"Doubtful. I hope you can get your money back for this ring." A line popped in August's cheek. His giant hand was beginning to sweat inside of hers. Was he worried? Obviously. He wanted that bank loan as much as she wanted her trust fund released.

They were almost to the hostess station when one of the passengers squeezed past them toward the exit, crowding Natalie closer to August's big, warm body. The air was beginning to cool, thanks to the approaching sunset, and she'd accidentally left her black silk jacket in the car. In other words, the heat he gave off felt incredible on her goose-bumped arms. And when she didn't immediately move away, he angled toward her slowly and corralled her closer with a forearm to her lower back.

"You want my jacket?" he said gruffly, his breath stirring her hair.

That dreaded pulse started beating between her thighs, her toes twitching in her heels. "Oh sure. After catching me off guard, embarrassing me on purpose, and proposing publicly without so much as a discussion, now you want to be chivalrous."

"How long are you going to stay pissed, Natalie?"

"It only happened ten minutes ago!" she whispered furiously. "We could have had a civil conversation and arranged everything properly. But no. You had to have the upper hand."

"I'm sorry. All right? Is that what you want to hear? Because I am." He jerked his chin toward the opening of the train. "You almost said no."

"I *should* have said no." Natalie shook her head. "I should just bite the bullet and ask my father to amend the terms."

His sturdy frame stiffened, long moments passing while those words hung in the scant space of fading daylight between them. "Hey." He dropped his mouth to her ear. "We're in this. Quit talking about backing out. I'm taking this seriously now."

"Do you really think you'll be able to take this ruse seriously for an extended period of time, though? Because, according to my mother, we have to share an address, August. For the marriage to be considered viable *and* for the purposes of the loan. And all you want to do is make me look stupid. I don't trust you." Her heart thunked noticeably, dropping lower and lower by the moment. "Oh my God, what have I done?"

He surprised her by pressing their foreheads together. "Natalie."

"What?"

Three seconds passed. Four. "I will never, *ever* let you down again. Is that clear?"

The strangest thing happened in the wake of that unexpected vow. The clamminess of her skin subsided and her pulse slowly returned to normal. She found herself nodding, even, because how could she do anything else when she'd never seen him look so serious? Or heard that thread of honor so deeply woven into his tone. This was August the Navy SEAL.

Still, she wasn't 100 percent ready to take that leap into trusting him. Not after everything. Not when they were so fresh from the stunt he'd pulled. "We'll see, I guess."

"You *will* see," he countered without the slightest hesitation. "Now are you coming with me to the Lovers' Nest or not?"

When had August pulled her closer?

Better question. When had she pushed up on her tiptoes so her arms could reach around his neck? She started to retract her touch, but he shook his head. "If I were your real fiancé," he said quietly, for her ears alone, "this is how I'd hold you. All the time. So this is how we should stay."

"Right." The big slabs of his pecs were inches from her mouth and she had the strangest urge to sink her teeth into them. Maybe even had a premonition that he would enjoy it. *There will be none of that.* "Later, we can h-have an actual discussion and lay down some ground rules. Come up with a timeline for our respective goals. But first and foremost, let me reiterate, there is going to be absolutely zero sex. I cannot stress that enough."

"It *has* been stressful, princess. Believe me." His thumb brushed across her lower spine and a hot shiver went through her, head to toe. "Remind me again why we can't have sex."

His voice cracked on the word "sex," right there against her ear, and a swallow got stuck in her throat. "The reasons have changed, obviously, with this shiny new development. Lines that need to be clear will . . . blur . . . if we go there. But the underlying logic is the same. I can't let my guard down around you."

That big hand flexed on her back. "Do you always let your guard down during sex?"

"I mean . . . I *have.*" She drew the words out, registering her answer even as she spoke it out loud. "Sort of. Let it down. But I definitely can't let it down with someone who is gleeful about pointing out my shortcomings and poking fun at my insecurities. That's just self-sabotage."

He frowned down at her. "What about the fact that you poke fun at my insecurities, too? Wouldn't it be self-sabotage for me, as well?"

"You are a man. You'd be getting sex. You wouldn't care."

"Valid point." His eyes narrowed further. "So you're saying you *would* care?"

"I'm saying I'd beat myself up over giving in while you snored it up on the other side of the bed."

"You're so sure you wouldn't be snoring right there beside me?"

"We're not going to find out."

"I'm inclined to agree to anything right now to make you happy, Natalie, but I'm not agreeing to any no sex rules. Sorry. We're grown adults and if we both want something, we should be able to take it without consulting some arbitrary rulebook." His chest rose and fell as he pulled her in closer. "If you don't directly ask me for sex, I'll respect that. But if you want to be fucked, you're going to get it. Period, the end."

Oh damn. That pulse was back and now a damp sensation had been thrown in.

She was aware of every erogenous zone she owned. Her hip blades, the insides of her ankles, her neck and throat and breasts.

This evening could not end quickly enough.

"Ah, here they are," crooned a man's voice behind Natalie. She turned to find the general manager of the wine train approaching with his hat sitting jauntily on his head. "The newly engaged lovebirds. Follow me this way, please." Finally, Natalie unhooked her arms from around August's neck and trailed after the manager, cool air once again making her arms prickle. "I'll take you to the Lovers' Nest."

"Caw," August chirped in her ear, sounding like a dying crow. "Caw."

Natalie elbowed him in the stomach.

He chuckled.

And dropped his jacket around her shoulders.

I will never, ever let you down again. Is that clear?

His words bounced around in her head over and over again on their way up to the second floor of the train. He couldn't possibly *mean* that, could he? No way. Just lulling her into a false sense of security. Still, her mind continued to replay that intense vow, the seriousness of his tone. Almost like he'd been trying to engrave those words on her brain. Yet he'd left something unspoken, buried between the lines.

But no. *That's ridiculous.*

The manager led them to the farthest corner of the train's second floor and stopped in front of a high-backed, red velvet swivel chair, the sides curved for ultimate privacy. It could face the train car or the window, depending on how it was turned. With a smile of pure anticipation on his face, the manager hit a button and a small fireplace bloomed to life beneath the picture window that would display their view of Napa's rolling hills on the train ride.

But . . .

"There is only one chair," Natalie pointed out.

"Oh, is there?" The man feigned surprise. "Surely it's big enough for two. You won't know unless you try!"

"Have you seen this man?" She jerked a thumb in August's direction. "He's the actual Yeti. He probably won't even be able to fit into it by himself."

The man looked momentarily thrown, but he rallied with a tip of his hat. "I'll leave you to your own devices," the manager sang, backing away, clearly committed to the belief that he was doing them a favor. And even Natalie had to admit . . . the setting was nothing short of sickeningly romantic. The pink-gold sunset burnished the velvet swivel chair in a glow and the fire crackled. A bottle of wine sat open on a side table with two glasses. Had her relationship with August been real, she'd be obligated to ovulate.

Natalie turned to August with the intention of informing him they would just sit in a couple of the regular seats, like the handful of inaugural ride passengers who were now making their way up to the second floor. Before she could open her mouth, however, he dropped into the deep swivel chair, stretched his long legs out, and patted his thigh. "Your throne awaits, princess."

"I am not sitting . . ." Realizing the other passengers were within earshot, she lowered her voice to a whisper. "I am not sitting on your lap in this public pleasure den. What do they expect us to *do* here?"

August considered the curved and extended sides of the swivel chair that were obviously meant to block them from view. "Some groping at the very least."

Please tell me that my nipples aren't tingling. "Grope me and live to regret it."

"Fine." He sighed, running a hand down his tie. "You can grope me."

"You mispronounced 'strangle.'"

His answering laugh fell silent after a moment and he leaned forward. "Natalie." He tucked his tongue into his cheek. "We're not convincing anybody."

A familiar laugh came from the direction of the stairs and Natalie glanced over to find Hallie's blond curls among the crowd of newcomers to the second floor. Which meant her brother wouldn't be far behind. Hallie was speaking with the British woman who owned the donut shop in town, Fudge Judy, and if memory served, she loved to gossip. Everyone from the mayor to the teenagers of St. Helena frequented the shop. Behind them were several other business owners and ladies who lunch—all eager to get eyes on the newly engaged couple. Being standoffish with her supposed fiancé would be noticed and commented on. Maybe, according to her mother, even reported back to Ingram Meyer?

Natalie looked down at August, who was now staring into the fire. Back in the tent, she'd made a split-second decision. Either jump into this subterfuge with both feet and form a convincing union . . . or call it off immediately—and put herself back at square one. She'd looked down at August on one knee, his expression earnest and hopeful and . . . she'd felt something unnamed, but poignant, move inside of her, causing her to choose the former. Natalie and August were now engaged in the eyes of the St. Helena elite.

This marriage of convenience had been her idea. August arriving out of the blue like a wrecking ball had caught her off guard outside, but right now? If she didn't swallow her pride, this plan was going to sink them both before it even started.

In finance, her credo was *go big or go home.*

Obviously it hadn't always paid off, considering she'd gone big and . . . gotten *sent* home.

Doubts were piling up about the wisdom of this arrangement. But it was the solution to her problem. A way forward. And if she didn't seize it with both hands, the chance would pass her by. Through the crowd, she met Hallie's eyes. Saw her brother's tall frame moving into view and it occurred to her, if she brought shame on the family name, all of Julian's hard work to restore the winery would go down the drain.

God, she couldn't do that. No chance.

There was no more time to waffle.

With a deep inhale, Natalie set down her clutch on the side table, hesitated a moment, then parked her backside on August's thigh. Obviously he'd expected her to stand for the whole ride or sit somewhere else, because his eyebrows shot up, that big paw going to the small of her back automatically, his fingers splaying on the base of her spine.

"I should probably just keep my mouth shut," he said, his voice lower by several octaves, "so I don't say anything to fuck this up."

"That would be the smartest thing you've ever done."

"Yeah, wow. Engaged for twenty minutes and I'm already a changed man." She watched in the reflection of the window as August's attention ran down the slope of her neck. Felt his heart accelerate against her shoulder. "But I can't help but point out . . ."

"God, you refuse to get out of your own way."

"That maybe you're afraid to kiss me."

She pinned him with a look, her pulse quickening over their position—faces no more than a few inches apart, his hand braced on her back protectively, fingertips curling slightly as if he wanted to pull her closer. All the way into his lap. His five-o'clock shadow, which hadn't been visible upon his arrival, was beginning to darken his jaw and his tie was slightly crooked. A rugged soldier forced into a suit and a marriage. For her. With her.

They were a team whether she liked it or not. Natalie had a feeling the next thing out of his mouth would put her firmly in the *or not* camp.

"Why am I afraid to kiss you? Besides your overall repellency, I mean."

He gave a cocky shrug. "You're scared to enjoy it."

"Do you actually think I'm going to fall for this?" she sputtered.

"Fall for what? It's the truth. You can't stand my ass, but if we kissed, you'd forget."

"To hate you?" She scoffed. "Not likely."

As if to call her bluff, a loud whistle went off and the train lurched forward, sending Natalie crashing into August's chest, her butt sliding neatly into his lap, where she was galled to find that it fit like a glove. He hissed in a breath, his hand leaving her back in order to grip the edge of the velvet chair. "Look, might as well warn you, I'm going to get hard."

"Seriously?" His fly swelled beneath her bottom rapidly, turning her skin flush. *Not excited.* She was *not* excited. Maybe if she kept repeating those words, they would become true. "Been a while?"

"Ten minutes or ten years celibate, I'd still be hard with that butt in position for a good time, Natalie. But, yeah, since we're on the subject, it's been a while. You?"

She couldn't quite hide her surprise that he'd admitted a dry spell out loud. Surprised enough to speak her own truth without thinking. "Yes. You were *supposed* to be my rebound."

"Rebound from what?" he asked sharply, his chest muscles hardening against her.

That's right. He didn't know. Of course he didn't. Why would he? "I was engaged." She strove to keep her tone light. "In New York. Now I'm not."

It took several moments for him to process that, a veritable canyon forming between his eyebrows. "Why?"

"I don't want to talk about it, okay? Not right now."

Those long fingers flexed on her back. "Is he still in the picture?"

"No." For some reason, she felt compelled to look him in the eye and impress her answer on him. "No. You and I just got engaged, August. Obviously he's not."

Relief seemed to make his pupils expand. "Good."

"Good?"

Several seconds ticked by wherein she found herself studying the indent in the center of his bottom lip. The stubble appearing just over the firmer top one. And why was there something . . . annoyingly sexy about her feet not touching the ground while sitting in his lap? "That's what I said. Good," he repeated, something flickering in his eyes. "Wouldn't want to have to fend off any competition for my fake fiancée, right?"

"Right." That tiny sink of disappointment she felt was incredibly unhealthy. "Well, you don't have to worry about that."

A muscle snapped in his cheek. "Good."

"Stop saying 'good.'"

"*Great.*" Tension coiled between them like a copper spring and she couldn't quite place a finger on the source. Arousal—his, *not* hers—was the obvious answer, but there seemed to be something more. She was being challenged in some way, though, that much was obvious. August had leaned in, bringing his mouth within an inch of hers. They were completely shielded from the rest of the train car. Napa danced by in all its rich, sunset-drenched splendor, vineyard vines threading toward rolling hills and fading sunlight, but she was barely aware of any of it. Only this man's breath on her mouth and his strength surrounding her. "Just so we're clear, Natalie, I wouldn't have any problem fending off some city boy in loafers."

Please tell me that my vaginal walls did not flex in response to that. "Jesus. Leave it to you to have a pissing contest with someone you've never met."

Why was she breathing so fast?

Her words tripped over themselves on the way out and he only moved closer, his hand opening wide on her hip and squeezing, his lips making the barest contact with hers. "Rebound, huh?"

"Is that what you're mad about?"

"Who said I'm mad?"

"Your face."

Their lips were all but flush now. "Maybe I'm just pissed I missed my chance to help you move on from your broken engagement."

"I *have* moved on."

"Prove it, princess." Ever so briefly, his tongue touched the seam of her mouth and fingers of lust raked up her inner thighs. "Convince this train full of your fellow wine snobs that you're dying to walk down the aisle with me."

Bastard. "To this day, no one in St. Helena has ever beaten my record for shots taken at a party. Sixteen shots, August. I should by all accounts be dead. Before me, the record stood at fifteen."

"Proud of you, girl, but why are you telling me this?"

"So you understand that I don't lose. Not when I'm challenged."

A rumble went off in his chest. "Getting that mouth on mine won't be a loss."

Slowly, she wound his tie around her fist and used her body to guide him back into the dark interior of the Lovers' Nest chair, turning so her breasts were pressed high to his chest. "Are you sure about that?"

"Sure as I've ever been about anything," August said with confidence.

But when she twisted a little in his lap, he gulped.

"Fuck" was the last thing he said before Natalie settled her mouth over his and kissed him in a way that was pure foreplay. Wet lips dragged right to left, teasing, showing him what her mouth could do elsewhere. And based on the rigid rise of his erection under her butt, he was definitely thinking about it. A lot. She framed his bristled jaw with her right hand and tugged his chin down, opening his mouth, giving her the access to lick deep, once, twice, three times, leisurely and savoring, tasting his hearty groan and feeling his muscles tense to the point of snapping. "I see what you're doing now," he uttered between kisses. "You're going to get me hot and leave me hanging, aren't you?"

"Congratulations," she panted. "You're not as dumb as you look."

He tilted her chin up, glazed eyes looking down at her. "You're underestimating how much I love a challenge, too, princess."

She would not be making that mistake again.

Before she knew what was happening, August's fingers slid up into her hair and fisted a thick bunch of it, using his grip to tilt back her head. Expose her neck. And then . . . oh. Oh God. His teeth and the tip of his tongue and his lips moved like a sensual trio up the curve of her throat, then over to the right. To a spot behind her ear that had her toes spreading so quickly, one of her heels fell to the floor with a *thwack.*

"I can't believe you waited until we're on a train full of people to kiss me again." His teeth closed around the shell of her ear and razed up and down, up and down. "Maybe you did it on purpose because you know exactly what we'd be doing if we were alone."

"Fighting?"

"Fucking." He licked a circle behind her ear, traced a path back to her mouth, and suctioned her lips into a hard kiss. "But I'd start with two fingers in deep between your legs and I'd keep them there until you're wet enough to take it hard."

More vaginal flexing. Accompanied by a soft moan she tried to disguise with a cough.

Fooling no one.

The tables were quickly being turned.

She could see him in her mind's eye, moving roughly on top of her in a mess of bedding, her ankles locked behind his big, flexing back. They would be agitated and sweaty and trying to outdo each other and it would be *mind-blowing*, but she would regret it afterward. Giving in to this man who thought she was nothing more than a spoiled brat.

Time to regain the upper hand.

"Maybe I'd be giving instead of taking," she murmured, dragging a finger down the front of his shirt and toying with his belt buckle, reveling in the way his breath stuttered. "It might be so good you wouldn't even make it to home base."

"Princess, if I had to slide home on a bed of razor blades, I'd make it to that base with you." He bit off a sound. "Stop moving that tight ass, or I swear to God . . ."

"What?" She caught his bottom lip between her teeth and rotated her hips, enjoying the privilege of watching his eyes glaze over. "What are you going to do about it?"

"Cry, probably."

A laugh hopscotched out of her. A genuine giggle at his strained admission.

Eyes closed, he smiled against her mouth.

Something unexpected leapt in Natalie's chest and her lips paused in the act of teasing him into another kiss. What the heck was that? Under no circumstances should anything be happening in the place between her brain and her vagina. He'd been ready to leave town. He *would* have left town if it wasn't for her offer to help him secure a loan. He'd pegged her as a spoiled rich girl. They weren't even in a real relationship, yet he'd already firmly rejected everything about her. It would be a waste of time and energy trying to prove him wrong. Especially when their potential arrangement was founded on the release of her very healthy trust fund.

She'd be wasting her breath.

"Come back here," he rasped, studying her. "Torture me. I can take it."

Get up. She needed to get up.

They'd almost definitely been spotted kissing in the reflection of the window. The purpose of the Lovers' Nest had been served. So why was she leaning in again, craving the fullness of his lips and the way his hands traveled over her slowly, memorizing the dip of her side, the shape of her kneecaps, everywhere.

Natalie's mouth was half a centimeter from August's, her heart pounding riotously. The gauntlet between them was blurring. This kiss was going to be all about pleasure. Exploring. Them. Desperately, she tried to recall all the insults about her drinking and the way he'd intentionally blindsided her in the tent, but all she could feel was his heart banging like crazy and her own leapt in response to the proof that he was so affected—

"Natalie."

It took her a full five seconds to realize her mother was speaking. From where?

Natalie lifted her head and leaned to the side and there was Corinne, arms folded across her trim middle, regarding her with an impassive expression. "Oh my God," she whispered. "Caught making out by my mother. Did I accidentally board the train back to middle school?"

"Could we speak privately, please?" Corinne continued.

"One minute."

Natalie ducked back into the privacy of the chair, willing her face back to a normal temperature.

August's head dropped back on a groan. "Christ."

"Antichrist is more her vibe, actually."

His chest rose and fell on a pained laugh. "You'll have to give me a minute. Or . . . sixty. For this thing to go down."

"In that case, definitely don't think about *me* going down," she said, fluttering her eyelashes.

"Natalie," he gritted out.

She dropped her mouth to his ear and let out a warm breath that made him shiver and clutch at the side of her dress. "Looks like I win, rat king."

His jaw popped. "This time."

"*This* is the only time *this* will happen. We've made our point."

"Unfortunately I've still got mine," he muttered, nodding at his lap.

"Gross," she snapped, even though she felt the fluttering of a laugh build in her throat, and climbed off his lap. "Get yourself together while I"—she locked eyes with Corinne—"speak to my beautiful mother."

Corinne rolled her eyes and walked away.

Natalie followed, smiling and thanking people who congratulated her as she passed. When they reached a quiet corner of the train car, Corinne kept a serene smile on her face, but there was no mistaking the temper in her eyes. "Don't you think it would have been nice to give us a little prewarning before roping your brother and me into this stunt?"

"Yes, I do, actually. That was my intention—"

"In the space of thirty minutes, you and this . . . ape have turned us into a spectacle."

All at once, Natalie's blood rose to a rollicking boil. "He's a war veteran. A Navy SEAL. Don't ever talk about him like that again."

Her mother's mouth snapped shut, but she regrouped quickly. Natalie, however, did not. Since when was she so passionate about defending this man who was supposed to be her enemy? She could insult him until the cows came home, but someone else attempted it and she bit their head off? "You threw wine in this man's face at the Bouquets and Beginners competition two days ago. Do you not think everyone in town knows about it? Do you not think they're wondering how you could go from enemies to engaged so quickly?"

Natalie's cheeks heated. At this rate, she was going to burn off a layer of skin. "Couples argue. You should know that better than anyone. It's not so hard to swallow the idea that we were in the middle of a spat."

The other woman was already shaking her head. "You are going to humiliate this family, the same way you did in high school."

Natalie reared back like she'd been slapped. Her body retreated from the sharp reprimand—and her back came up hard against an immovable object. Startled, she tilted her head to find August behind her, frowning. First at her and then at her mother. "Everything okay, princess?"

Corinne scoffed at the nickname. Natalie watched her mother wage a war between manners and her obvious anger. Surprisingly, the anger won. Instead of shaking hands with August and saying something to smooth over the uncomfortable situation as she normally would, Corinne sailed past them with a tight smile

and approached a different group, launching into a boring round
of small talk about the train's restored vintage fixtures.

"How much did you hear?" Natalie asked without turning
around.

A beat passed. "Some."

Based on his gruff tone, he'd heard the part about her humiliating the family. "Great. I guess I spoke too soon." She didn't
know what to do with her arms. Cross them. Gesture without
purpose. Hug her middle. "You win tonight's battle."

They stood in silence a moment. Then August surprised her
by taking hold of her right hand and leading her back toward the
Lovers' Nest. He dropped into the seat and pulled her down after him. She didn't have the energy to fight him or pretend his
warmth wasn't welcome and, a moment later, she found her head
tucked beneath August's chin, her legs draped over his thighs,
watching Napa go by in the silence.

"Let's call it a tie for tonight," he rumbled.

Natalie, experiencing the shock of a lifetime, closed her eyes
and nodded.

His voice turned soothing against her ear. "I'm going to rent a
tux and you're going to put on a pretty dress. Or pants. I value my
balls, so I'm not telling you what to wear, I just like your legs. A
lot. Basically, they belong in a museum." She sniffed a thank-you
and he patted her on the head. "We're going to say the vows and
then I'm going to bring you home to my psychotic-ass cat. We
might even bond over trying to defend ourselves against her
feline evil. If we manage to survive each other—and Menace—
we are going to stick this thing out until you have the money to
start your firm. Okay?"

Had anyone ever made an effort to reassure her like this?

Maybe Julian, when she first returned home and felt horribly out of place being back in St. Helena. But her brother's efforts didn't strike like this. Not so thoroughly.

How odd that it would be August to calm her down after he'd spent so long riling her up.

"Okay," she agreed, testing a hand on his chest. "And your loan."

A pause went by. "Yeah, princess. That, too."

And she left her palm over his heartbeat, feeling the steady pound, while the train trundled on against the endless sky, his chin eventually coming to rest on top of her head. Maybe this wouldn't be so bad after all.

Ha.

Chapter Seven

$\mathscr{F}$amiliar faces smiled back at Natalie from the surface of her laptop screen. Every time she logged in to social media to check on her New York colleagues, their expressions and even their names became less and less recognizable. The pictures of her former coworkers on a private rooftop had been taken only yesterday, maybe even while she'd been making out with her archnemesis aboard the wine train, but it was like looking at photographs from the past.

The longer Natalie was away from New York, the more these people and their glitzy activities grew unfamiliar. The bounce of euphoria after a successful swap, the adrenaline that surged when the opening bell rang—her memories of those things were starting to fade along with the scent of victory cigars. Those pieces of her life were growing muffled and she wanted them back. Sharper. She wanted to experience it all again, *in person*.

When she'd first arrived in St. Helena, there had been an almost desperate sense of FOMO. *Must get back as soon as possible. Must not let them forget about me.* It was still there, beating like an extra pulse in her bloodstream, but the urgency had started to lose its grip on her—and that simply wouldn't do. She needed it back. Five minutes in New York equated to five years anywhere else. People forgot. Business moved on. The road paved right over yesterday's star and called them a speed bump.

She belonged on that roof, making the toast. Celebrating a breakneck trade that added value to the fund's coffers. Zeroes on the screen. When she'd been adding those zeroes, she'd been embraced. She'd been a member of the winning team.

Here in St. Helena?

She was the bumbling, cartoonish mascot.

Although yesterday, for a very brief window, she'd been on a two-person team. With the most unexpected of allies. August. Maybe that's why she was awake so early—again—trying to sear images from her desired timeline into her brain. Because it had been a little too easy to call a truce with August and let herself just . . . be. Be okay with that big arm slung around her hip and his prickly chin resting on top of her head, nuzzling her hair every so often.

Was it a show for the crowd?

Natalie sighed and stroked a few keys on her Mac, going to a location on the internet she absolutely should be avoiding like the pork special at an all-night diner.

Her ex-fiancé's Instagram.

She hesitated briefly before tapping enter—and then there he was in all his suited, boyish charm. Her stomach turned sour at the memory of him calmly asking for her engagement ring back. He'd been even calmer while explaining that while he might love her, he couldn't let their relationship cost him a career he'd worked so hard for.

Calmer still while he asked her to leave.

August wouldn't break up with her that way—that is, if they

were *actually* together, instead of merely pretending. There would be shouting and door slamming and insults from both of them. They would bring the house down. Why was she even thinking about this? Moreover, why was she suddenly taking note of Morrison's shoulders and musing that they could fit into her fake fiancé's shoulders three times? It wasn't a competition—

Natalie drew in a breath as a new image popped up on the screen. Just posted. A picture of Morrison on the balcony where she used to have her coffee overlooking Central Park South. Beside him was a familiar blonde in a white bathrobe sipping green juice from a glass, rolling her eyes over having the photo taken. That blonde . . . Krista, right? Natalie knew her.

One of their board member's daughters.

He'd traded up.

Feeling out of breath, Natalie smacked the laptop shut. She stood up and walked a half circle around the bed. Her heart wasn't breaking. That damage had already been done and, if she was being honest, it had been the easiest part to mend. But her confidence? That was a different story—and it took another pounding now, an invisible mallet flattening her like a chicken cutlet between two sheets of wax paper.

"Deep breath," she murmured to herself, stretching her arms up over her head and letting them float down slowly. Back up, back down. She could spin this jarring discovery that her fiancé was already moving on into something positive. What didn't kill her would make her stronger. The fact that her ex was sleeping with a billionaire's beautiful daughter would only make her comeback more satisfying. She'd belong again. Not exactly as before, but with a similar life. She'd get back that sense of . . . being wanted. Being seen.

Deciding to grab a cup of coffee before getting in the shower, Natalie opened the guest room door as quietly as possible and crept out, not wanting to disturb Julian and Hallie, who were sleeping on the other side of the kitchen. God forbid she wake them up. The bed would be creaking in ten seconds flat and honestly, bearing witness to someone else's orgasm quest was the last thing she needed this morning.

She stuck a pod in the coffee maker, placed a mug under the spout, and pulled the lever down, selecting the strongest setting. And waited.

Why was August's face the first image to pop into her head literally five minutes after finding out her ex was dating someone new? She didn't know. But it was definitely a sign to redraw the battle lines today. They might be working together for a greater cause in public. In private, his favorite pastime was scorning her for being born into privilege while he'd done life the hard way.

Although . . . she didn't know *a lot* about the path he'd taken.

Maybe she should find out. Just in case anyone asked.

She should probably know at least the *basics* about her fake fiancé.

"Psst," came a hiss from the darkness.

Natalie lurched for the knife block, pausing only when Hallie stepped into the dim kitchen wearing a Stanford shirt that went well past her knees.

"Jesus," Natalie breathed, slapping a hand to the middle of her chest, positive her heart was about to explode straight out of her rib cage. "What are you doing sneaking up on me like an old Victorian ghost or something? I almost hurled a butcher knife at you."

Hallie pressed a finger to her lips. "Shhh."

Natalie tilted her head. "Now you're really freaking me out."

"Sorry," Hallie whispered, creeping forward barefoot, each of her toes painted a different color, an ankle bracelet jangling softly. "I don't want to wake up Julian."

"Really? You seem to love waking him up. Along with the dead."

Her brother's girlfriend pinkened slightly, but she wasn't thwarted by the innuendo. No, she appeared to be extremely focused for six A.M. "Can we chat?"

"Um . . ." What was going on here? Natalie picked up her freshly brewed coffee and sipped it black for an initial kick before heading to the fridge for milk. "Sure. What's on your mind?"

Whatever the reason for this predawn rendezvous, Hallie was deadly serious about it. "I'm here to offer my services."

Natalie did a double take while adding a splash of milk to her coffee. "In what way?"

Hallie frowned as if the answer should be obvious. "Why, for your fake wedding, of course. I'm here to help."

"Don't get comfortable calling it that. There are eyes and ears everywhere in St. Helena, you know." Natalie mock shivered. "We're just going to exchange vows at the courthouse, but I suppose if you want to make me a bouquet—?"

Hallie's giggle stopped her short. "The courthouse. That's adorable. Didn't you hear your mother demand a proper wedding?"

Natalie's smile vanished, dread curling in her stomach. "Yes, but there's no way she could plan a wedding within the time frame we need. Right? What do you know?"

"Your mother told Julian to have a tuxedo rented by this Saturday." Hallie took her time continuing. "And then she had to get off the phone because the caterer was calling on the other line."

"Caterer?" Natalie choked out.

She should have seen this coming. No way Corinne could get

down with a courthouse ceremony. Not with the pageantry and tradition of the Vos name to uphold.

What was August going to say about this?

And why did his very name transport her back to the wine train, where he'd wrapped her in warmth and slowed the rate of her heart down to a normal pace with soft words in her ear, his strong arms giving her the sensation of weightlessness? He'd made her feel almost . . . peaceful. Protected. How could the same man who made her want to screech like a banshee get that reaction out of her? No way to know. But the effect of him . . . lingered. Hard.

"There was also some talk of giant tent rentals. *Giant.*" The corkscrew blonde tilted her head, but it was hard to discern whether she was sympathetic or excited. "You're getting the full Napa wedding treatment whether you like it or not. Corinne is taking the flash-and-awe approach to fooling the local flavor and I want in, too. I'm an agent of chaos, Natalie. I can't help it, I crave the danger."

"How do I know you're not on an undercover mission?" Natalie narrowed her eyes over the rim of her mug. "Are you wearing a wire, Welch?"

Without a moment's hesitation, her brother's girlfriend lifted the Stanford T-shirt to reveal a pair of rainbow panties and two very impressive tatas. She dropped the shirt again after a moment and Natalie hummed into a sip. "What kind of services are you offering?"

"Floral arrangements, obviously. But also . . ." Hallie stepped forward, coming farther into the light. "Literally anything nefarious. Namely bachelorette party planning. I got you."

"You're a little nuts, aren't you, Hallie?"

"I wrote your brother secret admirer letters and got jealous when he wrote me back."

"Good point." Natalie tapped a finger against the side of her mug. "Aren't you going to ask why I'm entering into this phony union with someone I once called diseased foreskin? Or are you *not* asking because you already know?"

"Julian and I have been talking about . . . you know." Hallie flushed so rapidly, it was a wonder her legs had enough blood in them to keep her upright. "Marriage. To each other. And he might have mentioned something about a trust fund that will be released once that happens. He's, um . . . well, he asked if I'd be opposed to him putting that money back into the winery. When the time comes."

A pang caught Natalie in the throat. "Well, he's a lot more selfless than I am."

"No." Hallie shook her head. "He's just in a better position to help at this moment."

"I would help if they asked. If I thought they wanted my help—" She cut herself off with a wave of her hand, forcing a smile. "I appreciate your offer to help, crazy pants. I accept. I will feed your need for chaos as long as you keep my secret among family."

Hallie closed her eyes slowly, hands pressing together between her breasts. "Thank you. I hereby declare myself your secret minion."

"Just don't ask me to call you that." Natalie switched off the coffee maker and sauntered toward the hallway, half a cup in hand. Before exiting, she stopped in front of Hallie, who was all but quivering in excitement. "My brother has no idea what he's gotten into, does he?"

"Actually, he does." The gardener's eyes sparkled. "He's fully aware that I'm capable of destruction and he loves me anyway. Maybe he's the crazy one."

"Maybe so," Natalie muttered, shaking her head. "I've mentioned I like you, haven't I?"

"I like you, too." Hallie winked and melted back into the darkness, whispering, "Let's fuck shit up," as she vanished into the black.

Natalie stared into the dark for long moments, guilt beginning to tickle her throat. Now she'd dragged her entire family *and* Hallie into her scheme? Was this going to be the lie that multiplied into a thousand more, when the whole charade could potentially be avoided with one humbling phone call to her father in Italy?

Yeah.

Her head fell back on her shoulders, a silent groan issued at the ceiling. One phone call. She could do it. Preferably before she did any more damage—or implicated any more loved ones. But man, was it going to suck.

NATALIE DOODLED FURIOUSLY on a notepad, dragging the tip of the ballpoint pen back and forth in a blue trench that slowly turned black. In her ear, the sound of a call connecting to Europe buzz-buzzed. She broke out in a cold sweat, glanced at the clock, and did the time-difference math again. Eight hours ahead in Italy. It would be early evening. She had no idea what her father's schedule was like, no idea if this was still his phone number, even. But she didn't want to look back in ten years and wish she'd made this attempt to avert catastrophe.

"Hello."

Brisk. Gave nothing away. That was her father.

God, there was no one on earth more intimidating, and she'd come across some giants while in finance. Dalton Vos had judgmental eyes and no time. Always rushing, on to the next best thing, as if he had a fear of leaving the world without putting his mark on it. He'd been frantic in his desire for his to be the most lucrative winery in Napa. As soon as that was accomplished, he'd gotten . . . bored. With St. Helena. His family.

The fire four years ago seemed almost unacceptable, like he couldn't admit a natural disaster had gotten the better of him. After ending his fraught marriage to Corinne and signing over Vos Vineyard, he'd shifted his obsessive focus to a Formula One team, no doubt investing a giant chunk of money that the winery could desperately use.

It was the reminder of what Dalton had done to her mother that made Natalie throw down the pen and sit up straight. "Hello, Father, it's Natalie."

"Yes. Your number came up," he said, almost distractedly. "How are you?"

"Fine. I'm in St. Helena, actually."

"Ah." A short pause. "How is Corinne? Exhausted, I'm guessing. It's not easy operating a vineyard, as I'm sure she's realized by now."

"She's thriving, actually," Natalie said without hesitation. Sure, there might be tension between her and Corinne, but there wasn't a chance in hell she'd let this man think he'd been the strongest thing about her mother. Or that she was worse off without him. Any woman worth her salt would have done the same. "Better than ever."

No response. In fact, she could hear him typing something on the other end.

Aloof and dismissive as always.

She needed to make the request before she started shrieking. "I'm calling because I have the opportunity to start my own investment firm in New York. My colleague, Claudia, and I are branching out—"

"I know you were fired, Natalie. The bad trade that almost tanked your entire firm earlier this year." He cleared his throat. A chair creaked. "I'm still an avid investor. Your company might have kept it quiet, but my broker was able to track down the behind-the-scenes details."

Nausea rolled into her belly like fog over a lake, a stabbing ache forming in the dead center of her forehead. He'd known about her getting fired and he'd just carried on with life as usual. Why would she expect anything different? *Recover. Keep it together.* "Yes, well. I'm down, but not out. I'm already on my way to recovering from that, actually, which is why—"

"Which is why you're calling about money."

"Yes." She took a deep, silent breath, willing herself to keep down the coffee she'd drunk. "I am. Calling about my trust fund. I think you will agree that in this day and age, the language is wildly outdated."

"I made the money, Natalie. It is up to me how to distribute it. If you'd made smarter decisions, you wouldn't be having this issue."

"What do you want me to say? I screwed up? I know I did." *Leave it at that.* He just needed to hear he was right. Letting him score points would burn, but she had to keep the goal in mind.

But then he went there. He went *there.*

"Maybe the idea of getting married is not so wildly outdated after all. Perhaps you're more suited to family life than business, Natalie."

In other words, get back in the kitchen.

Every hair on her body stood straight up. "Frankly, Father, I don't think a man who abandoned his own wife is in a position to extol the virtues of marriage."

A snort from Dalton. Then the line went dead.

She closed her eyes and let the phone drop to her lap.

The wedding was definitely on.

Chapter Eight

August swiped a hand across his sweaty brow and tossed down a wrench.

One of the best parts of leaving this winery behind would have been never seeing this horizontal press ever again in his lifetime. After he sold the property, the antiquated equipment would become somebody else's problem. Now here he was, fixing the temperamental piece of garbage for the eight hundredth time.

Giving winemaking another pointless try.

Maybe this time his Cabernet would actually kill somebody.

August took a few steps toward the worktable that ran along the right side of the barn and plucked up his water bottle, draining most of the contents in one gulp and dumping the remnants over the top of his head. Sighing, he leaned back against the table and scanned the barn, his gaze lingering on the row of oak barrels that contained fermenting grapes and their juice, which, in theory, should age into wine.

Truth be told, he'd been a little anxious about leaving those barrels in his rearview. He'd grown their contents from the soil, picked the grapes with his bare hands, and if he could just find the right manipulation of yeast, something would click. Right?

August snorted, remembering how many people he'd watched spit his wine up like babies after a full bottle of formula. He'd had such high hopes the first time he walked in. The place would be packed full of people drinking wine with his best friend's name on the label. Somewhere, somehow, Sam would see that and do that clap and laugh combination that August could hear in his sleep.

Although his attempts to sleep had been interrupted by someone else entirely last night. Natalie. Memories of them sharing that Lovers' Nest on the wine train.

Vivid memories that were making his cock a very unhappy camper.

God, her ass fit so perfectly into his lap.

August's head fell back on a groan. Why couldn't he just beat off and get it over with? He wanted to. Badly. The mouth of hell opening up in his front yard normally wouldn't even stop him from stroking one out, if necessary—and Christ, it was necessary now. Weirdly, his upstairs brain seemed intent on bombarding him with nonsexy thoughts, though, interrupting the whole self-hand-job process in its infancy.

Mainly, he didn't like the memory of Natalie deflating at her mother's criticism.

He'd definitely enjoyed the way she'd curled into him for comfort—couldn't help it—but he didn't like the cause. Not one bit. Natalie being sad made his dick soft before he could get a good rhythm going. What the *fuck*.

When the source of his discomfort appeared in the doorway of the barn holding a notebook, looking like a young professional on her way into the board room, August could only stare. Was she still upset about last night or feeling better?

Because his dick had no idea how to act.

He got his answer when she wrinkled her nose. "God, I can smell you from here."

Definitely feeling better.

With a humorless laugh, he swiped up the wrench from the ground. "This is what manual labor looks like, Natalie. Have you ever seen it in real life or just in movies?"

Her withering sigh filled the barn. "I grew up on a winery, moron. I know what manual labor looks like."

"Nope. You know what it looks like when *other* people are doing it."

She opened her mouth to respond, but snapped it shut just as quickly, avoiding his gaze. Immediately he wished to have it back. Why did he continue to fall into this trap with her? Why did they fight every time they were in the same room? Did she steer them into disagreements or did he continually put his foot in his mouth where she was concerned? "I came to discuss the . . . exchange of vows," she said, presenting him with an unconcerned smile, even though her eyes were vulnerable in a way that made his gullet pinch together. God save him from his kaleidoscopic woman. "Unless you slept on it last night and decided to back out."

"I'm not backing out." That long breath she let out made him want to shake her. Or kiss her. Or something. "So we're doing notebook-level planning, huh?"

"Guess you have to put a shirt on. Unless you've ripped them all down the middle pretending to be the Hulk in the mirror."

"As opposed to asking my mirror if I'm the fairest one of all like you do, oh evil one?"

"Beware of poison apples once we're married. I could inherit this place and actually make some decent wine."

"You mean you could hire other people to do it?"

"Better than stubbornly trying to do it alone without any expertise whatsoever."

"Do you think you can do better, princess? Because as far as I can tell, you have nothing to do with the actual producing or bottling of your family's wine. Only the drinking of it."

The shutters went down.

She went from animated to robotic in one second flat.

And his brain, the upstairs one, started to recall the other times he'd poked fun at Natalie for her penchant to get tipsy on a frequent basis. Had she reacted the same way those other times? Yeah . . . August suspected maybe she had, but it was hard to tell when they were swinging from one barb to the next like monkeys on vines.

"Do you want me to stop needling you about the drinking?" he asked, approaching her from the other side of the barn. "I can."

She flipped open the notebook to the first page and pretended to make a note, even though he could see the cap was still on her pen. "It hardly matters. Everything you say to me goes in one ear and out the other."

"No, the drinking thing bothers you."

"You're making a big deal out of nothing."

"Because I'll stop."

"We're setting parameters now for insulting each other?"

"Yeah. Looks like it. The goal isn't to hurt your feelings."

That surprised her. And got her attention. Good. "What *is* the goal?"

"You're so determined to put me in my place on the peg below you. Maybe I'm just trying to get you down to the same level so we can . . ."

"Have sex? God, you're so predictable."

"I was going to say, so we can see eye to eye again."

"In bed."

"Among other places."

Like cuddling on trains. Not that he could say that out loud without her crucifying him.

He could, however, get this one problem solved, couldn't he? This woman shouldn't have to put up her guard around him. It bothered him a great deal that she did. He liked her sitting in his lap and trusting him a hell of a lot more. "Your mother said something last night about . . . an incident when you were in high school?"

Her muscles braced, as if she didn't expect him to bring that up and was now preparing to layer on even more armor. Not happening.

"Natalie, I burped 'Wanted Dead or Alive' by Bon Jovi into a microphone at my high school talent show when I was seventeen. In a wig and tasseled knee socks. I'm not here to pass judgment."

A gasping laugh snuck out of her. "Last place, I'm assuming?"

"They didn't really grasp my artistic vision."

She ran her eyes over him, as if trying to picture the scene, and pressed her lips together to smother a smile. Hesitating. Then with a jerky shoulder roll, she confessed, "I do tend to use alcohol as a coping mechanism. Of course I do. I'm an adult living in this world." She chewed the inside of her cheek, her expression running the gamut of emotions so quickly, he had to concentrate on keeping up. Damn, she was something. "Back in high school, though, it was more . . . the impetus to act out and get the attention I needed. Julian came by it so easily. Attention for his achievements and his wise way of reasoning through a problem. I didn't have any of his attributes and I panicked, I guess. I'd started to feel invisible. When I drank a lot and acted reckless, people at least paid attention. They thought I was funny. The party girl."

August was dying to shout that everyone who didn't pay attention to her must have been utter morons, but he was afraid to interrupt with the wrong sentiment and cause her to shut down. God knew they were already at odds due to his penchant for saying the wrong shit.

Didn't stop him from wanting to verbally defend her. Maybe cuddle some more.

"My parents checked me into rehab for two weeks, to scare me, more than anything. I'd pulled one too many stunts—I think the straw that broke the camel's back was me bleaching a giant number sixty-nine into the football field the night before homecoming—"

"Nice."

They fist-bumped.

Then looked shocked that they'd done it.

". . . and my reputation was beginning to cast the winery in a negative light. Sounds familiar, doesn't it?" Her smile was tight, but she was looking down at her fist curiously, as if still absorbing the fact that it had bumped into his. "It worked. I was really scared."

Those words, delivered in such a matter-of-fact tone, caused denial to rip through August. "*Who* scared you?" he barked.

"Me." A wrinkle formed in her brow. "Me. Once I didn't have the party magic to hide behind, all I had was me. I needed to figure out what I was good at. *Besides* throwing keggers."

August really wished he was in a position to pick Natalie up and bear-hug her—and make her swear to God no one had scared her at rehab—but this was important information. He needed to *listen* instead of just reacting. "So when I make fun of you for drinking too much wine, you feel unhappy," he said very slowly, piecing it all together. "Because you want to be acknowledged for the other things you're good at? Like Wall Street shit?"

She didn't quite hide her amusement. "Way to work through it, big guy."

He let out the breath he'd been holding in a heavy rush. "Is my nose bleeding?"

"No. It's still ugly, but you're good." Her lips twitched, then stilled. "I guess . . . yeah. I'm not so good at the Wall Street shit right now, so when you constantly joke about the drinking—"

"It reminds you of being seventeen. When drinking and partying was all you had."

"And I feel not great." The color of her cheeks deepened. "About it."

A wheel of fire spun in his stomach. "I don't like you feeling less than great. That I made you. I'm sorry." He took a step toward Natalie and tilted up her chin, marveling over the smooth lines of her neck, the way her eyelids drooped slightly at his touch. How could he continually be at odds with someone so delicate? "No more jokes about the wine."

"Everything else is fair game?"

"I mean, I have to pay you back for that ugly nose comment, right?"

For the barest of seconds, Natalie leaned her face into his palm and sighed, before shaking her head and stepping back. "Do you think we can avoid fighting for half an hour while we figure out how to put the 'civil' in civil ceremony? Because Corinne has been busy—"

"Yes, ma'am," he drawled, following her with a wink. "But I'm leaving my shirt off. You're welcome."

"My God." She waved her hand frantically. "The *stench* of you."

"Hard work comes with a price. You'd know that if you ever tried it."

"You mean, like, digging a hole big enough for your grave? Because I'd be willing to try that."

"Bury me with a six-pack of—" August halted mid-stride on his way out of the barn, cold washing down his insides and hardening into ice. Simultaneously, his eyes started to burn and his body snapped to attention, hand whipping to his forehead in a salute. It wasn't necessary. Not in this setting. He wasn't even in uniform. But muscle memory performed the action at the sight of his commanding officer walking toward him across the lawn. "Sir."

"At ease, Cates."

His arm dropped. He forced himself to look the man in the eye, even though a hole was being torn straight down his middle. "I didn't know you were coming."

The barest flash of amusement. "You know I like to have the element of surprise on my side."

August forced a laugh but it came out rusted. Nearly three years had passed since the last time he'd seen his commanding officer, and it had been under the worst circumstances possible. The funeral of his son and August's best friend, Sam. Though looking Commander Zelnick in the eye was extremely difficult, August didn't allow his gaze to falter as the man tread closer, his attention drifting out over the vineyard with open curiosity.

August became acutely aware of Natalie behind him. Having her present for this reunion was the equivalent of making an incision from throat to belly and letting her see everything on the inside. Totally exposed, utterly vulnerable, nowhere to hide.

He turned slightly, meeting Natalie's interested gaze and holding out his hand to her. He wasn't sure why. Only that it seemed natural to reassure her that the unexpected appearance of a stranger wasn't a threat of any kind. Or maybe he needed to feel the warmth of her against his suddenly clammy palm. She didn't hesitate for a single second before taking his hand and squeezing it. Skirmish forgotten. Interesting how they could flip that switch so quickly. What did that mean?

"So this is the place you've built for my son." Commander Zelnick stopped, clasped his hands behind his back. His tone was brisk as ever, but warmth seeped through. "Had a week off and finally decided to come see it for myself."

Christ. He'd almost left it behind two days earlier. Out of necessity, sure, but this man would have arrived and found an abandoned vineyard. If it weren't for Natalie.

He pulled her closer without thinking. "Yes. For Sam. It's a work in progress," he managed around the object in his throat. "Sir, I would like you to meet Natalie Vos. My fiancée." Perpetuating the phony relationship to his CO didn't exactly feel great, but the words were out in the open before he could think better of them. Just hanging there, feeling like the truth. "Natalie, this is Commander Brian Zelnick."

Zelnick nodded, visibly impressed—and a little surprised. "Good to meet you, Natalie."

Of course he would be surprised. Not only was Natalie beautiful in a polished way, she had an air of sophistication and success that she wore like an aura. In other words, not the kind of girl who ended up with a loud asshole who liked to trade battle wound stories and had long ago earned the nickname Bullhorn among his fellow SEALs.

"It's very nice to meet you," she said, going back to scrutinizing August. He could feel that she wanted to ask about Sam and he pressed a thumb to the small of her wrist, hoping she would know what it meant. That he'd explain later. And somehow she did. She interpreted the action with a nod. "I'll let you two talk." To August, she said, "I'll be inside."

Natalie tugged on her hand three times before August realized he was still holding it in his grip. Finally, he released her and they watched her walk toward the house, go inside, and close the door. August and the commander turned together like a single unit and walked side by side toward the edge of the vines, the earthy, sun-heated aroma of greenery and grapes carrying in their direction on a light breeze.

A bead of sweat rolled down August's temple as he waited for his CO to speak.

This man had assured him once that he didn't blame August for what happened to Sam—and the CO never repeated himself. Nonetheless, August had to swallow the deep urge to ask for those words one more time. God, he needed to hear them and yet, they made no difference. He'd let his friend get killed fifteen yards away from him.

Fifteen fucking yards.

"I appreciate what you've done here, son," said Zelnick, his voice more gravelly than before. "Sam would have, too."

August cleared his throat hard. "To tell you the truth, I'm a shit winemaker, sir. I think he'd probably be laughing his ass off."

A low chuckle from his CO. "I did my homework. I know it

hasn't been an ideal experience for you. That's the other reason I'm here." He remained silent a moment. "You've always been a battering ram. Kick down the door, ask questions later. But there are certain things in life that require patience and diligence. You must have learned some of that lesson already, if you've convinced that woman to marry you."

Patience and diligence.

Is that what he'd been needing with Natalie?

He memorized those two words and tucked them away for later.

"You're saying I can't expect perfection right away," August said. "That it takes time."

"Yes." Zelnick crossed his arms and braced his legs apart in a stance that was so familiar to August, reminded him so much of Sam, that he had to look away. "That being said, I know that spending time on a project like this equals money. A lot of it. That's why I'm here to invest."

Chapter Nine

Natalie stood at the window peering through the blinds, Menace making figure eights through her legs. She studied the ripple that went through August's back, her fingers restless on the sill. It took her a moment to realize she was tracing the exact shape of that scar on his right shoulder and she immediately stopped. Backed away from the blinds. Went back and looked out again.

So this is the place you've built for my son.

Okay. Wait. What?

What had she missed?

And why was this new unknown tying her stomach in knots?

An idea occurred to her and she stepped back from the window once more, turning, hesitating for a moment, then striding into the kitchen and throwing open cabinets. Searching for a bottle of wine. Maybe an answer to the riddle would be included on the label, which she'd never bothered to read very closely.

Nothing. Not a single bottle of August's wine in the house—he'd given them all away.

She pulled out her phone and performed a Google search with the name of August's winery. Several critical reviews popped up. Her gaze snagged on the words *undrinkable, fermented in a dumpster, kill it with fire.* But of course he didn't have a website. She'd just moved on to the second page of search results when the front door of the house opened and August stood outlined in the frame, his thick body nearly blocking out all of the sun.

His throat appeared to be stuck in the middle of a swallow.

Natalie couldn't seem to move, could only watch him as he took a few absent steps into the house and closed the door behind him, his heavy footfalls making the floorboards groan. In the distance was the sound of a car engine starting and moving out of earshot. His commanding officer was leaving already?

"Did the . . . meeting not go well?"

August paused in the hallway leading toward the bedroom. "It went fine." Briefly, he glanced back at her over his shoulder and she hurriedly cataloged the trench between his brows. "Thanks for going along with the whole fiancée thing in front of him. He's going to tell everyone back on base that I'm marrying a knockout."

When he kept walking, leaving that knee-weakening compliment in his wake, Natalie started to shiver. He wasn't being himself. It reminded her of the afternoon of the wine tasting competition. How he'd retreated deep into that big, goofy head and couldn't seem to find his way out. So she followed him. All the way to the bathroom. When she opened the door, he was standing with his hands braced on the sink, his head bowed forward.

"August, who is Sam?"

After a moment, his head came up, and he turned toward her, his expression weary. "He was my best friend. He . . . died in combat. Killed during a raid. Last one in. He was the *last one in.* I'm still not sure how we missed the target coming down the staircase. Faulty intel, they said, as if it helps." While she digested that awful and jarring information without being able to take a breath, August's fingers drummed on the side of the vanity. "Sam had this dream to be a winemaker. We all laughed about it. Called him Napa Daddy. But he was serious about doing it. Leaving the teams one day and buying a small vineyard, like this one. This is his dream, not mine. I'm just the one fucking it up."

Natalie's stomach hung down somewhere in the vicinity of her ankles. Every terrible thing she'd ever said to him came roaring back in perfect clarity, making her throat feel like it had been cut to ribbons. "August . . ."

"You're right." He pushed off the sink abruptly, his hoarse laugh filling the small bathroom. "I smell god-awful. I'll take a quick shower and then we can talk about wedding stuff, huh?"

He didn't wait for an answer. Just leaned into the shower stall and twisted the handle, the sound of water pelting the tile wall filling the silence. Feeling numb down to her toes, Natalie backed out of the bathroom and closed the door behind her. Guilt burned inside every one of her organs. Made her limbs feel like dead weight. All this time, he'd been trying to fulfill this dream for his late best friend and everyone had been ridiculing him for it?

The reality of that was too much to bear.

Natalie's hand still rested on the bathroom doorknob and she watched through gritty eyes as it turned in her grip, letting her back into the now-fogged-up space. *What am I doing? No idea.* But she knew that she'd been extremely unfair to the man on the other side of the shower curtain. He was clearly hurting after having painful memories dredged up . . . and she wanted very badly to comfort him. In any way she could.

Maybe the *only* way she could in this exact moment?

Natalie untucked her T-shirt from the waistband of her skirt, pulling it off over her head. Her skirt dropped to the floor, followed by her sandals. Her fingers hesitated for only a moment on the front clasp of her bra before releasing it. Baring her breasts to the hot, foggy room. Too eager to touch him to realize she still wore her mint green panties, she walked slowly to the curtain and drew it back, stepping into the stall.

Or . . . squeezing into it, rather. August occupied nearly every inch of space.

He stood with his head hanging forward beneath the spray, but the sound of the curtain being pulled back and her stepping into the shower had the meat of his shoulders flexing dramatically—and he turned with an incredulous expression.

"Natalie? What are you . . ." If he was a cartoon dog, his tongue would have rolled out of his mouth. "Are those your *tits*?"

"No, they're somebody else's."

Apparently the sarcasm didn't register. He was too busy bracing his hands on the wet shower wall and leaning down to look at them. "Oh my *God*. They're incredible." He choked a sound and winced. "Jesus. My balls have never gotten so heavy so fast in my life. Pretty sure every drop of blood in my head just went south. Give me like . . . eight seconds to make sure I'm not going to pass out."

Seriously, that wasn't a problem.

With his eyes clamped shut and his bottom lip being pulverized between his teeth, Natalie was given the opportunity to look him over. Starting from the top of his wet warrior's torso covered in dark hair, down his egg-carton stomach to the . . . whoa, mama. His balls were not the only thing that was hard. If the financial sector didn't work out, maybe she had a future in snake charming. Her sex clenched and turned warm, so warm.

So ready. And if she was being honest with herself, this wasn't instantaneous arousal. This physical attraction had been brewing for months. Plaguing her. Keeping her awake at night. God, it felt incredible to stop fighting it. To let her heart race and her body soften and know that relief was on the way for both of them. Finally. *Finally.*

"Okay," he exhaled above her head. "I think I'm good." His mouth dipped and found hers roughly, two sets of lips slippery from the steam, suctioning her into a kiss that made her whimper in her throat, her palms flattening on the ridges of his pecs, her nails scraping down through the patch of springy hair. "Scratch that," he groaned. "I'm so much better than good."

"It's going to feel even better inside of me," she whispered against his panting mouth, her fingertips traveling lower, lower. "It's long overdue, isn't it, babe?"

"Babe?" He caught her wrists before she reached his erection, his breath pelting her forehead. "Hold up. What is this, Natalie?"

"I . . ." She tried to tug her wrists free, but he didn't let go, eyes narrowed on her through the swirling mist. "I want you. That's what this is. We want each other."

"No shit. But why now?"

Natalie opened her mouth but nothing came out.

"Is this because of what I told you?" Slowly, August pinned her wrists high above her head, his mouth hovering an inch away from hers. "Do you think I'm going to let you pity fuck me, princess?"

Being called out, even if it was only the partial truth, rankled. "Based on the way your hard-on is trying to enter my belly button right now? Yes, I do."

"It's been a while. He's confused." He pressed their foreheads together, looking her square in the eye. "You're confused, too, if you think I'm going to let you explain this away later with some nonsense about feeling bad for me. Not happening."

"You were trying to do something noble," she whispered in a rush. "All this time."

His jaw ticked. "That has nothing to do with us." They breathed against each other's mouths so long, she lost track of who was inhaling or exhaling. Only knew her chest ached as much as the flesh between her legs, and August was so hard, she could almost feel the pain and hunger in every vibrating inch of his body. "I can't fuck you when your head isn't in the right place." His mouth moved to her ear, open lips raking side to side over it, then up into her hair. "But I'd sell my soul to yank those panties down and finger you, Natalie. The fact that I've never made you come eats me alive. *Do you get that?* It's the first thing I think about when I wake up in the morning. Still haven't given Natalie an orgasm. Day eighty-two of *not* making those two hot legs shake and kick the lamp off my side table. It's hell. Day in and day out."

Her brain was struggling to make sense of his words. They were sexy words. Her body liked them very much. As for logic and her power of deduction? Circling the drain. "You . . . don't want me to make you—"

"Come? Yeah. Another time. When the reason doesn't piss me off." He tucked his coarse index finger inside the center of the waistband of her panties, so close to the top of her slit that she moaned, her head landing with a thud against the tile wall. "Say yes if I'm allowed to push these panties down to your knees."

"Yes," she said on a shuddering exhale. Wasn't she supposed to hate the abrasive way he spoke to her? Yes? Didn't she normally? When had that same method of communicating become a verbal drug to her senses? "Yes . . . you're allowed."

With a groan that shook her head to toe, he fisted the front of her underwear so tightly that she swore he was going to rip it off, but instead he pulled them down hard, his labored breaths loud in the shower stall. Braiding together with her gasps. Gasps that only increased in volume when that huge, thick-fingered hand dragged up her inner thigh and he gripped her pussy roughly, massaging it while he held her in thrall with splintering eye contact. "Nearly had this thing months ago. I've been hating myself for blowing my shot."

Her teeth were literally chattering. "You can take your shot right now."

"No," he gritted out, parting her flesh with a middle finger and entering her so swiftly with that single digit that she screamed, going up on her toes as she was plastered to the wall by his strong body, his mouth flush with hers. "No, I want a lot more from you now."

"Please, please, please." The shower spray came from over his shoulder and rained water down between them, the fall of warm moisture parting around his hand where it started to work her, pumping that finger in and out slowly, too slowly, all while he watched her face. He seemed to hunt for every little reaction and exploit it, pressing deeper when she whimpered, pulling back when she started to breathe hard and rock her hips. "Please, August. I need something."

"You'll get it. You'll always get it from me. Just let me enjoy you." The joint of his thumb pressed to her water-slicked clit and rubbed, making her back arch compulsively off the wall, stars dancing in front of her eyes. "Jesus Christ. You are so fucking gorgeous, Natalie. Bet you rub expensive lotion and shit all over yourself twice a day to look so . . ." He licked her. From the curve of her shoulder all the way up the side of her neck and jawline, all while pressing his finger high and deep. "Damn. Damn, it's so smooth. You'd slide all over me like a fucking dream, wouldn't you, princess?"

She couldn't take the dirty talk anymore. It was overwhelming her, along with his touch, which she definitely hadn't expected to be so . . . *skilled*. And the sudden proof that he'd definitely done this before made her irrationally annoyed. To the point that when he stamped his mouth down over hers, she bit down on his bottom lip and pulled hard. "You're too good at this," she said on an expulsion of breath. Then, on a quieter breath, "I love it. But I hate it."

Watching her with a furrowed brow, he slipped his middle finger out, joined it with his ring finger and rubbed her clit, slowly at first, then with more pressure. Faster. Leading to an embarrassingly whiny moan from Natalie that she swore came from someone or somewhere else. "Tell me why you hate me being good at this," said August, his lips grazing hers, side to side. "And I'll keep this up until your knees buckle."

"I don't want m-my knees to buckle."

"Yes, you do." Faster. *Oh my God.* "You know I'm going to catch you."

"Do I?" she whimpered.

His teeth snapped at her jaw. "Yes."

Dammit. She did know that. Why did she know that? The reason wasn't clear, nothing was clear right now save the fact that a fuse had been lit, the fire racing across the ground toward the powder keg that was Natalie's body. Going to blow, going to explode.

When that touch slowed slightly, she cried out.

"You want me to keep going, don't you?" he asked, mouth busy on her neck.

"Stop and I'll kill you."

Those two fingers delved inside her, twisted deep, and pushed high. "Answer me, then, Natalie," he growled against her mouth while she silently screamed, eyes blind, release shaking the exit gates. "It's only supposed to be you and me. That's why you're thrown off by my knowing how to touch a woman. That right?"

Yes. Was this jealousy? She couldn't remember. Hadn't felt it since high school. Not about anything that wasn't job related, at least. "I'm not admitting that out loud."

"The murder in your eyes did it for you." With their breathing shallow and steam clouding every corner of the shower stall, bodies glossy with condensation, August added a third finger. He swallowed her moan with a kiss, working high, higher, until he found this . . . this place that she was positive had never been so sensitive, and he toyed with it using the pads of his blunt fingers. And *oh no, oh no.* The palm of his hand pressed down on her clit, tighter, tighter, until her butt was flattened against the shower wall. "I can't even fucking remember what it's like to want anything but this pussy, princess. Yours. I don't look right or left. No exceptions. Got that?"

That sounded dangerously close to a vow of faithfulness—and she really shouldn't have been relieved or gratified to hear it. Not in this setting. Alone in his shower, where they were the only ones to witness it. That made the exchange real. Not a farce. Furthermore, she shouldn't be lifting up onto her toes and sealing their mouths together, kissing him as if to reward him, those fingers simulating sex between her thighs. Picking up the pace along with their kiss until she could no longer concentrate on both and her head fell back on her shoulders, a gasp of his name tripping over her lips as the orgasm crested—

"August, Jesus. Yes. *Yes.*"

"Good girl. I've got you."

Got her? Right. Because her knees *had* buckled, as predicted, and she didn't even have the room to be miffed or embarrassed about the bracing left arm he'd circled around her back to keep her upright. She was too busy shaking through the most intense orgasm in recent memory. And he knew how to get her through it. Knew to stop advancing and hold firm, wedging his right palm tight to her pulsing flesh and twisting, groaning against her mouth like a satisfied beast as if he were the one getting relief instead of Natalie.

So hot. His being so turned on by her pleasure was so stupidly hot.

And unexpected.

This whole encounter—and August himself—was turning out to be unexpected.

As soon as Natalie's climax started to cool, her open mouth on his shoulder became scarily intimate. The lazy coasting of his lips over her temple and into her hair was decidedly . . . affectionate?

Whoa. What had just taken place here? Getting physical with August was not part of the plan. They were supposed to be in a fake relationship.

But their wet, tangled limbs felt the furthest thing from fake.

They were getting married so she could secure her trust fund. So he could get a bank loan and put it toward a second attempt to run this fledgling winery. They were doing this for money. What did it mean if they sealed their union while in an actual relationship? Did that make the marriage real? *Legitimate?*

A true love match between her and August Cates.

That was the most insane possibility she'd ever heard.

For one, she had to get back to New York. Her life was on pause until she picked up the broken pieces of what she'd built. Two, they would end up murdering each other.

And three, she was fresh from being booted by her fiancé without warning, literally left out on the curb like yesterday's trash. The idea of opening herself up to *this* man as a follow-up? This man who made a sport out of pinpointing her flaws? No. She might as well hand him her diary and a megaphone.

All right, they were physically attracted to each other. No tiptoeing around that fact.

She'd gotten it out of her system, right?

Yes . . .

Yes.

Totally.

Unfortunately, August was still hard against her belly, his mouth moving dangerously close to hers again. His eyes clouded with need. If he kissed her, she'd sink down again and forget the commonsense pep talk she'd just given herself. There could be no having a crush on her phony husband. That would only lead to entanglements. Ones that could potentially keep her in St. Helena, where she would never, ever feel like more than an inept and unwanted teenager.

She needed to get the lust out of August's system, too, though, didn't she?

Otherwise the itch scratching would be one-sided. The rebound would be left . . . unbound.

He'd have something to hold over her._

Going up on her toes, she slanted their mouths together, her fingertips skating down his stomach—and once again, he trapped her wrist at the very last second. "You don't have as much of a poker face as you think you do," he rasped against her mouth. "I'd rather leave my cock hard than let you stroke it just to return the favor."

A finger of panic swept through her middle. Partly because this man seriously didn't let her get away with anything, which made her feel naked in more ways than one. And partly because . . . there was a genuine urgency inside her to give him the same pleasure he'd provided for her. "Isn't returning favors how sex works?"

He shook his head. "That's not how it's going to work with us."

"*Us?*" That panic was going off like fireworks now. She'd really muddied the waters here. Especially considering that traitorous little pop of satisfaction she got over the word "us." *You need to stop.* "This is a marriage in name only, my dude."

August visibly judged her steadiness before removing his arm from around her waist, slapping that newly freed hand onto the tile above her head. "Guess you weren't thinking about that when you climbed into my shower in nothing but panties."

"Don't worry, it won't happen again."

Dripping wet, hair stuck to the side of her face, Natalie propelled herself out from behind the curtain and started snatching clothes up off the floor.

"Hold up. Can we rewind a second?" August said behind her, cursing under his breath. "I'm not good at arguing while my dick is in eggplant form. By the way, this was never a problem until I met you. My whole fucking system is out of whack." He whipped a towel off the rack and wrapped it around his waist, then raked frustrated hands through his hair. "I just . . . Look. I'm a little touchy about . . . pity. Being *pitied* over Sam dying. You know? I have a hard time accepting it from anyone. But especially you."

Natalie paused in the act of fastening her bra. "Why especially me?"

"I don't know. I grew up working for everything I had. I was taught to be proud of making ends meet. Grinding. The affluent Napa crowd looks down on that."

"And I'm a great big representation of this place to you."

He dragged a hand down his face. "Shit. I need to shut up until there is some blood back in my fucking head. I just keep making this worse."

"You think I can't grind? You think I can't work hard?" *Stop, girl.* She really needed to quit talking. She had a goal and was working on securing the means to achieve that goal. There was no room for side trips or rabbit holes. Still, she'd had it up to her eyeballs in implications from this man that she was a pampered princess who didn't know the value of a day's work. Especially right on the heels of that phone call with Dalton. "I could turn Zelnick Cellar into an operational winery with a decent vintage with one hand tied behind my back."

His muscles stiffened. "Look, the loan is one thing. But the hands-on stuff? That's mine. For Sam. I didn't ask for your help making his wine." Then he added quietly, almost contritely, "Please. Just stay out of the barn. Okay?"

Out of everything they argued about, why did his rejecting her aid seem to hit the bull's-eye?

"I need to be an official employee at Zelnick Cellar to fulfill the other condition of my trust fund," she reminded him, trying to keep the sting of his denial out of her voice. "And employing me, having my name tied to your wine, helps get *you* a loan. I don't like being a member of this dysfunctional team any more than you do, but let's not go through this for nothing. Use my knowledge as well." She gave him a meaningful look, yet she knew he probably wouldn't understand the importance of her being allowed to help. "I won't ask again, August. I don't like to re-peat myself."

"Sure about that? You've called me a dumbass at least ninety-four times."

Yup. Her words had gone in one ear and out the other.

"There are exceptions to every rule."

"Good. Especially if there is a rule against kissing my fake wife."

"As it happens, there is."

His jaw flexed. "Can't wait to break it."

"I'll break your ugly nose before that happens," she snorted, stepping out of the bathroom into the hallway, sandals cradled to her chest.

"Wait. I thought we were going to talk about wedding stuff," August boomed, following behind her, his giant, wet feet slapping on the floorboards. "What time are we meeting at the courthouse on Saturday?"

"We're not."

"*What?*" She looked back over her shoulder to find him stricken. "Just like that, the whole thing is off? I blew it?"

Every once in a while, a comment slipped through the cracks that made her very aware that he was lovable *just* under the sur-face. Why couldn't he keep that fact hidden? It made her want to turn and walk into his stupid muscular arms and whack him in the head with an encyclopedia at the exact same time.

And, dammit, her anger at him took a drastic nosedive.

Natalie picked up speed, heading toward the door. "Relax, we're still getting married." She stopped. "I did want to get your thoughts on the timeline. Considering everyone knows about our public fight and subsequent engagement, they probably assume it's going to be volatile and flame out fast. One month should be enough time to achieve our goals before . . ."

August narrowed his eyes. "Before what?"

"Before we end it, of course. Legally." He said nothing. "Are we agreed on one month?"

When he only remained silent, she had no choice but to accept his lack of argument as a yes. What else could he possibly say? He thought they should stay married *longer*?

"So, um. My mother has taken the lead on planning. That's mainly what I came here to tell you. Tradition and keeping up appearances, those things are important to her. It's probably going to be the snobbiest event this town has ever seen. Swans and harps and canapés on gilded platters. You'll need to rent a tux." She paused with her hand on the door. "I understand if you have second thoughts."

Exactly five seconds ticked by. "I want a DJ. My only request is the song 'Brick House.'"

"Oh my God." Refusing to acknowledge her relief, she yanked open the door, a laugh bursting out of her on the way down the steps. "*Why?*"

He grinned. "You'll see."

Natalie halted beside her car, stopped in her tracks by the sight of August standing in the sunshine in a towel, light playing over his Mount Rushmore of chest muscles—and a very prominent erection tenting the white terrycloth. What struck her most was how unabashed he was. He didn't make a single attempt to hide it. "Yes to the DJ. Hell no to the song," she managed, mouth dry, pulling open the driver's-side door with a little too much force.

"Natalie," he called, before she could climb in.

"Yes?" she responded over the roof of the car.

"Can we write joint showers into our vows?"

"No. And honestly, why would you want that?" Pointedly, she nodded at his lap. "Didn't exactly work out for you."

He braced his hands on the doorframe over his head. "You're leaving my place with smeared lipstick and bare feet. I'll take a hundred more showers just like it."

"Jackass," she muttered, climbing into the car and slamming the door.

But for some stupid reason, she was smiling as she drove away.

Chapter Ten

The last person August expected to see when he opened his front door the next morning was Corinne Vos. Convinced she was a figment of his imagination, he blinked several times and rubbed his eyes, but there she remained. Arms crossed, features pinched, blocking his path to the outdoor workout area he'd built behind the barn.

He searched her face for similarities to Natalie and found none. Maybe there was a glimmer of Natalie's live-wire quality deep in the golden depths of the matriarch's eyes, but it had been smothered in judgment.

"How are you this fine morning, Mr. Cates?"

Good question. The word "stunned" came to mind.

He'd spent a lot of the night pacing, wondering if he'd done the right thing by accepting the two-hundred-thousand-dollar investment from his CO. He didn't want to deprive the man of the chance to support his late son's dream. God, no. But August was also painfully aware that accepting the money from his CO meant . . . he no longer needed a small business loan from the bank. Which meant he technically didn't need to marry Natalie.

When he married her, it would be purely so she could get her trust fund.

How would she feel about that if she knew?

Not thrilled, August's gut told him. She'd probably rather change Menace's litter box than be indebted to him. Yeah. If he told her about the investment, she would walk—and he really didn't want Natalie biting off her nose to spite her face. She *needed* that trust fund. He wanted to help. And hell, what if she married someone else instead? Someone who *would* benefit from her family's influence?

Fire singed the walls of his throat.

Maybe in this case, some things were better left unsaid?

At least until the timing was right.

"I'm doing all right," he finally answered. "You?"

"I'm as well as can be expected, I suppose," Corinne clipped, dragging him out of his worry spiral.

"Would you like to come in?"

"No." She looked past him, briefly. "I'm fine out here, thank you."

Of course she didn't want to come inside for coffee. This woman probably never stepped inside anywhere that didn't have a full staff and—lest we forget—original *vintage* fixtures. With an exhale into the cold morning air, she gestured to the barn. "Getting an early start on production? We can talk while you work."

"Actually, no. I won't get started until later today. I have a makeshift gym behind the barn." He jerked his chin straight ahead, though it wasn't visible from their vantage point. "That's where I start my mornings."

"An outdoor gym on vineyard grounds. Really." She blinked approximately six hundred times. "Well, don't let me keep you from your unorthodox routine."

He couldn't exactly hold a conversation while pushing a massive tire end over end, so he shook his head and mimicked her stance, crossing his arms and leaning back against the porch rail. "This is about Natalie."

"Yes." She studied him for a long moment. "I know what you must think of me. That I'm stuffy and controlling and . . . well, to put it plainly, I'm sure you think I'm a bitch."

"I'm not going to pretend I liked the way you spoke to my . . . to Natalie. But I don't know you well enough to say that, Mrs. Vos."

"You would think I'm a bitch, let's be honest. Perhaps I am." She paused, dropped her crossed arms in favor of folding her hands at her waist. "But that doesn't mean I don't want what is best for my children. I might have an odd way of showing it, but their happiness is no small thing to me. Especially since they've come home, I . . ." She cleared her throat and lifted her chin. "Well. I've become slightly more vigilant when it comes to our relationships. Unfortunately, the damage is not always easy to reverse. For instance, it's very hard to take back years of criticism—what I thought was the constructive kind—instead of just showing . . . support. But I'm trying to do that with Natalie . . . in my own way."

Discussing Natalie without her there to answer for herself felt disloyal and he didn't like it. A weight sat heavier on his chest the longer she spoke. "Which way is that?"

A beat passed. "I guess I'm still figuring it out." She smoothed her shirtsleeve. "I don't really have an example to pull from."

August said nothing.

"I always thought she would find her purpose far away from Napa. She *did* for a while. Then again, this place, my family, became my anchor when I was Natalie's age. Maybe she needs to be here. Maybe she needs to be shown that roots aren't always ripped out as easily as they were in New York. Family ones are stronger."

Damn.

What exactly was the catalyst for her leaving New York?

It took everything inside him not to pry, but he wouldn't dig up a story that Natalie wasn't ready to tell. He thought of her in the bathroom, listening to him explain about Sam. How she'd come to him offering comfort. What if he got the chance to do the same for her? He'd give her whatever she needed, emotionally, physically. No questions asked.

Maybe she needs to be shown that roots aren't always ripped out as easily as they were in New York. Those words occupied every inch of space between him and Corinne.

"I might not be very adept at showing affection, but I am *here*. She knew she could come home to me. I am permanently planted in her life and my roots run deep. Eventually she'll realize that not everyone rips out their roots and leaves. But it would seem to me that a fake marriage with no actual commitment value would have the opposite effect."

August's pulse galloped. He'd used all of his brain power yesterday trying to get to the bottom of Natalie's alcohol hang-ups, but he would try mining for more. "If you could tell me exactly what you came to say, Mrs. Vos, it would be much appreciated," he said finally.

She inclined her head. "I should put a stop to this right now. This out-of-the-blue wedding and inevitable quick split has the potential to embarrass my family and the reputation I've worked so hard to carry through bad times and good—and there have been times that reputation is all we had. A farce like this one threatens to make us a punchline." She tapped a finger against the back of her hand. "I'm supposed to pay the caterers today. But before I spend a fortune on crab rangoon . . . what would you say if I offered you a certain sum of money to leave and never come back?"

"I'd say burn it." He said it without a thought. Didn't need one. "And hell yeah on the crab."

"Somehow I knew you'd tell me what to do with my money." Her eyes narrowed slightly. "I saw . . . something. In the way you acted toward my daughter the other night on the train. I can't really put my finger on what it was. Perhaps . . . protecting your investment? After all, being married to a Vos will earn this place a lot of attention." August started to speak up, not sure exactly what would come out of his mouth, only that he took serious objection to Natalie being referred to as an investment. But Corinne held up a hand before he could speak. "Somehow that theory didn't stick. So I've come here to ask you one thing. If you can give me a satisfying answer, I will pay the caterers and smile my way through your wedding vows."

"Ask me anything," August said, looking her dead in the eye. Bring it on. He'd once walked nineteen miles in the pitch-black with a snake bite. His commanding officer might have been cordial during his recent visit to the vineyard, but he'd once asked August if he had a pile of shit for brains. There wasn't a question on earth that could scare him.

"Do you have genuine feelings for my daughter?"

All right, maybe that one.

Did he have feelings for Natalie?

August almost laughed.

Honestly, he should have just said yes. That would have been more than enough. It would have been true—and there wouldn't be any mistaking that. But for some reason—and this probably had a lot to do with the fucking feelings themselves—he wanted this woman to approve of him, fake son-in-law or not. God help him, in this moment, he didn't want the arrangement to be phony. He wanted, maybe needed, someone to tell him he was worthy of Natalie.

"I've lost count of the feelings I have for your daughter. Pardon me for saying this, but lust is really high on that list." She rolled her eyes, so he rushed to continue. "But that's only the beginning, really. I, uh . . . I worry about her. You know?" That confession ripped a seam open and the rest just came pouring out. "Sometimes she looks sad and I goad her into a fight just to get the kaleidoscope turning in her eyes again. And when it comes back, it's a lot easier for me to concentrate. I'm not going to lie, sometimes she irritates me, but way more often, I'm just trying not to laugh. She's really goddamn funny. Like, the girl can verbally cut my balls off and I respect that, even when I'm pissed. Does that make sense?" Corinne's face remained totally blank, except for an eyebrow that was slowly creeping higher. "I don't know what else to say except . . . if someone hurt her, I would go ballistic, ma'am. My head aches even thinking about it. I'm actually afraid to find out what happened in New York, because . . ." *I've managed to hold my cards pretty close to the vest, but if I find out someone wronged her, she's going to know I'm the furthest thing from casual when it comes to her.* "Like I said, I don't like her being sad. I'd rather have her angry and I'm pretty good at making that happen. I'd also really like her to be *happy* with me more often than she's annoyed. I'd . . . love it, actually. Happy Natalie is a mission I want to go on and never come back. Have I gotten off track here?"

For long seconds, there was nothing but the sound of the wind. "I think I got what I came for."

Jesus, that sounded ominous. "Is that a good or bad thing?"

"That remains to be seen."

"Are you always this cryptic?" Was that a flash of a smile? Yeah, he thought it was. For that brief little window of time, he could see a resemblance to Natalie and his heart clunked. "You're not going to try to stop the wedding, right?"

He held his breath after asking that question. "I don't know," she said, turning and gliding away. Back toward her silver Lexus. "Am I?"

"I'm starting to see where Natalie gets her venom."

Corinne paused at the driver's side, looking startled. And a little pleased? "Thank you."

August shook his head until his future mother-in-law had driven away.

He pushed the tire a lot longer than usual that morning.

"WELCOME TO YOUR officially unofficial bachelorette party."

Natalie stared at Hallie, trying to make sense of the words that were coming out of her mouth. She'd just walked into a bar named Jed's that was more than a little out of the way—off Grapevine Way and a good three blocks down a side street. Until a moment ago, when she'd stopped in front of the rustic lodge facade and double-checked the address, she wasn't aware this place existed.

Before she could respond to Hallie, a loud thud echoed through the buzzing establishment, loud enough to make her jump and spin around. "My God. Is that man throwing an axe?"

"Yes." Hallie clapped her hands together. "It's an axe-throwing bar. I've been dying to come here and this was the perfect excuse." She looped her arm with Natalie's and tugged her through the throng of people in jeans, T-shirts, and flip-flops, making Natalie feel utterly ridiculous in her black silk tunic dress and studded gladiator sandals. "My friend Lavinia got us a table in back where it's semi-quiet so we can go over the details for Saturday, aka the big day!"

"Great," Natalie said. "I'm not throwing an axe."

"You'll change your mind after a drink or two."

"Yes, lower my inhibitions, then hand me a weapon. What could go wrong?"

Before Hallie could answer, a woman stepped into her path and enfolded her in a hug, the scent of sugar and chocolate wafting off her clothing with such potency that Natalie's tastebuds tingled. "Well, if it isn't the future bride 'erself," crooned the woman in a thick British accent. "I wanted to rent strippers, but it seems we'll be getting split in half by axes, instead."

Natalie couldn't help but laugh at that. "I suppose both would have been too dangerous?"

The woman tossed back her blond hair. "We can't have wangs getting chopped off, darling. It's bad luck before a wedding."

Hallie ushered them both to a table in the corner. "Natalie, I would introduce you to Lavinia, but I think you've just been thoroughly acquainted."

"Speaking of wangs . . ." Lavinia continued, dropping into her chair across from Natalie, "it's nice not to have any around for once. Fuck off, lads. It's ladies night."

"How did you pry yourself away from my brother?" Natalie asked Hallie, swallowing a smile.

"Actually, he is kidnapping August as we speak."

"August?" Natalie breathed. She hadn't seen him in two days. Not since the Shower. He'd texted her once, asking for guidance on his tuxedo rental. "Should I go with purple or powder blue?" he'd asked. To which she'd replied, "Get one with a bib for those inevitable spills at dinnertime," accompanied by a baby emoji. He'd also sent a meme about shotgun weddings that depicted a man standing beside a woman at the altar with a gun barrel pressed to his back.

A case of wife or death read the caption.

Ridiculous. Still . . .

Why did hearing his name make her feel awake for the first time in days?

Both women were staring at her. "Uh . . ." Natalie crossed her legs hastily. "Is it even possible to kidnap a Navy SEAL?"

"Maybe he'll go willingly when he finds out it's his impromptu bachelor . . ." Hallie hedged. "Well, I would say party, but . . ."

"But it's my brother and they'll probably just watch *Jeopardy!* and eat ham sandwiches?"

"Julian is learning to be more adventurous," Hallie said, flushing clear up to her temples. "He didn't mention *where* they were going, but I'm guessing somewhere quiet where Julian can read August the riot act."

Natalie frowned. "The riot act?"

"You know . . ." Hallie waved at the waitress. "Hurt my sister and I'll kill you."

"Right." Natalie snorted. "That sounds like Julian."

"Doesn't it?" Hallie sighed, obviously missing Natalie's sarcasm.

For the last four years, she'd barely spoken to her brother. Not when she'd gotten engaged to Morrison. Or made partner at the firm. Just the obligatory birthday and Christmas call and nothing more. He didn't even heart her Instagram posts. As children, he'd been the one to console her, defend her from unwanted male attention at school—in his albeit sharp and emotionless manner. But when she'd emerged from rehab at seventeen, an embarrassment to the Vos name while he was already thriving at Stanford, she'd sort of assumed his lack of contact was his way of showing disapproval. Or worse, that he wasn't aware of her at all.

No matter what she did, the reverse of that disapproval never came, from Julian or her parents. Not after she'd improved her grades and gotten into Cornell. Not after she'd climbed her way up the ladder in the boy's club that was New York finance or jointly purchased her condo with Morrison on Central Park South. It had taken them accidentally sharing the guest house together to make her realize Julian had been dealing with his own issues that whole time. It didn't excuse his silence, but she understood him more now.

I'm glad you're here.

She could still hear those clipped words coming from her brother as they'd walked up the path toward the main house one night just over a month ago. The night she met August at the Wine Down festival, actually. Until then, she hadn't realized exactly how starved she'd been for any form of affection from her family. Hearing that Julian had given up his Thursday night in order to get better acquainted with August . . . meant something. It meant a lot.

Even if he'd been bullied into it by his girlfriend.

For the next hour, they went over wedding plans. At Corinne's behest, Natalie and August would be married in the front yard of the main house, overlooking the vineyard, at sunset. A dream wedding, really, if only it were real. Hallie had outdone herself with the flower arrangements, creating a tasteful color scheme of cream and crimson with pops of black ribbon, somehow grasping Natalie's style without her having to say a word. Corinne had taken charge of the ceremony arrangements and a tent for the reception was already in the process of being erected and decked out. Natalie's only request had been "Small, please," and it had obviously been vetoed.

Hallie shuffled some paperwork around. "If there are any specific songs you'd like the DJ to play—"

"Anything but 'Brick House.' Please."

"An anti-playlist," Lavinia chimed in, her fourth martini hoisted in the air. "I love it. Can we please add 'Mambo No. 5'? There isn't a person alive that looks good dancing to that song. We need fucking *Abba*—and that's it, really. Abba."

"Fucking Abba. Check," Hallie chirped, making a note. "I also need to know which song you and August would like to dance to."

For some reason, her whole body flushed hot.

Dancing with August while he held her close.

In front of everyone.

Would she even have to fake her enjoyment of that?

"How about 'You're So Vain'?"

Hallie's nose wrinkled. "By Carly Simon?"

"The very one." Satisfied with her choice, already picturing the look on his face, Natalie smiled around the rim of her glass on the next sip. But the cold liquid didn't make it down her throat, because the door opened and August strode in with Julian.

Wow. The whole place went silent. Or maybe the sudden, rapid pounding of her heart was drowning out the shuffling chairs and laughter? Her brother by himself would have caused a stir by walking into any bar. He carried himself like nobility and looked perpetually annoyed—and yeah, she supposed he was pretty darn handsome.

But August.

He entered Jed's with an air of danger that she'd never quite noticed before. Maybe the first night they met, when she'd clocked the navy tat and deemed him the strong, capable, heroic type. Ever since then, however, he'd more or less become the loudmouth goofball to whom she was nursing a destructive attraction. She should have found it exasperating that he walked into the bar as if trying to establish himself as the alpha. All swaggering and huge and scanning the place for trouble—and the exits. *Oh. That's right. You're marrying a SEAL.*

There had to be two dozen women in the bar, but his gaze didn't stop on any of them.

Not until it landed on her.

Oh, this was bad.

She was two cocktails deep and the memory of his knowing fingers was too fresh.

Also, dammit. Something akin to joy leapt inside her at his appearance. As if a suppressed part of her was happy to see the jerk.

"I can't believe he picked the same bar as me. An *axe*-throwing bar," Hallie murmured to Natalie's left. "Next he'll be getting his septum pierced and vaping."

"Well, I'm not about to be the fifth wheel." Lavinia drained her drink and plonked the empty glass on the table. "The husband is due his bimonthly shag anyway." She saluted them on her way toward the door, calling over the noise, "I will see you at the wedding on Saturday. I'll be the only one in a fascinator, since you Americans refuse to respect their majesty."

"Bye, Lavinia," Hallie called, drawing Julian's notice.

Julian's eyes widened slightly and he gravitated toward Hallie, as if entranced, a smile curving his mouth. As much as listening to her brother and his girlfriend slam the headboard into the wall every morning had scarred her for life, Natalie could admit to swooning just a little at the straight-edged professor's reaction to spotting the troublemaker gardener. But as Julian and Hallie reunited with quiet murmurs to her left, she could see only August. Obviously. His head almost brushed the low pendant light that hung from the ceiling.

One did not miss a being so enormous.

In fact, a lot of women in Jed's were having the same problem.

Some women really went for the whole muscle-bound hero thing, apparently.

Natalie tried not to care. She really did. But when a young woman fanned herself in Natalie's periphery, she found herself pushing up out of her chair and planting one on August's surprised mouth. "Hi," she said brightly, brushing back her hair. "You're here."

"Yeah." His gaze ping-ponged between her mouth and eyes. "Can we try that again? I wasn't expecting it. My tongue is ready now."

"I don't think this is an appropriate time for tongue."

"When will it be?"

Natalie dropped her head back so she could groan at the ceiling. "Literally thirty seconds into this conversation and I'm exhausted."

"You think you're tired now?" He winked. "Wait until after tongue time."

"Don't ever say 'tongue time' again. Or I swear to God."

August chuckled, his hand settling into the curve of her waist naturally, brushing his thumb up and down her rib cage, as if he did it all the time. She wanted to push his hand away, because that light touch was stiffening her nipples. Ironically, that was the same reason she wanted his hand to remain exactly where it was. "Should I be worried that we're in a bar where weaponry is readily available?"

"Yup." She chopped the air with her hand. "Watch your wang, Cates."

He shuddered, glancing over his shoulder long enough to watch someone throw an axe—badly—missing the bull's-eye by a good two feet. "You're not the only one I have to worry about, princess. Pretty sure Julian would bury one of those in my back at any sign of premarital discord. Be nice to me for once, huh? I'm too young to die."

"Say 'tongue time' again and we'll test that theory." A waitress stopped in front of them and held up her notepad with a smile, prompting August to order a pint of Blue Moon. "What did my brother say to you?"

Natalie tried to be casual about posing the question. She must not have pulled it off entirely, though, because August seemed to look deeper. "Usual brother stuff."

"I don't know what that means."

"Why not?"

She shrugged a shoulder. "We haven't been close. I mean, he didn't even meet Morrison, let alone threaten him with axe violence."

"Guess I'm special like that." August blew out an extra-long breath. "I'm not going to ask about the ex-fiancé. I'm not going to ask about the ex-fiancé."

"That's probably for the best. It's not a pretty story."

A low rumble reached her ears.

Was he . . . *growling*? Why?

Natalie had no idea. But a subject change probably wasn't the worst idea. The last person she wanted to talk about was her ex-fiancé. "So about the wedding—"

"You know, tonight isn't the only time Julian has threatened to kick my ass. The first night you threw a drink in my face? He told me if I ever spoke to you like that again, he'd break my nose. It's kind of the reason I like the dude."

"Really?" She laughed. But her throat was suddenly so tight, the word emerged a little choked. "I didn't . . . I didn't know that."

"Yeah." Her future husband watched her closely. Like he could see everything going on in her head and it fascinated him. Probably squirreling information away for later so he could pull it out and use it during their next argument, which, at best, would likely take place in the next five minutes. "He cares about you, Natalie. Your mom cares about you, too. But it's like you're all trying to keep your love a secret. Why is that?"

"I don't know," she said, half defensive, half . . . honest. She *didn't* know. "Did your family go around making big professions of love all the time?"

"Not exactly. Not *all* the time. But it was said. In birthday cards. Or when my mother had too much to drink on New Year's and got sappy and started sharing memories." He accepted his beer from the waitress and took a long gulp, staring at an invisible spot over her shoulder. "But I think my parents put more importance on telling me they were proud of me. I worked a summer job so I could afford a beat-up Honda Accord. When I signed the paperwork, my parents said they were proud of me. When I joined the navy, they were proud. Looking back, I think maybe that was more their way of saying 'I love you' than the actual words."

It unnerved Natalie how much she wanted him to continue talking about his family. But wanting to know the background of the person she was fake marrying was healthy and normal, right? "Which is more important to you? Love or pride?"

He studied her face. "You answer first."

Was it crazy to be having this deep conversation in the middle of a loud bar? Probably. For some reason it didn't feel strange, though. There were no formalities with this man. Just jumping in with both feet and being pulled along in the current. "I guess . . . pride is more important to me. Pride is something that can be kept. Love is too often squandered when you give it away. People might be careless with your love, but they can't touch your pride. Or put it on their shelf like a trophy. It's yours."

Something about his demeanor changed. Sort of a swelling of his shoulders and lifting of his chest, as if he was preparing for a fight. On her behalf? "Your ex was careless with you."

Not a question, a statement.

Flustered by her willingness to share so recklessly with this man, she reached for her drink and stared into its depths. She took a sip, cooling her throat, feeling his rapt attention on her the whole time. "Your turn. Love or pride?"

"Love," he answered without hesitation.

Why did something inside her bloom like a rose over his answer? "Really?" Her voice was more uneven than a middle schooler's. "You just told me that whole story about Honda Accords and your family valuing pride."

"I know." He appeared thoughtful. "But love seems more important now."

Don't ask why. "Why?"

"Because I can tell you don't believe in it. And I want you to."

She definitely shouldn't ask why to that question. Or try to read between the lines for something that wasn't there. "That's very generous of you," she said quickly, feeling a rare ramble coming on and too flustered to avoid it. "I mean, the two are very closely related at the end of the day, right? Love means letting go of your pride, after all."

He looked at her as if she'd just said something really smart. "Holy shit. Does it?"

"I don't know, August. I'm not an expert." He continued to stare at her. For so long that she started to fidget. "What?"

"I want to know exactly what happened in New York."

Natalie shook her head. "No."

"Who is up for some axe throwing?" Hallie sang, coming along beside them, face flushed, a very cocky looking Julian sauntering up behind her. "We can do teams. Couple versus couple."

"Screw that." Natalie set down her drink and hauled Hallie against her side. "Men versus women."

A smile threatened the corners of August's mouth. "Who am I to object?"

"Battle of the sexes." Hallie flexed a biceps. "Let's do this."

Julian and Hallie left to secure their foursome a lane, leaving August and Natalie sizing each other up in the middle of the growing crowd. "Care to make it interesting?" he asked. "Not that I haven't already won just getting to watch you throw an axe in that short-ass dress."

"I'm going to get you sexual harassment training as a wedding gift."

His expression brightened. "Are we getting each other gifts?"

Natalie opened her mouth with the intention of calling him a bonehead—again—but the group to her back surged forward without warning and she stumbled, pitching forward. August moved like lightning, catching her around the waist with his free left arm, spilling not a single drop of his beer in the process. She successfully avoided falling, but her nose buried itself in the middle of his chest, smack dab between his pecs, and the smell of grapefruit soap and shaving cream momentarily made her brain fuzzy. And it grew fuzzier still when he pulled her closer. Protectively. Giving the people behind her a dark look. "Okay, princess?"

"Yes, I'm fine." She inhaled—discreetly—a final time.

Or maybe not so discreetly, because his lips twitched.

Finally, she managed to pull back, smoothing the front of her dress, wincing at the breathlessness in her tone when she said, "You were saying something about a wager?"

Chapter Eleven

It is a universal truth that people don't make the best decisions while drinking alcohol. In fact, people came to places like this with the *express intention* of making questionable decisions. To stop being responsible for a while and let fate stir the pot. Case in point, axe throwing in a bar. As a man who'd undergone extensive weapons training and knew how shit could go wrong in the blink of an eye, he wanted to carry Natalie out of there over his shoulder. The fact that she was anywhere near several blades was unsettling him to a degree that couldn't be ignored.

The increasing protectiveness he felt for his fiancé told August . . .

This wasn't temporary.

They weren't.

Sorry, princess. Sucks to be you.

This woman standing in front of him was his destiny. Part of him had known it the night they met, when she'd made him laugh and made him horny in the same breath. Jesus, she looked beautiful tonight with all that dark, smudgy makeup around her eyes and her hair . . . it kind of looked like sex hair. Like she'd been rolling around in the sheets. Was that intentional? Fuck. He would give up watching baseball for a decade to sink a fist into it right now. Move her head right to left, tug it back so he could get a look at that mouth up close.

Don't get me started on her legs.

If someone brandished an axe within ten yards of those pins, he'd throw them out of this place through the plate glass window. And her face. Man, he loved looking at those kaleidoscopic features as they brightened and dimmed and shifted. They were the reason he'd gotten severely off track.

Bottom line, he knew in his bones that in fifty years, he'd still want to look at her face.

Pretty sure he'd be starved for the opportunity.

He was protective by nature—and by trade—but the way he felt about Natalie's safety was on a whole other level. It wasn't just her physical safety he seemed to worry about at all times, it was the safety of her feelings. Her heart. *I'm responsible.* But just like any operation, he needed to get in there and find out what he was dealing with. He needed intel.

That was where their path from temporary to permanent needed to start.

And if Natalie knew he'd taken the loan from his CO and was marrying her purely because he wanted her to achieve *her* goals—and fine, because he couldn't stand the thought of never seeing her again—she'd stab him to death.

So he'd just leave that a secret for now. At least until she stopped hating him.

Love means letting go of your pride, after all.

Those words circled around and around his head. Was he ready to stop trying to win their ongoing battle of wills? Maybe not completely. Totally letting his guard down around Natalie might lead to his balls being amputated. He could damn well begin making inroads, though.

"August." She waved her hand in front of his face. "Battle of the sexes. The wager."

"Wager. Right."

If the men win, you agree to grow old with me.

Too much.

"If the men win, you tell me what happened in New York."

Also too much, but his big trap had already released the challenge—and damn, he really did want to know what had driven her back to Napa. If he was being forced to pry the information out of her, it couldn't be good.

Natalie's expression had grown shuttered on the heels of his throwing down the gauntlet, but almost immediately, she straightened her shoulders and pinned him with a look. "Fine. And if I win, you have to let me help you with your wine production."

Oh boy. No way.

Natalie had teased him so brutally about his shit winemaking, allowing her into the inner sanctum of his production line would make him feel like an exposed wound. "Do you actually want to help or are you just trying to one-up me?"

She pursed her lips, pretending to consider it. "Both."

Let her help. What's the big deal?

Making the wine was supposed to be his gift to Sam. Not just a gift, though . . . more of an atonement for letting him die. It was August's penance to serve and he was protective of the job. It was *his* work to do. *His* amends to make. No one else's.

"Pick something else. Anything else."

Instead of being exasperated by his stubbornness, she seemed kind of fascinated by it. "Um . . . okay, fine. For the entire month that we're married, you're not allowed to complain about how long I take to do my makeup."

"Done." Thank God she hadn't made an issue about the wine thing. He didn't want to explain out loud why he was so defensive about the operation. "But we kiss to seal the wager."

"You can't just make up rules as you go, rat king. A handshake seals it."

He scoffed into his beer. "Someone's scared."

"Oh, I'm scared?" Speaking of pride. "Pretty sure I'm the one who climbed into that shower. Or did you forget?"

Tits.

Beautiful, beautiful tits.

"Princess, that is a core memory. It'll be with me in the fucking afterlife."

She tossed her sex hair. "Good." So flippant. Except he caught her blush.

Did she like knowing he'd remember their shower for eternity?

Yeah. She did.

"Get over here and kiss me."

She snorted, gripping the front of his shirt and pulling him down. But she hesitated before their lips could touch. Wetting hers and staring at his. "Fine."

As if it was no big deal.

Right before their mouths met, however, she looked up at him and proved herself wrong. It was a very big deal. They kissed in the middle of the bar like they were alone. August absently set his beer onto the closest table so he could finally, blessedly, sink all ten fingers into her hair and go to fucking town on that mouth.

Tongue, lips, teeth. He used everything at his disposal to make her moan while they slanted their parted mouths, sampled, took deeply. And deeper still. *I'm going to figure us out*, he told her with the kiss, meaning it with every breath in his body. *I'm going to marry you, make this work.*

When they pulled back for air, Natalie looked more than a little startled.

Hell, he was startled, too. Every time they kissed, he needed more. *More* of her.

She gathered air into her lungs with their lips still only inches apart. "We better stop—"

"Before I carry you into the back alley and rip those panties down again?" He dragged her bottom lip down with his thumb. "Yeah. Guess we better."

Natalie knocked his hand aside and marched past him toward the axe-throwing booth, her gait more than a little unsteady. "W-we were just sealing the wager."

"Whatever you need to tell yourself, princess," he drawled, picking his drink back up and following in her wake.

A few moments later, when August picked up his first axe, he didn't even put his beer down. He looked Natalie right in the eye and threw a bull's-eye, then drained his pint glass while she and Hallie stared at him with their jaws on the ground. "What the . . ." Natalie sputtered. "You just—"

August pointed to himself. "SEAL. Remember?" He signaled the passing waitress with his empty glass. "Word to the wise, never make a bet with one of us. Especially when weapons are involved. What were you thinking?"

"I'm thinking . . ." Natalie shrugged a jerky shoulder. "I

haven't had my turn yet." She stepped up to the wooden, waist-high shelf that blocked the bar from the axe-throwing lane. "I could still win."

"That's right," Hallie piped up, patting her on the back. "You got this, Natalie. Never underestimate beginner's luck."

"Or a woman with her pride on the line," August said with a smile.

You're doing a great job of making this relationship permanent, buddy.

"A *beautiful* woman," he added quickly.

Natalie looked at him like he'd lost his marbles. Maybe he had.

After all, he was needling her while she was holding a sharp object.

As August watched, staring at her ass for only a few well-worth-it seconds, Natalie picked up the axe and sank it straight into the red bull's-eye. And she lit up. Her mouth fell open, light flooding her eyes. She gasped, hands flying up to her mouth. Like a woman did during a proposal. Like she might have done if he hadn't turned his proposal into a giant joke.

Dammit.

Swear to God, the whole bar blurred around them as she celebrated.

Jump into my arms. Do it. Please do it.

Spoiler: she did not.

She gave him a prim sniff and took her place off to the side, way too far from him. "Can you please come over here, Natalie?" he said.

"Why?"

"People are throwing axes in here."

"Way to recognize the theme." She waved him off. "I'm fine."

"Please? I'd like to be close enough to step in front of you if necessary."

Her features momentarily softened and she eventually rolled her eyes and sauntered over, nestling in beside him out of necessity, thanks to the bar being so crowded, especially in the throwing zone. Whistling casually, he let his arm creep up and settle onto her shoulders, earning him a pointed look, but thankfully she didn't try to pull away. They stood like a real-life, honest-to-God couple while Hallie took her turn—a throw that nearly ended up in the ceiling—and then Julian, whose throw landed in the ring just outside the bull's-eye. That lack of perfection really seemed to annoy him.

"We can't all be a hero on the first toss," August said, slapping the professor on the shoulder.

"There are different kinds of heroes," remarked Natalie, drawing his attention.

"Meaning?"

She looked like she wanted to take back her comment. Both Julian and Hallie appeared to be surprised, too, by the statement. Possibly even a little uncomfortable about it? "Meaning . . ." Natalie's throat worked. "My brother. He . . . rescued me from the fire." She laughed, but it didn't quite reach her eyes. "Didn't I tell you that?"

August was having a hard time hearing over the squeal of tires in his brain. "*What fire?*"

"Stop shouting," Natalie whispered, nudging him in the ribs with her elbow.

Was he shouting? "What fire?" he said again, sounding strangled. *Feeling* strangled.

Everyone remained silent for long moments. Julian became fascinated by the axe-throwing rules posted on the wall, crossing his arms and observing them as if they were a painting in a museum. "Four years ago," Hallie said finally, quietly. "The fire that went through Napa? It did a lot of damage to Vos Vineyard. Julian and Natalie were home for the harvest when it happened, and they were able to help evacuate their parents, staff, and as much equipment as possible, but Natalie got trapped in—"

"Okay. Whoa whoa whoa." August was beginning to sweat. "Natalie? *Trapped?*"

"Are you all right?" asked the woman in question.

"Yeah." Nope. Not at all. "Where did you get trapped?"

"Hallie was trying to tell you," Natalie pointed out.

"It was a lot of information at once." He swiped at his forehead with the hem of his T-shirt. And his pulse was racing too fast to enjoy the fact that Natalie bit her lip hard at the flash of his stomach. "I'm ready for the rest now." *I'll never be ready for the rest.*

It didn't escape August's notice that Julian was no longer reading the rules, but watching him very closely instead. Who could blame the guy? August was rapidly losing his cool. Because Natalie had been in danger from a fire four years ago. Really? A fucking *fire*? He hadn't even been in the country four years ago. Not close enough to do anything. Thousands of miles away.

"The fire approached much quicker than anticipated. Hours faster than they told us it would." A groove sat between Julian's dark brows. "She got caught in the shed while transporting equipment back and forth to the truck. There's only one entrance and it was blocked by the flames."

"But Julian got there in time. He ran in, covered my face, and hustled me out." August didn't realize how stiff he'd turned until Natalie shoved him a little and he almost pitched sideways like a toppling statue. "And it's a good thing, too, because I'm alive tonight, in this bar, to kick your ass in axe throwing."

Hallie whooped and held up a glass of wine. "I know that's right."

"Your turn, August," Julian prompted. Was he smirking?

August couldn't even feel the axe in his hand when he picked it up. He turned it over a few times, looked down, and found it shaking. Damn. "Uh, does someone else want to take a turn?"

"Turns must go in order," Julian said, pointing at the rule sheet.

Having no choice, August made sure no one was standing too close, then threw the weapon—watching with a sour stomach as it landed in the outer ring. No one said anything when he stepped back and gestured for Natalie to take her turn. She looked at him curiously on her way up to the barrier, picking up the handle of her blade. This time, she caught the middle ring, followed by Hallie doing the same. Julian got a bull's-eye. They were all talking and planning the next round, but August couldn't concentrate on what was being said. All he could see was Natalie trapped and scared, and he needed to get some air. Now.

"I'll be right back." August tried to smile but was pretty sure he just looked ready to hurl. "Just stepping outside for a minute."

"Hey." Before he could take a step, Natalie reached out and caught his wrist. "You're not mad because you lost the wager, are you?"

"What wager?"

She blinked. "Come on, let's go." She pulled him through the crowd toward the door. "You're having a mental breakdown. Either that or you just realized you gave up the chance to ridicule me over a thirty-minute makeup routine, so you're faking amnesia."

Christ, he needed to pull himself together. "I remember." They stepped into the crisp evening, onto the empty sidewalk outside Jed's, the last remnants of the earlier sunset giving the air a purplish glow. Or maybe he really was just having a mental break. Could air taste purple? "But I was kind of counting on winning."

"What happened?" Natalie asked.

"I'm not very good at feeling helpless. That's how I felt hearing that story." He looked her over, head to toe, barely resisting the urge to reach out and run his hands all over her skin. "You're okay? You didn't get burned anywhere?"

Her mouth opened and closed, her stance shifting side to side. "No. It was really scary, but beyond the fact that I triple-check my smoke detectors now, I'm fine."

"Good." A beat passed. "How can you doubt your brother loves you when he ran into a burning shed to save you?" August said it without thinking, raking a still unsteady hand down his face. God, he really needed to thank Julian for what he'd done. He *would*.

Soon as he got back inside.

In fact, he was going to ask him to be his best man.

"It's . . . his nature. He always does the right thing." Natalie's cheeks were deepening with color. "It gave him a terrible panic attack afterward. He's had this anxiety since we were kids and I made it worse because I wasn't paying attention."

"Yeah, Natalie. So inconsiderate of you. Next time, try to predict the fire."

"Wow. Nice. Using logic to make me feel better. That's low." Her lips twitched slightly to let him know she was joking and his fucking heart just sort of wrapped itself in a bow for her. "I spent a lot of time thinking he blamed me for his episode after the fire. But he . . . doesn't. He *told* me he doesn't. We're a lot better now that we've spent some time together."

"But?"

Her chin lifted. "How do you know there's a but?"

"Nat-tuition."

Lips twitching, she sized him up for a couple of seconds. "We all go it alone in this family. But they . . . were all ready to go it alone long before I was. Now Julian and my mother are getting closer and *I'm* the independent one. I'm kind of like, hey, remember everyone telling me to get my shit together and go stand on my own two feet? Well, I did. And no one . . . cared or noticed. Now I'm supposed to make this big effort to reconnect? No. I found what I was looking for somewhere else. For a while. And I just want to get it back."

"In New York."

"Yes, hence our impending nuptials." She seemed jumpy. "Can we go back inside now?"

"No." He took a step in her direction and tilted his head, seeing her through fresh eyes. Still as tough as ever, but wounded. *Patch it up.* That's what he wanted to do, but he had no idea how. "They should have noticed. You should always be noticed."

That caught her off guard and she fumbled through a thank-you.

"It's a hell of a balance, wanting your family to be proud while also keeping them at a distance so you can be your own person." What he wanted to say next felt too personal. It was about his best friend and his knee-jerk reaction was to keep it to himself. Still, he forced the words out, even though they felt like they were traveling through barbed wire in his throat. "Sam struggled with that a lot—having his father as a commanding officer. They cut off the father-son part of their relationship out of necessity. So there would be no distracting emotions in the mix—those can get a man killed in our line of work, you know? But when they had some down time and wanted to reconnect, it wasn't so easy. Probably because they'd seen how smoothly each could . . . detach, you know?"

"Yeah," she breathed. "That's exactly right."

Holy shit, was he on to something? Did he have the potential to actually *help* simply by being honest? The barbed wire was still there, along with the desire to hold all of his Sam memories close, but he was determined to make Natalie feel better. If opening up a little about Sam, at least for tonight, was how he accomplished that, he'd do the hard thing. "That's why Sam and I were so close. He stayed with my family on holidays. My mom sent him birthday cards with twenty-dollar bills tucked inside. My dad took him fishing, even when I wasn't around. We were brothers."

Emotion shone in her eyes. "Were you surprised to see his father the other day?"

"That's putting it mildly." The scar tissue on the back of his shoulder throbbed. "I retired early from the team after we lost Sam. I just couldn't operate the same." *Not after what I let happen on my watch.* "The CO and I didn't part on bad terms, but it was . . . I don't know. It was like he didn't welcome me doing something so drastic over Sam when he was just planning on staying in the exact same place. Does that make sense?"

He appreciated the way she thought it over for a moment. Then, "Yes. It does."

"Mostly, I wish Sam were here to see how much his dad cared

all along. I wish he were here for . . ." Momentarily unable to speak, August gestured between them.

"For the wedding."

August cleared his throat hard. "Yeah."

The evening hummed around them, the buzz coming from inside making the sidewalk seem all the more silent. Intimate. He couldn't read Natalie's expression, but he thought there might be a touch of wonder in it for some reason. And then, "I got forced out of my hedge fund in New York," she blurted. "For making a seriously bad trade that lost the company *a lot* of money. Like enough to buy three private islands and still throw a party. Lost a lot of respect in the process. I was the youngest partner. The only woman. But overnight, I became a liability and they fired me. My fiancé broke off our engagement because I no longer fit into our world." She lifted a shoulder and let it drop. "That's what happened in New York."

Damn. He couldn't imagine this woman making a mistake painting her fingernails, let alone one that cost a bunch of suits their mansion funds. And even more pressing, what man in his right goddamn mind would let *Natalie Vos* get away?

He wanted to shout a bunch of words—"that spineless mother-fucker" chief among them—but this was a vulnerable moment for her. Even he could recognize it wasn't a time for threats and anger, despite the fact that he sorely wanted to let loose on the wrongs done to her. Still, he reined in the burst of adrenaline and kept his voice steady as possible.

"If he bailed that quickly, Natalie, he never had enough integrity to deserve you in the first place." He kept his expression serious. "Thank God you found me."

Her lips sort of quivered up into a smile.

August smiled back.

And he wasn't entirely certain, but he was pretty sure they'd made some headway tonight. Not to mention, he'd learned something. When he shared things with Natalie, she shared back. He needed to remember that, because he wanted to know everything going on in her head. Wanted that badly. For now, he was going to bask in the glow of progress with a woman who'd once called him a walking sewage plant.

"Should we celebrate this meaningful conversation with a kiss? Maybe some light petting?" He held up his hands, palms out. "Or heavy petting. I'm down either way—"

She was already walking past him with an eye roll. "Just when I thought you might be capable of basic discourse."

Coming up behind her, he blew a raspberry into her neck. "Told you I'd never let you down."

She swatted him away. "Your interpretation of letting someone down is ass backward."

"Ass backward sounds even better than heavy petting," he said, waggling his brows. "Where do I sign up?"

"Right here," she sang, flipping him the bird.

"Uh-huh." He winked. "I remember how much you love a nice middle finger."

Natalie's groan mingled with August's booming laugh on their way back into the bar.

Chapter Twelve

I'm sorry. Did you say you've got us a potential investor?"

Natalie skidded to a halt on her way across the grounds of Vos Vineyard. Her former colleague and future partner, Claudia, had dropped that good-news bombshell on her, then proceeded to shriek at someone for stealing her cab while Natalie held her breath three thousand miles away.

"Claudia?"

"Yes, I'm here. Hold on, though, let me order an Uber." Precisely twenty-six seconds later, she was back. "William Banes Savage. Made his money in tech in the nineties. Something about Pentium processors, like anyone knows what the fuck that is. But he's old and bored, with money to burn, and wants to get his feet wet with the young scamps. If you can get here by next Friday, I can arrange a dinner meeting."

"Next Friday? As in a week from today?" With the sounds of New York City in her ear, the vineyard around her felt almost like an alien planet. "I'm getting married tomorrow."

"*Married?*" Claudia made a gagging sound on the other end. "What the hell for?"

"Rent money for our new office space. Equipment. Funds to take Pentium processor man out to dinner—"

"I've got the gist. Damn. So he's loaded?"

Why did she even reveal the marriage to Claudia? Now they were discussing August the same way they'd been discussing William Banes Savage—as though he were a means to an end— and she didn't like that at all. He was a lot more than that. Last night, after she'd returned from axe throwing, she'd lain awake in bed, replaying what he'd told her about Sam. About his own family. How he held these people so close to his heart. Treasured them. What would it be like to mean so much to August? "Never mind," she croaked. "Set up the meeting for next Friday and I'll do my best to be there. Worst case scenario, we cancel and tell Savage I'm meeting with someone more important. He'll be blowing up my phone."

"Go off, Anna Delvey. There's the bitch I used to know."

Natalie's smile felt stiff. "I never left."

Claudia snort-laughed. "My Uber is here. I'll let you know when I've got details. Bye."

"Bye."

For several seconds after she ended the call, Natalie stared down at the device in her hand trying to calm the weirdly un-settled sensation in her middle. A couple of weeks ago, she would have sold her soul for a chance to get back on a plane to New York and meet with a potential investor. Her trust fund would establish the new firm, but they would quickly need clout. They would need someone to come on board and send a signal to other investors that Natalie and Claudia were not only a safe play, but a shiny new endeavor.

But leaving only six days after the wedding?

Of course, she wouldn't be leaving for *good*. Just long enough to meet with William Banes Savage. Could she sneak out of St. Helena for a couple of days without the masses taking note? Would it hurt their chances of appearing legitimate if she left on a solo trip less than a week after tying the knot?

How would August feel about it?

Natalie swallowed hard and kept walking toward her destination—the Vos wine cave.

It's not like they were going on a honeymoon or anything, right? Business was business.

Eventually, she'd be leaving permanently and August was well aware of that. This was what they'd both signed up for. Temporary.

She took a hasty turn into the production facility, smiling at the employees who glanced over. After they got over the surprise of seeing her there, they nodded back, returning to their tasks. Harvest had taken place toward the end of the summer, followed by the pressing of the grapes. Now, firmly into fall, they were in the fermentation phase, which was a very careful science that could take months. Row after row of barrels were racked on their sides, employees carefully stirring the natural yeast to keep it from settling at the bottom of the wooden vessels, giving the wine oxygen, cultivating the flavor.

Natalie journeyed past them to the rear of the facility, opened the metal door, and started the long trek down four flights of stone stairs. When she reached the bottom, the scent of wet mushrooms tickled her nose and the sight of thousands of aging wine bottles greeted her, along with even more barrels. Tables were arranged throughout the cave for guests who toured the winery and wanted to explore the grounds beyond getting tipsy at the welcome center.

Did Zelnick Cellar have a wine cave? She needed to ask August about that. A lot of wineries in Napa had one, though they ranged in size. Maybe he could bring her on a tour of his underground cellar. Not that she wanted to be alone in the dark with him, it was purely out of professional *curiosity*, since she was now, technically, an employee of his vineyard—

Her heart jumped into her throat when she heard voices approaching from deep in the cave. Corinne and . . . was that Julian?

"It's an imaging service that takes high-resolution aerial photographs of the vineyard," Julian explained briskly. "That way, we can see which vines are overstressed, understressed. It can teach us a lot about why the taste is inconsistent and how to irrigate—"

"I don't even want to ask how expensive aerial photographs run," Corinne cut in.

"It's becoming a built-in expense for a lot of wineries," Julian returned in his usual calm and concise manner. "Over time, it actually helps reduce costs because resources are being directed to the right places, rather than wasted."

"Sounds like a winner," Natalie piped up, stepping into view from behind a rack of barrels. "When did you two start meeting in an underground cave like supervillains?"

Corinne looked startled at her daughter's sudden appearance, but Julian only seemed curious to find her there. "Shouldn't you be at your final fitting?" Corinne demanded to know. "It's not easy to find a tailor willing to make alterations on a wedding dress practically overnight."

"Don't worry. I just came from playing pin cushion," Natalie said, transferring her attention to Julian. Trying her absolute best not to let it show on her face how it felt being left out of the family meetings. All the time, now that Julian had gotten involved in operations. She might as well be a ghost. "What was the imaging service you were talking about? That sounds interesting."

Before Julian could answer, Corinne spoke again. "You never explained what you were doing down here."

Natalie jerked a shoulder. "I don't know. I just came for the quiet."

That was partially true. As a kid, she liked to sneak down to the wine cave and sit with her back pressed up against the chilly stone wall. She'd sit there for hours imagining a search party being formed to find her up above on the surface. She'd fantasize about how relieved everyone would be if and when they actually found her. They'd snatch her up in a big hug and make her promise never to hide away again without telling anyone where she'd gone.

That fantasy never came true, but pretending made her feel better.

This afternoon, she hadn't come down to the cave to fantasize about a worried posse of loved ones searching for her with flaming torches through swamps and valleys. No, she'd come to do a little soul searching. She'd stopped in town today to buy a couple of bottles of wine . . . but drove away empty-handed. Drinking wine had become a coping mechanism rather than a tool of enjoyment. If she really thought about it, she hadn't enjoyed wine *at all* in weeks. Soon, her trust fund would be released and she would need a clear head to take advantage of the opportunity. Her only one.

"Hmm," Corinne said, observing her the way a scientist examines a glass slide. "Do you want to come by later and do a quick rundown of the wedding arrangements?" The barest glimmer of a smile teased her mouth before it fled. "You're getting married tomorrow afternoon, you know."

Natalie wondered if she'd imagined that tiny smile. Heaven knew Corinne wasn't *happy* about Natalie getting hitched to August. "Yes, I'm aware. And . . . sure. I'll stop by after dinner."

Her mother inclined her head. "Ingram Meyer was the first to RSVP. He holds your trust fund in his hands, lest you need reminding. It won't reflect well if you appear to have no idea what's going on tomorrow."

This was why she drank. "Understood." Before Corinne could remind her of any more pressing responsibilities, Natalie continued, "I'm packed and ready to vacate the guest house. Hallie offered to drop my things off at August's place this morning while I attended the fitting, so I'm sure that mission was completed promptly and on time."

Julian snorted. In an affectionate way. His girlfriend didn't operate under the constraints of time and clocks and calendars. As a result, his inclination to schedule every second of the day had begun to wane. Drastically. And he appeared to be quite happier for the change. Why, he wasn't even wearing a tie and were those . . . flip-flops adorning his feet?

Before she could comment on her brother's startling choice in footwear, Corinne cleared her throat. "We're discussing business right now, Natalie."

Natalie plastered a smile on her face, refusing to let the hurt of dismissal show. "Julian, when you have a chance, shoot me the name of that imaging service you were speaking about. I'm just curious."

"Stay and talk about it with us," he said, splitting a thoughtful frown between Corinne and Natalie. "I haven't even gotten started on their methods of disease detection."

"Whoa. I'm too young to die of excitement." Natalie laughed, holding up her hands and backing away. "It's fine. I'll see you guys back on the surface."

"Natalie," Julian called when she reached the stairs, but her smile was beginning to wane, so she kept going, as if she didn't hear him.

It's fine.

Next Friday night was right around the corner. That was when she would prove herself.

That was when she would shine.

God knew she was never meant to do that here.

August propped a picture of Sam against the gravestone, sat back, and cracked open a cold one. "Cheers, buddy."

He'd woken up even earlier than usual this morning to make the drive down to San Joaquin Valley National Cemetery, where Sam was buried. Calling his parents and informing them of the news about his wedding had been fun. Fun like a root canal. His ears were still ringing from his mother's outraged screech. They were on a cruise to Alaska—which he didn't even know was a thing—and obviously couldn't make it to St. Helena by tomorrow. He'd managed to escape with what remained of his hearing by promising to bring Natalie to Kansas to meet them soon.

Maybe he should just crawl into one of these graves right now, because he didn't know when or even *if* he'd be pulling that off.

But it sure was nice to think about. Considering they were both tough as nails, Natalie and his mother would probably square off across the dinner table, refusing to blink. August was *here* for it.

Propping himself up from behind with his left fist, he lifted the beer to his lips with his right hand, tracing the name on the gravestone with his eyes. "I came here to ask you something important, man. Will you walk me down the aisle?"

Sam stared back at him from the glossy photograph, half smiling. August had snapped the shot with his phone at the end of day one of BUD/S training, where they'd met. Sam looked dog-tired in the photo, but there was a touch of exhilaration there, too, like he was relieved to get through the first twenty-four hours.

"Wait, you're telling me only the bride gets to walk down the aisle?" August reared back a touch. "That doesn't seem fair. I've been working on my runway strut for nothing."

He listened for a minute, trying to imagine what Sam would say.

"Natalie? Yeah, she's . . ." He let go of a breath. "Way out of my league. Remember how I used to tell you no woman would ever get me under her spell? Well, this one could. She could have me whipped in the time it takes to crack an egg."

The wind drifted through the sunny cemetery, rustling the trees.

"I'm already whipped, you say?" August smiled into his next sip of beer. "I don't recall asking for an opinion." He cleared his throat. "But seriously, you know, I have no idea what I'm doing these days. I'm trying to open your stupid winery and I suck at it. Out of nowhere, I've got a fucking *cat.* Stop laughing." The beer was sour in his mouth now. "You were really good at the things I wasn't. I taught you how to fish, you reminded me when it was time to buy new socks. I told you the mustache made you look like a serial killer, you talked me out of mining for Bitcoin. The balance is off now. But, uh . . ."

He swiped at his eyes and shifted into a different position.

"I don't feel off-balance when she's around. I mean, I do. She definitely makes me feel like I'm juggling dinner plates. There's also this feeling like . . ." He thought about it for a few seconds. "You know the feeling you had when I took this picture? Like the hard shit is over? I feel that with her. Or that it's possible with her, I guess. I don't know. Like if we just get through the difficult shit, all the strain we went through to reach the other side . . . I'll remember it like it was a joy, instead of being hard."

August listened to the wind.

"Yes, she's hot, too, you dog. The hottest. Don't get any ideas."

Beer empty, he let the bottle tip sideways in the grass, then decided to do the same himself, lying with his cheek pressed to the ground.

"I knew you'd ask about the wine sooner or later. Like I said, it's going terribly. Harvest is the easy part. Pick the grapes at night, keep them cold. Crush the grapes—yes, I left the stems and skin on during fermentation to bring the tannins to life. We're making a Cabernet. I know *that* much, dick." He exhaled. "Now the red stuff is in the barrels and that's where I got tripped up last year. Did you know people add egg whites and clay and sulfur and all kinds of shit to bring out the flavor of the grape? There is no recipe. It's all . . . trial and error science. And that was your deal. I'm the one who gives *wedgies* to the scientists."

He rolled over onto his back and looked up into the clouds, sighing a little when one of them took the shape of Natalie's lips.

"If you were here, I know what you'd be saying. Ask for help, August." His throat tightened up unexpectedly. "It's weird, though. I know I should, but I can't. I was supposed to do this for you. I was supposed to . . . have your back at all times. I failed. I'm sorry."

When his voice cracked, he knew it was time to go.

With one more hard clearing of his throat, August rolled back up into a sitting position, collected the picture, folded it on the crease, and carefully tucked it into his pocket. "I'll be back soon, if you're lucky." He fist-bumped the gravestone. "Love you, man. Wish me luck."

Chapter Thirteen

It was the antithesis of how Natalie had pictured her wedding.

The theme of her thwarted nuptials had been modern. Chic, black-tie, smoky jazz, and chandeliers. A rooftop ceremony at dusk, followed by champagne and mingling with colleagues. Making professional inroads at her own wedding had been a given. Although, in a manner of speaking, she was doing the same here. Marrying in the name of returning to the world of finance. The fast-paced, often ugly, no-time-to-cry business of investing.

But she never, not once, envisioned herself getting married in St. Helena in the front yard where she had once woken up beneath an overturned unicycle and Ludacris blaring from her Bluetooth speaker. Don't get her wrong, the setting was unmatched. Mount St. Helena was clear as a bell in the distance, smothered in sunshine. The vineyard seemed to be putting its best foot forward today, rows of lush greens and rich browns rolled out like shiny ribbons in the flattering afternoon light.

Natalie walked around the perimeter of the tent where the reception would take place into the evening. It was smaller than she'd expected, based on her mother's description, thank God.

She'd convinced her mother to keep the guest list on the intimate side and for once, they hadn't argued about it, though only one man on the list seemed to matter today—Ingram Meyer. At least to Natalie and August. For Corinne, the wedding was as much about image as it was about helping them succeed. Wasn't it?

A hundred yards ahead, Natalie could see Hallie bustling around in ripped jean shorts and a sky-blue halter top, securing big, bright boughs of crimson roses to the aisle chairs where the ceremony itself would start in about an hour.

Natalie didn't even have her dress on yet.

Hair and makeup was done—she'd taken care of that herself.

Everything was being handled. All she needed to do was get fake married.

Just get through today, stay married for one month to make the union believable and not blemish the Vos name with a scandal. Then she'd be on her way.

It took Natalie several moments to realize she was scanning the yard for August.

Shouldn't he be here, with only an hour to go before the ceremony?

Had he changed his mind?

When they'd parted ways two nights ago after axe throwing, everything had seemed fine. Meaning she'd called him a lumbering twat and he'd made kissing noises at her until she'd slammed the door of her Uber on him. All perfectly normal.

Funny, while pondering the possibility that August had gone AWOL, she didn't immediately think of her trust fund. She was kind of . . . worried? That maybe he was having a hard time going through with the wedding without Sam?

She reached into the pocket of her robe and took out her phone, smoothing her thumb over the glass screen. Should she call him? See if he needed to chat? As little as a week ago, the very idea of holding a conversation of any length with the world's worst winemaker would have been laughable. And hey, they weren't best friends now or anything. Ha! That would be the day. But talking to him didn't quite suck as much as it had before? It was kind of nice how she could be as mean and sarcastic as she wanted and he simply rose to the occasion. She didn't have to pretend. She'd even been honest with him about her family woes and afterward, she'd been just a little bit lighter.

Maybe pretending to be married to him wouldn't end in World War III.

It wouldn't be a walk in the park, either. But they *might* not kill each other.

Right as Natalie was preparing to call her missing fiancé, his truck roared into the parking lot and skidded to a halt, kicking up a dust cloud. Everyone on the lawn stopped and turned to watch the giant groom climb out of his truck—carefully cradling a marmalade-colored cat to his chest, patting its head soothingly.

Menace was here. Wearing a cat tuxedo.

Natalie ducked back behind the tent to laugh, getting it out of her system as quickly as possible, before schooling her features. When she heard August exchange a hello with Hallie, she stepped out into the open.

August spotted her, jerked back, and held the cat up in front of his face. "Jesus Christ, Natalie. I'm not supposed to see you."

She implored the sky for patience. "You're not supposed to see me in the *dress*, August."

Still he didn't lower the cat. "That's not the dress?"

"It's a robe."

"Ahhh." Finally, the cat was back against his chest. "Whatever it is, you look hot in it."

Natalie shook her head at him. Too bad so many locals were within earshot, setting up tables inside the tent, caterers arranging champagne flutes and place settings. "You look very nice in your tuxedo, as well."

The lie detector test determines . . . that is not *a lie.*

August Cates was *fine*. Rugged. Totally at ease with his enormous body and thick muscles, which were accentuated to perfection in the starched black jacket and pants. She could tell he'd shaved, but growth was already apparent on his cut jaw and upper lip, somehow making the bow tie look softer. Like it could be whipped off at any moment. He'd tried to tame his hair, but the wind in his truck must have gotten hold of it, because some pieces were refusing to stay in line. Honestly, though, who cared about hair when his shoulders could seat a party of four?

He sauntered closer, his right hand stroking the cat's back absently. "Yeah, I can see you like me in a tux, princess."

She smirked at him, hoping the heat in her cheeks wasn't turning them red. "Nice of you to show up."

"Aw," he drawled. "Were you getting worried?"

"That you slipped in a puddle of your own caveman drool and hit your head? Yes. I was."

His smile showed off a row of strong, white teeth. "Were you able to get a dress made of Dalmatian fur on short notice?"

"Had one in my closet already, as a matter of fact. I just had to find a good man." The corners of her mouth lifted. "And by good, I mean standing upright, with a pulse."

"Gosh, Natalie. You sure know how to make an Adonis feel special."

"It is our wedding day, after all." Now that she'd made sure they were on even footing, in that safe bickering space where they tended to live, Natalie was comfortable enough to draw an object from her robe pocket and hold it out to him. "You mentioned wedding gifts and I just picked up a small thing. It's really just a *very* small thing. Like you said, this was short notice and . . ." *Stop rambling.* "I found your Facebook profile, which you haven't posted anything on in like, seven years, but there was a picture of Sam, and . . ."

She couldn't seem to stop moving as he turned the laminated picture over in his hand, reading the words that were printed there. Then back. Right side up again. He said nothing, just looked down at the small card with his brow puckered.

"This is the U.S. Navy hymn," he said quietly, finally looking up at her.

"Yes." She tucked a strand of loose hair back into her low chignon. "I had to google it obviously. I don't just know hymns off the top of my head."

"Natalie . . ."

"Sam can't be here, but you can put that in your pocket and . . . I don't know. Maybe it'll feel a tiny bit like he is. Like I said, it's just a small thing—"

He moved quickly, his firm mouth pressing to hers and cutting her off mid-sentence, staying there for a long moment while neither one of them seemed to breathe. "No, it's not," he said, releasing her lips, but staying close. So close she'd tilted her head all the way back to receive the kiss. "This isn't small, princess."

She couldn't think of an adequate response to that and talking at all seemed like it might be difficult, so she just nodded, the pressure on her chest increasing the longer he held her eyes, searching them.

"Your present is back at the house," he said, carefully tucking the picture into his breast pocket.

"Great." She had to swallow because her throat was utterly dry. "I can't wait to open my lube from the gas station. Which flavor did you get me?"

"Tropical. Obviously."

"Pity we'll never use it."

"I know, right?" He let his gaze trail down her body to the knot of her robe. "You don't need any help in that department. Not when you've got me to look at."

"That's beautiful. If only we'd decided to write our own wedding vows, you could have included it."

"Who says I didn't write my own?"

That gave her serious pause. Was he joking? "Did you?"

August held up the cat's paw in a little wave and strolled past her toward the house. "I don't know, did I?"

"August!"

"Meet you at the end of the aisle, Natalie."

Her intended had just moved out of earshot when her phone buzzed in her pocket.

When she saw her father's name on the screen, the warm fuzzies she'd—admittedly—gotten from her conversation with August vanished. It couldn't be a coincidence that he'd called on her wedding day. She stepped into a small tent at the edge of the property that appeared to be set up as a coat check. And she answered.

"Father."

There was a short burst of Italian on the other end, then Dalton's voice came through clear. "Natalie." His sigh was woven with resignation. "You're going to call off this ridiculous spectacle immediately. What are people going to think when I'm not in attendance at my own daughter's wedding?"

That rendered her momentarily speechless. "Who told you I was getting married? I know damn well it wasn't my mother."

"I have a lot of friends in the Valley. A better question is: Who *didn't* tell me?"

"And just to recap, you're more upset about how this reflects on you . . . than the fact that you aren't close enough to your family to be *invited* to your daughter's wedding?"

His long-suffering sigh was interrupted by someone else speaking to him in Italian, a woman this time. Dalton responded to her in kind. Before he spoke again, Natalie knew she wouldn't get a satisfying answer to her question. But she never could have expected what he said instead. "Is this what you want, Natalie? To force my hand?" A pause ensued. "Fine. Call off the wedding and I'll release your trust fund."

"You . . ." Natalie was immediately winded. "I don't understand. Now y-you're offering to release the money? What made you change your mind?" The ground seemed to be quaking beneath her feet, so she sat down on an overturned crate. "Is this only about saving face in Napa? You don't even *live* here anymore, but you're still worried people will think your daughter might be marrying for money?"

"Marrying a *nobody* for money," he snapped in an ice-cold tone. "A nobody who is a laughingstock who doesn't know a grape from an olive. Tying himself to *my* legacy."

"Actually, it's *my* legacy," Natalie pushed through her teeth, anger sweeping through her at such an alarming rate, she almost fell off the crate. "My life."

And she would be best served marrying August. Because she would hate herself for the rest of her life if she gave in, took the easy road, after Dalton had abandoned them. Without apology or regret. It was more than resentment that kept her from outright agreeing to take her trust fund in exchange for jilting August, though. She couldn't quite describe the nausea that roiled in her stomach at the thought of calling off this wedding. Was she actually . . . excited to walk down the aisle, because of the man who would be waiting at the end?

No way she was going to answer that definitively. Not even to herself.

One thing she did know, this piece of work she called a father wasn't going to insult a man who'd literally stopped in his tracks on the way out of town and stayed to help her.

Not a chance.

"And I'm sorry to disappoint you, Dalton, but it is a real marriage. August Cates is an incredible person, actually. Did you know he moved to St. Helena to open a winery in his friend's name? His friend had this dream, but he died before he could fulfill it, so August is doing it for him. Yes, even though he's awful at winemaking. I don't expect you to understand integrity like that. You made wine because you wanted to be the best. He makes it to honor a friend. August . . . he listens to me and tries to understand me when I can barely understand myself most of the time. He wants me to believe in love. He said that. Out loud."

She stood up and started to pace.

"He's reliable. And funny. He's one of the only people I've ever met who genuinely makes me laugh. I don't have to fake it. And

I care about him." Oh God, was she really doing this? Marrying August for some indefinable reason when her ticket back to the East Coast was within her grasp? Yes. Yes, she was. "I'm not calling off the wedding in exchange for getting the money now. Your rules are bullshit, but apparently . . . I'm following them anyway. I'm marrying him."

"My rules might be bullshit, but you're going to wish you didn't have to follow them. Turn down my offer and you'll be obligated to convince Ingram Meyer that you're not a couple of brazen cons—and believe me, it won't be easy."

"Good. I welcome the opportunity. Arrivederci, Father."

AUGUST'S PALMS STARTED to sweat at the very moment the wedding march started.

All right, this was really happening.

This was his wedding day. August had never imagined his own wedding, per se. But he'd always assumed his parents would be there. Sam, too. He'd figured on a lot more people in naval uniforms and fewer people in statement scarves. He didn't know anyone in attendance very well. Julian stood to his right, giving him a steady professor look that caused August a beat of panic. Did he forget to turn in his homework? No, this was his wedding day and he . . . needed some reassurance. Someone to smack him in the head and remind him he was marrying a ten.

Because he was. That was what he really needed. To see Natalie. She knew him. They knew *each other*. She was his closest friend in the tent, for better or for worse.

I'll make it for better. Won't I?

Yeah, you will, said Sam's voice in his head. *You're more than stubborn enough.*

August's hand automatically rose to his pocket, his pulse calming when he felt the outline of the laminated picture—

Oh shit.

Oh . . . shit.

August's emotions were raw to begin with, but when Natalie appeared at the top of the aisle, the breath quite literally fled from his lungs. He thought she'd looked incredible in the robe. But now? Why was he getting emotional over a fucking dress? It had no significance to him. It was expensive looking, with long, flowing, sort of see-through material on the bottom and a sparkly . . . boob booster on top? It didn't have straps, just a tight section of sparkling beads that pushed up her tits.

How was he just supposed to act normal when she looked this way? The combination of the dress and her hair and makeup . . . this was a bride.

His bride.

She was walking toward him on a satin runner, all by herself, no man to guide her there. Was she all right coming down the aisle alone? He wished they'd discussed that. Julian could have done it, right? So maybe she *wanted* to do it alone? Natalie's brother stood across from Hallie, who held a bouquet of roses and baby's breath in her hands. A lot like Natalie's, but much smaller.

His future wife was halfway down the aisle now. Getting more and more beautiful with every step she took. Damn, even her shoes were sparkly.

The music swelled along with August's throat.

How did he get here? *How?* He had no earthly clue, but he knew one thing. The richest man in the world couldn't pay him to be anywhere else.

Especially when Natalie's eyes found his and held on, as if gathering strength. She was nervous. Sweat was slipping down his spine, so yeah, he could relate. They shared an exaggerated breath while staring at each other and . . .

Jesus Christ, was he crying?

Yeah. Actual moisture flooded his eyes. Too much to blink away.

Natalie paused ever so slightly, looking dumbfounded.

"Sorry." He laughed, swiping his sleeve across his eyes. "Who's cutting onions?"

The tent full of strangers laughed. Except for Julian, who August could feel staring at him, speculating. Corinne sat in the front row, Menace curled at her feet, looking back and forth between August and Natalie and for some reason, her shoulders seemed to relax over whatever she saw. August would have given a million dollars to find out what it was, because he had no idea what was happening in his chest. A fucking racket, that's what.

She'd brought him a picture of Sam.

She'd printed it out, found the hymn. Had it all laminated.

Until she handed over the card, he'd had no idea how badly he needed it. Again, he felt the slight weight of it behind his pocket square and it calmed him. Someone had his back. The person he'd grown to trust the most out of anyone in his life . . . was present. In his thoughts, if not physically. And he had the woman in front of him to thank.

The woman clutching her flowers with white knuckles.

Calm her down.

"Your tits look insane."

She looked like she wanted to clock him over the head with her bouquet.

But at least the blood was back in her fingers.

Damn. He had it so bad.

Chapter Fourteen

*N*atalie watched in horror as August unfolded the piece of paper that he'd removed from the pocket of his tuxedo. Yellow legal-pad paper, to be exact, on which lines had been crossed out and arrows had been drawn.

It looked like the first draft of a football playbook.

What in God's actual name was he going to say?

More importantly, had she *actually* passed on an offer to get her trust fund and remain single? With her money in hand, she probably could have even afforded to reimburse Corinne for the catering. Sure, the last-minute flake out wouldn't have been good for her relationship with Corinne or the Vos family reputation, but neither of those things were stellar at the moment to begin with!

Although, wow. If she'd taken the money and skedaddled, she would have missed the sight of August in front of an altar—a portable one, sure—looking at her in a wedding dress with total, unabashed awe. It wasn't every day a girl was privy to that compelling of a moment.

My goodness, he's beautiful, too. A big, beautiful, battle-worn presence.

She'd meant every word she'd said to her father. God help her. What now?

Follow through on her word to the man. She owed him that. He deserved that much.

But that was all she could offer. All he could expect.

They were halfway through the traditional vows when August cleared his throat and flattened the wrinkled paper on his thigh. Out of the corner of her eye, Natalie noticed her mother shifting nervously in her seat. She knew August was a loose cannon who never tried to hide his disdain for St. Helena's elite and every guest at this wedding fit that profile, including Ingram Meyer.

August reached for the microphone and the pastor handed it over with a glance toward the wedding planner. He shrugged. August cleared his throat directly into the mic, sending a trill of feedback through the tent and a smattering of murmurs. "Natalie Vos. Wow. Here we are. Getting married." He turned the paper toward her so she could see he'd written those exact words, before going back to reading. "I promise to take your side in every argument—unless it's the one you're having with me, then it's fair game. But the point I'm trying to make is that we might fight . . ." He scanned the room with a pointed look. "But God help anyone else who tries to fight with you. They will answer to me."

Oh . . . my God. Why were her eyes burning?

This wasn't even real. Why did his speech feel . . . important?

Why did the whole day feel significant?

"I also promise to protect you from this day forward. From cat claws to fires to drunk people with axes. You're always going to be safe. I'll make sure of it. You can call me no matter where you are, and I'll come."

There was more.

A whole second half of a page. He couldn't seem to continue, though. Maybe because the guests were so silent. Maybe he got self-conscious. Whatever the reason, August coughed into his fist, folded up the paper hastily, and shoved the vows back into his pocket. "We can keep going now," he said with a brief smile, handing the microphone back to the pastor.

Instead, Natalie just dropped her bouquet of flowers, took a lunging step, and kissed him. Smack on the mouth, right there in front of everyone, her hands smoothing up the lapels of his black dress jacket. "Are you kissing me because of what I said about your tits, princess? Because I meant it. They are hot as sh—"

"For the love of God. Shut up."

"Done."

She kissed him again, ignoring the dangerous stinging behind her eyes. The kiss threatened to grow more intense until August squeezed her waist and broke away with a low whistle, his eyelids at half-mast.

They finished reciting the words that officially made them husband and wife, but she stumbled over every single sentence, thanks to the way August was looking at her.

APPARENTLY, THE BRIDE and groom didn't get to spend a whole lot of time together at the wedding. File that under information August hadn't been unaware of until today.

At least, they never got to be alone.

Everyone else under the tent seemed to be getting tons of face time with Natalie and he wasn't even going to pretend not to be jealous. Whenever he got her attention, someone came by and struck up a conversation with her. Men. Women. Children. Even the cat was in her lap for a while, rolled over on its back like a lazy queen.

Obviously everyone wanted to talk to his wife, she looked like a fucking angel.

In sixty years, when he thought back on his wedding, he was going to remember this—chasing her around the candlelit tent just trying to get her alone. So he could . . . what?

He wasn't even positive this wedding meant anything to Natalie. Not the way it meant something to him. If her motives went beyond unlocking her trust fund, they remained unclear. And he wanted to know where he stood with this woman every time he looked at her. Starting today, he'd do everything in his power to make it happen.

August-style, of course.

"It's nice to see you again, Mr. Cates. Under better circumstances, of course," said a voice to his right. August turned to find none other than Ingram Meyer standing at his elbow, holding a plate of cake. Who wore a straw hat to a wedding? Was it the guy's signature fashion piece or something? "I'm Ingram Meyer."

August shook the man's free hand. "Yes, I believe the last time we met, you told me not to let the door hit me in the tuchus on my way out of the bank."

"You weren't so polite, either, as I recall, but that's all water under the bridge now." The man was regarding him a little too closely to be polite, but August said nothing. Making a good impression on this man was important to Natalie. Ingram held the purse strings and August wouldn't mess up Natalie's chance to untie them.

"Enjoying the party?"

"I am. Corinne always outdoes herself." Ingram paused. "Although not usually on such short notice."

A prickle rode up the back of August's neck. "Natalie and I are grateful to her."

"Yes." Ingram canted his head to the left. "How *did* you and Natalie Vos meet?"

"Natalie Cates," August corrected, forcing an affable smile. "We met at Wine Down Napa." God, she'd been beautiful that night. And every night since. Back then, though, there wasn't a speck of vitriol between them. Just that weightless excitement. "She was there to represent the vineyard—"

"And she'd had a little too much wine, like we all do at those events," Julian said, approaching unexpectedly on August's left. Giving him a quick nod. "An online wine blogger was trying to snap Nat's picture in a tipsy state, but August blocked their shot."

Did I?

Yeah, he guessed he had. The whole night was a blur of anything but . . . her.

The way she'd smiled. Her smoke-and-flowers scent.

How he'd lost his balance the moment he saw her and never got it back.

"I was positive in that moment we'd be seeing a lot more of him," Julian finished, raising his glass and sharing a fleeting smile with August. "And I was right."

Ingram considered both of them in turn. "What a nice story." He took his time taking a bite of cake, chewing it while looking over the crowd. "Corinne invited me to dinner at the vineyard on

Monday night. I'm looking forward to hearing more about how this union came to be." He tipped his straw hat to Julian and August. "Enjoy your night."

"Same to you," August said, smiling with teeth.

"Bastard," Julian muttered near his ear.

"Yeah. Someone find a princess to kiss that guy and turn him back into a frog," August agreed, rubbing at the nape of his neck. "Thanks for having my back, man. I forgot about the whole thing with the photographer."

"I didn't." Julian swirled his wine. "I also remember when she threw wine in your face and you only looked angry at yourself for arguing with her in the first place."

"Yeah, that sounds like me."

Julian shook his head. Sighed. "You're in love with her."

Suddenly, August couldn't swallow.

The music swelled in his ears.

Was he in love with Natalie? No idea. If the key to her happiness was at the bottom of the ocean, he'd strap on some flippers and goggles to dive down and get it. If she showed any signs of illness, even a common cold, he would consider bringing her to the ER. If she asked him to dress like Zack Morris at Halloween so she could dress like Kelly Kapowski . . . he'd already have suggested it first. Did all of that equal love?

To him? Yes.

He loved her. Really, really bad.

It couldn't have seemed less natural for Julian to lay his arm across August's shoulders, but he did. Briefly. "I have faith in you." He stepped back. "I also have faith that she wouldn't have gone through with this unless something was there."

"Thanks, Julian," he managed through his parched throat.

"And if you hurt her, I'll break your nose."

"Heard you the first two times."

When Julian returned to his girlfriend's side, August picked up an uneaten plate of food from one of the tables and dug into it with a tiny fork. Cold sea bass was not the most appetizing of choices, but God knew he'd eaten worse.

How to get Natalie's attention. How to get . . .

The DJ booth released a slow plume of fog out onto the dance floor.

August smiled mid-chew, finally landing on a plan.

A few minutes later, the opening strains of "Brick House" filled the tent and Natalie's shoulder blades twitched, then she was turning around and sending daggers at him with her eyes. He only winked back. When the lyrics kicked in, August strutted out onto the dance floor and pointed directly at his new wife with an open challenge. At first, he was positive she was going to throw the closest heavy object at his head, but to his everlasting happiness, she joined him in the center of the floor, causing the drunk guests in attendance to applaud.

"Are you serious?" Natalie mouthed at him over the music.

August unbuttoned his tuxedo jacket with a flourish and dropped it on the dance floor, moving on to the cuff links next. Rolling up his sleeves. And then he started to dance—although even he could admit that that term should be used loosely when applied to his series of exaggerated disco moves and jump spins. Not to mention *a lot* of finger guns. He'd developed this routine years ago as a way to shake the malaise that often overcame his team when they'd been away from their families too long and, frankly, it was ridiculous. But it was *him*, whereas this wedding was definitely not.

Not unless he counted Natalie.

This woman was . . . him. She was why he'd come.

"I'm not dancing to this," she shouted over the music.

"Are you serious? This song was *written* about you," August called back, grooving closer.

"I wasn't even born when this song was written."

"The Commodores must have seen you coming." He snagged her wrist and spun her around, noticing the beginnings of a smile creeping in. "On the other hand, I did not," he said, leaning down to speak into her neck. "See you coming, that is."

Her eyes shot to his, a furrow appearing in her brow. As if trying to decipher whether or not he was putting her on. "The only reason I'm going to dance with you right now is this. My mother picked '(I've Had) The Time of My Life' from *Dirty Dancing* as our first dance song. I don't know what in the hell she was thinking. Everyone expects a lift at the end of that song. Or a dancing flash mob. She clearly didn't think it through."

"Her oversight is my gain. Which song did *you* pick?" He rubbed his chin, as if he hadn't already spent hours pondering this. "Let me guess. 'You're So Vain'?"

Natalie's mouth dropped open.

"Knew it. Get moving." He performed a pretty stilted version of the hustle. Not because he wasn't amazing at it, but because Natalie was on the verge of giving up the fight. She was starting to bump her shoulders to the music and Lord, when Natalie allowed herself to enjoy him, even for just a few minutes, it was like holding a puppy in one hand and a foot-long hoagie in the other. Bliss. "For the record, though, I could have lifted you Johnny Castle style."

Natalie was already shaking her head. "This dress has about

forty pounds of crystals sewn into it. I would have knocked you out."

"I'm known for absorbing blows to the head without losing a step."

"Should we test that theory?"

"No, but we should definitely test the lift theory when we get home."

They were in the middle of the dance floor having this conversation, and August was pretty damn sure Natalie had no idea she was dancing. As if he didn't already find this woman attractive beyond human comprehension, she had to go and look good cutting a rug, too. Just effortless and fluid and sexy. In rhythm. How was it even fair?

"You're proposing that, after we've both consumed our fair share of champagne, we go home and try the *Dirty Dancing* lift?"

He winked at her. "You're damn right, princess."

She pitched toward him, laughing. "Do you think they'll give us lollipops if we're brave enough in the emergency room?"

"Maybe we'll get lucky and end up on *Sex Sent Me to the ER*."

"In your wildest dreams, Cates."

"In *your* wildest dreams, Cates."

Natalie jolted slightly. "Oh my God, I'm Natalie Cates now."

His bow tie was suddenly way too tight. "It has a certain ring to it."

The *shake it down, shake it down now* portion of the song started and he hit the running man while she effortlessly worked the Batusi. Shit, he was falling deeper for her the longer this song went on. His team would love her. They'd worship the ground she walked on for not putting up with his crap but occasionally giving in, wouldn't they? "We're doing the lift."

"We're so *not* doing the lift."

"What are you afraid of?"

"A concussion, for one."

He scoffed. "You seriously think I would ever drop you? My beloved *wife*?"

This time when she laughed, her eyes were sparkling, the sound piercing him right in the middle of his chest. Although he wondered if she would be laughing if she knew he wasn't laying it on all that thick. She danced for another few seconds, then rolled her eyes up at the ceiling. "Fine, we'll try it. But if I end up with an injury, you'll be waiting on me hand and foot until I've healed."

"I'd do that anyway, if you asked me to."

If the music wasn't blasting, August was pretty sure he'd have heard Natalie gulp. "You'd wait on me hand and foot?"

"Yes. At least until I annoyed you enough to be banned from entering your room. Even on my best behavior, that could happen pretty quickly." She was biting her bottom lip to keep her full smile from blooming again. They were close enough now that he could see the indentation of her teeth and the light sheen in the hollow of her throat that was proof of a good dance session. His hands were on her hips before he realized they were moving and, praise Jesus, her eyelids drooped on contact, followed by a measured intake of her breath. "We fail at the lift, I become your servant. We succeed . . ."

He pressed and dragged his thumbs along the curve of her hip bones, tugging her close by the skirt of the wedding dress.

"What?" she said, though he could only read her lips as he looked down at them from above. She must have been whispering.

"I give you a proper wedding night," he said.

She huffed an incredulous laugh. "Pretty sure that's a prize for *you*."

He brought his mouth to her ear and felt his own eyelids grow heavy at the waft of her scent. "No lies detected. I'm gonna love going down on you, princess."

Her quick release of breath bathed his throat, making his stones feel weighty, the nape of his neck beginning to sweat. "That's . . . your prize?" she asked, finally, her tone threadbare.

"Uh-huh." He slid his palms around to the small of her back and crushed her closer, letting her feel the resulting rumble in his chest. "It's kind of a two-part prize, to be fair. First, I finally, *finally* get to fucking taste it, Natalie." They both shuddered. "Second, every time you look at me in the future, you'll have this knowledge in your eyes. That I know exactly where your clit is located and what the hell to do with it."

The song ended.

She shoved away from him with a flushed face.

Applause broke out from the perimeter of the dance floor, startling her. And it gratified August to no end that when she was alarmed, she reached for him instinctively, fingers curling in the starched white material of his shirt. Before she could recover and step away from him again, August wrapped an arm around her waist and tugged her closer, leaning over to plant a kiss on the crown of her head, the wedding photographer snapping away with pops of light.

Oh yeah. His heart boomed. *They were in this.*

The applause and whistles died and Natalie eased away, leaving the dance floor with a wary backward glance in August's direction. Correction: *he* was in this.

In order to get his heart off the chopping block, he needed to bring her along.

Starting with an overhead lift. *Jesus.*

On the way off the floor, he pulled his phone out of his pocket and started googling.

Chapter Fifteen

The limousine ride back to August's home was short.

But effective.

Everything today involving this man classified as potent.

She couldn't even blame it on the champagne, because she'd barely stopped talking long enough to drink two glasses. After they'd walked out of the reception and everyone threw handfuls of obligatory rice at them, August had pulled her into his lap in the back of the limousine and proceeded to pick the tiny, white grains out of her hair, his fingertips brushing the nape of her neck repeatedly. Out of self-preservation, she'd crawled over to the opposite seat, giving him an affronted look.

But the damage was already done.

She was turned on by her fake husband.

Not just buzzing with an electrical current of attraction, either. This was a full-on meteor shower of hormones, the likes of which she'd never experienced in her life. Not for her former fiancé. Not for anyone.

She needed to shut this down immediately.

This was a marriage inspired by advantages. Money. Eventually it would be over and they would walk away, hopefully better off than they started. This was not a long-term situation and introducing the complications of sex was a very, very bad idea.

God forbid it turned out to be good.

What would she do then?

Don't pretend you don't already know it would be good.

The fact that August had even mentioned her clit boded extremely well, let's be honest. It wasn't something that typically rolled off a man's tongue—before *or* during the act—unless he valued the woman's pleasure as much as his own. She would not have assumed that about the hulking SEAL who had somehow gotten red wedding cake frosting in his hair, even though they'd both been handed forks.

On the other hand, maybe it was a signal that he *did* excel at . . . giving pleasure?

"You're thinking about me going downtown, aren't you?" August drawled from the other side of the limousine, the cat fast asleep between his feet, purring loud enough to drown out the limo's engine. "How does it feel? I've been thinking about it for over a month."

They slowed to a stop in front of his house and the driver alighted, his footsteps on the gravel loud in the sudden silence. "I think we should put this bet off until we're both totally sober."

An eyebrow went up. "You had one, maybe two, glasses of champagne, Natalie."

Had he really been paying that close attention? "If that's true, why am I considering a dangerous dance lift with oral sex as the prize?"

A grin spread across his mouth. "Maybe you're drunk on my charisma."

"Nope." Her stupid heart wouldn't slow down. *Slow down.*
"That's definitely not it."

The door of the limousine opened and August exited, cat cradled in his left arm, reaching in to help her out. He released her
from his grip only long enough to tip the driver a twenty and
throw him a salute, before recapturing Natalie's hand and guiding her up the steps of the house.

"You said there was a wedding present waiting for me at
home," she said, bracing herself. "Is there a bucket of water inside,
resting precariously above the door?"

"Even I am not dumb enough to ruin a woman's wedding-day
makeup," he said, chuckling. "By the way, if you can drop the
word 'precariously' into a sentence, you're stone-cold sober."
He set the cat at his feet, gave the feline a quick scratch behind
the ears, then unlocked the door, pushing it open. Natalie was
too distracted by the streak of fur disappearing into the darkness to realize August's intention—and then it was too late.

She was in his arms being carried over the threshold.

"This is highly unnecessary."

"It's tradition among the Adonis culture."

She snorted and tried not to enjoy herself.

"Natalie . . ." He stopped in the middle of the kitchen, still
holding her without any signs of exertion—which made her
chances of coming out on top of the bet feel slim. "I got your
present before you gave me mine. The picture of Sam. I was a
little slow on the uptake and I didn't realize . . . we were swinging
for the fences, you know?"

"That wasn't . . ." Her laughter was halting. "I wouldn't call
that swinging for the—"

"Yes, it was." His tone was final. A tad rusty. "It was."

Charged silence took up the air around them. "Okay."

"And essentially, I got you a piece of paper."

"A what?"

He finally set her down, but only so he could slap his hands over his eyes. "I'm a shit gift giver. I'm absolutely awful at it. When I was seven, I gave my mother a pancake for Mother's Day. Only, I'd been planning ahead, so it had been wrapped in my closet for three weeks. I haven't gotten any better." He gestured to her room. The door was open and she could see a frame propped on the small nightstand. "I framed a ticket stub from Wine Down Napa—you know, the event where we met?" He shook his head. "You'd probably rather forget that night."

Had she swallowed a fistful of feathers? "No. That was a good night," she murmured, recalling the first time she'd seen him in his Kiss the Vintner apron, a head taller than everyone in the room. That booming laugh. "But you were an exhibitor at Wine Down. You wouldn't have needed a ticket. Where did you find this one?"

He jerked a big shoulder. "I might have asked a few people." He coughed. "Few dozen."

Oh my.

"Let's do the lift," she interrupted, surprising both of them.

"Wow." His voice went from surprised to gruff. "You really switched gears there."

Hello, understatement. A few minutes ago, she'd been intent on redrawing the boundaries and battle lines of this relationship. Now she was throwing her common sense in the dumpster because of a framed ticket stub.

Maybe this annoying attraction to August had simply built to a fever pitch. Toss in the undisputed fact that Napa weddings could make a corpse feel romantic, let alone a warm-blooded woman, and her immunity to him was currently paper thin. Whatever the reason, she wanted an excuse to be touched by him and this was the perfect opportunity. Even if she ended the night on a gurney in the back of an ambulance.

You won't.

You know you won't.

August wouldn't drop her. Ever. End of story. Was that why she wanted to do the lift? Did she enjoy the way he made her feel physically safe? Maybe. Yes. It was refreshing to have that confidence in another person. A rarity. So she backed across the kitchen, all the way to the far corner, to give herself enough running space. And then she went for it.

Ran right toward him in a wedding dress and heels.

The man didn't even blink.

He simply caught her around the waist and lifted her up over his head, turning her in a slow circle, giving her a lopsided smile from below.

"Don't say it," she whispered. "Don't ruin it."

"Nobody puts Natalie in a corner," he blurted, followed by that rich, abandoned laugh that collided with her groan. "It's out of my system, I swear."

"Too late, I'm already flooded with regrets."

"No, you're not."

"No..." She sighed as he set her down, pulse beating a million miles a minute. "I'm not."

Holy hell.

His mouth was close. Very close. The fingertips of his right hand traced her cheekbone, their lips gravitating toward each other until they were trading breaths. "I win," he rasped, touching the tip of his tongue to the center of her upper lip. "Promise it'll feel like we both did, though. Yeah, Natalie?"

Was she nodding?

She let him take her wrist and hustle her down the hallway, past the bathroom to his bedroom. He drew her inside, kicking the door shut with a definitive slam. And then they were making out. Although was that really the proper term for the way they were mauling each other? Hands seeking and clutching and exploring while his tongue swept deep in her mouth, turning her delirious.

August walked her back to the bed and down she went, his thick forearm snaking beneath her hips and pulling her up the bed until the back of her head landed on a pillow. His heavy body pinned her in place like he damn well belonged there. And in that moment, he did. He belonged there like air belonged in her lungs.

He wasted no time bringing his mouth down on hers again, groaning while angling his head right. The sides of their noses mashed together as his hands gathered the hem of her wedding dress higher and higher. Up her calves. Knees. *Oh God.* When the heavy skirt scraped up her thighs, he lifted his hips to move the bunched material out of the way and dropped his lower body into the cradle of her open legs, firm bearing down on soft. *Pushing.* They both cursed, Natalie's breath escaping in a trembling rush.

"I want to have sex," she gasped, twisting her fists in the sides of his tuxedo pants, tugging him hard. Into her. Relishing the stiffness there. "I never miss a pill, and I want to have sex."

His face buried in her neck with a strangled growl. "Natalie, I want to fuck you so bad, I'm surprised God didn't strike me down when I walked into that tent today." He rolled his hips and the friction made Natalie's vision go black. "But I could fuck you until your thighs turn into rubber and you'd still hate yourself for giving in when the sun comes up. Until I know for damn sure that you'll wake up beside me without regrets, you only get my tongue."

She couldn't argue with his point.

If she broke her no-sex rule on night one, hour one, she'd chalk the indiscretion up to temporary wedding hysteria or bad decision making. Or she'd tell herself she'd scratched the itch and it couldn't happen again. August didn't seem to want her to have regrets.

August was already talking like there would be a next time?

A mixture of panic and relief had her nearly gasping.

Of course he was talking in the future tense.

What man *wouldn't* want built-in benefits to any relationship?

Her thoughts scattered like broken necklace beads when he reached between their lower bodies and gripped her sex hard, sawing his middle finger through her panties, along that sensitive valley. Parting her, wetting her. "You'd love to get filled the fuck up. I know. But I promise you, princess, this is going to be a hell of a consolation prize."

This wasn't her first time at the rodeo. A few men had tried their God's honest best down there. Techniques had been employed, toys had been engaged, and once, even edible lube had entered the mix to no success. Just sticky sheets and the artificial smell of banana hanging in the air of her bedroom for a week. But she remembered the way August had touched her in the shower and how he'd gotten the drop on her, so she braced herself, taking two fistfuls of the comforter. She was going to be prepared this time—

"Holy. Sh-sh . . . *iiit*," she said on a blasting exhale when he kissed and nuzzled her. He drew the panties down to her ankles, threw them unceremoniously over his shoulder into the darkness, then buried his face in the juncture of her thighs like he was competing in a pie-eating contest. His groan held equal parts relief and lust. She could feel his five-o'clock shadow coarse against her softness, his breath hot. Fast. Anticipatory.

"I swear, Natalie, when I'm not dreaming about your pussy, I'm *day*dreaming about it. I've gone down on you so many times, imaginary August has lock jaw. Now I finally get to see you up close. And my imagination? Apparently it sucks." He dragged his tongue through her slit and pulled back slightly, licking his lips, shaking his head. "I haven't been doing this pretty thing justice. That changes now."

He quickly worked the front buttons of his shirt and tossed the garment away, followed by the no-nonsense stripping of his tight, white undershirt, the rigid flex of hard-earned muscle causing her fists to yank the sheets, her high heels to dig into the mattress.

"Oh," she said, sounding dazed. "I forgot to take off my shoes—"

August pushed her thighs open and dropped down onto his front, one big knee digging into the bed and pushing forward. His open mouth met her flesh and he suctioned it, *the entire thing*, moaning, before delving his tongue between her folds again, raking it from entrance to apex, where his lavish attention made her eyes cross. His tongue stroked her clit like it was his long-lost love. Not hurried, just thorough. *So thorough.* Damn. *Damn.*

In the space of a minute, the whole situation went from cautious optimism to imminent blastoff. She was on a roller coaster, cranking vertically to the highest point of the ride. Preparing to take the plunge. Her stomach turned weightless and a ticklish throb began way down deep, back where she'd never felt it before. This wasn't going to be like one of her self-inflicted orgasms. It was going to build and build and bury her, wasn't it? Oh God, *oh God.*

"August, please," she whimpered, her fingertips flying from the comforter to his hair, wrapping around the short strands, holding him in place even though he clearly had no intention of vacating the premises. "K-keep doing that. Do it. Do it. That."

He nodded, squeezing her thigh. Why was that intimate reassurance so sexy?

Right there.

I can't believe I'm this wet.

And he was living for it, using her readiness to his advantage. He pumped two huge fingers inside of her while flicking his tongue against her clit. *Oh. Mama.* Was he serious? "Babe, please," she panted, no idea who she was calling babe. But saying it again, anyway, in the next breath, because what else to call a man making her feel this good? Her whole body was surface-of-the-sun level hot. Knees shaking. Throat strained like she'd just left a Harry Styles concert. Had she been screaming? Was she screaming now? "Harder, babe. Please. Okay?"

What was she asking for?

No idea.

But he gave it to her, almost completely pulling out his fingers, then thrusting them deep and holding them there while his licks turned rougher. Pinpricks of light appeared in her vision, forming constellations on the ceiling, and she tipped her head back, letting the pleasure plow through. Unequivocal hedonism. That's what this was.

With strands of his hair wrapped around her fingers, she raked her hips side to side against his mouth and he kept his tongue stiff for her, adapting on the fly, trusting her to know what she wanted in that moment of euphoria, also known as the best climax of her life. She was trembling and mumbling to herself when she came down from the highest peak. August kissed the insides of her thighs, looking like he was already considering round two, shoulder muscles bunching as if he was just waiting for the green light.

"Red light," she slurred, slapping a hand to her forehead, trying desperately to calm her breathing. No way she could let him do that to her again. Who knew what lust-drunk Natalie would do next? Round one: call him babe. Round two: offer to bear him sons.

"I'd be happy with a son or daughter." He grinned. "As long as they're happy and healthy, right?"

Right. Great. She'd been talking out loud.

How thoroughly had this man scrambled her brain?

In the middle of kissing her thigh, he smirked.

"So smug, aren't you?" she said, still short of oxygen, which really took the sting out of her rebuke. Her tone was more fawning than critical.

This couldn't stand. The night could not end like this.

He'd have the upper hand and he would be insufferable. She'd totally lost herself in the act and he would miss no opportunity to remind her how she'd essentially erupted like Vesuvius, called him an endearment, *and* lost power to her limbs. Minutes later and her legs were limp. Resting on his shoulders. When did that happen?

There was only one way to even the scales.

"You don't think I could make you call me babe?"

His mouth paused in the act of nuzzling the inside of her knee. "Natalie . . ."

Having a purpose breathed new life back into her limp body. She allowed her legs to slide from the rocky slopes of his shoulders onto the bed, gathering herself into a kneel and turning around, gesturing to the zipper of her dress. "Can you help me out of this?"

"I-I don't . . ." His voice had dropped lower than a baritone. "That might not be a good idea."

"I needed help to get into this dress." She blinked at him innocently. "Now I need help getting out of it. Simple as that. Besides, it's tradition."

One of his eyebrows winged up at the T word. "Really?"

She nodded earnestly, giving him her back.

The heat of August's hands met the area below her shoulder blades. He hesitated with his fingers on the zipper. "What exactly are you wearing under this dress?"

"Nothing exciting."

Without him making a sound, his skepticism was obvious. "I know when you are lying."

She scoffed. "No, you don't."

"It's the only time you sound casual."

Natalie frowned. Was he right?

"I'm going to ask you again, what's under this dress, princess? I need to be prepared."

"A strapless bra and panties. My God. You're acting like there might be a sniper."

"Same level of danger as a strapless bra on those tits, as far as I'm concerned. I wasn't lying when I told you they look insane."

"Unzip the dress, banana brain. Or I'll be sleeping in it." She looked back at him over her shoulder and broke out the big guns. "Please, August?" she half whispered, trying to look as helpless as possible. "I need your help."

His lips parted on a long intake of breath, eyes darkening. "Come here," he rasped, pulling her backward into his lap and drawing the zipper down slowly. "I've got you."

She had him, too.

Right where she wanted him.

As soon as the opening was loose, she pushed the dress down, lifting her hips to divest herself of the heavy material. She used her foot to slide it off the bed into an ivory heap, her rear end landing soundly back into August's lap, eliciting a groan.

"Can't help but notice you're half naked in my lap all of a sudden," he half slurred.

"Noticed that, did you?"

"Tradition means nothing to you." His warm breath slid along her neck, knuckles from both hands traveling upward on her rib cage. "This was a trick."

"Evil of me, wasn't it?" She circled her hips on his lap. "There has to be some way I can make it up to you."

"Natalie . . . " he warned through his teeth. "I told you. We're not having s—"

"You can touch my boobs."

"Under the bra or over?" he blurted, that big chest heaving at her back.

The corner of her lips ticked up. *Gotcha.*

She pulled down the cups of her strapless bra and guided his hands there, surprised when they didn't just grab on or handle her breasts too roughly. She should probably stop being surprised by August now. By the way he gently played with her nipples, dragging his thumbs over them, side to side, his mouth beginning to lick and nip at her neck. Oh. *Wow.* If she didn't keep control of this situation, she would wake up tomorrow without the upper hand. She might as well raise the white flag and surrender any leverage she had left.

Climbing off August's lap, she turned around on her knees, allowing herself a second to savor his choked curse at the sight of her bare breasts—

And then she shoved him onto his back.

She raked a hand up and over the distended crotch of his dress pants, stroking him firmly through the material. "My turn."

"Blow job?" he asked, hoarsely. Openly hopeful and visibly shocked.

She nodded.

"Oh. Okay. Wow. Jesus." A monster shudder went through his giant frame and he dropped fully onto the bed, his muscular chest rising and falling at a rapid rate. "When you're fucked, you're fucked," he muttered thickly, seemingly to himself.

He reached down and started unbuckling his belt.

It shouldn't have been so hot. Really. It shouldn't have.

But those big mitts fumbling with the metal buckle and the eager flex of his abdomen made her tongue heavy in her mouth. So eager that she was kissing his stomach, biting the sinew that ran in a downward-pointing V along his hips.

"Bite harder," he said, laboring to breathe, his hands dropping away from the belt. "Harder, please."

Oh God. When he begged her to bite harder, she wanted to.

Badly.

She sucked a gust of air into her lungs and shot forward, sinking her teeth into the meat of his hip, drawing a shout from August that resonated through her entire body. "Fuck yes," he growled. There was a brief pause before he lifted his head to look down at her. "Don't bite my dick, obviously."

Natalie giggled.

He grinned back. A big, bad warrior with an inconvenient charming side. It was alarming, the severe pinch she felt in her chest at that moment, so she closed her eyes and licked over the rope of muscle that ran along his sides, then down to his belly button, wetting a path through those coarse whorls of his hair. Her right hand delved into his pants and . . . okay, she'd expected this.

Of course it was XL. *He* was XL.

But she couldn't even get her hand around him.

"Just do the best you can," he gasped, one hand gripping the sheets, the other one cupping the side of her face. But not to guide her down. It was almost like pregratitude. *Oh my God, Natalie is about to suck me off. Oh my God.*

Had she ever felt confident during sex before? She'd always assumed so. She even liked to think of herself as adventurous.

But now, with this man almost hyperventilating at the thought of her mouth on him, she felt like a goddess. Seductive. So confident in herself and his imminent enjoyment of her that she was almost purring when she drew August's shaft out through the opening of his pants.

"Wow," she whispered, swallowing. "Wow."

It swelled further and August bit off a curse, hips twisting right. "Now that's the reaction a man wants on his wedding night."

What was her whole plan about keeping the upper hand?

Whatever it was, she couldn't recall the details. Could only lean in and run her tongue up the side of his gorgeously thick shaft, watching his thigh muscles bunch in response. A burst of steam escaped his flared nostrils. From one lick.

She'd never held a man's balls in her hand, but instinct had her reaching for August's, rolling them gently in her palm, and really, there was no way to avoid them, because they were, for lack of a better word, prominent.

"*Son of a bitch.* I'm sorry, there is going to be a lot of cursing here tonight. Now. Oh *fuck*, tug them a little. Rub them fucking rough. Yeah . . . oh . . . *yeah.* Now do it again while you've got that mouth gift-wrapped around my cock. *Yes.*"

Natalie's confidence climbed higher. Wow, he was really, really enjoying everything she was doing. She didn't have to wonder if her tongue was in the right place or if she was stroking him too hard in her fist, because August was sending a clear message and it read *Holy shit, I've never been touched so right. Never felt anything this good.*

That fear of rejection or criticism she normally dreaded was quite simply . . . gone.

The absence of that burden made her more eager to give him pleasure, lips traveling past the point she thought possible, not worrying whether or not too much saliva was visible or if it was weird to be moaning while giving someone oral. As if the pleasure was hers.

Wasn't it, though? With him?

Whoa.

Easy, girl.

"Call me babe," she whispered, gently tracing her teeth from root to tip and whirling her tongue around his swollen head. "But only if you want to finish."

"Babe, baby, princess, love of my life, I'll do and say anything you want. Just don't stop. Don't stop for me. I'm so close."

Okay, he did not mean the whole *love of my life* part, obviously. He was just lost in the moment. So why did it make her nearly swallow him whole, her pulse tapping wildly in her temples? Her lips stretched around his ample length and when the tip of him brushed the back of her throat, his knees jerked up, the hand that had been cupping her cheek sinking in her hair now, ruining her updo in a split second.

"Fuck," he ground out through his teeth. "Natalie. *Fuck!*"

Her fist moved up and down in rapid strokes, sensing the beginning of his peak. Was she still moaning?

Get a grip on yourself. He didn't taste *that* good.

Liar. His taste was singularly incredible.

The scent of that grapefruit soap clung to his pubic hair and wires must be getting crossed in her brain, because smelling the fruit while taking him in her mouth made him almost taste like it, and somehow she knew she'd never pass up grapefruit again at the supermarket.

"If you don't want to swallow," he panted, throat muscles strained, "now would be a good time to stop, but please don't stop. Please. Babe. But if you have to, please let me roll you over and come on your tits. I'm asking as an upstanding citizen and service member."

There was simply no way she could stop now.

Not when he made her *smile* during a *blow job*.

That had to deserve some kind of award—and she was in the position to give him one.

Continuing to rapidly fist him up and down, her mouth followed her hand a little lower each time and she heard his breathing stutter, the groan building in his chest. He alternated between squeezing his eyes shut and watching her mouth bring him deep, skate back to the tip, then go deep again. And finally, the veins on his abdomen turned blunt and . . . he . . . *roared*. Her name.

His spend hit the back of her throat so fast and in such abundance, she had to struggle through swallowing it quickly enough, her hand still busy. Still working his slick shaft. His grip was twisted in her hair, but she could feel him resisting the urge to push her mouth down and hold her in place. And considering the animal state he was in, she found that oddly touching. Was she losing her actual mind?

August deflated, his arms falling to his sides.

His sex remained at half-mast, sticky and smooth. Somehow still appealing.

"I can't believe what you just did for me," he said between heavy breaths, reaching down to haul her up against his chest. "Natalie, the way you . . ." He shook his head, plowed his left hand through his hair, looking totally and utterly dazed. "Damn, woman."

She preened, testing a palm on his chest, her head on his shoulder.

Just temporarily. Until they caught their breath.

"Look, I've got about three point eight seconds before I'm unconscious, thanks to you. So I'm going to use it to tell you to stay. Sleep right here. On me." He leaned over and kissed her forehead hard, his lips remaining there for a few seconds. "It's the safest place you'll ever be."

She ignored the flutter trapped in her throat. "Maybe it's tradition."

"Tradition," he agreed.

They passed out cold less than ten seconds later.

Chapter Sixteen

August rolled out of bed with a smile on his face.

It took every ounce of strength in his body to ignore the impulse to whistle while pulling on his drawers. Damn. Now that was how two people kicked off a marriage. An oral sex competition where there were no losers.

The sun hadn't yet risen in the sky, but he was an early bird out of practice. He'd throw some eggs down his gullet, catch a workout behind the barn, and get started on production. But first he stopped at the foot of the bed and admired the view. Watching people sleep was creepy as hell. No one would blame him for stopping to check out his own wife's ass, though, right? It was in plain view. No panties or anything.

"What am I? A monk?" he muttered under his breath, turning at the door for one final, prolonged peek before closing it behind him and heading into the kitchen. As quietly as possible, he poured himself a glass of orange juice and scrambled up five eggs, eating them in as many bites. He paused in the act of chewing, his lips twitching when a snore reached him from the bedroom. He didn't remember any snoring from last night. Then again, he'd been passed out cold after the best blow job of his entire life.

Natalie snored. *Good.* They'd drown each other out.

He'd once been told by his teammates that he sounded like a grizzly with a cold.

With a smile on his face, August set his egg bowl in the sink and rinsed out the empty glass that had held his orange juice. He high-fived himself and slipped into the front yard, locking the door and testing it twice, now that he had a woman to protect. Stretching an arm across his chest to loosen up the muscle, he strode toward his makeshift workout area, reaching into the barn to flip on the rear light.

Then he got to work on the pullup bar.

Day one as a married man.

Their sexual chemistry was fire. More than life itself, he wanted to go crawl back into that bed with Natalie and kiss her awake. Get between those legs and work himself into a sweat giving her orgasms. Now *that* was the exercise he really wanted. But something wouldn't let him take it all the way with Natalie yet. Not until they got on the same page. He wasn't sure how he would feel if they had sex and she still carried on like their marriage was a sham.

Wrong. He knew exactly how he would feel.

Devastated.

No further proof necessary that he was falling deeper and deeper in love with his wife. That damn bow-wielding cherub had lodged a double arrow in the dead center of his chest. Either it was going to pierce his heart and kill him or give him a new reason to live.

You're already living for her and you know it.

August dropped down from the pullup bar with a gulp and trod across the flattened grass to his squat rack, which he'd bought off the local gym when they upgraded their equipment. He ducked his head underneath and braced the heavy bar across his shoulders, stepping back and kicking off a round of squats.

He and Natalie couldn't be that far from reaching common ground, could they?

She'd slept with her back plastered to his chest, thigh to thigh. They might have a lot of shit to work out between them before the marriage was solid—or "real" or whatever—but she was comfortable with him, right? At the very least, she trusted him in her sleep.

Man. He really wanted full trust from her when she was awake, too.

Wanted it with a fierce pain in his stomach.

What was holding her back?

His mission was to figure that out and eliminate whatever it was.

August had just returned the squat bar to the rack when his phone rang. Frowning over who would call him this early, he slipped his phone out of his back pocket, his shoulders tensing slightly at his CO's name on the screen.

"Sir," he answered briskly, his spine straightening out of habit. "Good morning, sir."

"Cates. I'm sorry to call the morning after your wedding. I'm sure you're busy."

If only. August mentally sighed, flicking a look at his bedroom window. Who would know if he just crept over to the window and took one more quick look at that butt?

"It's no problem, sir."

"I'm calling because the transfer of funds is coming in today.

Two hundred thousand." He paused to clear his throat. "I've made the investment in Sam's name."

A cord pulled in August's sternum. "That's . . ." Shit. It hurt to breathe. "You knew him a lot longer than me, of course, but I think . . . I know this would mean a lot to him, sir."

"I might have known him longer, but unfortunately, I don't think I knew him better. This dream of a vineyard was something I never understood. Or *tried* to understand, I suppose." The stilted nature of the CO's words made it clear that the admission was difficult. Hell, having a personal discussion at all wasn't really the man's style, let alone one involving an emotional topic like his son. "Maybe this is my way of remedying that. After the fact."

August tilted his head back and breathed deeply. "I'm going to do my best with the money, sir. I'm not great at this. Not like Sam would have been. But I'm going to try and do you both proud."

"Don't try, Cates. Just do it."

Determination hardened his muscles. "Yes, sir."

The CO hung up. For long moments, August remained in place with the phone still pressed to his ear. *Don't try, Cates. Just do it.*

Yes, that was exactly what he would do. Stop fucking around and create a lasting legacy in Sam's name. Sam's honor. Didn't his friend deserve that? This was up to him. There was no one else who could make this dream happen. No one else who would dedicate the time. This dream was on his shoulders and he needed to focus harder. Make it a reality.

The front door of the house opened and there was Natalie, framed in the doorway. Hair tangled all around her head, his sheet wrapped around her body like a toga. She squinted at him across the misty yard. "I'm having the weirdest dream." She yawned. "I got up to go to the bathroom in the middle of the night and you were working out."

"This isn't a dream." August flexed his biceps. "You're really married to this."

"No." She rubbed at her eyes and affection stuck in his belly like a spear. "It's still dark out."

"It's five o'clock in the morning, give or take a few minutes." He sauntered toward her across the lawn, guilt kicking around in his stomach over the phone call he'd just taken. "This is when I get up."

"Oh." Another yawn, bigger this time. "In that case, I want a divorce."

"Sorry, I won't sign."

Her smile was sweet and sleepy. "Arsenic poisoning it is."

"You'd have to know how to cook something in order to poison me, princess."

That one might have zinged a little too sharply, based on her flushed cheeks. He was on the verge of apologizing when she said, "I can't *believe* I slept with you."

"We haven't slept together yet. When we do, you'll know it."

Why. *Why* couldn't he stop antagonizing her? His brain was trying to reach down and clap its hands over his dumbass mouth, but obviously its arms weren't long enough and it couldn't reach. "Then I guess I'll never know it," she said, shrugging. A beat passed and she looked down at the phone, still in his right hand. "Did I hear you talking to someone?"

"No."

Fuck.

His stomach sent a wave of acid up toward his mouth.

His mind gave him a clear road map toward fixing the lie immediately. All it would require is telling her about the investment from his CO.

Easy.

Sure.

He'd just tell Natalie he'd gone through with the marriage because of his feelings for her. That he loved her and was powerless to do anything but help her succeed. Not because of her family's influence with the local loan officer. She'd be totally fine with that and wouldn't kick his nut sack at all.

A pause lingered between them, a line popping up between her brows. She took a final look at the phone—he'd lied and she knew it.

Fix it before you cross the line of no return.

Having her suspicious of him was worse than weathering a little anger, right?

"Natalie, I have to tell—"

"I'm going to New York," she blurted. "In five days."

"*What?*"

Without answering, she turned and slammed the door, leaving him panting out in the cold, his breath forming clouds of condensation around his face. Did that just happen? What *was* happening? He'd been eating her out less than six fucking hours ago. Now apparently he wasn't the only thing going south. Their short-lived, unspoken truce was joining him.

"*Natalie,*" he growled through his teeth, storming into the house behind her. Just in time to watch her disappear into her bedroom, the white sheet trailing behind her on the ground. The cat pounced on the dragging linen, wrestling with it briefly before shooting off into the darkness. "Come back here."

He tried the handle, expecting to find it locked, and he wasn't disappointed.

"Open the door."

"Why?" she called through the heavy wood.

"You can't just drop a bomb like 'I'm going to New York' and strut away."

"Oh, I'm the one who struts, bicep flexer?"

"That's fair." He laid his hands flat on the door, willing it to dissolve. "I'm sorry for implying that you don't know how to cook."

"I don't," he thought he heard her say, very quietly.

And that tiny admission set his throat on fire. "Natalie, please. I just want to talk."

No response.

She's not angry about the cooking joke, fuckwit. She's locked you out because you lied and she's more than smart enough to see through it. "I was on the phone with my CO." August scrambled to open the call log, got down on his knees, and slid his phone under her door. "We're both early risers."

The longer the silence stretched, the more he wanted to bang his head against the door. But finally, there was a low creak of the floorboards in the bedroom, a shifting of shadows. He exhaled inaudibly and closed his eyes, the pressure ebbing slightly from his chest. He needed to tell her the rest. Confess why his CO had called. But he needed to clear up one thing first.

"Did you think I was on the phone with another woman or something?"

That would be the day. Other women might as well be invisible since he'd met this one.

"No," she said right away, and he relaxed his shoulders. "I didn't think that."

He dropped his forehead against the door. "Good."

"Although technically . . . we're only married on paper. I-I guess you're allowed, right?"

His shoulders bunched right back up, accompanied by a sharp twist of denial in his middle. "Wrong. There's only you for me." God, saying that out loud was like free falling and landing on a cloud. "And there's only me for you."

"Until this is over."

"Right," he said, grinding his jaw. "Please open the door."

Seconds passed. "I'd rather not."

August inhaled slowly through his nose, then let it back out. "Babe."

Was that her breath catching? "Is that a code word now or something?"

"Yeah. It is. Because we probably both think it's a stupid endearment, am I right?"

She hummed in the affirmative.

"So if I'm willing to humble myself enough to say it, I'm serious. And vice versa." A heavy beat passed. "Babe."

"Oh, for crying out loud," she grumbled, opening the door and thrusting his phone out at him, which caused her to nearly drop the sheet keeping her modest. She gathered it back up with hasty movements, but he wasn't really registering anything but the paleness of her face. Something had changed. She wasn't as comfortable with him as she was before. Even if she was trying to pull together a casual air. "Look, I overreacted." She pushed five slender fingers through her hair. "Morrison used to be secretive, and I guess it's a sore spot. We were hired by the firm at the same time, so we were in competition a lot in the beginning. It never really went away. He liked to compare portfolios, but only when *he* was ahead. When his numbers were down, he hid it. Hid money. In-sisted on keeping separate finances. Anyway . . . it's not important."

The floor had turned into quicksand, and he was sinking. Some of this sounded sickeningly familiar. "It sounds important."

"Maybe it is. Yeah." She thought for a few seconds. "My father has been holding money over my head, too. Maybe I do think it's a red flag when people use money as a weapon. Or hide their finan-cial status. What else are they hiding, you know? I just think be-ing up front is a sign of good character." She waved a hand. "Like I said, I totally overreacted. You were just having a phone call."

His stomach felt like a tomato that had been left out in the sun for a week. Holy shit. Natalie's ex had played mind games with money. Her father continued to do the same. Now he was hid-ing a two-hundred-thousand-dollar chunk of green from her? Also known as the supposed reason he was marrying her in the first place. She'd gotten married based on how he'd represented himself—a winemaker who'd run out of capital.

That hadn't been true for nearly a week.

Prior to their whole-ass wedding.

What would she do if he told her the truth now? Nothing good. She was already threatening to fly three thousand miles away and he hadn't even confessed yet.

"What's this bullshit about you going to New York?"

"There's an investor who is willing to meet with me."

August reared back slightly, taking note of the way she held that sheet like a shield and hating it. "Why do you need an inves-tor when your trust fund is being released?"

"My trust fund is a good start, but additional funds could make us more viable from the jump. A notable investor would make us competitive and attract more of them."

"So six days after our wedding, you're going to bail. How's that going to look?"

He didn't give two craps about how things looked, but he was willing to say just about anything to prevent her from leaving St. Helena when they weren't yet on solid ground.

"I'll only go for one night. No one will notice I'm gone."

"I will."

Lips parting, she searched his face. "Right. I'm sure you want to get the ball rolling with the small business loan. I'll call on Monday morning and set up a meeting."

"No," he said too quickly, clearing his throat. *Hand me a shovel so I can dig myself deeper and deeper.* What else could he do but keep his true reasons for marrying her to himself? It was more than obvious she was about a hundred steps behind him in the love department, not even *close* to drawing even. The truth might knock her off the track completely. "I mean, we're having dinner with Meyer at your mother's on Monday night. I can set it up then."

She took in that information with a deep breath and nodded. Wet her lips. "Okay. That works, too."

His heart pounded, his arms aching to wrap around her. There was definitely still some new distance between them that he disliked immensely, but their connection was stronger than when she'd opened the door. Right?

He had to test that theory. Or he wouldn't relax for a single second. He'd be in turmoil.

Propping his forearm on the door, he leaned down very slowly, bringing his mouth within an inch of hers. Turning his head slightly, he nuzzled her nose, brushing their lips together in a way that made them both breathe faster.

"Don't go to New York, princess."

Natalie turned her head and their mouths slanted hard over each other, lips opening and seeking, tongues delving. Just once. And then she pulled away, leaving his body hard and his breath coming in harsh pants.

"See you in the real morning, August."

The door slammed. Again. And he couldn't help but worry that an emotional one had been locked between them, too.

Chapter Seventeen

Natalie woke up for the second time that day, but now it was midafternoon and she was gritty-eyed and disoriented. Her argument with August in the wee hours of the morning felt like a dream, but the queasiness in her stomach told her no, it had definitely happened. She'd attempted to people before coffee, before her brain fully woke up—and she'd acted like a bozo.

Had she really stormed off in a sheet because he wouldn't initially explain his phone call? *Dear God.* This marriage was supposed to be a business arrangement. She'd been the one to propose it. And on day one, she'd acted like some kind of jealous lover.

Furthermore, she'd slept in his *bed.*

As far from a business agreement as one could get.

Nervous energy—and a dire need for distraction—forced Natalie out of the comfortable mess of sheets where she'd fallen asleep around six A.M. Slowly, she creaked open the guest bedroom door and peered out, finding Menace staring back at her curiously from the middle of the kitchen table. But no August. Thank God. She needed to thoroughly wake up and get ahold of her long-lost faculties before coming face-to-face with her husband again.

Retreating back into the bedroom for clothes and her toiletries bag, she closed herself in their shared bathroom a moment later, sighing as the heavy aroma of grapefruit snuck up and ambushed her. Memories rushed in from the last time she stood in this shower, getting pleasure from August. Scenes, naked ones, bombarded her, making her movements clumsy as she twisted the handle, setting the water temperature to scalding.

She went through the motions of showering—only allowing herself one or two itty-bitty sniffs of August's homemade soap—while contemplating her new role as a fake wife and employee of Zelnick Cellar. Her title didn't have to be in name alone. She could help this place run successfully. At the very least, she had a whole month to give August a running start.

Natalie turned off the shower, climbed out, and got dressed in a pair of shorts and a loose, long-sleeved shirt. She went back to her room, dried her hair, and left the house with a purpose: find a way to help. She should just stay locked in the guest room and pray for her trust fund to promptly arrive in her bank account. But she'd spent so much time laughing off August's attempts at winemaking when the cause was a good one. A worthy one.

And maybe she wanted to be a part of it somehow.

Maybe his happiness meant a little something to her.

Natalie stopped in the entrance to the production barn when she saw August standing before the row of barrels, stirring the settled yeast. The temperature in the barn was slightly warm for this time of year and there was every chance it was affecting his process. Granted, he didn't have the budget for a more advanced facility, but they could certainly find a way to cool down the barrels by a few degrees. Had he tested the nitrogen content of the grapes?

August turned suddenly, his expression going from surprised to slightly guarded. "Sorry, what was that?"

Voicing her private thoughts out loud without being aware of it was a fun new habit. "I was just wondering if you'd tested the nitrogen content. Of the grapes."

She wanted to go closer. Wanted to peer into the barrels herself and sort through the tools on the nearby table, just to see what he was working with, but August's stiff shoulder muscles cast an invisible barrier. Or maybe she was imagining that?

Sure, he'd asked her to stay out of the barn. But that was pre-wedding and they'd been in the midst of an argument. Had his request been serious?

"Um . . ." She squared her shoulders and tried again. "How soon after the first racking did you remove the layer of gross lees?"

"Gross what?" After what felt like an eternity, August cleared his throat. "Are you talking about that thick layer of shit that appeared on the surface after I pressed the grapes and put them in the barrels?"

She exhaled. "Yes."

The fact that they were on the same page relaxed his shoulders. "I don't know. I guess . . . about a week."

Problem number one detected. The gross lees should be racked off after one or two days. But she didn't say it out loud. She simply nodded when he looked back at her over his shoulder.

"I've got this, Natalie," he said. "It's all right if you want to go back to the house. Or . . ."

"Oh," she said, a little caught off guard. She was no stranger to going toe-to-toe with August, but he'd never outright dismissed her. "I thought we were going to dig into the issues you're having with production."

"Yeah. It's just, uh . . ." He coughed. "It's just that I feel like I have to do this for Sam alone. It's my responsibility. I *want* the responsibility."

Natalie ignored the wound that formed in the center of her belly. Just like Corinne and Julian, August wanted things done a certain way and it did not include Natalie. She was not welcome. Both vineyards could be sinking into the red and still, her assistance would not be required. Same old story. But why did it hurt more that August wanted to manage on his own? That he didn't want any help—*her* help—with the winemaking? She was used to her family being dismissive of her efforts but August . . . again, he wasn't *supposed* to push her away. It stung, even if she understood that his grief over Sam caused him to react in ways no one could fully comprehend.

Setting aside the hurt, she took a moment to try to see things from his perspective. He'd gone on this mission for his best friend. August was the only one standing here who knew what Sam wanted. "I haven't lost anyone close to me, but I think grief can be expressed in a lot of different ways."

August's shoulders drooped a little, his eyes casting guarded gratitude in her direction. "I wouldn't talk to the guys about Sam's death. I didn't even tell anyone but my CO that I was coming here, buying the vineyard. I didn't want any of them to ask to be involved. Isn't that fucked up?" He rubbed at his throat. "It's just that I was closer to him than anyone else and . . ."

"You want to carry all the weight yourself."

"Yeah. If I give anyone else some of the weight, it feels like a cop out. Or like I'm shirking responsibility. So I just have to do it alone."

Natalie marveled over the fact that she could experience such a piercing sense of sympathy for someone she'd once thought was a bumbling ogre. Occasionally still did. "Do you think he would want it this way? You carrying all the weight?"

August stopped in the middle of nodding. "No." He let out a gust of breath. "No, he definitely wouldn't. But that doesn't change anything."

"Yeah," she said softly. "You have to do it your way, August. You're the only one who knows what that is." They stared at each other across the barn for several moments, before Natalie realized she was the intruder. Was he waiting for her to leave so he could continue? The possibility made her speak a little too quickly. "Anyway, I'll let you get back to work. Sorry for acting like a jealous wife this morning."

"I liked you being a jealous wife—" Immediately, he backpedaled. "No, wait. No. I didn't mean that. I didn't like you being jealous, but I loved you expecting more from me."

A weight slowly traveled from her throat to the center of her chest.

He said the most impactful things sometimes. And he meant them.

But the poor bonehead couldn't see that simply *letting her help* would have the biggest impact of all. Explaining that to him would force him into sharing before he was ready.

Maybe he would never be ready.

"Oh well." The barriers she'd been too tired to engage at the crack of dawn were now up and running, thank God. She stepped backward out of the barn with her chin raised. "I'm going for a walk. I owe Claudia a call back—"

"Wait a few minutes," he said quickly, fumbling the long wooden spoon a little. "I'll come with you. Show you around."

"No, thanks. I'm fine to go alone." Before she could turn away from his frown, she remembered something and she snapped her fingers. "Oh wait. I've been meaning to ask you. Does this property have a wine cave?"

"Uh . . . yeah." He swiped a wrist across his forehead, but the frown remained. "Yeah, there is an entrance at the rear of the event barn. Or what was *going* to be the event barn."

"You had one event."

"And I sold negative three bottles of wine. I'm not even sure how that math is possible."

"Half of one ended up on your face."

"Negative three and a half. I'm coming on your walk."

She waved him off. "I can find the cave myself."

"I haven't been down there in months, but I remember there is no lighting and the stairs are steep—" He started to fan his armpits. "I'm sweating thinking about you in the cave alone. Just give me a second to wrap up here."

"Don't be ridiculous. I know my way around a cave—and I have my flashlight app."

"Wait for me," he growled.

"No."

This whole argument was beginning to feel like it had a hidden meaning, and she'd woken up this morning—the second time—and decided to uncomplicate their relationship. The more time she spent with August, however, the more convoluted their responsibility to each other seemed to become. And they'd been married less than twenty-four hours.

God save us.

He followed her across the dirt path between the two barns, taking off his gloves and leather apron as he walked and leaving them on the ground in his wake. Ridiculous.

She picked up her pace.

He matched it.

And now they were running, because nothing made sense anymore.

"Goddammit, Natalie."

She rounded the corner of the event barn and spied the concrete staircase with the rusted metal handrail. "Why can't you understand that I don't want company?"

"Too bad. You're getting it."

"I like being alone when I'm in the cave." When that statement sounded confusing to her own ears, she tried to clarify. "The one at Vos, I mean."

He was right behind her now. Mere steps. "How much time do you spend down there?" They were even now, damn his long legs. "And what the hell for?"

"It doesn't matter."

"Sounds like it does matter."

"No." She stopped abruptly at the top of the stairs and turned to face him. "I mean . . . it doesn't matter. That I'm down there. No one ever notices I'm gone."

"*I'd* fucking notice," he shouted down at her.

She fantasized about punching him in that moment. Hard. She truly did. That he could be so caring and protective, but *still not realize* how much it burned when he locked her out of his grief, out of his winemaking—it was frustrating. And since when did she let him have that power over her? How did he manage to sneak inside her and rearrange things?

"You don't notice as much as you think you do," she said, pushing him back a step, then stomping down the concrete stairs toward the cave entrance. After a moment, his tread followed behind her and without turning around, she could sense his poor man-brain working overtime. She almost felt a trace of pity. Almost.

Natalie opened the door slowly and welcomed the scent of earth and mold. Being that this cave hadn't been used in a while, there was more dust in the stale air that escaped, but the cold, familiar darkness was welcome nonetheless. She opened her flashlight app and shined it in front of her, noting that August was right. The stairs were treacherous. But they were dry and the handrail wasn't rusted as it was outside. She felt safe enough to venture inside, descending slowly into the underground.

"Natalie . . . " August said thickly. "Hold on. I think I should go first."

"I promise you, it's okay. I'm not scared of a bat or two."

"Bats?"

"Sure. They love caves. You could have a whole colony down here—"

"You're going too fast. Slow down."

Ignoring his odd tone, Natalie swung the flashlight left and revealed a long, oval-shaped room. Cobweb-covered racks lined the wall, empty, and discarded bottles of wine littered the stone floor. More darkness lay beyond in what looked to be a second, smaller room. "Oh my gosh, this is incredible, August. You could fix this up and have private parties down here. Or you could make it a storage room. There are so many different techniques . . ."

She trailed off when she realized August hadn't answered her in a while.

Pausing midway down the stairs, she turned, using her flashlight to illuminate his face—and found him white as a ghost. His eyes were closed, sweat clinging to his forehead.

"August," she breathed, alarm gripping her windpipe.

"I'm sorry. I don't like this. I don't . . ." He reached for the center of his chest, almost like he expected something to be there. Then he smacked at his waist, his outer thigh. Searching for a gun, she realized. Obviously coming up empty.

That was when the situation they were in started to register differently. They were in near total darkness, traveling into an unfamiliar space. Did this remind him of being in battle?

Did this remind him of . . . what happened to Sam?

"Natalie, I just need you out of here, okay?" he rasped haltingly.

"Yes. Yes, okay."

She started to retreat up the stairs as quickly as possible, but August met her halfway and scooped her into his arms, jogging the rest of the distance and into the sunlight. He took the outer concrete steps two at a time, at which point his legs just seemed to give out. Still holding her in his arms, he dropped into a kneel in a shaded patch of grass and instinctively, Natalie curled herself around him. She wrapped every available appendage around this shaking man and clung, moisture pooling in her eyes.

"I'm sorry. Oh my God. I didn't . . . it never occurred to me the cave might bring back bad memories—"

"Of course it didn't occur to you. It shouldn't." His voice just sort of unraveled into her shoulder. "I don't *want* you thinking about terrible shit like that."

Natalie tightened her arms around his neck and slowly, slowly, he laid them down sideways in the grass and she could feel that his T-shirt was soaked in sweat, his heart still going a million miles an hour. "I shouldn't have barged my way down there. I was just trying to find a way to help where I wouldn't be in the way."

He blew a rocky breath into her hair and pulled her closer. "You're not in the way, but I appreciate that."

She stroked his back with her fingertips and he sighed, the tension in his muscles ebbing slightly. "Has this happened before?"

"No." He cradled the back of her skull in his hand and pressed her face more securely to his neck, as if the position comforted him. "No, I left the team after Sam died. I didn't see any more combat. I couldn't. There are dreams occasionally, but no flashbacks or panic attacks. Nothing . . . this fucked up."

"This isn't fucked up," she whispered fervently.

He made a sound like he didn't believe her. A long minute passed, his pulse beginning to slow. Then he said, "Winemaking was the heart of him. He wanted it so bad. And I already . . . I failed him once, Natalie. I wasn't supposed to let him die. I was supposed to protect him." A heavy swallow. "He wouldn't have let it happen to me."

Natalie's tears were soaking into the shoulder of his T-shirt now, a torturous wind in her middle. "I'm not a soldier, August, and I don't know anything about war, but I know your character. And I know if you'd had the slightest hint of a threat to anyone you love, you'd have done something to stop it. I know that like I know the sun will come up tomorrow." She kissed his salty skin. "It wasn't your fault."

They held on to each other tightly in the afternoon sun, time passing without measure. Natalie pushed the lingering sadness she felt about August refusing her help as far away as possible, weighing it down with sympathy and understanding. And an encroaching, never-experienced-before feeling that was too scary to name.

Chapter Eighteen

Going to dinner at his mother-in-law's house.

August never thought he'd be so excited.

He and Natalie were dressed in business casual attire as they walked out of the house together and called goodbye to the cat. August opened the car door for Natalie so she could slide into the passenger seat and balance a homemade pie on her lap. This was the kind of evening that made the marriage feel real, and goddamn, he loved it, especially since they'd been orbiting each other without touching or speaking much since yesterday.

When he'd lost it in the wine cave.

Yeah, there hadn't been a lot of conversation since they'd spent hours clinging together outside the event barn, inhaling each other's exhales, her heartbeat like a song that he could follow out of the darkness. There'd been a lot of staring, however. A lot of passing each other in the kitchen or on the way into the bathroom and looking. Wanting to touch.

August knew damn well Natalie was waiting for him to make a move—and believe him, not taking her to bed was unmitigated torture, but if yesterday had proven anything to him, it was that he needed Natalie to be in his life permanently. He needed to take this slice of time seriously and not get distracted by her smoking-hot, one-of-a-kind rack. He needed her for sixty years, not sixty minutes. What else was a man supposed to believe when the idea of her getting injured made every molecule in his body scream like a child who'd accidentally walked into a theater playing *It*?

Descending into that cave had been eerily similar to entering the hideout with Sam three years ago. The same dusty waft of decay, the silence and pitch-blackness of it all. And all he could think was *I can't lose her, too. I can't.*

It would be so satisfying to make love and forget about all the obstacles in their path to matrimonial bliss, but if he took that route, he'd wake up one day and she'd be leaving for New York. His dick would have gotten a workout, fine. But she wouldn't be any closer to loving him back. Or believing they could go the distance.

At this rate, cheesy eighties songs were writing themselves, but who could blame him when she looked so gorgeous in his passenger seat, her left knee bouncing up and down in a nervous gesture that threatened to upend the pie.

"Hey." He took his right hand off the steering wheel and brushed his knuckle along the outside of her knee, which turned out to be a big mistake, because Lord God almighty, she was smooth and that kneecap would fit right into his palm. *Focus.* "Are you nervous because Ingram Meyer is going to be there? Because we've got this, Natalie. By the end of the night, he's going to be so positive that we married for love, he's going to send us a second wedding gift. Fingers crossed on a chocolate fountain."

She appeared to be on the verge of rolling her eyes, but cut him a sly look instead. "You know, the one from Williams Sonoma doubles as a fondue pot."

He smacked the steering wheel. "Are we positive no one bought us one of those?"

"Hallie took our gifts home, and opened and arranged them. Not a single chocolate fountain that doubles as a cheese cauldron, but then again, I wouldn't put it past Julian's girlfriend to steal it for herself. She once robbed a cheese shop in broad daylight." She nodded solemnly at his incredulous eyebrow raise. "How are you so confident we'll convince Meyer?"

Because if that man can't see I'd die for you, he's blind.

"I'm great at dinner parties. Although in Kansas, we call them barbecues."

Her laughter was kind of dazed. "Dinner with my mother in her formal dining room is far from kicking back with a cold one in someone's backyard."

"That bad, huh?" His stomach begged him not to ask the next question, but hell, he did it anyway. "Did you ever bring your ex-fiancé home for dinner?"

"Morrison? No."

"*Fuck* yeah." His fist pump was so involuntary, he almost punched a hole in the roof of the truck. *Pull back, tiger.* "I mean, I'm glad you didn't have to go through the whole sticky process of detaching your family from the dude, as well. You know how that goes. You don't just break up with someone, you break up with their family and friends. Such a mess."

Natalie stared.

Any second now, she was going to call him on that fist pump and the bullshit that followed. Instead, she asked, "Do you . . . know how that goes? Have you had serious girlfriends?"

Somehow, August got the sense that this was a dangerous topic. "My father used to say that women ask questions they don't really want answered, and it's our job to figure out which ones are safe and which ones aren't. And we will always be wrong."

Natalie scoffed at that, readjusting the pie on her lap. "What are you implying? That I don't really want to know about your past girlfriends?"

"I can relate, princess. I want to hear about this Morrison prick about as much as I want a staple gun pointed at my nuts."

"You asked."

"I live with a woman now. Maybe she's rubbing off on me."

"Whatever. Just answer the question." She chuckled.

Oh no. That chuckle was deceiving.

Trust your gut, son.

Or was it his dick? Because his dick said to tell Natalie anything she wanted to know. Give her anything she wants without delay.

"Yeah, I had a serious girlfriend," he said slowly. Cautiously. "One. In high school. She lived next door. Matter of fact, I think she's still in the house beside my mom and dad."

"What was she like?"

O-kay. Natalie was still smiling. This seemed fine. "Carol? She's a sweet, down-home Kansas girl. Her pickles won a blue ribbon at the state fair."

"Oh." The smile looked a tad forced now. "Wow. She sounds like my total opposite."

Hold up. Things were getting dicey.

"Why did you break up?"

"Natalie, are you sure that pie isn't too hot on your lap? I can—"

"I mean, if she's so *sweet*, what happened?"

"Did I say sweet?" That was just what his mother always called

Carol. A sweet, down-home Kansas girl. It must have stuck. "Well. She wanted to settle down and get started on a family right away, and I wasn't ready for that. I wanted to serve." He recited these truths very slowly. "So she gave me back my class ring and now she's married to the church pastor. Last time my mother updated me, they have four kids."

"Oh." Natalie slumped back in her seat. "And you're happy for her?"

"Of course I am. Why?"

"It sounded like she was the one who got away."

"No, that was my next girlfriend." He winked at her. "Just kidding, princess."

"You know, I'm holding a pie," she said calmly. A few beats passed and he started to sense he wasn't in the clear yet from the dangerous nature of this conversation. "But speaking of pie, I'm just . . . curious. You're very good at . . . you know. Indulging in a little pie yourself. So when did all this practice occur—"

He was already shaking his head. "*Natalie.*"

"I'm just saying, it couldn't have been with the pastor's pickle-making wife."

"This conversation ends now. I only have eyes for your pie."

"Just tell me," she cajoled.

"No."

"We're both adults!"

"Oh my God, I . . . yeah, okay. Fine. I lost my virginity when I was twenty-two. Kind of late and *thirteen years ago*, Natalie. The girl was a friend of a friend's girlfriend and I can't even remember her name, but she . . . she looked at *it* and said, *You better learn how to make a woman stupid before you even think of bringing that thing into the mix.* She showed me a few tricks and I listened. Okay? And that is the *end* of this conversation."

"Are you sure you don't remember her name?" She had the nerve to sound disappointed. "I was hoping to send her a Christmas card."

"Very funny." His face was on fire. "I can't believe I told you that."

"Why?"

"Because you're my *wife*. You're supposed to believe I've existed only for you since day one." In his self-directed irritation, he'd become a loose cannon and could no longer keep himself from erupting. Maybe he was worried that his confession had put doubts in Natalie's head or maybe he was just tired of keeping the truth to himself. But for whatever reason, he chose the moment they pulled up outside of the Vos estate to spill his guts. "And when I look at you, I swear I have. Existed just for you all this time. It feels like I have."

She was utterly beautiful and vulnerable in that moment.

Also pale and full of terror.

Awesome.

"Are you just . . . are you method acting because we're getting ready to fake it in front of Ingram Meyer, or—"

"Nope. I meant what I said." It was an understatement. A massive one. But her visible fear told him to rein it in. "I have feelings for you, Natalie."

She opened her mouth, then closed it. Glanced over his shoulder, where he could hear the front door of the house opening. Footsteps approaching. "Can we talk about this later?"

I HAVE FEELINGS for you.

Natalie walked into her childhood home trying desperately not to fumble the pie. Her fake husband had just admitted to having feelings for her. What *kind* of feelings? They didn't get that far. Did he mean lust? Did he mean he cared about her? Because she'd already sort of sensed both of those things, but they weren't supposed to speak about it out loud. That made it real. That made it something they would have to deal with.

"Do you want me to carry the pie?" August asked, resting his fingertips against the small of her back. Goose bumps sprung to life on the nape of her neck as a result, her eyelashes fluttering, thanks in part to the conversation they'd been having leading up to his confession. She'd gone from jealous to turned on faster than an upside-down roller coaster loop. Perhaps she was in the minority, but a man who listened to a woman's advice on sex, going from pupil to master? That was unforgivably hot, no matter which way she sliced it.

Still, she wasn't supposed to get tummy flutters over phrases like *I only have eyes for your pie.* Yet here she stood. Fluttering and flushed and trying to come to terms with this huge presence in her life now having feelings for her on top of everything else.

Maybe even her own feelings for him. Big, daunting ones.

"No, it's okay," she whispered. "I've got it."

"Do you want me to carry you *and* the pie? Those heels look uncomfortable."

Briefly, she glanced down. "I used to wear shoes like this every day of the week." She used the pie to gesture at the dining room ahead, where voices could be heard, including one belonging to Ingram Meyer. "The heels make me feel more confident. I . . . need some confidence at family dinners."

August searched her eyes, nodded—and Natalie was flooded with the strangest sense that he'd seen exactly what was going on upstairs in her noggin. "I got you, princess."

She blinked up at him. "You've got me?"

"What did I say in my wedding vows? I will take your side in every argument, unless it's with me. Were you listening or just standing there looking like a goddess?"

She was blinking very fast now. "I was listening."

"Good." He leaned down and nudged her forehead with his own. "I got you."

It took Natalie a moment to realize they'd walked into the dining room together, but the extended silence finally registered. They hadn't immediately taken their eyes off each other and now everyone—Corinne, Julian, Hallie, and Ingram—was observing them curiously. It was a slow, reluctant peeling of gazes and she felt almost delirious over being that close to his mouth without getting kissed. She watched as August finally focused on Corinne, who stood stoic at the head of the table, offering her a grin. "Hey, Ma."

Natalie caught the ghost of a smile before Corinne rolled her eyes. "Come in. Dinner is almost ready. We're having lamb." She extended a hand toward the man sitting to her left, who for once didn't have a straw hat perched on top of his head. "I'm sure you'll remember Mr. Meyer from the wedding."

The loan officer gave a lazy salute with his wineglass. "Lovely to see you again."

"Likewise," she and August said at the same time.

Corinne pointed at the pie in Natalie's hands. "Who made that?"

"August," Natalie said. "Obviously. Or I'd be carrying its remains in a ziplock bag."

She only vaguely noticed August frowning down at her. Why? It was no secret she couldn't make food to save her life. By refraining to do so, she saved everyone else's. And hadn't he made fun of her about her lack of kitchen skills as recently as yesterday?

Corinne remained standing until August and Natalie took side by side spots at the table, then everyone was seated.

"So," Hallie half squealed, leaning forward. "What have you been doing together since the wedding?" Corinne coughed and Julian smiled into a sip of wine, and immediately, the curly-haired blonde jogged back the question. "I-I mean, besides . . . besides getting to know each other better a-as husband and wife . . ." She winced, obviously realizing she'd only dug the hole deeper. "I mean—"

"Well. I've been working on my fermentation technique," August slipped in smoothly. "When Natalie isn't working on her laptop, she's been exploring the grounds. Settling in."

That wasn't the greatest start toward convincing the loan officer of their undying love, and August seemed to realize it right away. He reached for her hand under the table, where no one could see, and squeezed it, appearing trapped in his thoughts.

Meanwhile, Ingram Meyer swirled the ruby-red contents of his glass. "Natalie is technically an employee now at Zelnick Cellar, is she not? With her vast array of winemaking knowledge, she must be a huge help to you."

There was a wrenching sensation below Natalie's collarbone and she reached for her water. A huge help? Not likely. He wouldn't even let her in the door. August watched her sip water with a deep groove between his brows, then visibly shook himself into answering. "She . . . yes, she's got a lot of knowledge to offer. I'm very lucky."

"I'm sure she's going to be more of a help on the administrative end of things," Corinne tacked on without missing a beat. Two women hustled out from the kitchen and started forking salad onto one of the smaller plates in each setting. Corinne said something to one of them, then redirected her attention to Ingram. "My daughter has a head for numbers, and I'm sure that will be a major advantage for Zelnick Cellar. As far as the production side, her company title will likely run along the lines of official taste tester."

Natalie had just forked up a bite of salad, but paused while everyone chuckled at Corinne's jest, though she noticed that August didn't laugh. At all. "It's true. I know how to stay in my lane. Especially if it's the checkout lane at the wine store." More laughs. But none from August. "Zelnick Cellar might give Vos some stiff competition in a few years."

Corinne raised an eyebrow at August. "Wouldn't that be something?"

"It sure would," Ingram agreed. "I'm sure a small business loan would go a long way toward making that future a reality."

Corinne gave Natalie a meaningful look.

"Yes," Natalie said to Ingram. "It would." When August said nothing, she squeezed his hand under the table, and he nodded once without meeting her eyes. What was going on with him? He knew this dinner was important. Well, if he wasn't going to make it count, she would show up for the both of them. "It's not so far-fetched, actually. I've never seen anyone so dedicated to teaching himself the art of winemaking with so few tools at his disposal. August came to St. Helena with a dream and a serious work ethic, while so many just show up with millions of Silicon Valley dollars and state-of-the-art equipment, and they never truly understand the finer transformations that take place within the grape. But August continues to try and fail and try again—and eventually he's going to get it. I know he is. And when he does, it's going to be amazing, because he's doing it by hand. By the sweat of his brow. It's going to mean something more than money."

She'd gotten so lost in her speech, she didn't realize Ingram had lowered his glass to the table and was regarding her seriously. Minus the smirk for once. "We should all be so lucky to have someone believe in us the way you believe in your husband, Ms. Vos."

"Mrs. Cates," she corrected with a flustered smile. And there was no way not to be flustered when August was using his grip on her hand to pull her closer, all but physically dragging her into his lap. "Stop it," she whispered.

"No." His voice had thickened. "People sit on other people's laps at barbecues."

"I told you, this isn't a barbecue," she whispered back, laughter in her voice. "Barbecues don't have salad plates."

"I don't acknowledge salads. I see nothing."

Outright giggling now, Natalie slapped at his tugging hand and August finally settled for having their chairs pressed together, their outer thighs flush. Finished with their impromptu play fight, they tore their eyes off each other and found the room riveted.

"Anyway," Natalie said seriously, with a quick smooth of her hair, "I foresee great things."

"So do I," August agreed, looking down at her.

But she had a feeling they weren't talking about the same

thing at all and the possibility made her heart hammer. Made it hard to look at him directly. He was so *much*.

Corinne finally broke into the extended silence they'd left in their wake. "So, Ingram. Julian and I have been looking into the value of aerial crop monitoring. Of course, I'm not sure this is the season for it. We're in a rebuilding year after all."

Julian sighed and set down his wine. "Yes, we're in a rebuilding year, but that's even more of a reason to make use of the technology . . ."

Natalie perked up. Ever since Julian had brought up Vine-Watch, she'd been examining their company history and playing with numbers and statistics. To be honest, she'd been doing this research while she should have been working on strategy for her upcoming client meeting. The one taking place in New York on Friday—four days from now. She couldn't help but be fascinated, though.

"Natalie," August said suddenly, "aren't they talking about the company you've been stalking on your laptop for the last few days?"

Everyone's attention swung toward Natalie.

He'd . . . noticed what she was doing on her laptop?

"Uh . . ." Beneath the table, August placed his hand on her thigh and the warmth was somehow exactly what she needed. "Yes. I did look into VineWatch."

"And what are your thoughts?" Julian asked, openly curious.

"Natalie isn't really up to speed on what's happening here at Vos," Corinne remarked. "The technology might be cutting-edge and right for some of the more thriving wineries, but we're not ready for it quite yet."

"With all due respect, Mother, by the time you're ready, you'll have to play catch-up," Natalie said, shocking herself. She started to wave off her own statement, but August squeezed her leg beneath the table again, nodding at her once. Slowly, she set down her fork and wet her lips. "VineWatch offers a way to reduce the winery's environmental impact by conserving water and allocating fertilizer in a manner that helps eliminate significant waste. It detects diseases that could potentially spread throughout the region and affect other wineries." She paused, a little surprised to still have everyone's attention. "I think it's great that Vos is rebuilding, but it needs to rebuild *correctly* and that includes embracing new science. Responsible science. If it were up to me, I wouldn't simply be considering them as a service provider, I would be looking to invest, because someday very soon, this kind of technology is going to be a requirement for winemakers, not a fun side option." She straightened her water glass. "I've been in contact with their chief operations officer. As it happens, they are bringing on an investor already. A competitor of yours. The tax breaks alone being afforded to green companies will make their investment worthwhile times ten—and they will be called visionaries while everyone else piles on after the fact."

Natalie sipped her water.

No one said anything for several moments.

She glanced up at August to find him looking . . . awestruck? Corinne's jaw was hanging open halfway to her salad plate and unless she was hallucinating, Julian wasn't bothering to hide his pride. Hallie was gleefully topping up everyone's wineglass.

It was the first time she didn't feel like a child in her childhood home.

"Well." Her husband slapped a hand on the table. "Now that

we're all satisfied that my wife is freaking brilliant, it's time to break out the baby photos, if you don't mind."

THERE WERE NOT enough baby pictures.

One measly album? A thin one at that?

August was outraged.

Where were the bad haircuts and Little League photos? His mother would have had Natalie on her couch in the den for a week methodically going through each year of his life on film, and Natalie deserved that same consideration. To Corinne's credit, the lack of photographic evidence of what must have been a beautifully impish daughter seemed to give her pause.

"There has to be more," said his mother-in-law, attempting to refill Ingram's wine for the third time since dinner ended. To put it bluntly, the guy was soused. They'd won him over before the main course and he'd let his guard down, but the closer they got to the end of the evening, the more August's guard went in the opposite direction.

When Ingram refused the refill and stood up, slapping the straw hat back on his head, everyone stood with him. Everyone but August.

"Tonight was a pleasure, as always," he said, shaking Julian's hand. Kissing Corinne's. "The only thing that could have made it better was Dalton's presence. St. Helena surely misses that man. I hold out hope that we'll lure him back from Italy sooner or later."

Corinne maintained her smile at the mention of her ex-husband. Meanwhile, Natalie sent August an eye roll, and he loved that. He loved that they were sitting beside each other on the couch, his arm around her shoulders, and now she was gifting him little nuggets of exasperation. Still, his dread remained and a moment later, he knew why.

"I'm quite satisfied that this is a strong match between two upstanding young people. I only wish Dalton were here to see it for himself," Ingram said, tipping his hat. "I'll file the necessary paperwork in the morning to release Natalie's trust fund."

August expected Natalie to thank him. To stand up and cheer. Something.

Instead, her chest seemed to be cranking up and down. "And . . . a meeting with August to speak about the small business loan? Could that be arranged, as well?"

"Yes, of course," Ingram replied, having no idea that August didn't require a loan any longer. No, the investment from his CO had arrived in full that very morning, hadn't it? "Though my calendar is jam-packed this week. I'll take a look at my schedule when I arrive at the bank tomorrow morning."

Finally, Natalie exhaled. "Thank you."

August's throat was on goddamn fire. Their plan had worked. Natalie was going to get her money. That was what he wanted. But it put her one step closer to no longer needing him.

When Natalie blinked up at him and said his name softly, August realized he was staring into space, imagining the desolate world he'd be living in when she left. She'd get her trust fund and forget his name within a year or two, while he was still hung up on the *real* one who got away.

Unless.

Unless he could find a way to convince her they were great together before Friday. Before she left for New York. Because once she had that investor in her pocket, it would be over.

Not ready to admit defeat in any way, shape, or form, he drew Natalie onto his lap, dropped his chin onto her head, and flipped back to the start of the baby picture album.

"Again."

Chapter Nineteen

It was a startling contrast, the way August could let her get close in some ways, but he continued to doggedly fend her off in others. Last night at her mother's house, they'd been each other's one-person hype squads. They'd comforted each other with touches and ... God, at some point it started to feel like she was actually introducing her husband into the family. She'd forgotten about their arrangement right up until Ingram stood to leave for the night.

She'd wanted to forget again on the ride home, but the silence was too deafening.

Was he waiting for her to announce her returned feelings?

Was he waiting for her to announce she wanted him as her real husband?

Reading August was next to impossible this morning, when he was working in the barn with the door closed, a clear sign to stay out. She wasn't welcome there. And it was too much of a reminder of how she'd been raised. Allowed to participate only when it was convenient for everyone else and there was no chance she'd screw up.

Maybe she would screw up his operation, even worse than it already was.

After all, she'd flamed out brilliantly in New York.

If he were hurting her intentionally, maybe she could find the heart to be mad at him.

But really, he was just a stubborn, determined man who saw only the goal, not sparing any thoughts about who he climbed over to reach it. And instead of being mad at him, she missed him. Missed sitting shoulder to thigh with him like she'd done last night. Missed the sound of his big, obnoxious laugh—and it had been only one day.

Whether she'd hurt him by protecting herself and not vocalizing her feelings or he was shutting her out, she still wanted to hear that laugh. She wanted this time with him and she wanted to experience it to the fullest because it . . . made her feel a way she couldn't admit yet. Not without questioning her vision for the future.

Natalie's attention drifted away from her laptop and around the kitchen, landing on a package of cookies above the stove. Should she make August some food? Heaven only knew the last thing he'd expect was for her to bring him a snack.

An idea struck. A perfect way to hear his laugh again.

She closed her laptop and made sure the door was locked, then she spent the next forty-five minutes setting her plans in motion.

At one time, she'd been known in this town as the prank queen. But it had been a while since she'd played a prank. Funny how the series of pranks excited her more than the chance to guarantee a billion dollars in financing, but that was a problem for another day. For now, she desperately needed to lighten the tension between her and August. And in the process, she'd get him back for making her dance to "Brick House" at their wedding.

Close to an hour later, Natalie plated the cookies she'd been working on, schooled her features, and walked out to the barn. She stopped just inside the door and watched August pulverize the grapes like they'd stolen his bike. Shaking her head, she picked up the cookie on the right edge of the plate and nibbled on it, bumping her hip against the creaky barn door to draw his notice.

When he turned, Natalie was caught off guard to find him looking a little haggard. She considered calling off the whole plan she'd hatched, especially when he saw her and brightened, that weariness vanishing without a trace. Like maybe he'd been out here feeling just as unbalanced as she'd been at the kitchen table.

"Hey," he said, taking a rag out of his back pocket and mopping his brow. An eager step forward. "You found my Oreo stash."

"Mmmm." She took a proper bite out of the one in her hand. "I'm not sharing. I just brought these out here to taunt you."

At her customary barb, she saw relief landslide down his entire body and it made her stomach hurt. She was right. He'd been out here feeling just as terrible.

"You brought me out a snack, princess. That counts as cooking."

She rolled her eyes. "No, it doesn't."

"Anything you put on a plate is a culinary creation."

"Stop trying to walk back your bad cook insults. It's not working."

"You're smiling. It's working." He came closer and snatched one of the Oreos off the plate. "How about this? In our household, if it's on a plate, it's considered an entrée."

Trying not to look too smug, Natalie sighed. "If you insist."

"I do." He sank his straight white teeth into the Oreo and chewed. "Hey, that's my second 'I do' in less than a week—" He froze. Chewed a little more. Then doubled over and spat the chewed-up glop onto the ground. "Christ, what did you do? Replace the frosting with *toothpaste*?"

"The old Colgate switcheroo," she confirmed over his dry heaving. "Too easy."

"Tell that to my esophagus," he choked.

A laugh blew out of her.

August looked up and smiled, his teeth caked in cookie, turning her laugh into a full-body guffaw. "You realize you've incited a war," he said.

"Yes, sir. The only war in which I can—and will—beat a Navy SEAL."

He threw back his head and let out a punctuated *ha*. "Not in your wildest dreams."

She checked her manicure. "I hope you have good medical."

"You are toast, Natalie. Pumpernickel. Rye. Sourdough. *Toast.*"

They were standing at the entrance of the barn, grinning at each other like dummies. Natalie didn't want to acknowledge how much steadier she felt already. So she wouldn't. Nor would she acknowledge the fact that she wouldn't always have the option of going out to the barn and antagonizing him until they got to the other side of whatever was bothering them.

For now, though . . . thank God she did.

Because the thought of being anywhere else made her shudder. She'd have to get over it. Another day.

Natalie turned and speed walked toward the house, feeling almost buzzed from the giddiness. She couldn't seem to stop giggling under her breath, the lightness in her chest almost sweeping her up off the ground. Must be the prank. Had to be the prank.

"You know, in my high school yearbook, I was voted Most Likely to Replace Your Hand Sanitizer with Glue."

August's laughter boomed across the front yard. "Oh yeah? Well in my high school yearbook, I was voted—"

"Class Clown. Fart Champion. Guy We'll Miss the Least."

"Wrong, princess. Most Likely to Surprise You." There was a short pause. "I do think that was in reference to the fact that I used to sneak up behind people and fart, but still."

She had to stop halfway up the stairs to the house, because she was almost blinded by tears of mirth. They were streaming down her face, her sides trembling. This was definitely worth the time she'd taken to lick the frosting out of five Oreos. Especially when August followed her into the house a moment later and turned toward the bathroom. "I'm going to take a shower and then it's on. You're not getting the best of August Cates." He traveled halfway down the hallway and stopped. "You didn't do anything to the shower, did you?"

"What could someone do to a shower?" she asked innocently, sitting back down at her laptop. "I'm going back to work."

Eyes narrowed into slits, August turned again and, a second later, closed the bathroom door. Natalie bit down hard on her lower lip, listening to him open cabinets and slowly pull back the shower curtain, as if wary of a snake jumping out. She even heard him uncapping the shampoo bottle and taking a big sniff of the contents, which she had to admit was pretty wise.

Just too predictable.

Calmly, she stood up from the table, opened the drawer containing the plastic wrap, tore off a long piece, and attached it across the hallway entrance. She squinted an eye to judge August's exact height and left the plastic there, waiting. That was when she heard the shower start, the pelting spray interrupted by his large frame.

And the resounding "What the *fuck*?" that carried though the house, sending the cat skidding from one dark hole to another.

Ready to explode from excitement, Natalie sat down at the table and pretended to type, but kept one eye on the hallway. Sure enough, August burst out of the bathroom a moment later, towel wrapped haphazardly around his hips, blinded by the chicken bouillon cube she'd hidden in the shower nozzle. And just like a dream, he walked straight into the plastic wrap, the film clinging to his slimy features until he tore it off.

"Something wrong, honey?" she asked with mock concern.

"You're . . ." he sputtered, turning in the direction of her voice while searching the immediate area for something he could use to wipe his face. "You're a criminal."

Natalie gasped. "That's no way to speak to your bride."

"Fine. You're a criminal bride. Coming to CBS this fall."

All right, that deserved a paper towel. When was the last time she'd laughed this hard? Or didn't feel like the uncertainty of the future was hanging above her head like a hundred-pound sack of fish guts? "Here," she said a little breathlessly, standing up and handing August the paper towel roll he kept on the counter. "I think you've had enough. For now."

"You, on the other hand . . ." He swiped at his face hastily, cleaning his eyes off enough to pin her with a predatory look. "Haven't even begun to feel the wrath."

"*Oooh*, look at me. I'm shaking."

"You should be."

There had to be something terribly wrong with Natalie that she'd never been more attracted to anyone in her life—and he was currently wearing chicken-flavored slime and his mouth probably tasted like mint hell. Yet if he kissed her in that moment, she would have been moaning for him to take her to chicken town in a heartbeat.

Gulping through the humiliation of that, she swiped the screwdriver off the counter where she'd left it, handing it over. "For the showerhead." She shrugged. "I don't think they make a tool big enough to fix your pride."

He shook his head slowly. She expected a hot take to come out of his mouth. Instead, she got "Sam would have adored you." His gaze carried over her face, as if memorizing her features. "That's not a prank."

"Thanks. Thank you," she sputtered, because she couldn't think of anything else. Or process thoughts into words when an erosion was taking place inside her.

Looking sort of at a loss himself, August turned on a heel and creaked back toward the bathroom. "Sleep with one eye open, princess," he shouted before closing the door.

She caught his smile right before it closed.

AUGUST WAS COOKING something on the other side of her bedroom door.

It smelled incredible.

She didn't trust it.

After round one of the Prank War, they'd retreated to their battle stations. He'd gone back outside and flipped his tire for a while before occupying the kitchen with so much presence that she'd fled like a coward to stop herself from doing something stupid like sliding between that thick, badass body and the counter, leaving the rest up to fate.

It was getting darker outside and there seemed to be some correlation between the sunset and her libido. The damn thing had a personality now and it wanted to know why it hadn't been pampered since their wedding night. She definitely hadn't exfoliated and lotioned herself to death hoping something might *accidentally* happen again. Of course not.

They were in the midst of a war!

What was his first move going to be?

She didn't know his prank style yet. What if he shaved off one of her eyebrows? That was exactly the kind of nonsubtle action her husband would take. Had she gotten herself in too deep? Why was exhilaration spinning in her tummy like a Ferris wheel? Who got this much enjoyment out of a fake husband? Was she doing it wrong?

Obviously, yes.

A ping on her laptop signaled an incoming email. She was on the verge of assuming it was an advertisement when she noticed Claudia's name. Why was her business partner emailing her so late? With no subject line?

Frowning, Natalie opened the email and found a short message: *Sorry if I'm the first one to tell you, just didn't want you to be blindsided this week.* Below that cryptic statement was a link to a *New York Times* article.

No, an engagement announcement.

For Morrison and his new girlfriend.

Her whole body beat once, a tingle at the crown of her head. Mostly out of shock. After that, she waited for the jealousy to rise up and drag her under.

It never did.

They were like two fictitious characters on the screen, smiling and two dimensional and so far away. What did those two people do for fun? Probably not a prank war. They definitely wouldn't dance to "Brick House" at their wedding. But she hoped they had their own versions of those activities. She really did. Like, wow. She actually found herself truly hoping they would be happy. How evolved was that?

Thanks for letting me know, Natalie typed back. *I'll send a fruit basket.*

She hit send and sat on the edge of the bed for another moment, still a little wary of the total lack of shits she gave over Morrison's being engaged. What did that mean?

A gruff rendition of "Love Train" being sung in the kitchen drew her attention. She set her laptop on the bedside table and promptly forgot about the news. It was time to face her fate. No more putting it off. Whatever comeuppance was in her future, she would take it like a woman and immediately begin plotting revenge. Would it be sugar replaced with salt in an evening coffee? Or maybe even an old-school whoopee cushion. That *smacked* of August—

As soon as she opened her bedroom door, a bucket of water turned over and rained down on her head. It was like that famous scene from *Flashdance,* except she wasn't wearing a sexy leotard and the absolute soaking wasn't voluntary. No cinematic value whatsoever.

Standing at the stove and laughing like a psychotic hyena, August snapped a picture with his phone. "Photographic evidence. Bet you wish you'd thought of that."

Natalie was still rendered speechless by the deluge. Not to mention, the fact that her embarrassment was now immortalized digitally. But when the bucket came loose from the door frame and plunked her square on the head, she thought on her feet, grabbing onto the opportunity for quick revenge with both hands.

"*Ouch.*" Her hand flew to the spot where the empty bucket had connected and sucked in an unsteady breath, blinking rapidly, as if holding back tears. "Ow, my head. Ouch."

August went still as a statue, the blood draining from his face. "Oh my God." He dropped his phone and it bounce-skidded under the table, but he didn't seem to notice. "Are you hurt? Did I hurt you?"

She gave a long, brave sniff and looked at her hand, wincing like she'd spotted blood. "I . . . I don't know. I probably only need a few stitches."

"*Stitches?*" August roared, stumbling into the table and upsetting the saltshaker. The poor man looked on the verge of passing out. His hands were shaking as he turned off the stove burners with jerky movements, reached for a dish towel, and stomped toward her, chest heaving up and down. "Come here, princess. Oh fuck, I'm so sorry. The bucket wasn't supposed to fall."

"I'm feeling a little faint," she rasped, pitching to one side and clinging to the doorframe of her bedroom. "Do you think it's a concussion?"

"No," he breathed, horrified. White as a sheet. "No, no, no . . ."

Okay. Jig's up. The man had suffered enough.

Right before he could tug away her hand to examine the nonexistent wound on top of her head, Natalie smiled. "Gotcha, babe."

It was like watching an air mattress deflate in fast motion. The air just sort of blew out of him and he doubled over, bracing his hands on his knees. "That's not funny, Natalie," he wheezed. "I thought I split your head open."

"You do. But only with migraines."

He lifted his head, his complexion still lacking in color. "You're really okay?"

Suddenly her heart weighed four hundred pounds.

And was roughly the size of a watermelon, the whole thing seeming to pry apart her ribs and protrude from her chest. Perhaps she needed an ambulance after all. "Yes, I'm okay. I was just getting you back."

"Consider me gotten."

He commenced a breathing exercise—in, in, out, in, in, out—she suspected was designed to calm him. And it was just barely working. Come to think of it, she was having a pretty difficult time breathing, too, her heart galloping like a Derby winner.

I'm falling for my husband.

Hard and fast.

Might even be well past . . . *fallen* for him territory.

Oh shit.

And he wiggled a little deeper into her heart when he straightened suddenly and crowded her into the doorway, brushing around the wet hair on her head gently, looking down at her from above. "I just need to check for myself," he said, his warm breath on her forehead. "I don't see anything. Thank God." He closed his eyes, pressed their foreheads together. "You scared forty-six years off my life."

"That's a very specific number," she whispered, staring at his mouth.

Did it always look so delicious?

Yes. Always.

"That's the number of fights we've had since we met," he said, almost to himself, his lips lingering on her forehead. Kissing the center and remaining there for long seconds. "Which, coincidentally, is the number of times I've wanted to kick myself afterward. And bad news, I don't see me learning my lesson anytime soon. I'm a glutton for punishment." He brushed her hair back from her shoulder. "Yours."

Her knees wobbled like they might send her splattering to the ground. "I'll do my best to keep meting it out."

"Good."

Natalie wet lips that had become parched, despite the fact that a bucket of water had been overturned on her head. "I better get out of these wet clothes." She tilted back her head so their mouths could rest on top of each other and just like that, they were struggling to breathe. "Want to help me?"

August swallowed audibly, then took a long inhale and exhale through his nose. "It's not a question of wanting to. I always fucking want you. Every minute, every hour of the day." The words weren't even finished coming out of his mouth when she kissed him, their mutual groans coming from deep within. "But I told you the night we got married. Before we go there, I want to know you're not going to wake up with regrets. Don't you dare roll over in my bed tomorrow and act like this was a one-night stand. It's not."

"What is it?" she whispered against his mouth, almost terrified of the answer.

Funny, he didn't look scared at all. Only determined. "We're going to find out." The determination flickered a touch and some vulnerability shone through. "Tell me how you feel about me, Natalie."

Her heartbeat spread to her entire body, pulsing in every limb, every hair follicle. "Oh my God, who just puts somebody on the spot like this?"

"I'm done wondering." He backed her into the bedroom one slow step at a time. Mouth to mouth. His fingertips traced gently down the sides of her face, her throat. Then they took hold of the neckline of her T-shirt and tore it straight down the middle, making her cry out. "I'm done obsessing about you every waking second and having no idea if you're obsessing about me, too."

She stared down at her ripped shirt in shock, eyes shooting back up to meet his increasingly intense ones. "Do you *want* me to obsess about you?"

"*Yes.*" With gritted teeth, he unsnapped the front of her bra and tugged it down her arms, throwing it clear to the other side of the room, along with the remains of her shirt. "Maybe you've been with men in the past who don't want to label shit or be tied down. Well, that's not me. Not when it comes to you. I want you to count the minutes until we're breathing the same air again, the way I do."

There was quicksand shifting beneath her feet, preparing to suck her down. "W-we only married for money—"

His mouth stamped down on hers at an angle and she went from protesting the existence of her own feelings to kissing him eagerly, whimpering into the possessive stroke of his tongue. "Go sell that lie somewhere else, princess," he rasped, pulling her yoga pants and panties down to her knees, dragging his nose upward over her stomach and between her breasts on the way back to looking her straight in the eye. "Now am I just giving you head again? Or are you going to admit how you feel about me so we can fuck like animals?"

Her sex gave a very dramatic, very enthusiastic clench in favor of the latter. But speaking of animals, her heart was still hammering like a jackrabbit. Just admit how she felt? Who did that? Obviously people who had never been on the receiving end of a *No thank you, I'll pass.*

Natalie stood poised on the edge of a canyon being asked to walk a tight rope to the other side. But the longer she looked into his seeking eyes, the steadier that rope became until it turned into a full-fledged bridge. "I do it, too," she whispered in a rush. "I count the minutes until we're breathing the same air again."

"Okay." He wrapped his arms around her, his relieved exhale blowing her hair in several directions. "Damn. Okay. That wasn't so hard, was it?"

"That? Was like standing in the woods smeared in honey."

His chuckle was halting. "Brave girl." He smoothed his palms down her naked hips, back up the sides of her rib cage, his lips moving on the side of her neck. "*My* girl."

In that moment, it was the truth. Her body belonged to him. Her heart lay defenseless.

Just asking to be mauled.

When his strong hands finally closed around her breasts, Natalie's neck lost power, her head tipping back on a breathy moan. In one swift movement, his ropy forearm wrapped around the small of her back and he knelt on the mattress, dropping her down beneath him. Her yoga pants were around her knees. Never taking his eyes off her, he pulled her pants and underwear down the remaining distance, letting them slap wetly onto the floor. They joined the rag that used to be her shirt as he licked her nipples. Just once each and she was *shaking.*

"Have I told you lately that your tits are insane?" he murmured into the valley between the two mounds, his thumbs brushing circles around the puckered peaks.

"On our wedding day."

He lifted his head, grinning. "Took away the nerves, didn't it?"

Don't smile back. Don't—

Too late. She was beaming like a headlight. "It shifted my priorities. From trying not to faint to trying not to sock you in the junk."

"My junk is deeply grateful." Eyes twinkling, he winked at her. "And I promise to make you deeply grateful for my junk."

The laugh snuck out before she could trap it. "You're such a bozo."

"I'm your bozo." The words were half muffled because he closed his wet mouth around her right nipple and suctioned lightly. His tongue provided friction at the same time and God, *God*, her legs jerked up around his hips, her back arching in a half-moon shape. He used his mouth on her breasts for so long, lapping and biting softly and thumbing her peaks, she almost reminded him they'd agreed on sex. But when she started to grow hot and agitated, she realized—once again—that this man knew exactly what he was doing.

"August."

His hand slid up and cupped her face, tongue still working, working, working her swollen nipple and now . . . there was some kind of tugging cord between said nipple and her core. It vibrated and hummed, sending reverberations throughout her body. "Hmmm?"

"Can you please."

"Please?"

"Be inside me now?"

The movements of his tongue were so slow and savoring, she was caught off guard when he lifted his head and she found his pupils taking up nearly his entire irises. "I'm not entering the palace without paying homage to the queen, Natalie," he said, out of breath.

"What does that *mean*?"

"It means . . ." He licked up the hollow of her throat, all the way to her mouth, capturing it in a blistering kiss. "I thought I'd blown my chance to have you like this. I'm not sure how I was able to go on living. Still a mystery." He sank his fingers into her hair, angled her head, and took her mouth in several slanting kisses that scrambled her brain, all while his big, fully dressed body kept her pinned hard to the mattress, his thickness trapped between their bellies like a taunt. "Bottom line, I'm not going in like some eager young puppy. Bad as I want to unzip my jeans and give you hell, princess, if your life doesn't flash in front of your eyes when I finally get my cock inside you, I don't deserve to call myself your husband."

Natalie mentally reeled.

Opened her mouth to disagree that unzipping and giving hell was a negative thing.

But August had already stripped off his shirt—oh, the *muscle*—and rolled over onto his back. "Come here." He ran his tongue along his bottom lip, that broad chest beginning to heave faster and faster. "Let me lick it."

Her brain had gone offline. "I don't understand."

August either didn't hear her or was choosing to ignore her confusion, because his teeth were sinking into that glossy bottom lip now, his palm stroking the ridge in his jeans. "Christ, just thinking about you sitting on my face might finish me."

"You want me to—"

"I'm not above begging."

Forget the fact that she'd never done that before. Not from the top position. But she'd experienced the force of nature that was August's tongue on their wedding night and the memories were not just glorious, they were fresh. He didn't need to beg. He didn't even need to ask her twice. She straddled the mile-wide mountain range that was his chest, whimpering when he took two rough handfuls of her backside and dragged her onto his mouth.

Dragged.

Grinding her there. On his stiff tongue.

And now, ladies and gentlemen, she would never again underestimate the effects of nipple stimulation. There was no awkward moment or easing into the act of being pleasured from below. Not when he'd already gotten her this wet, this *sensitive*. There were only the desperate writhes of her hips, the shallow, hiccupping sounds emanating from her throat, August's moans, and the wild urgency to climax.

He entered her with his tongue, pushed it as deep as possible—and her womb itself constricted, her thighs going rubbery. "Oh my God. *Oh my God.*" His middle finger teased her rear entrance, that magical tongue driving in, out, in—and *goodbye reality*, she was now a resident of the stars. She rode on a rainbow unicorn over the Milky Way and waved at an astronaut. Her body was still in the bedroom, thighs squeezing the sides of August's head, fingers clutching shakily at the headboard while wave after wave of pleasure rocketed through her lower body, tightening and releasing muscles, brutalizing her in the best way possible.

Even after the orgasm crested and she came back down the other side, she was still trembling, her skin speckled in sweat.

She actually had to blink several times to align her vision again and look down into August's face. And he was so turned on by her reaction to what they'd done, so visibly heated, that somehow, against all odds, her own lust rose back to the surface. Unrecognizable, eager sounds fell from her mouth as she scooted backward down his body and found he'd already lowered his zipper. Taken his shaft in his hand.

"The pill, you said?"

"Pill. *Yes.*"

"Doctor said I'm good, Natalie."

"Same."

"No condom?"

All she could do was shake her head.

"*Then sit,*" he growled through his teeth.

Speaking of eager young puppies, that's exactly what she did—taking his thickness all the way home, not stopping until he shouted her name.

Deep, so deep.

Fragments of light exploded behind her eyes, her hips moving of their own volition. In a split second, they were fulfilling his promise of fucking like animals, her sex, never wetter in its life, bringing him inside over and over again, her butt slapping down on the top of his thick, hairy thighs.

"Don't stop, don't fucking stop," he panted, fingertips digging into the meat of her butt cheeks, his lower body slamming upward to meet the breathless bucks of her hips. "If you squeeze up around my tongue that goddamn tight when you come, can't wait to feel how you grip that dick. You're going to ride it until I find out."

"Uh-huh. Yes, August."

Oh yeah. This was the new her, apparently. Obedient as all get-out.

How else was she supposed to behave when this man had unlocked secrets to her pleasure that she didn't even know were being held prisoner? He was magic. And his erect penis, God help her, was pure perfection. Normally Natalie would have called it too large. She *had* called it that at first glance. But the foreplay—the mothereffing *foreplay* turned that . . . eight? Nine-inch? . . . monster into a jungle gym. And it had a curve in it. She actually had to throw her hips back to accommodate that slight bow and in doing so, her clit rubbed against the solid, *so solid* base of his sex, turning her into a moaning, sweating mess.

"There's a lot happening on your beautiful face, but nothing coming out of your mouth." He sat up suddenly and she whimpered, because every time this man moved, she found a newer, better angle with which to happily torture herself. "Tell me what you're thinking," he demanded against her mouth. "While you're fucking me so fucking good, Natalie, say what's on your mind."

"I love your dick," she blurted in a rush, holding on to his shoulders so she could maneuver herself even faster. "I love it."

His eyes were almost black by now, upper lip curled. "What do you love about it?"

Why was she shaking so violently when she wasn't even having an orgasm? Did this man give her pre-orgasms? Was that possible or should she donate herself to science? "It's . . . y-you made me ready for it," she gasped. "With your mouth."

"When I sucked your tits?" He spanked her hard and she screamed into his shoulder. "Or when I stuck my tongue in your pussy?"

Actual moisture was beginning to overflow from her eyes, her teeth chattering. *So good, so good, so good.* "Both!"

"Tell me the truth. You thought I would throw you into missionary, come in sixty seconds, and fall asleep. Didn't you?"

"Yes. No," she babbled, rocking furiously in his lap. "I-I don't know."

"Not with my wife." Without warning, he flipped Natalie onto her back and drove her up the bed with one savage pump of his hips. "I'll be earning the right every single day to come inside pussy this good."

The orgasm slapped harder this time and she soared, loving it, loving being objectified and fucked and revered all at the same time. It was in the way he leaned down to kiss her, letting her know with that cherishing stroke of his tongue that he would be there to take care of her when it was all over. That he adored her.

She could feel that.

He *made* her feel it.

Now she wanted to return the favor. "You've more than earned it," she whispered, scraping her fingernails along his scalp. Raked them down his back and his eyes glazed over. Then she contracted the intimate muscles between her legs and watched his control stumble, his jaw flexing, a stuttered version of her name tumbling out of his mouth. "Although . . ."

"Yeah?" he asked hoarsely, hips moving faster. "Yeah, princess?"

She positioned her mouth against his ear, flexed again, and buried her nails into his back. "Do you really need to earn anything when I want your come so bad?"

"*FUCK*," he bellowed, gripping onto the headboard with his left hand, yanking up her right knee in his other one. The bed creaked ominously beneath them, faster and faster, while he worked through his finishing thrusts, finally flattening her with a snarl and filling her with liquid heat. She took hold of his ass cheeks and yanked him in tighter, purring in his ear. He cursed, panted, and groaned through a renewed series of pumps, their flesh connecting and smacking, hands straining to touch, to gain purchase. From above, his huge body dominated her smaller one in a way she instinctively knew she would crave for the rest of her life.

Moments later, they were nothing but a tangle of sweaty limbs, their labored breathing slowing in the small room. August's mouth traveled along the slope of her shoulder, kissing her beneath the ear as his fingers twined themselves with hers. "Holy shit," he muttered into her hair, sounding completely dumbstruck. "Holy shit."

"Hmmm."

"Seriously, I should get a medal for staying hard that long. You . . ." He rolled her closer, nuzzling his mouth into her neck. "I've *needed* you."

"I've needed you, too," she whispered, a sting creeping in behind her eyes.

He lifted his head to frown down at her. "You sure that falling bucket didn't hurt you?"

Natalie felt herself plummet deeper into the feelings that had been building for this man and wouldn't seem to stop, despite their very opposite objectives. Despite the outward reasons they'd married and the different directions they were heading. "I'm sure."

Her heart gave a heavy thud, so intense that she reached out suddenly for the glass of water on the bedside table, just for something to do with her hands. In the process, she bumped her laptop and the screen brightened. She barely noticed at first. Not until August tapped her bare hip. "Who is that?"

"Who is who?"

August pointed over her shoulder at the *New York Times* engagement announcement still very much visible on her screen. The glass of water paused halfway to Natalie's mouth.

Chapter Twenty

Every time things between him and Natalie started to feel right, a snake had to slither through the grass, jump up, and bite him square in the testicles. Swear to God. As soon as her shoulders stiffened, he knew something was up. And he knew he wouldn't like it.

A significant part of August didn't want her to confirm the identity of the suited, smiling golden boy in the photograph, because he'd already put it together. Central Park spread in the background gave it away. That fucker with the whitest teeth he'd ever seen was Natalie's ex-fiancé. They'd just had sex so incredible that he'd heard "Lucy in the Sky with Diamonds" by the Beatles playing when he came and this was going to ruin it, huh?

"Who is who?" Her question lingered in the air, her eyes zipping to the screen, widening, the glass of water stopping before she could take a sip from it. "Oh."

"Oh?"

She took a long drink from the glass and set it back down on the bedside table. "That would be my ex, Morrison, and his new fiancée." Her smile was tight and brief. "I wasn't internet stalking. Someone sent me the announcement."

"When?"

Jerky shoulder shrug. "I don't know, a little while ago."

It was all coming together now. His stomach pitched first, followed by the scraping out of his chest, leaving it hollow.

No, not totally hollow.

There was a big billow of green smoke wafting in, carrying jealousy on its back. Sticky, grimy, and impossible to escape. "A little while ago, as in, right before you asked me for sex."

"Asked you for . . ." She opened her mouth and closed it, nose wrinkling up. "I don't understand where you're going with this."

August lunged off the bed to his feet, zipping himself back into his jeans with numb fingers. "You need me to spell it out for you?"

"Apparently I do." Her voice had grown louder to match his. "Yes."

Unable to stand the sight of Morrison's smiling face another second, he crossed to the other side of the bed and closed the lid of the laptop. "You were feeling shitty about your ex getting engaged and I was a convenient ego boost."

That marked the first time he'd ever rendered Natalie speechless.

And it didn't feel a *tenth* as good as he expected it to.

In fact, it felt the opposite of good. It was awful.

She stared up at him for several beats, then seemed to blink back tears while turning her face away. "Get out of my room."

It took him a moment to find his voice. "Deny it."

"No, you have it completely right. Everything I said about having feelings for you was a big, elaborate lie so I could get some ego-boosting sex." She stood up and shoved him toward the door, but he didn't budge an inch. Couldn't seem to move at all. "Doesn't that sound exactly like me?"

Nope.

Nope, it certainly did not.

Now she was covering herself with a pillow. Hiding from him.

Apologize. Right the hell now.

"Tell me this isn't one of the reasons you're going back to New York," he growled instead, because he had obviously lost full control of his faculties. The green smoke growing thicker and thicker inside his chest was manning all battle stations. This finance guy was utterly perfect for August's wife—who he was fucking in love with, by the way—and the whole time they'd been making love, she'd been sad about the asshat marrying someone else.

She'd just turned him inside out in that bed and the possibility she'd been on a different page was eating him alive.

"I am not required to deny anything to you," Natalie said, lips barely moving. *Uh-oh.* Now there was a whole slew of snakes gunning for his balls, fangs out. "Nothing has changed between us. The original agreement still stands. We're in this for the money and that's it. Now get out of my room."

His heart climbed up into his mouth and he swallowed it, the whole aching mass of it getting stuck in his throat. "Once I'm out, it's going to be really hard to convince you to let me back in."

"Oh, you have no idea, shithead."

"I'm jealous, Natalie," he said hoarsely. "I'm jealous."

"You know what, August? I don't care. You don't get to say whatever you want because you're feeling a particular way. That doesn't excuse anything. You have to learn to take the information given to you by your brain and stop your mouth from interpreting it first."

"Because it hurts your feelings."

"Yes," she whispered, then seemed to regret it. "No. *Out.*"

More than anything, he was angry with himself in that moment. Pissed beyond measure. Frustration built higher and higher, any remaining thread of control slipping from his fingers. He couldn't do anything right. Couldn't make Natalie happy for longer than a few measly minutes at a time. Couldn't do justice to Sam's dream. Couldn't interpret brain shit, either, apparently. What good was he doing anyone?

Giving Natalie breathing room was probably the right thing to do, but he couldn't seem to make himself leave the room. He simply remained there, an inanimate object with his hand on the knob. No, he couldn't walk away. That's what they'd both done at the end of every fight, since the beginning, and it had hurt their relationship every time.

He'd *lose* her unless something changed.

Her feelings were hurt because of him, and he wasn't just going to abandon her.

August turned around. "What can I do to make this better, Natalie?"

Her chin snapped up. "Besides light yourself on fire?"

"Preferably."

"I don't know, August." She sighed.

"Tell me how you feel right now." He ventured a cautious step toward the bed. "That seems like a good start."

"Mad." For a second, he thought she might leave it at that, but she threw up a hand and let it drop. "A little empty."

A hoarse sound left him. And it occurred to him that storming away was definitely easier. *This* was the hard part. Hearing what he'd done wrong and how he'd hurt her. Was that what made a marriage last? Doing the hard shit? "Why empty?"

"Because I was . . ." She glanced down at the messy sheets. "I let myself trust you and you didn't trust me back. You made me drop my armor and then, I don't know, it's like I'm being punished for it."

Her words dug into him like slivers of glass. Christ, that was worse than he'd imagined. What would he have learned by now if he'd just spoken to her like this after all of their arguments? He'd be wiser than Doctor Strange. "God, I'm sorry."

"I know." She laughed without humor. "That's the thing. I know you're sorry. I know that so many of your choices aren't made to hurt me, even though they do."

So . . . *many* of his choices?

What else was he doing to hurt her?

He racked his memory bank and came up with nothing. "Natalie, what am I . . ." Out of nowhere, an idea lit up the nether regions of his brain. "I can read you the rest of my wedding vows. Will that make you feel better?"

Was that reluctant interest he sensed? "There was more?"

"Yup. Don't move." On a mission now, he jogged through the house, which sent Menace into near hysterics, and barged through the half-open door of his bedroom. Where did he put them? Where?

Bedside table.

August snatched up the yellow, lined piece of paper and ran back out of the room, skidding to a halt a few seconds later at the foot of Natalie's bed.

He cleared his throat dramatically, but she wasn't ready to smile yet. Fair enough. He'd be lucky if she simply lost that hollow look in her eyes by the time he finished reading.

Don't ever hurt her feelings again, you son of a bitch.

"You can call me no matter where you are and I'll come. That's where I left off, right?"

She nodded.

Good. He loved knowing she remembered exactly what he'd said at the altar.

"Okay. Natalie Vos, I vow to hug you when you're sad. Encourage you when you're down. And take the blame for a fight if it means we don't go to bed angry."

"No way." She snorted. "It doesn't say that."

He flipped the paper around and held it out, so she could see he was reciting the vows verbatim. "Read it and weep, princess."

She glanced at the page, then studied her nails, trying and failing to hide a glimmer of interest. "Anything else?"

"Yeah." He pressed a knee into the bed. Then another. Walking himself closer to her despite the growing stiffness in her shoulders. "If I ever make you cry, you get to give me a purple nurple. Says it right here in bold print."

"I'm not crying."

"You were close," he said miserably. "I hated it."

"Don't come any closer. I'm not purple nurpling you."

"Those are the vows."

"You didn't say them in front of God. They don't count."

"I just said them in front of a goddess. They count." He threw aside the piece of paper and tackled her backward onto the bed in a bear hug that made him feel like crying. If he'd left, if he'd walked away after the fight, he wouldn't have his arms around her right now and that would forever be the wrong choice. He needed to keep his arms around this woman come hell or high water.

When she sniffed a little, he reached for her hand, bringing it up between them.

Pressing her fingertips to his nipple.

"Make it count." His wife didn't need the reminder. She secured two knuckles around his nipple and twisted with nothing short of savagery until he yelped, discomfort shooting through his pec. "Ow, ow, ow, ow, *ow*."

She twisted harder.

"Natalie! *SHIT*."

Finally, she let go. And had the nerve to look innocent when he lifted his head to show her his incredulity. "You asked for it," she said, blinking up at him. Smiling.

He'd made her smile. After a fight.

The bliss of that almost eclipsed his pain. Almost.

"I'm afraid to look down and see if my nipple is still there," he choked out.

She yawned. "Male nipples don't really serve a function anyway."

They laughed and he held her tighter, turning them bodily onto their sides and molding himself around the perfect back of her. "That does it," he growled into her neck, kissing her soft skin in between each word. "You have to sleep with me tonight. That's your punishment for trying to kill me."

"Oh my God." She elbowed him in the ribs. "I had no idea I married such a big baby."

"I'm probably bleeding," he muttered, tucking his knees up behind hers, smiling when she snuggled him back. "We good, babe?" He pressed his lips to the back of her neck. "Please tell me we're good."

Little by little, the tension left her muscles until she was completely relaxed in his arms and his heart constricted in response. "We're good, August."

He believed her.

But he also believed his dick/gut and it was telling him they were far from out of the woods. New York was still on the horizon. Not to mention the investment from his CO he'd neglected to tell her about. And earlier, hadn't she said *I know that so many of your choices aren't made to hurt me, even though they do?* Whatever she was referring to, his eyes needed to be more open to it now. He'd do better.

Because he wanted to fall asleep holding her forever.

Chapter Twenty-One

A boom of thunder jolted Natalie's entire body upright in bed, August's heavy arm dropping from around her shoulders down into the sheets. Within seconds, that muscular limb was curling around her thigh, hoarse, unintelligible murmurs coming from her husband. No doubt about it, the man was beautiful when he slept. A big, cozy brute with obvious morning wood. She'd expect nothing less—

Another roll of thunder seemed to shake the entire house. With a gasp, her gaze flew to the window. The storm sounded like it was coming from their backyard. Her distress must have finally woken August because he sat up beside her in bed, bare chested, his brow chiseled with concern. Instantly on alert.

After a quick glance at the window, he studied her face. "Are you okay?"

"Yeah."

"Bad storm," he said, pushing a set of fingers through his bedhead. "We might be stuck in here all day." That same hand disappeared beneath the comforter and she knew exactly what he was doing under there. The flex of his forearm muscles gave him away.

"Can't think of a single thing we might do to occupy ourselves. Can you?"

A little over a week ago, she would have taken an immediate jab at him. Claim she was calling the police to request immediate evacuation. Or ask in mock horror if they'd be forced to drink his wine if they ran out of rations. But now, she simply turned wet, already starved for August's weight on top of her, the friction their warm morning skin would make as he moved. Slow at first. Then hard. Then fast and ferocious.

They would talk after that.

They had to talk.

Either they stopped ending up in bed like this, acting like a real-life married couple or . . .

Or they adjusted their plan from one month to . . . longer?

A goose egg stuck in her throat. Dear Lord, the very idea was scary.

What if she actually tried to make it work with this man who she had deep, messy feelings for? What if they remained married permanently? It would require *a lot* of shifting. Her expectations and aspirations and . . . well, everything. She'd have to reimburse Claudia for all of her time and hard work, make sure her friend wasn't left hanging. She'd have to find . . . a purpose here. The financial sector didn't operate out of Napa. Wine was her only option and so far, August had only thrown up roadblocks to prevent her from helping.

He hadn't yet carved out a place for her in his daily life. Starting each morning, he'd shut her out while he worked, instead of accepting her help. Letting her in.

Perhaps his rejection was unconscious, but he did it nonetheless. Explaining her reservations to August would only force him to make changes too soon and she couldn't fast-forward his grief process. But could she gamble her entire future on him letting her in eventually? What if he didn't and she signed up for another life like the one in which she'd been raised? Always being kept on the periphery of the Vos family, never let into the inner circle.

August leaned over, skating his mouth over hers. Urging her down into the sheets and coming down on top of her, licking into a moaning kiss that shot bullet holes through her worries. "Woke up starved for that thing between your legs." He groaned into her neck. "Not sure if you're still a little pissed from last night, so I'm asking very nicely if I can eat it."

She really should give him another purple nurple for referring to her vagina as *that thing*. Unfortunately, she liked all the words coming from his mouth and wanted more. Immediately. "Yes," she murmured, letting her knees fall open while his mouth trailed eagerly downward—

Natalie's phone rang on her bedside table.

"*No*," August wailed. Directly against her sex. "Please God, no."

There was no way to trap the giggle. Any other time, she would have ignored the call, but she happened to glance over and see Julian's name on the screen. Her brother wouldn't pick up a phone unless there was a good reason. She had to answer.

"Sorry, it's my brother," she said, pushing her fingers through her husband's hair. When August admitted defeat and rolled over, misery etched in every line of his face, she finally picked up her phone and hit talk. "Hello?"

"Hey, it's me," came her brother's voice from the other end.

"Julian, hey—"

"Are you watching the news?"

"What?" she pulled away from the phone momentarily to check the time. Nine A.M. "No, I just woke up. Is something happening?"

"Yes. Is August there? He's not answering his phone."

Natalie frowned, a weird sort of clinch happening in her middle. "He's here. I'll put you on speaker." She tapped the screen. "Okay, you've got both of us."

"There's been a flash flood in St. Helena," said Julian, without preamble. Brisk, as usual, but slightly choppy. "There's helicopter footage on the news. A whole road turned into a river and there's a minivan stuck in the middle of it." He paused. "Kids and a mom."

"Oh my God," Natalie breathed, tossing aside the sheets, her feet finding the cold floor.

"Search and rescue are dealing with similar situations all over the region. They're bringing in reserves from other counties, but the roads are causing delays. The police are at the scene, but their first attempt to reach the van wasn't successful—"

August pulled up his pants and disappeared from the bedroom. Just *boom*. Gone.

His feet pounded across the floorboards of the kitchen. The creak of a door opening and closing in the hallway, a distinct click she recognized as the linen closet. Was he taking a shower? Or was that wishful thinking? Because she had the sudden fear that her fake-for-now husband was heading straight to a flash flood.

"He's . . . I don't know what he's doing. Hold on." With Julian still on speakerphone, Natalie jogged from the bedroom with her stupid heart lodged in her throat. "August?"

She found him in the hallway. But this man was a stranger.

Gone was his golden retriever, tongue lolling out, lazy beers at the lake kind of demeanor. He'd been replaced with a soldier. His expression was hard, focused, the movements of his hands precise and efficient. And from somewhere in the linen closet she'd opened multiple times, he'd unearthed a gigantic backpack. He checked the contents now, nodded, threw it on his back, and strode for the door.

"You're going?" Natalie moved like a ghost in his wake. "You're going."

"I'm going," August said without stopping.

"He's going," Julian echoed, sounding relieved.

Relieved? Natalie felt like someone had shoved a stick of dynamite into her chest. Her feet were barely functioning, but she ran after August, anyway, barefoot in a nightshirt. Outside. Within seconds, she was soaked to the skin. So was August, though he seemed almost at home in the rain, cutting through it like some kind of deadly assassin in sweatpants and no shirt.

He was going to help the family stuck in the flash flood.

Just like that.

Her heart was torn in two directions. Obviously, she wanted those children and their mother to be rescued, but she'd seen what nature was capable of four years ago during the fire. Floods were dangerous. He was one man—not a team of SEALs.

Was he going to be all right?

Natalie hung up on Julian, blood pounding in her temples. She watched August climb into the driver's seat of his truck and didn't even hesitate before springing to the passenger side and throwing herself into the vehicle.

"*Out,*" he barked, pointing at the house, intimidating her for the first time ever in their entire acquaintance. But not enough to send her out of the truck to watch him drive off into the storm from hell.

"No. I'm coming. I can't just sit here w-wondering if you're okay." Warm, salty moisture splashed down her cheeks, like a cartoon version of crying, and she batted the tears away with shaky fingers. "Don't make me do that. Please."

"Natalie . . ." He shook his head, rested two fists on the steering wheel. "If it comes down to rescuing you or literally anyone else in this fucking world, it's going to be you. I'll be focused on you. I won't be able to think about anything else."

"I will be fine. I will make sure I'm fine." She put on her seat belt with difficulty, because her fingers were going numb. "We're wasting time."

A beat passed.

With a curse, he gunned the truck in reverse and shot down the tree-lined driveway while her heart pumped in time with the windshield wipers.

It was so much worse than she'd imagined, and she'd been picturing the apocalypse. No fewer than two dozen emergency personnel vehicles were parked at haphazard angles along the road leading to the flooded street. A helicopter circled overhead. The occupants of news vans were fighting with police officers to gain entry to the cordoned-off scene. And all the while, the deluge continued to pour, thunder and lightning arguing with each other in a way that suggested they were in the thick of this storm.

August screeched the truck to a halt at the police barrier, the window already rolled halfway down. "Petty Officer Cates, formerly of SEAL team five. I can help."

They waved him through and he hit the gas.

"H-how exactly are you going to help? Do you have a plan?"

"Nope."

"Fuck oh fuck oh fuck."

"I'm trained in swift water rescue, but I need to assess the situation up close from the ground level. See what kind of landscape and manpower I'm working with. And then I'll have a plan." He hit the brakes and threw the truck into park. "*Your* plan, Natalie, is to stay in this truck or so help me God, it will be the worst fight we've ever had," he ended on a shout.

"I'm not scared of a fight," she shouted back. "I'm scared you'll get hurt."

August took a long look at her face, seeming to register her terror for the first time. How polite of him. And he momentarily softened, cupping the side of her face. "I'm adding it to my wedding vows. I won't get hurt. It's written in stone now, just like the rest of them." He kissed her hard and took one last look at her face. "My God, I am fucking crazy about you."

With that, he shot from the truck with the backpack over one shoulder, leaving her reeling, her heart bleeding profusely. But instinct kicked in a second later and Natalie moved into the warm spot left behind by his body, watching him through the windshield, the scrape of the wiper blades suddenly becoming the soundtrack to a horror film. He shouted at a group of huddled men, joined them. After a brief exchange, they moved as one big unit toward the top of the road—and that's when their location finally registered.

She'd taken this shortcut a million times throughout her life. When town was jam-packed with tourist traffic, this road was a way to avoid it. Elevation wise, she supposed it was much lower than the surrounding area, but that fact had never seemed important until now.

Up ahead, August disappeared around a bend in the road with the huddle of rescue workers and without her husband in view, everything inside her screamed to throw herself out of the truck and sprint after him. But she would not distract him in a dangerous scenario like this. Absolutely not. If he made a mistake and got hurt or killed because of her, she would never forgive herself. She was staying in the damn truck.

But there was no one around to stop the truck from creeping forward a little.

Just so she could keep tabs on any developments.

August had left the motor running, so she put the truck into drive and inched slowly around the police vehicles and their flashing lights, stopping when the very top of the rushing water came into view below.

And her blood ran cold.

The van was halfway submerged in turbulent water.

Teri Frasier, Zelnick Cellar's one and only customer, and her triplets were holding on to one another for dear life on the roof of the van.

For the first time, she noticed a man on the scene with a blanket wrapped around his shoulders, wearing what looked to be a sodden suit. His hysterical tone reached through the rain and windshield and though the voice was muffled, Natalie somehow knew it was Teri's husband. Helpless, watching the water slowly rise around his family.

"Oh no. Oh no." A chill rent through Natalie, making her shiver even harder than before. Her rickety breaths were causing the windshield to fog up so she turned on the defroster, retreating into the seat and pulling up her knees to her chest. "Please, please, please, August. Get them. Get them and be okay. Please."

A few minutes later, a yellow raft approached from upstream and there was August, steering it, two officers behind him. They'd put August in a helmet, but the life vest was obviously too small for his king-sized body, so it just hung on him loosely, flapping open in the wind. He shouted something at Teri, smiled, and she nodded.

"I love you," Natalie whispered. "I love you. Come on. Please."

The timing was barbaric. Why did she have to realize she loved the big lug right before he was about to do something life threatening? It couldn't have happened while he was cooking eggs or trying to reason with the cat? Natalie was never more positive that she *hadn't* loved Morrison, because this big, wild, terrifying feeling had happened only once in her life.

Right now. For August.

She understood now. Love turned the heart into a liability. If something happened to him, she'd never get the damn thing to beat properly again. It seemed to be beating for him now.

Time seemed to freeze when August reached the side of the submerged road. From his backpack, he pulled out what looked like . . . a grappling hook? He raised it high and buried it in the dirt and rock formation that ran along the road, twisting and screwing it into the earth. One of the officers leapt out of the raft onto the rocks and worked to secure it further, wrapping the attached cable around his forearm several times. August threw the excess cable to the other side of the road, where a waiting officer caught it, securing a latch to the front of his vehicle.

As soon as the man turned and gave August a thumbs-up, he jumped into the raging current of water and Natalie almost puked.

It carried him several feet toward the submerged van and she started to cry, the heels of her hands digging into the hollows of her cheeks. Hard enough to hurt. But her breath caught as August stopped suddenly and Natalie realized he'd hooked himself to the center of the cable that ran perpendicular to the road.

"Okay," she breathed, shaking uncontrollably. "Is that okay? Is that good?"

No one was there to hear her nonsensical questions. Or hear her chant her husband's name over and over again, her fingernails digging into her knees, the seat. The fact that the truck smelled so heavily of grapefruit wasn't helping. Or was it the *only* thing helping? She didn't know. She could only hold her breath as August moved toward the minivan, instructing Teri and the three children to climb onto the hood of the van, which was partially beneath water.

The woman hesitated, visibly nervous to step into the water at all, but whatever August said seemed to reassure her and finally, she stepped in, handing the first of the three children to him. He took off his life jacket and wrapped the small child as tightly as possible with the belt, then he put the young boy on his back and started moving toward the side of the road by pulling himself along the cable, hand over hand. Natalie could see he was talking to the crying child and more than *anything*, she wondered what he was saying. Probably just the best things in the world, because he was August freaking Cates.

When the child was reunited with his father, Natalie expelled a breath she didn't realize she'd been holding, her heart still fluttering as fast as a hummingbird's wings.

"What the hell. I'm married to, like, Captain America or something." She sniffed, the scene blurring in front of her. "I can't watch this three more times. I can't."

But she did.

By the time it was Teri's turn to hop on his back, the woman no longer looked worried. Her kids were out of danger.

And then it was over. The rain continued to come down in buckets, but it was over.

At which point, nothing short of an act of God could keep Natalie in the truck.

Chapter Twenty-Two

August trudged up onto the shore, sweatpants waterlogged, skin scraped from the debris that had passed him in the water. He accepted a blanket from one of the emergency workers and waved off the applause, relieved and gratified enough just to see the Frasier fivesome reunited. But he had one destination in mind. The truck. The woman.

Getting her the hell out of there and back into his house, where it was safe.

And he didn't need to wait long to reassure himself she was all right, because Natalie was running toward him in her nightshirt.

It was the most beautiful thing he'd seen in his entire life—and easily the most terrifying. They were still in a volatile situation with the rain continuing to come down at an alarming rate. If the road behind him could be flooded in seconds, the one they were standing on could, too. Don't get him started on landslides and falling trees and power lines coming down.

"Get back in the truck," he called, his voice hoarse from shouting.

Of course she kept coming. Didn't slow down at all.

The nightshirt clung to her, black hair stuck in damp curlicues to her neck and cheeks. No shoes. Was she hoping to round off this fine fucking morning with a tetanus shot? Or was she more of a hypothermia girl?

If only she wasn't the most beautiful sight he'd ever beheld in his life, maybe he could hold on to his anger. But he was aching everywhere, all over his body, for her touch, because he'd had the same recurring thought during the rescue.

What if the last time I saw her, I was shouting at her? What if that's how she remembers me? After all, there was always risk involved with every mission, no matter how big or small.

Around ten yards away from August, she stubbed her toe on the road and the dinner they'd eventually gotten around to eating around midnight nearly came back up.

"Natalie," he growled, ready to admonish her for leaving the safety of the truck when he was damn well on his way to be with her, anyway. But the lecture died in his throat when she leapt into his arms with a sob, her body shaking like a washing machine during the spin cycle. "Hey." He kept his voice as soft as possible, but it was thicker than pancake batter. "Everyone is okay, princess. Everything is fine."

"What the hell," she strangle-whispered into his neck. "Like, what the *hell*?"

August carried her over to the open passenger-side door of the truck, but he walked slowly, because there was nothing in the goddamn universe better than holding this woman, except for maybe holding her in a safe, dry location. "What's the matter? You've never seen a flash flood before?"

She clung harder. "No!"

"Civilians." He sighed, tickling her ribs a little. "Stay off this road during storms. The elevation puts it lower than the creek bed." She said nothing, so he poked her. "Promise me, Natalie."

"Okay. I promise." She leaned back a little and her puffy eyes and red-tipped nose nearly made him stumble. "Of course, if I ever got stuck out there, you'd just strap on a harness and come rescue me. Totally calm and casual, as if you're heating up a microwave dinner."

He took stock of his body, cataloging the chaotic buzz at the base of his throat, the vibrations in his fingertips. The rippling of his heart, which whipped into breakneck speed at her words. "For the record, I'm not calm. I've got enough pent-up adrenaline to flip this truck and maybe run a half marathon. If *you* were the one I had to rescue, Natalie . . ." He shook his head, and kept right on shaking it until he probably looked insane. "I wouldn't have been coolheaded enough to put on the harness. I'd have jumped in and swum."

The picture she'd painted in his head—of herself stranded on the island of her blue car in the middle of a swift current—made his arms and knees weak, so he set her down sideways on the passenger seat before he did something humiliating, like collapse in the middle of the road. He was attempting to rein in his stampeding adrenaline and it took him a moment to notice how she was looking at him. Softly, with teeth-marked lips and eyes heavy with moisture, her breasts shuddering up and down. Vulnerable in a way he'd never seen her before. Walls down.

"I don't think one month is going to be enough anymore," she said haltingly, swiping at her eyes and hiccupping through a gulp of air. "We might need to renegotiate our terms."

Oh shit. There went his heart. Booming like a cannon. Did

she mean what she was saying? Or was she shaken up over the water rescue? He didn't care. He just wanted his bride. "Forget negotiations." He leaned down and pressed their foreheads together. "I don't need any fancy language to know you belong with me."

She gave him a tearfully dubious look. "It's not that easy."

"I don't *want* easy," he said through his teeth. "Neither one of us wants easy."

"So . . . what? I can't just . . ." The rain was so loud on the roof of his truck, he had to press his ear almost to her mouth to make out the next part. "I can't just . . . give up New York."

August's lungs flooded with oxygen so fast, he got lightheaded. The way she said those words didn't sound all that confident. No, she sounded open to negotiation. As in, she was considering the alternative to returning east? Holy hell. "Yes, you can. You can stay with your husband, who would throw himself into a flood for you."

"That's . . ." Was she having trouble breathing? Should he perform CPR? "That's extremely romantic, but we're probably jumping the g-gun because we just went through something scary."

He shook his head. "I can't believe that all it took was a standard water rescue to make you consider staying."

A watery laugh burst out of her. "There was nothing standard about that. You were heroic. You were . . ." The muscles of her throat worked. "You could have died."

"Me? Nah. I'm too stubborn." Why did his response seem to upset her more? Was her lip trembling now? God, he didn't like that. Not at all. *Make her laugh.* "Out of curiosity, how scary does living with me permanently sound to you? On a scale of TV dinner to flash flood."

Not even a beat of hesitation. "Like back-to-back flash floods."

"Thanks for your honesty," he responded dryly. "We'll try and work it down to a summer storm with no possible fatalities."

Her attention dipped to his mouth and the damn thing went dry, like she'd snapped her fingers and wished it. "I love that," she murmured. "I love some parts of the storm between us." For long moments, they looked into each other's eyes. Hers were uncertain, but hopeful, and so beautiful, so fathomless, a chicken bone seemed to be stuck behind his jugular. And it only doubled in size when her legs parted, ever so slightly on the seat, allowing his hips to move in closer to her heat. "Am I really considering staying longer than a month? I don't have a real job, my family could take me or leave me, and you . . . we barely get along—"

"We are the fucking dream team and you know it. We *got* this."

"Not yet. Not completely." She closed her eyes. "Right now, this very moment, we do, though. I've got you. You've got me. Can you please bring me home and take me to bed?"

Frantically, August performed another check of his vitals and found the adrenaline hadn't ebbed *whatsoever.* If anything, it had skyrocketed at the very real possibility that Natalie might consider staying in St. Helena. That he might actually have a shot at turning their marriage from one of convenience to one that would last.

Forever. *Forever,* if you asked his heart.

Or his dick. Because the damn thing was forever a backseat driver that wouldn't be silenced. At the mere suggestion of sinking into Natalie's warm, wet pussy, dude was growing like Jack's magic beanstalk. *Fuck.* He was going to love on that thing so hard, he'd snap the headboard in half. Unfortunately, he might snap the girl of his dreams in half in the process. "You need to give me twenty minutes to flip my tire when we get home."

Puzzlement knit her forehead together. "Huh?"

"The leftover adrenaline, Natalie. I need to work some of it off first or . . ." He pointed at the apex of her very smooth, very spreadable thighs. "I'm going to offend the queen."

She did a double take. Squinted one eye. "Wait, so I'm the princess and my vagina is the queen?"

"And I'm her loyal subject. Yes."

Silence fell.

But it was interrupted a moment later by her laugh.

A clear, musical sound that twisted his chest up in a knot and forced a hoarse chuckle from his own mouth. Foreheads flush, their bodies shook with mirth in the middle of the still-raging storm. "You're such a weirdo," she gasped.

"You can learn to live with it."

She nodded, turned serious. "Maybe." Her fingertips traveled down the front of his torso and he saw actual stars when they tucked inside the waistband of his sweatpants. "I don't want to wait for you to flip the tire."

"Need to flip the tire. I don't want to hurt you."

"Do you think this is turning me off?"

"I don't know. I just stay one hundred percent honest with you and hope for the best."

"Oh dear," she whispered, brushing her lips along his jaw-line. "That turns me on, too. We're not even going to make it home."

Jack's magic beanstalk was almost at full height. "Tire."

"Forget the tire," she purred, touching her tongue to his earlobe.

Colors and shapes blurred in front of his eyes. "What t-tire?"

Footsteps approached from August's right and he moved on instinct, stepping back from the V of Natalie's thighs and pushing her knees together. There was only one person that had the privilege of seeing her panties and that person had been reduced to monosyllables.

Someone slapped him on the back.

"Thank you again for your assistance, Cates."

August looked back over his shoulder to find one of the police officers holding his hand out for a shake. But thanks to his beanstalk being at full maturity, he could only turn partially and slap his hand into the officer's waiting palm. "Don't mention it." The guy just stood there nodding and grinning, shifting in his boots. Oh man, August knew that look. He was seconds from getting invited out for a beer with the bros. "I need to get my wife home before she catches a cold."

Natalie ran a knuckle down his happy trail and he almost swallowed his tongue. "The only thing I'm going to catch," she whispered for his ears alone, "is this di—"

"All right, you take care, man. Let's have a beer sometime," August blurted, pushing Natalie's legs into the truck, his blood thickening like hot gravy. At this point, he didn't even care who saw his boner, as long as he got the woman home in the next ten minutes. Rest in peace to his headboard. In a few long strides, he was around the front bumper, diving into the driver's side and reversing through the maze of emergency vehicles. "Oh, you are going to get it, Natalie queen princess Cates."

She slid gracefully across the front row of his truck, pressing her mouth to his shoulder. Kissing, licking . . . and biting down in way that sent his balls up into his throat.

"Fuck."

"Yes, please." She gripped his cock through the wet material of his sweatpants and in one big, shuddering breath, he fogged up every single window of the truck. "And I don't need you to take it easy on me. Our make-up sex was interrupted this morning. Maybe it *should* be a little . . ."

"Rough." He fumbled for the defroster with a growl. "You have no idea how bad you're making it hurt, princess."

That magic hand of hers started to stroke him up and down. "Pull over and show me."

"Natalie," he groaned, trying to blink away the tiny dots of light spinning in front of his eyes. "I think you might be short-circuiting my brain."

"I'm sorry," she said, not looking the least bit contrite. Jesus, what was coming next?

When she stripped the soaked nightshirt over her head, he had his answer.

In a mere scrap of panties, she resumed jacking him off, but this time her hand had entered the end zone. It was inside his sweatpants doing the Lord's work, playing with his balls and tugging on his cock gently, with a grip that increased in pressure, then got *rough*.

"*Son of a bitch*," he hissed through his teeth, forcing himself to breathe and focus on the road. If he crashed his truck with Natalie in the passenger seat, he'd probably die from the horror alone. "I can't pull over into the woods, Natalie. I'm not risking you getting struck by lightning or . . . God, another flooded road—"

"I'm safe as long as you're with me."

Now she was stroking his ego, too? He was man enough to know when he'd lost a battle. "You're damn right you are, princess."

Her hand was going for broke now. Was someone singing opera in the rear cab of his truck or was that all in his head? "Taking a quick break from our argument to let you know this is the best hand job I've ever had in my life. And about ninety-nine percent of those were performed by me, an expert on my own dick. You're absolutely nailing it."

Those lips curved into a smile against his jaw, her low-pitched hum coursing through him. "You know what would feel even better..."

"Your pussy? Yeah, it's pretty much the only thing I'm capable of thinking about."

"Pull over," she cajoled, cupping and massaging his balls.

August gritted his teeth and searched for a break in the trees. There was one around here somewhere. He'd used it to make a K-turn a hundred times after forgetting to buy cat food at the store. Come on, come on. Point of no return. He was going to come in his pants.

There.

Every ounce of blood in his body was located in his lap, making his dick so stiff that he was dizzy by the time he parked the truck, threw open the driver's side door and dragged Natalie across the seat. Out into the rain. He couldn't get a breath, couldn't think about anything but getting inside her, where it was warm and he belonged and she'd get pleasure. Christ, he wanted that more than anything. To bring her off so hard she'd be delirious for a week. "All right, let's go." Door closed, he lifted her up against it and pinned her there. Rough enough to rock the vehicle. *You're twice her size.* "Natalie, I ... the adrenaline ..."

"I know what I'm doing," she breathed, arching her back. Giving him a long, hot look at her tits. Those stiff, rosy nipples. "I know what I'm in for."

"Just to clarify, though . . ." *My cock is going to explode.* "Very rough sex. With me. Now."

"Yes."

"No foreplay."

"No," she said, her tone reedy. "Please. Please. I want you to use me to get rid of the adrenaline. Now, August."

Her panties were ripped to one side, his sweatpants shoved down and he entered her in one fast, upward punch of his hips. And a series of images from his life flashed in front of his eyes. Learning to ride a bike, Hell Week, shopping for socks that would actually fit his big-ass feet. Not a single moment in his existence compared to this. Filling up his woman and finding her soaked as fuck, on the verge of coming from one thrust. "Damn, princess," he grunted, rattling the window of the truck with a series of quick drives. "Speaking of flash floods—"

"No."

"Sorry."

Their mouths locked into a kiss and she heaved a broken sound from her throat that made him feel sick with need. And she was ill with want, too. He could tell by the way she closed her eyes so tight during their breathless kiss, her legs wrapped so securely around his hips, he swore they were becoming a part of him. The way she had an orgasm almost immediately, her eyes flooding with anticipation, then going utterly blank, head falling back against the window, thighs quivering uncontrollably. "Oh Jesus, August, yes. Yes. *Harder.*"

This woman was a treasure. His hips were moving in a battering rhythm, cock harder than a fucking mallet, her ass squeaking up and down the wet door of his truck, and she was asking for more. "Anything you want."

"No, anything *you* want." She was shaking so hard mid-climax, he almost couldn't make out her words. "That's what I want."

"Oh yeah?" The tether inside him loosened and he snapped his teeth against her ear. "I want you to bend over like a good girl so I can hit it filthy from the back. How about that?"

August learned something about their relationship in that moment.

This woman didn't let him get away with jack shit.

Not unless he was giving her orgasms.

So apparently he'd be doing a lot of that.

August pried Natalie off the side of the truck and wrenched the driver's door back open. She dropped her legs from his waist and spun around, gripping the edge of the seat, hips tilted up, her panties half in tatters. He tore them the remaining distance down her legs, licking the crack of her ass on the way up, which was something he wouldn't mind doing every hour for the rest of his life, especially when she moaned and inched open a little wider. She panted his name, her smooth back puffing up and down. And hell, he was powerless to do anything but lick that pretty pucker some more, pressing between those tight cheeks and worrying his tongue against it. "*August.*"

"Mmmm."

She squirmed back against his face. It was truly a thing of beauty. "*August.*"

If he kept this up, he was going to try something he had no goddamn business trying today, when he couldn't be slow or gentle to save his life. "Coming, princess."

He lunged to his feet, pressing forward over Natalie's back and jerking her up onto her toes, her ass tucked like a dream into his lap. Then he reached down and pushed his cock home, shuddering over the enthusiastic way she welcomed him. She cried out and lifted her butt, giving him that deep access he needed so bad his nuts almost swore out loud.

"*God*, I love fucking you," he growled against her spine, gripping her hip in his right hand, holding on to the steering wheel with his left. "I love fucking my *wife*. I feel it in my chest, you know? It's never been like this. It's never going to be like this again for either of us. All right? We found it." He pressed his mouth to the nape of her neck. "You love fucking your husband." His palm slipped downward from her hip, delving between her pussy and the edge of the seat, massaging her clit with two fingers. "Say it back to me."

She heaved two big breaths, tweaking her hips back to meet his fast and furious pumps. "I love fucking my husband."

"Why?"

"It's so good. It's just so good."

"That's not all that's good, Natalie." He took his left hand off the steering wheel and plowed it into her hair, tugging her head back. Locking eyes with her from above. "It's good outside of bed, too. You know it is. We're just figuring it out. I . . ." This was what he'd secretly been worried about, all hopped up on adrenaline. Saying those three words too early. Scaring her. *Don't push for too much too soon.* "I need my wife. I'll *always* fucking need my wife."

Her breath caught and she blinked rapidly several times. Her response probably could have been delayed until later. There was a lot going on, between the pouring rain, thunder, the fact that he was thrusting into her body like humankind depended on him hitting that release button. But she surprised him, moved him, by pushing her back up against his chest, nuzzling her hair into his hand until his fingers loosened automatically to stroke her face. "I need my husband so badly, too."

Oh boy.

That did it.

His dizziness increased due to the palpitations of his heart and the pressure between his legs. It was system overload. Desperate to bring her with him, never wanting to go *anywhere* without her ever again, he rubbed her clit the way he knew would roll her eyes back in her head—and with a pair of strangled moans, they lost it. August dropped his face into the valley of her neck and came like a motherfucker, roaring through some rough punches of his hips, making her scream, kicking that second orgasm into overdrive until they were in a heap, draped over the front of the driver's seat.

He kissed her hair with what little strength he had left. "As long as you need me, Natalie, I'm with you. Whatever you decide, whatever happens, I'm your goddamn man."

"I know."

Several seconds ticked by, his chest swelling with every single one. "I love that you know." *I love* you. He kept those words from running loose by dragging his lips along the slope of her shoulder. She'd admitted she needed him, that she wanted longer than a month. He needed to be grateful and patient. For now. "Going to take you home—our home—and do everything I can to make sure you don't forget."

Chapter Twenty-Three

*N*atalie would say this for August.

He was making a very convincing case for staying in Napa.

She'd lost count of how many times they'd made love last night—the only marathon she'd ever participate in. They'd collapsed into bed after returning from the water rescue that afternoon, their naked skin pressed together head to toe, limbs intwined like they'd never let go. Hours later, she'd woken up aching for him. *Aching.* So badly that tears had escaped her eyes while she rode him, his fingers buried and twisting in her hair, his hips slamming upward while they feasted on each other's mouths.

The rest of the night and subsequent morning—a lot of which had been spent together in the shower—were a blur. But this wasn't. He was back in the barn without her, and it hurt more and more every time. And maybe it shouldn't. He'd hesitated in the doorway a few hours ago, doubling back and suggesting she help with the administrative side of Zelnick Cellar, like Corinne had suggested . . . but it felt a little like being placated. Or distracted.

So much of August's heart was made up of honor, but it was all tangled with Sam's memory. The way he toiled over the wine on his friend's behalf. The labor *was* his heart. But locking her out of the process meant he was still guarded. Not letting her in the whole way. And she was truly done settling for half measures when it came to love. That was what she'd gotten from her family, her friends, her colleagues, and Morrison.

It was all or nothing now. With August.

Maybe this was another definitive sign that she loved him.

Full trust was all she could accept.

She needed to focus on the positive—they both continued to evolve within the relationship.

He'd stuck around without storming off during their most recent fight. He'd made vows. Beautiful ones. Built her up in front of her family. Made her feel safe and cherished. Made her *laugh*. Told her he needed her.

That he was her man.

Did that mean she could simply call Claudia and shut down their concept in its tracks? Her last remaining New York friend had been loyal enough to promise to leave her job and come on board with Natalie. She'd done a ton of leg work over the last month, filing paperwork to register them as a business, making endless calls to find willing investors.

Now it was Thursday morning, one day before the scheduled meeting with potential investor William Banes Savage. This could be liftoff for them. The payoff.

Was she really ready to scrap their blood, sweat, and tears . . .

Not to mention the comeback she'd been dreaming about for months?

Her eyes strayed to the locked door of the barn, an impossible-to-miss dagger twisting in her breastbone. Was he making progress in there? Could she help in a roundabout way—and distract herself from life-altering decisions in the process? Yes. She'd call the bank and set up his loan meeting with Ingram Meyer. That wouldn't step on August's toes, would it?

Then she would call Claudia. Let her know that the plan to return permanently to New York was slightly less firm now. That way, if by some miracle she decided to stay, Claudia wouldn't be blindsided. They would have time to make sure her livelihood was protected.

Secure in her plan, Natalie picked up the phone and called the bank.

"Hello. This is Natalie Cates for Ingram Meyer, please?"

A moment later, Ingram's familiar voice filled her ear. "Mrs. Cates—I had a feeling I would be hearing from you. I assume you noticed the new zeroes in your account. Unless there is some kind of delay, the money should be there by now."

Zeroes.

Account.

Her trust fund. She'd actually forgotten to check if it had been transferred.

If that didn't tell Natalie her heart was here with August, nothing would.

"Thank you. Yes. I'm sure it's fine." She looked across the front yard to find August stepping out into the sunlight, pouring a thermos of water over his head. An unexpected swelling hit her in the dead center of her chest, her heart pumping so fast she struggled through an indrawn breath. Love. For better or worse, she was in love. "I'm actually calling about the loan appointment for August. Are you sure you can't sneak us in this week?"

AUGUST WATCHED NATALIE approach from the house and everything in his head went momentarily silent. Kind of like dropping from a helo into pitch-black water, everything just cut out except for the sound of his heart. *Boom boom boom.* If he got lucky enough to watch his bride walk toward him on a regular basis for the next sixty years, he'd . . . die a happy man?

No, not quite.

As long as she was breathing, he'd be negotiating for more time with the man upstairs.

Surely God would understand. Natalie was his finest masterpiece.

"Hey," he said, feeling totally and utterly tongue-tied in the presence of her looking so . . . relaxed. Soft in a loose denim dress with gold buttons down the front, hair in some kind of knot that looked like it could fall out at any moment. Maybe if he kissed her, it would just tumble down? Hell yeah. Sounded like a great idea to him.

You won't persuade her to stay with sex.

What was the key ingredient? What was he failing to give her? The answer seemed just within his reach, but the elusive thing always slipped away before he could define it.

She distracted him from his troubled thoughts with a smile. "Great news. I got us an appointment tomorrow morning to meet with Ingram about the loan for Zelnick. Eight thirty. He's going to sneak us in before business hours, since he has meetings for the rest of the day."

And August's stomach hit the dirt.

Right.

He still hadn't told her about the investment from his CO.

That he didn't need capital from the bank at all.

From the beginning, this had been about Natalie getting what she needed. Would she believe that, though, after so many men in her life had used money to control her? August wanted to trust that Natalie knew better than to think that about him. That he was different. But right now, when he'd just gotten her to consider staying in Napa, was not the time to spring a falsehood on her. Anything that might cause her to make the East Coast her final decision. They'd made a deal—and he'd been lying by omission the whole time.

If she left now, when they were so close to finding common ground, he'd fucking break.

So what did he do here?

If they went to the meeting, Ingram would take a look at his bank account and question why he needed funds when his numbers were already healthy, thanks to his CO. And if he *didn't* go to the meeting, Natalie would question him.

Come on, universe.

He just needed a little longer to make sure she was his—permanently.

"August?" she prompted, her smile turning puzzled.

"Yeah, princess. Tomorrow morning at eight thirty sounds good."

AUGUST HAD A habit of asking Sam for advice when he had no idea what to do. So that was where he went in the wee hours of the morning. He left the most incredible woman on the planet sleeping naked in his bed—painful, by the way—and he made the drive to the cemetery, making sure to leave enough time to get back for the bank appointment.

If he went through with it and didn't end up calling Natalie to cancel. Maybe it was wise to tell her the truth in front of witnesses.

The sun was just beginning to peek over the horizon when August sat down exactly five feet and nine inches from Sam's headstone, not wanting to sit on his friend. He wasted no time burying his head in his hands and blurting out everything that had taken place since the morning of the wedding. "If I had one wish, it would be for you to meet her, man. She is such a badass." Christ, he was welling up. "It feels like . . . one misstep and I'm going to lose her. I hope it doesn't feel this risky forever, but even if it did, I would stick like glue. She's worth walking through an endless field of landmines." He blew out a breath. "Tell me what to do about this bank meeting, man."

Usually, he could conjure Sam's voice out of thin air. Imagine what his friend would say. But this time, his imagination didn't comply. The sound of his friend's voice was growing more and more faint; he couldn't get the tone right, had no idea what advice Sam would give him—and the lack of reassurance and fogginess of Sam's memory was too much on top of everything else.

He lay back in the grass and closed his eyes, taking deep breaths so his emotions wouldn't run away with him. Not when he needed to be present this morning, because establishing his marriage to Natalie was his sole focus.

But when he closed his eyes, the stress of indecision caught up with him.

And he fell asleep dreaming of Natalie's smile.

8:52.

No August.

Natalie looked down at the screen of her phone, willing him to return her calls. Or one of the numerous texts she'd sent. They were late for the loan meeting with Ingram and honestly, they might as well not even bother going inside now. Ingram had only a thirty-minute window to spare and much of that was gone now.

This wasn't like him.

Then again . . . maybe it was?

They'd been married for only six days. Maybe it was totally within his character to leave before she woke up without any prior warning. And not just to push his tire—but to leave. Off the property. She'd gone looking for him around the house and in both barns, the unsettled feeling in her stomach yawning wider by the moment. Was something wrong? Did he have an emergency? Why didn't he wake her up to help?

Then she'd finally found the note, attached to her favorite coffee mug.

Went to see Sam.

Until that moment, she'd never speculated on when August might bring her to see Sam. Or if he ever would. But as close as they'd been yesterday and last night, the way she'd been so vulnerable with him, August going to the cemetery alone felt a little like being shut out. Again. Perhaps it wasn't a rational reaction, but tell that to her heart while it sank like a setting sun. August had a whole private part of his life, his grief, and he guarded it like a lion.

It was a part of him she'd never touch. She just had to accept that.

She'd just given herself to this man, not only in name now, but emotionally.

Less than a day later, she felt as if he'd dropped her without a safety net.

Reluctantly, she started her car and pulled out of the parking space in front of the bank. She didn't feel like going home, though. To August's house. It was too quiet without him there and she was looking for some reassurance, not more questions.

To be fair, she should have known that the Vos estate was the last place she should go. Maybe she was a masochist or maybe she had a tiny bit of hope that her relationship with Corinne was getting stronger. She'd surprised her mother with her research on VineWatch, right? Plus, if she and Corinne could relate to each other about anything, it was a man disappointing them. So home she went, with a frisson of hope in her chest.

It was doused the moment she pulled into the circular driveway and she saw two hybrids parked outside. The VineWatch logo was silk-screened onto their windows. Two men and one woman in khakis and navy blue polo shirts had just alighted from the vehicles. And Julian and Corinne were approaching them to shake hands.

She'd obviously just crashed their meeting.

A meeting they were having without her. As if she should be surprised.

Yet, she was? Obviously, she still had the capacity to be hurt by her family, because her stomach turned completely around and all she could do was stare.

Julian must have caught sight of her, because he was suddenly standing beside the driver's-side window, signaling for her to roll it down.

"Hey," he said warmly. "I'm glad Corinne decided to invite you to the meeting. I told her—"

"She didn't invite me," Natalie said dully. "I'm here by accident."

If that didn't sum up how she felt about everything, this entire day, maybe her entire life at this very moment in time, nothing did.

Julian straightened his tie, openly befuddled. "I see. She didn't want to interrupt your first week as a married couple with business. For the record, I knew you'd want to be here—"

"It doesn't matter, Julian," she said, sounding numb. Feeling hollow.

What am I doing in this stupid town?

Nothing had changed. She would always be the odd one out. In her family. In her marriage. New York was the only place she'd ever been a consideration to others. It was the only place her input had ever been *valued*.

Not here.

Never here.

"I have a business meeting tonight in New York, so I'll be wining and dining a tech billionaire at Scarpetta if anyone needs me," she said, putting the car in reverse, blowing off her brother's request that she stay and talk. She ignored the phone when it started to ring on the way home, too. August. When her mother started calling, as well, she turned the device off altogether. And it felt good. It felt good to slip back into that mindset of her early twenties, when she'd needed no one but herself. Natalie against the world.

They wouldn't even miss her.

Thank God she'd never called Claudia to cancel the meeting with William Banes Savage.

As soon as Natalie walked through the door of August's house, she opened her laptop and swapped her midafternoon flight for the next possible plane to New York. Feeling in control for the first time in months, she sent the boarding pass to her phone and tucked the laptop into her purse. One hour until she needed to leave for the airport and August still wasn't home. Was he having a hard time with the visit to Sam?

Not my problem. He's made that clear.

Pain carved a slice out of her chest, calling her a liar. She had to pause in the act of packing her small carry-on bag in order to breathe. It seemed that shutting herself off from August wasn't going to be an easy process. Not like it had been before, with her ex. With every ex, really. If recovering from breakups was an Olympic sport, she would have medaled in all events. Vaulting over the truth. Sprinting away from accountability.

She wouldn't win gold so easily in the August relay race.

Her chest was a dumpster fire. And leaving for the airport without saying goodbye wasn't going to give her the vindication she wanted. The way she kept staring at the front door of the house, hoping he would walk through it, made that obvious.

The barn caught her eye through the window. Off-limits. She wasn't allowed to go in there and mess with his fermentation process.

Well, too bad.

Natalie shoved her feet into some flats and stomped out of the bedroom, stepping over the sprawled cat on her way to the front door. She yanked it open, hating the way hope that August's truck would be parked outside rose in her chest. It was not. There was nothing but an empty slab of concrete decorated with oil stains.

With her heart in her mouth, she paraded into the barn. She was surprised to find that the farther she ventured into August's off-limits workshop, the more the bowstrings inside her chest loosened. Sure, she didn't have his express consent to be in there, among his things, but she'd never consented to him making her fall in love with him, only to be compartmentalized. Kept at a distance. Close but not too close, the way her family kept her.

August wasn't supposed to do that to her, too.

Natalie realized she was staring across the rows of oak barrels through a veil of tears. Her nose was on fire and those flames followed a trail of kerosine to the dead center of her chest, lighting up that sad, suffering organ and turning it to ashes. Partially.

Some part of it must have remained beating, because she swiped at her nose and pulled out the stopper from the first barrel, immediately recognizing the need for filtration.

Nobody wanted her help, especially August.

Well, that was too damn bad, wasn't it?

I FELL ASLEEP. How could I fall asleep with her waiting for me? How could I do that?

When August pulled into his usual spot outside the house, his stomach was already a bubbling cauldron of acid. Because she wouldn't answer his calls, they went straight to voice mail and now, her blue hatchback was gone. Natalie's car. Was gone.

He dove out of the truck and without missing a beat, started shouting, "*Natalie.*"

She wasn't inside the house. He knew it, because if she was anywhere in the vicinity, he would feel that welcome presence. Despite that intuition, he almost kicked down the door of the house, because his fingers wouldn't work well enough to unlock it, shouting her name the whole time.

When he got inside, it was dead silent. Menace sat perched on the edge of a dining room chair, her expression nothing short of a narrow-eyed accusation. Panic rising, he took out his phone and called Natalie, cursing a blue streak when it went to voice mail again. Maybe she'd just gone to Vos Vineyard? Maybe she'd been pissed off at him enough to move some of her things back to the guest house? Because, yeah. His wife was not in the bedrooms or the bathroom and her fucking toothbrush was gone, a fact that made his windpipe shrink to the size of a pinhole.

"No. No, no, no . . ."

Julian would know if she'd gone to the guest house.

He'd call Julian.

August didn't notice his hand was shaking until he hit the number for Natalie's brother. "Yes?" answered the professor on the second ring.

"Is Natalie there?" August barked into the receiver.

"She was. But she left." A long pause, some creaking. "That was over two hours ago. She's not answering your calls, either?"

"If she was, I wouldn't be calling you!"

"Good point," Julian said—and August really, really didn't like the fact that this normally unflappable dude sounded worried. "All right. Take a deep breath. She was obviously upset, I just didn't think she'd really *leave*—"

"She's upset because I missed our meeting at the bank this morning. I know. I went to visit Sam and I couldn't *hear* him anymore and I fell asleep. She wouldn't just leave because of the meeting, though. Would she? She'd be here to fight with me. She's supposed to be *here*."

Julian remained silent a little too long.

"What?" August asked, dread curdling his blood.

"Corrine and I had a meeting with VineWatch this morning. It started just after nine A.M. When Natalie showed up in the driveway, I assumed she was here for the meeting. But my mother hadn't invited her." He cursed under his breath. "I should have done it myself."

August was frozen in the middle of the kitchen floor. "Why wouldn't you invite Natalie to a meeting with VineWatch? She knows that company inside and out. Better than both of you put together."

"You're right. She does."

How was he still breathing with a fifty-ton anvil sitting on his chest. "So . . ." His swallow got stuck. "So you're telling me I missed the appointment at the bank. And then she showed up at Vos and found out you were having a meeting without her."

My wife.

My wife.

We crushed her. I crushed her.

August was back outside now and the chill of panic had taken firm hold of his jugular and both lungs. Barn. She wouldn't be in the barn, but he had to look anyway.

He'd asked her not to go in there. Now he was desperate to find her inside.

Funny how fast things could change.

No. It wasn't funny at all. He'd asked her to keep out of this place where he performed the ritual of winemaking in honor of his friend. He'd refused to involve her, just like her family.

Pushed her away where it counted, while expecting *her* to come closer physically and emotionally. All the while . . .

He'd been the one putting up the barrier.

"Oh my God, I'm such a fucking moron."

"August . . ." Julian sighed. "I haven't told you the worst part. She said she was going to New York. Having a dinner meeting at some place called Scarpetta. It's hard to tell if Natalie is being serious sometimes, but obviously . . . she went."

Jesus. No. In the middle of the barn, August's legs weakened. He dragged his hand down his face and viewed the barn and all of his equipment through raw, gritty eyes.

No wonder my wine sucks. It needed her. I needed her.

He was no better than her family. She'd tried so hard to get in, to be important to them, until eventually she gave up. He'd been so outraged on her behalf. Who could keep their distance from someone so incredible and smart and dynamic and lively . . . ?

Meanwhile he'd done the exact same thing.

He'd rejected her help. He'd rejected *her*. Denied them a chance to be closer because he insisted on feeling his way alone in the dark. He was like a man who refused to pull over and ask for directions, but a hundred times worse, because being valued, considered . . . it meant so much to his Natalie. He was supposed to be her safe place, but he'd been hurting her all along.

Now she was gone.

Somehow August knew something had changed before he even reached the row of barrels—and after pulling out a few stoppers, the difference was obvious. The wine had lost a lot of its cloudiness. Was less sluggish. And the taste wasn't a 100 percent improvement—not so soon—but by God, it was a hell of a lot better.

She could have been helping all along. And his stupid pride had kept her locked out.

"I fucked up," he croaked into the phone, falling forward onto his elbows. "I have to go."

"August, wait." August barely had the strength to keep the phone pressed to his ear. "It wasn't so long ago that I almost ruined things with Hallie. I know you must feel like absolute shit right now. God knows I do—"

August wailed something unintelligible.

"My mother and I both owe Natalie a serious apology. But you're the one who has to reach her right now. Act sooner than I did with Hallie. You'll have less of a hole to dig out of."

"I've been digging a hole from day one, man. I've reached China at this point."

"Start climbing out of it now." Julian paused. "Women have the capacity for forgiveness and compassion that men will never fully grasp. She might decide to spare your life."

That's exactly what it would be. Sparing his life. He could already feel the will to live deserting him slowly. "I'm in love with your sister. I love her so much."

"We've established this."

"She's only been gone for a little while and I already miss her so much—"

"August, this is getting weird."

"Okay. Sorry." He cleared his throat, tried to put some steel in his voice, but it sounded suspiciously like a sniffle. "Later, man."

"Goodbye, August. And good luck."

August dropped the device and buried his head in his hands. "Goddammit."

She'd gone to New York. Three thousand miles out of his reach.

Then you better get your ass to the airport, roared Sam's voice, back and louder than ever. *They probably don't have any extra leg-room seats left, but you'll survive.*

If August could have plucked those words out of the ether and crushed them to his chest, he never would have let go. Of course Sam had gone silent. August's conscience had probably been blocking those mental echoes from coming through.

Come on, August, you can make this right. I believe in you.

That final dose of confidence from his best friend was exactly what he needed to sprint toward the house. If his wife was on the opposite coast, that was where he needed to be, too.

Chapter Twenty-Four

There was a low buzz in the back of Natalie's head.

It had been there since she'd landed in New York. It was still there when she checked into the hotel, just off Park Avenue, and it was growing louder now as the potential investor spoke to her from across the polished table, talking about his recent trip to Mykonos. That was how these meetings worked. They didn't talk about money or investment strategies, it was all social chitchat until the last five minutes. Up until that point, every tick of the clock was spent determining whether she had reached a high enough social standard to even associate with.

In the not-so-distant past, she didn't even have to *take* meetings. Her portfolio did the talking. But that approach didn't work anymore. Her company might have asked her to step down quietly, but after an extended absence and without a successful firm to back her up, her stock as a financier had dropped significantly.

"You wouldn't believe the water," said the investor, crunching into some kind of crostini with lobster salad on top. "We couldn't tell where it ended and the sky began. We're thinking of going back for Christmas. Too many tourists in New York in December."

Based on her research, he was from Florida, but fine. Hate on people just trying to have a stinking vacation.

"Greece in December," Natalie forced herself to respond in a bright, interested tone. "That's the time to go, so you can avoid the heat." Was that even true? Natalie didn't know. She needed to get her head in the game here, but she couldn't seem to concentrate. Had August found her handiwork in the barn? Was he angry that she'd overstepped his boundary or . . . maybe he was surprised he didn't utilize her solution sooner and would use it, even if he didn't come up with it himself?

Fat chance. He was too stubborn.

And it was really, wildly ridiculous to miss him so much that her body was sore.

Did they really sleep together for the first time this week?

It felt like they'd been making love for a century.

"Ah!" The investor broke into her thoughts by signaling someone over her shoulder. "I see one of my colleagues at the bar. Shall we settle up here and join them?"

My God, this whole night was getting away from her. She'd flown three thousand miles to secure a chunk of this man's money. Claudia had busted her behind to pin him down for Natalie. Now that she finally had the chance, she was blowing it?

Natalie mentally shook herself and leaned forward. "Before we do that, Mr. Savage—and tonight is on me, of course—I would love to talk to you about the new venture—"

"Listen, Miss Vos, I'll be plain," he interrupted, wiping his mouth with the white cloth napkin and setting it aside. She could see the rejection coming a mile away and all she could think was *I'm not Miss Vos anymore. I'm Mrs. Cates.* "I appreciate the fact that you've flown all the way from Napa to take this meeting, but I'm not sure us getting into bed together is the best play for me."

It took a physical effort not to openly gag at his phrasing. "I understand your hesitation completely, of course. I've been out of the game for a while, but that's an advantage, not a drawback. I'm coming in with a fresh perspective. You're going to get more than the same stale plays from me. Sure, my firm is the epitome of young, but you have a reputation as a maverick. You take gambles, as well. Early on in your career, you invested in microprocessors before that kind of tech became a standard addition to every portfolio."

He smirked. "*My* gamble paid off."

Those four words made one thing painfully obvious. Savage knew she'd been fired. Of course he did. News like that didn't stay quiet in the financial sector, especially when she'd been such a visible force prior to disappearing. Tonight was the first time she'd looked anyone from the finance world in the face and had her demise addressed. It was a lot easier than she'd imagined it would be. Almost like the sting was gone. Being revered by power players was no longer the most important thing in her life. What was?

Or more specifically . . . who?

Natalie breathed through a wave of loneliness.

"Yes. It did pay off. But lately you've played it safe. See these men at the bar?" Briefly, she glanced over her shoulder and her stomach lurched. Morrison was there. Her ex-fiancé had just pulled out a stool for his new intended, the bartender setting cocktail napkins down in front of the pretty couple, saying something to make them both laugh.

Oh God, why hadn't she chosen a different restaurant?

This was a typical haunt for analysts. She recognized several faces at the bar.

Natalie turned back around, praying her face wasn't fuchsia. *Keep talking.* "To these men, safe equals stagnant. It makes them begin to wonder if there is a cash flow. Or nothing but dusty stacks languishing somewhere, waiting to be inherited. Is investing with me a gamble? Yes. But it's also a signal to the sharks that you've got more than enough money. Money to set on fucking fire, if you want to. Maybe that's the equivalent to investing with me. Ringing a bell that says, 'I take risks, I know something you don't know'? It opens more doors. It puts your name in someone's mouth when they're considering who to bring in on the investment of the century. It makes you fresh."

Natalie sat back in her chair.

Familiar faces at the bar were staring. She could feel heat on her back. They were slowly noticing she was in the same establishment as her ex and his future wife. They were hoping to see fireworks. More than likely, they also knew she was there to court this man's influence and were hoping to get a hint at the outcome. Sharks, indeed.

Had her spiel worked? It was difficult to tell. Savage no longer had his smirk, but he looked more irritable than inspired by her speech. He was wiping a corner of his mouth over and over again, unnecessarily, while considering Natalie closely. "I need a little more time to consider it," he said finally, throwing down the napkin.

Okay. That was more promising than an outright *hell no*.

Where was the sense of victory? Or even hope?

Totally absent, that's where.

She'd given the pitch her best effort. For herself. For Claudia. Might as well admit it, though. She'd been hoping he'd say no.

"Thank you," she said, reaching out to shake his hand firmly. The waiter set the leather booklet containing the bill in front of her and she dropped her card on top without looking at the price, on purpose, which brought the smirk back to his face. After the receipt was signed, they both pushed back from the table and stood. "I appreciate your time, Mr.—"

"You'll join us for a drink before you jet back to wine country, won't you?" He raised an eyebrow while flicking a glance over her shoulder. "Unless there's someone you want to avoid?"

Obviously, he'd seen her ex arrive. This was either a test of her mettle or he just wanted to pay Natalie back for pointing out his lack of risk taking at dinner. "If I made a habit of avoiding uncomfortable situations, I wouldn't be here right now at all."

He inclined his head, as if to say, *Prove it.*

"One drink, then," she said, tightly, turning on her heel.

It was worse than she'd expected. Every eye in the place was fastened on her. She'd rubbed elbows with most of these analysts and portfolio managers over the years at this very place, smiling while they gloated over their client list. Attended a couple of their weddings, even. Now she was nothing but tomorrow's gossip at the office.

Making eye contact with Morrison was inevitable and everyone was watching to see how it would happen. No matter how she handled this, they would embellish the story or recast her as scorned and jealous. But in this moment, the only person who mattered was the investor she was trying to woo. Although, God, being tested by this dude was getting exhausting. She was beginning to lose sight of why it mattered.

She also just really, really wanted to go home to August.

Swallowing the fistful of tacks in her throat, Natalie followed William the remaining distance to the bar and let her gaze drift across to where Morrison was sitting with his fiancée. Giving them a wave and smile wasn't nearly as hard as she expected. Actually, it felt kind of *good*. Like closure. But that didn't stop everyone around her from whispering. Snickering in their single malt scotch. Having yet another laugh at her expense—

The thought died in its inception when someone else walked into the bar.

August.

August?

No, her eyes had to be playing tricks on her.

How . . . ?

It . . . was really him. There was no mistaking the giant ex-SEAL for anyone else. His wide shoulders had been wrestled into a navy blue suit jacket, his hair brushed back and semi-damp, his face clean-shaven. He sucked all the unwanted attention away from Natalie like an extra-large vacuum. Men who'd been hunkered over the bar stood up straighter now, as if commanded, trying to compete with August's height and swagger.

Dear God, the swagger.

He walked in like everyone owed him a hundred bucks, but he was too lazy to collect.

Where had he found a tailor who could craft a suit big enough to fit three normal-sized men? And there was no use pretending it didn't make him look like sex on two thick, tireflipping legs. Head to toe, her flesh flushed and turned *tight*.

I'm flustered. I'm actually flustered by my husband.

Probably because the last time she'd seen him, he'd been

feeding her orgasms like candy. Just popping them into her mouth like Mentos.

More, please, sir.

Wait.

Natalie shook herself. What was he doing here?

Time slowed considerably when she met August's eyes. He'd rounded the corner of the bar, striding in that overly cocky way right in her direction, and now she was actually jealous for the first time that night. Because that suit clung to his powerful body the way she wanted to—wrapped around every inch of him, tied in a knot and worn out.

When August was a few feet away, however, something else rippled through the lust.

Joy.

Flat-out joy to see him.

That she wouldn't have to wait to be back in St. Helena. He was here.

He should have been here all along. They should have been *together.*

That was what the buzzing in her head had been trying to tell her.

Natalie held her breath as her husband came to a stop right in front of her. The loud conversation in the bar area had died down to a hum. Or maybe the waves crashing in Natalie's head were drowning out the sound? And they crashed even louder when August leaned down and kissed her cheek, his hand landing possessively on her hip. Squeezing in silent communication. *I missed you.* Or was she projecting?

"Excuse me for a moment, Mr. Savage," she managed, walking them out of earshot from her potential client. The scent of grapefruit washed over Natalie and she gulped it down greedily. "What are you doing here?" she whispered, pulling him closer by the lapels of his jacket, careful to keep at least an inch between their bodies. An inch they both, very obviously, were eager to eliminate if the rushing of exhales was any indication.

"You want the truth?" He turned his nose into her hair and breathed deeply. "I've been through Hell Week, injuries, training that nearly killed me, giving myself stitches without so much as an Advil. And none of it, Natalie, is worse physical torture than being away from you."

Blood rushed to her ears and started pounding. Movements around them seemed to be happening in a dream, all grainy and distant. The inch between them shrank until it no longer existed, the fronts of their bodies meeting, pressing, the rate of her heartbeat tripling. "I would have been home tomorrow."

"That isn't soon enough. Another hour wouldn't have been soon enough."

If she didn't armor herself immediately, she was going down. RIP Natalie. "I'm still angry at you for missing the meeting. For—"

"Shutting you out. Good. You should be. I fucked up. I've been fucking up since the start with you." His fist twisted in the back of her dress. "I'm sorry. I'm not making excuses, but I went to see Sam yesterday and it wasn't the same as it usually is. I can usually pretend he's there talking to me and this time I couldn't. I just sort of . . . shut off."

Denial hit her like a truck. Oh . . . no. She'd left him to deal with that alone?

"Then I'm sorry, too, August." Was everyone in the restaurant staring at them? How could they not be? But with their prying eyes shielded by the wall of August's body, she was in a little I-don't-care cocoon. "It's hard to focus on that when you're wearing this suit."

In her periphery, she saw his eye crinkle at the corner, lips twitching. "Even better than my wedding tux?"

She sucked down another breath of grapefruit, then pushed him away slightly. On second thought, she tugged him a tiny bit closer.

I'm losing my mind.

August took hold of her indecisive wrists without a word and dropped his mouth to the space right above her ear, rumbling, "Babe."

It was the equivalent of putting a pin in a balloon. She just unloaded. "I don't think I'm going to get the investment and . . . instead of business, it just feels like another man using money to make me dance, you know?" She watched the lump move up and down in August's throat. "Everyone is staring at me. They think I'm a joke. And Morrison just arrived out of the blue with his future wife, sitting at the bar, making me the live entertainment for the evening."

August stiffened at the mention of her ex. "How do you feel about seeing him?"

He'd made himself vulnerable by giving her the truth when he walked in. She couldn't do anything but return the favor now. "I don't feel a thing."

His chest shuddered up and down, tension ebbing from his burly frame. "And when I walked in?"

"I thought . . . you should have been here all along."

A gruff sound left him, throat muscles shifting in a pattern.

He opened his mouth to say something, but they were interrupted by Savage.

"And who might this be?" asked the potential investor. Was it her imagination or had he intentionally dropped the register of his voice several octaves?

"Mr. Savage, I would like you to meet my husband, August Cates."

"Husband?" The man reared back a little and he traded a glance with a few of the men behind him at the bar. "It must have been a whirlwind romance." He put out his hand for August to shake. Her husband didn't seem thrilled about letting her go long enough to conduct the greeting. "Call me William, please. Good to meet you. Sorry you couldn't make dinner."

August nodded. "Nice to meet you, too."

Savage studied her husband. "Are you some kind of athlete or something?" he asked, rolling a shoulder.

"I'm a SEAL. Been retired just over three years."

"You're shitting me! A Navy SEAL." The man dropped his drink onto the bar, with no awareness that it splashed onto the jacket of the closest patron. "When I was a kid, I wanted to be a SEAL. Talked about it until I was blue in the face. My father even set up obstacle courses in the backyard and called it toddler training. I'd love to hear some battle stories."

Her husband looked down at her. "I'm sure you've heard plenty of them tonight from Natalie already, though, right? I don't know a lot about the financial world, but a woman on Wall Street would have to fight harder than anyone, I imagine."

Savage laughed. "Harder than a SEAL? I'm not sure about that."

August's eyes seemed to darken a shade. "It's a different kind of fighting. And she has fought her way back here with almost no support. No one encouraging her to do it. God only knows where her inner strength comes from, but I'll tell you something, it's more than I've got. It's enough to keep putting herself out there with no reward and I feel sorry for anyone who doesn't take someone with that much bravery seriously."

It took everything inside of Natalie not to burst into tears. He was right. She'd been kicking ass and clawing her way back and that effort had gone unacknowledged. By anyone. And she wasn't the only woman who went about her daily grind only for people to expect *more*, so she liked to think all of womankind celebrated with her in that moment. When her husband finally *got* it. When he finally saw her.

The investor had gone from jocular to thoughtful during August's speech. He turned his attention to her now. "If I trust you with my money, what's your first play?"

Natalie took a deep breath and let it rip. "Obviously we're going with a classic long/short equity strategy. We make the smart investments that put us ahead and give us room to play and then we short technologies, pharma, oil based on bold predictions and market trends. And I'm not just talking about the United States. We're going to monitor markets and how consumers respond in every geographical location on the face of the earth, taking everything down to the fucking weather patterns into account. If your money isn't tripled in the first quarter, I'll give you back every cent of your initial investment."

A muscle hopped in Savage's cheek. August's pride was evident in every line of his body, but she couldn't risk looking at him or she'd lose her cool.

"I'll move some numbers around and call you on Monday," Savage said finally, holding out his hand for another shake from August, then he traded a shake with Natalie one more time and rejoined his friends at the bar.

"Holy shit, that was incredible," August whispered to her out of the side of his mouth.

"Be cool. Pretend I go off like that all the time."

"Done. But let's get out of here, princess," he exhaled. "These pants are too tight in the ball region."

Natalie shook her head to hide the creeping amusement, breezing past her husband and beginning the journey toward the exit. "Only you would make the romantic gesture of flying across the country and ruin it with ball talk in, like, eight seconds."

August followed so close behind her, she could feel his body heat through the clingy material of her dress. "Eight seconds is a lifetime when a man has no testicular circulation."

"Is this a ploy?" she asked over her shoulder. "When we get to my room, you're going to tell me you're medically required to get your pants off as soon as possible?"

"Well, not *now*, since you've called me on it. I'll have to save that idea for next time."

"Next time?"

He grunted.

They were passing by Natalie's ex and his fiancée. Both of them sipped their drinks and looked coolly at Natalie and August as they passed. Or maybe they were just wary? If she recalled correctly, she and her partner's daughter had gotten along great at company functions. The situation itself was simply awkward. Just not for Natalie. For some reason, she felt totally comfortable stopping beside the couple, laying a hand on both of their backs, and saying a heartfelt congratulations. She'd never really loved Morrison, so what was the sense in begrudging the fact that he'd found love elsewhere?

Her ex smiled at his intended. She smiled back. Simultaneously, they thanked Natalie.

Then she took August's hand and after a little tugging—August clearly wanted to say something to her ex—they continued toward the elevator that would bring them down to street level. "What were you going to say to him?" she asked as they stepped inside, the gold doors snapping together in front of them.

"I don't know. All I could think of was Julia Roberts's line in *Pretty Woman*. You know? 'Big mistake. Big. Huge.' But then you decided to be mature about the whole damn thing. Kind of caught me off guard." He shrugged those big shoulders. "That's probably a good thing. I'd rather be remembered for quoting something like *Rambo*. Or *Happy Gilmore*."

"Wow. You really just summed up your whole personality in two movies."

He grinned over at her. "Your turn."

Natalie let her head tip back. Gone was the stiffness that had been building since she boarded her flight. Fun. She was having fun. Did she always have fun with this man, even when they were arguing? "*Wall Street*. And *Bridesmaids*."

"Bam. Beautifully done."

"Thank you."

Without warning, August backed her up against the wall of the elevator, his mouth stopping just a whisper above hers. "You know I'm trying to follow your lead and be mature, but I actually wanted to punch your ex in the face, right?"

Deep down, she had. She'd known that like she knew her own name. "Yes," she breathed.

"Good. Just so we're clear."

"Hmm."

Her brain said, *Sex. Sex right here and right now.*

Unfortunately, the elevator doors opened to reveal a dozen people staring back.

With a muttered curse, August took her hand and led her through the throng of people, toward the street. "Where are you staying?" he asked, guiding her through the glass door of the building and out onto the sidewalk. It was a Friday night in a part of town where not a ton of bars were located anyway, so most of the pedestrians were working stiffs who'd stayed late at the office. But traffic roared by at its usual breakneck pace, horns bleeping expletives, music drifting out of car windows, passersby holding conversations on their phones.

"I'm one block down," she called up to him over the street noise.

"Ah." He nodded, pulling her closer to navigate the sidewalk traffic with a frown. "I'm all the way east."

Natalie battled the disappointment. "You . . . booked a room?"

"Yeah, about that," he answered slowly. "Believe me, I wish we were in a place where I could assume I'm staying in your room. Fuck. You have no idea. My dick is like the end of a hockey stick right now. You remember the way it curves when it's hard . . ."

"Yes," she all but panted. "I remember."

"Good." He tucked his tongue into his cheek for a second, seemingly to subdue a smile, but it dropped just as quickly. "It wasn't right what I did." She tugged on his hand to indicate they'd reached her hotel and they ducked into the lobby together. The city sounds were replaced with the soft murmur of conversation and piano music. But she could barely hear anything over August's voice and the pounding of her heart, especially when he guided her to a quiet corner of the lobby and looked down at her with such earnest intensity. "I asked you to give up everything and stay in Napa. I asked you to drop your defenses for me when I wasn't willing to do the same. I've been keeping you out, by refusing to let you help me solve my main problem at the winery. I see that now, Natalie. And I acted really fucking superior, like I had my end of this relationship all figured out. I didn't. I was the weak link. And I'm sorry. I'm sorry."

He brought her hands to his mouth and kissed her knuckles, leaving her heart fluttering wildly in her throat. Over his touch. His words. The perceptiveness of them.

She'd underestimated him yet again, hadn't she?

"You have no idea how badly I want to come upstairs with you. Honestly, everyone in the lobby is about to see a grown man cry. My dick might just hop right off my body, assume a human form, and punch me in the face. But, uh . . ." He blew out a long breath. "I saw you in that bar tonight and you looked like you were in the right place, all classy and confident and polished. You knocked that motherfucker's socks off. This is where you *want* to belong, if nothing else. I should have listened to you in the beginning. Maybe, uh . . . maybe I'm *not* the best thing for you. Natalie . . ." He leaned down, kissed her mouth gently, remaining there and breathing hard for a moment. Then, swallowing audibly, he took a step back, misery written on every one of his features. "I have to protect myself from getting in any deeper here, because you're going to leave, maybe you *should* leave. And every time we're together, you and me being apart seems more and more unthinkable."

Being apart? He assumed her decision had been made to leave Napa. Permanently.

On the plane ride here, that was where her compass had been pointing. New York.

For good.

Now she wasn't so sure. How could she remove herself from this man's life when he'd walked in tonight and stitched her back together just by existing? She was deeply in love with August Cates and somewhere along the way, that started meaning more to her than a comeback.

A *lot* more.

Her indecision was causing him to suffer, so she needed to make a choice. Now. Tonight.

And when she looked up at this man, there really was no decision to make at all, was there?

Chapter Twenty-Five

So this is love.

A painful motherfucker.

That old saying, *If you love somebody, let them go,* actually had real-life applications and it was galling and horrible, to say the least. But Jesus, what he'd said was the truth. She fit into that bar full of millionaires tonight like sugar in coffee. A much-needed dose of sweet among the bitterness. Gorgeous and ready to take on the world—it was right there on her face.

He'd felt like a jackass walking in there, stuffed into his suit. Palms sweating.

The truth of why he'd come wouldn't stay out of his mouth. Hell, telling Natalie how he felt about her was becoming this thing he *needed* to do to breathe. But taking her to bed knowing she would come back to this city one day soon and stay? Might as well perform open heart surgery on him without the painkillers.

Those fancy hotel elevators would take them upstairs. To a room with a really nice bed and, yeah, that business formal dress she was wearing would come off so easily. Just slide right down to the floor. He'd get on his knees and eat her out until her head spun. She wouldn't be nearly as polished when he finished with her.

"August, about what you said . . . " she began, then paused to arch an eyebrow. "I can tell what you're thinking about."

August sighed, resisting the urge to adjust his erection. "I doubt that."

She blinked innocently. "You're not thinking of going down on me?"

Now it was August's turn to blink. And he did. About ninety-six times. "Did you not hear a word I said before? About protecting myself?"

"Yes, I did." She took a long breath. "I heard you and I understand. You're right. The more time we spend in bed together, the more difficult it would be to part ways."

That sounded like a pretty damn good reason to go upstairs, now didn't it?

August gnashed his molars together and tried to smile at the same time.

Everything hurt. His heart, brain, and dick were a trifecta of misery.

"I'll wait here while you go upstairs." He shoved both hands in his pockets to keep from reaching for her. "Call me when you're inside the room with the door locked. And a chair wedged under the door, too, princess. You wouldn't believe how easy it is to disengage those little safety latches."

"August—"

"Please, Natalie, you have to go. I'm losing my resolve. You have no idea how bad I need you right now."

Because, God, she was beautiful. The whole lobby had to be staring at his wife. If he could tear his eyes off her for a second, he might be able to confirm. He'd have flown back and forth between coasts for the rest of his life, just to be standing there to hear her voice. He also knew a long-distance relationship between them would never work, because he'd resent every second away from her and he still had a responsibility to Sam. And now to his CO.

The reminder of his commanding officer forced him to recall what Natalie had said back in the bar. *I don't think I'm going to get the investment and . . . instead of business, it just feels like another man using money to make me dance, you know?*

He'd come to New York to lay his faults at her feet, but he couldn't bring himself to tell her he'd kept a two-hundred-thousand-dollar investment a secret. She was already most likely leaving him, did he really have to make her hate him, too? Put him in a category with her father, the investor, *and* the ex-fiancé? His heart wouldn't withstand the blow.

What was going on in her head right now? A groove had formed between her eyebrows and she appeared to be trapped between a rock and a hard place. Was this it? Was she going to end things right here and now?

"August, I need you to walk me to my room—"

"Natalie . . ." His tongue thickened in his mouth and his hands felt stupid because they weren't on her. "I can't do that and not come inside."

Don't think of their wedding night.

Don't—

Too late.

He'd think of her mouth that night in his final moments on earth.

Right now, however, he needed to make it through a few more minutes. After which he would take a cab back to his hotel and get to his room as fast as possible. Then he would pull up those pictures that he'd added to his camera roll from social media and stroke one out to Natalie in her wedding dress. If that wasn't a sign that he'd grown obsessed with this woman, nothing was. He actually got off remembering the moment she'd vowed in public to be his wife. That couldn't be normal.

Natalie gripped the meatiest part of his arms and shook him. "August. I know. I know you can't walk me to my room without coming inside." She slid her palms up, along his shoulders and higher, cradling his face. It felt so incredible, he had to stifle a moan. "You don't have to protect yourself. That's what I'm trying to tell you. I'm coming home with you. To St. Helena. I'm staying there. With you. *Because* of you."

What?

August's lungs were suddenly empty, the lobby sounds dulling to a whisper around him.

Had someone slipped him an Ambien on the plane and he was dreaming this whole scenario, because he could have sworn Natalie just said she was coming home with him.

His entire body was one big pulse and he could barely gather his thoughts over the booming noise it made. "I don't understand. You're coming back to stay, even though I've been a jackass? Even though you have the trust fund? And the investor?"

"You're better than all of those things," she whispered, eyes shining.

He doubled over, bracing his hands on his knees, doubt finally giving way to joy, which spread through him like wildfire. "You better not be pranking me."

"Take me upstairs and find out."

They took a giant step toward each other at the same time, Natalie tucking her small, elegant hand into his larger one. Their fingers threaded together and held.

Christ, what a privilege. This was happening. It was actually happening.

The elevator ride to Natalie's floor was a blur. He couldn't even scramble enough brain power to kiss her, because it was all occupied with relief and shock and happiness. So much happiness. Doors opened, feet moved along a carpeted hallway, and with her room in sight, their official reunion imminent, his brain finally, blessedly came back online. Mostly.

When had he backed her up against the door? Their mouths were a breath away from touching, her tits flattened against his chest. He was *burning alive* with the need to give her an orgasm. Hearing her demands, feeling those fingers twist in his hair, her pussy clamping down—

"Stop thinking about it, August, and do it." She licked into his mouth slowly, dragging his bottom lip through her teeth. "Bring me inside. Put me up against the wall."

If a hotel guest happened by at that moment, they would have assumed Natalie was being mugged, he reached for her bag so fast. "Key, princess. Key."

A desperate sound bubbled out of her, both of them fumbling to get the clasp open on her purse and locate the card. He slapped it up against the sensor, groaning when the light turned green, and walked her into the room, kicking the door shut behind them. As horny as August was, spurred on by her request for wall sex, he expected to be the aggressor.

He was wrong.

Natalie shoved the jacket off his shoulders and started to unknot his tie, abandoning the task halfway through to work on his belt, leaving the tie sagging around his neck. Spoiler: nothing else was sagging. A fact Natalie discovered a few seconds later when she unzipped his fly and stuck her hand inside, molding it around August's cock.

"Oh my God," she moaned, riding her palm up and down the length of him, making him pulse. Making him grow impossibly thicker. "I know I'm being redundant at this point, but I need you to know you . . ."

He pressed her up against the wall, dragged her mouth into a frantic kiss. *I'm kissing my woman. Thank God.* "What?" he said, breaking for air. "You need me to know what?"

Her eyes were glassy, dazed. Needy. "You have the best dick," she whispered. "I mean, I-I was thinking about it on the plane. During a business dinner. If you mass produced a mold of this thing, a lot of people would be less angry."

"Nah, but it's just yours, Natalie," he rumbled, hiking up the hemline of her dress with rough hands, so turned on now he was almost in pain. If she kept talking about how much she loved his cock, he was going to nut right there in her hand. "You don't really want to share it with anyone else," he said in between kisses, his hips pumping, pushing his length in and out of her perfectly tight fist. "Do you, babe?"

He tugged her panties down, over her knees, letting them fall to her ankles.

"No," she gasped, trembling. "Never."

She looked vulnerable after the admission, so he made his own, something inside him demanding he match her step for step. Emotionally, physically. At all times. "I was preparing myself to live off memories of you for the rest of my life. It was going to kill me." He knelt down in front of her, drawing her right knee up and settling the arch of her foot on his shoulder. "Can't believe I get to live off you, instead. Can't believe you're *letting* me live."

The tenderness in her eyes undid him to the point of dizziness. "There's no letting here. You're the best decision I've ever made."

A gruff sound left August, his desperation to be joined with this woman growing to the point of pain. He wanted to lock himself to her emotionally, physically. Any manner available. She was his wife and she'd soaked herself in anticipation of his mouth, his cock. The sense of responsibility to deliver, to give her pleasure and heal both of their wounds, had August surging forward and kissing her mound. Traveling lower. Pushing apart her flesh gently with his tongue and finding that bud, greeting it carefully, then with more vigor as her moans increased in volume and her fingers ripped at the strands of his hair. *"August."*

"I know," he growled into the next lick. "I know you love that."

He trailed the fingertips of his right hand up her left inner thigh, leaving a trail of goose bumps behind. While she was struggling to breathe, he traced the seam of her pussy with his middle finger, then tucked it deep, all while flicking his tongue against her clit. And she just sort of melted back against the wall, her flesh clamping around his knuckle, begging for a second finger. So he gave it to her in one possessive shove, then kept his digits pumping in and out of her while he stood, taking her mouth from above in a starved kiss.

"Against the wall, yeah?" he panted. "Been thinking about that?"

"Yes. Because you're so strong," she blurted, immediately shaking her head. "I don't know why I keep saying these things out loud."

"Keep doing it." He lifted her up and pinned her to the wall, pressing their foreheads together and looking her in the eye. "Never hide from me."

"I won't," she breathed, lifting her knees and settling them on his hips. "I . . . can't."

Victory and elation and a million other emotions rocked August. *My wife. My wife.*

He punched his hips upward and sank deep, groaning into the wall beside her head while she whimpered through her first orgasm. "Left you primed for that one, didn't I? You love the way I tongue fuck it."

"*Yes.*" She continued to gasp and squirm between him and the wall, her thighs shaking around his hips, those golden eyes latched onto his. "More. More of you."

"As much as you need." He hooked his arms beneath her knees and started to drive hard. Fast. "As much as I need, too. Going to have you upside down and backward tonight, then carry you all the way back to California where you belong. In our home. With your man."

"Yes." She hiccupped, her thighs pressing in tight around his ribs, crying out when he yanked them open wider and increased the pace of his thrusts, boosting her up the wall with each one, her tits bouncing in the neckline of her dress. "Oh my God, it's so *good.*"

"*Mine* is good?" He bit down on the side of her neck. "Crossed the motherfucking country for this tight wife pussy." The way she clenched at that admission, growing wetter, hotter, around his driving flesh, burned away the last of his leftover self-preservation. There was only her. She was all he needed to survive and the truth of that, *his* truth, came pouring out. "Fuck it, I'm obsessed with you. I can't remember a time when I wasn't. Give me the orgasm. Give it to me, princess. Yours. *Come on.* I fucking need it."

Natalie speared her fingers into his hair and brought him in for a wild, almost animalistic kiss, eager little sounds coming from her throat. She was close, so close—and then her trembles turned to an earthquake, her lips releasing his to cry out, her body still getting pummeled up against the wall. His grunts turned to growls, his hips slapping upward between her thighs, eagerly experiencing her orgasm along with her. The throb and clench of his *wife.*

"Fuck, fuck, *fuck.*" August's climax was like reaching land after parachuting at night into the ocean. For a while there, he thought he'd die, and then came the relief. Relief so utterly thorough, his legs almost gave out halfway through, but his body wouldn't allow him to stop. He drilled her ass to the wall and held, shaking so hard his teeth chattered, muscles screaming from the strain. "Natalie. *Christ.* Oh Christ . . . *I love you. I love you.*"

His chest nearly caved in after saying the words, but he couldn't hold them back, because they belonged to her. *He* belonged to her, and she should know it. Maybe she wasn't quite able to say it back just yet. And that was okay. He should *expect* her to be hesitant after keeping her at a distance. He'd wait forever, for the rest of his life, for those three words from her, if necessary. For now, he should just be grateful she was coming home.

As soon as he'd finished completely, he stumbled on half numb legs to the bed, Natalie safe in his arms, and he lay down, pulling her as close as possible, kissing his way across her hairline. Her warm breath bathed his throat and he wrapped his arms tighter, drawing the duvet around their half-naked bodies as best he could when they were on top of the covers. "August, I don't think you realize what it means to me that you came all the way here," she said softly. "I don't think you realize how valued and important that made me feel. Thank you."

It took him a moment to swallow the sideways pencil in his throat. "You're the most important person in my life, Natalie. You always will be."

Her fingertips were busy for a moment in his chest hair, before they stilled and she exhaled slowly. "The day you rescued Teri Frasier and her kids from the flood . . . that's when I realized I was in love with you, but when you walked in tonight, I . . . you felt like my husband. You were my real husband for the first time, and I loved you so much. I love you so much—"

"Oh my God." August's body moved on its own, tackling her into the pillows, covering her entire body with his. Holding her down as if to trap the words before they fluttered away. His heart was no longer beating in his chest. It was up in the clouds somewhere. There was a strong likelihood he was crushing her and wouldn't that be ironic? Woman admits to loving man, is immediately smothered to death. But he wasn't in control of his own body. It was fucking shaking, he was so humbled and grateful and in love. So in love he didn't know how one body, even his big-ass one, could carry it all. "You love me, Natalie?"

"Totally. Completely. I *love* you, August."

A warm balm spread across his soul. "We're going home to run the winery together, okay? It's ours as well as Sam's. I'll do better."

She captured his face in her hands, her damp eyes looking into his equally moist ones. "I'll do better, too. You're not the only one who's imperfect."

"Agree to disagree." He kissed her hard. "Tell me again that I'm your real husband."

"You're my real husband," she breathed, a tear slipping down her cheek. "Now show me."

When she rolled over and pressed her bare ass into his lap, he needed no further encouragement. He'd show her every single day, for as long as he lived.

Chapter Twenty-Six

The morning after they'd returned from New York, the air tasted sweeter, her chest felt lighter, and she was more optimistic than she'd been in a really long time. Not the desperate, edgy kind of optimism that came with trying to climb the finance world ladder, but . . . a calm sense that she was in the right place. That she might just be enough on her own without having to prove herself over and over again.

While waiting to board their flight at JFK, Natalie had called and explained everything to Claudia and offered to compensate her for all the time she'd spent working on their start-up. Of course, she'd accepted, because smart was smart. Natalie's loyal friend may have even seemed a little happy that her marriage to August was going to stick. Not that she would ever admit it. Natalie had also left a message with Savage's assistant letting him know they would no longer require the investment. Unless he fancied putting his money behind a winery with a one-star Yelp rating.

No word back yet.

Julian and Corinne had been waiting in August's driveway when they pulled up, having been alerted of their arrival back in

Napa via text from August. Her mother actually apologized—
and meant it, unless Natalie was totally mistaken. Her mother
genuinely hadn't wanted to bother Natalie with business on
"her honeymoon" but would be including her in all interactions
with VineWatch going forward.

"Not only that, I'll be grateful for your input," her mother
had said.

Yeah. The air felt different today. Easier to inhale.

Natalie stopped short in front of the production barn.

Even after August's assurance that no part of the winery was
off-limits to her anymore, she still couldn't bring herself to simply walk inside. Her husband stepped into view inside the barn,
waving at her from the dusky interior, a leather apron pulled on
over his white T-shirt.

"Morning, princess."

Warmth trickled through her at the husky familiarity in his
voice and she had to force a sip of coffee past the lump in her
throat. "Morning."

He cleaned his hands on a rag a lot longer than seemed necessary, all while looking her over. "I was hoping you could help me
out in here today."

Her fingers flexed around the coffee mug, happiness popping
like bubbles below her throat. "You're sure?"

"Yeah," he said gruffly, his attention falling to the wine barrels
briefly, then shooting back to her eyes. "I need you."

Natalie shook her head. "You can take some time letting me
in, August."

He looked prepared for that response, because his expression
didn't change one iota. His voice remained even, though the latter seemed to require an effort. "You're in, Natalie. You're in deep

and that's where I want you. I can't do this for Sam by myself. I need you with me. I've needed you with me all along." He paused. "That's probably why I couldn't hear him the other day. He was giving me the silent treatment until I pulled my head out of my ass. He's back now."

Natalie breathed in and out very carefully, positive too big of an inhale would snap her in half. "I'm so glad, August," she whispered unevenly. "I'm glad he's back."

"I was trying to beat back my guilt for not saving Sam by doing this all myself, but the truth is . . . he never would have wanted that." He looked around at the interior of the barn, as if seeing it for the first time. "He never would have wanted me to succeed at his dream . . . at the cost of you." His eyes found their way back to her. "Because you're my dream. He'd want me to have you as much as he wanted this place. And . . . I'm the one who is still here. He'd tell me to cut the shit, quit feeling guilty, and live this dream with my wife."

It was hard to find words, let alone the right ones in that moment, so she simply spoke from the heart. "You were lucky to have Sam, August. But he was lucky to have you, too."

"Thanks." Clearing his throat, he shoved the rag into his pocket hastily. "Jesus, I can't believe I ever asked you to stay out now that I want you in here with me so fucking bad, Natalie."

"Okay, I'm coming," she said breathlessly, desperate to stop his flow of words before he said something, a final thing that would make her crumble. "Okay." She cradled her mug against her chest and approached him, her pulse ripping into an unruly rhythm the closer she came to August and his big leather apron. "You don't have to be so dramatic."

"I'm completely dramatic over you. Deal with it."

She slipped past him into the production facility, the fronts of their bodies brushing together and making their breath catch. "If I have to deal with your drama, you have to deal with my speech about the intricacies of a grape."

"Done." He followed behind Natalie, leaving her almost no room to breathe. "I'm all ears. And muscles, because obviously. Lay your intricacies on me, princess."

Natalie stopped in front of the racked barrels, noticing immediately that August had spent the morning filtering the ones she hadn't had time to do on Friday.

She looked at August to find a serious expression on his face, arms crossed.

He wasn't just paying her lip service, he was actively following her lead.

"Um . . ." She wet her suddenly dry lips. Why was her pulse going so fast? "Well. The character of a grape depends on a lot of factors. Climate, soil, whether the vines were stressed or understressed, the temperature at which they were picked and stored. I'm sure you're aware by now of tannins. They provide texture. They give the wine structure." She glanced back at the equipment behind her that was no longer in use. "You appear to have given the wine a short maceration time at a warmer temperature. That's a good practice for extracting those tannins. Where you're going wrong is the fermentation period."

"The filtration helped," August said without shifting his attention from her face. "I tasted some and didn't want to curl up and die. But it still needs a lot of work."

"Yes. We've removed the bacteria and excess yeast. But we need to continue to blend our wine. It hasn't been given enough oxygen."

"Sort of symbolic, isn't it?" He swooped in and kissed the side of her neck, lingering there for a second, wetter one. "The blending of two lives . . ."

"Are you going to be this romantic all the time?" She gasped as his lips moved hotly over her ear. "Or is it all the bacteria talk getting you worked up?"

"I'm going to give you all the romance you can stand, Natalie queen princess Cates." His smile was flirtatious against her mouth. "But mainly, it's all the 'our wine' and '*we* need to continue to blend' talk. It makes us sound like a team."

"That's what we are," she whispered, her emotions vibrating like a tuning fork. "Isn't it?"

"No, Natalie. Like I told you . . ." His forehead dropped to hers. "We're the dream team."

She smiled on the heels of their kiss. "I think you just named our first vintage."

"First of many."

A HANDFUL OF days later, on the way home from buying August socks without holes—seriously, he didn't own a single intact pair—Natalie had the craziest urge to pull over and buy flowers, too. The shopping trip was quite a departure from her usual routine of popping into one of St. Helena's many wine stores around four P.M. for a bottle—and backup bottle—of Cabernet. Who was this person she was slowly turning into? She hadn't even blow-dried her hair this morning, she'd just showered and let it dry in haphazard waves, because she couldn't wait to meet August in the facility, where he was already up and working.

Each morning, while she drank her coffee, she watched him from the window of the house, smiling into every sip as he continually glanced over his shoulder, waiting for her to come join him. Visibly eager to have his partner in crime out in the barn at his side. She'd gladly given up her blow-drying time in the mornings just to watch it. Observe how much he wanted her company. How much he wanted her around, all the time.

Now, Natalie pulled onto the dusty shoulder, parked, and got out. She had groceries in the back of the car so August could make them dinner tonight, because some things would never change. She wasn't going to become a chef, in addition to becoming a vintner. There was only one cook in the family, as evidenced by her pitiful attempt at eggs yesterday. Genius move, marrying a man who was accustomed to surviving on field rations—he'd choked them down without blinking and appeared only mildly seasick afterward.

On her way to the flower stand, her heart swelled so much that her entire chest felt like a struck funny bone. The gooey sensation melted down into her fingertips and tingled there. And she walked faster, wanting to get home.

Something inside her was healing at a rapid rate, not only because of this love stampede that had totally trampled her beneath its hooves. But because she'd pushed for exactly what she needed and deserved. She'd accepted nothing less and the *reward* . . .

It reminded her of the wild blooms that burst from all corners of the road-side stand. Colorful. Beautiful. Every time she looked at one of the bouquets, she saw something new, something different. She'd spent a long time on one side of a wall, with her fear of rejection, and August had been behind a different one. They couldn't see each other until they'd both climbed over and met in the middle. In a sea of flowers.

Or grapes, as it were.

"What'll it be? The roses or the lilies?"

Natalie's head came up, a puzzled expression on her face. She hadn't narrowed it down to two options yet. Was the flower vendor speaking to her?

A gentleman she hadn't noticed before had approached from the opposite end of the shoulder. Wait . . . she recognized the man. It was August's CO. Commander Zelnick. What was he doing back in St. Helena?

The commander glanced at Natalie from the corner of his eye and nodded politely, but he obviously didn't recognize her—and no wonder. Last time she met the man, she'd been in a skirt and blouse with perfectly coiffed hair and makeup. Currently, she was in a loose pair of boyfriend jeans, a tank top, and no bra, with sunburned cheeks, and she looked like she'd just been through a wind tunnel.

She approached the CO slowly, intending to reintroduce herself and ask what had brought him back to St. Helena, but he spoke to the vendor first. "I'm not sure. I met her only once, but I think she's more the roses type."

Was it possible . . . he was here to visit August and those flowers were for her? More than possible. It was likely. Who else could this man know in a town where he didn't reside?

As the flower salesman went about wrapping the roses in paper, Natalie approached, clearing her throat softly. "Excuse me, Commander Zelnick. It's me. Natalie. August's wife." There was no way to stop the smile that spread across her mouth after saying those words, so she simply let it grow and held out her hand for a shake. "I think you're buying me flowers?"

After a moment of clear confusion, he merely looked chagrined. "I'm sorry." He shook her hand once, firmly. "I didn't recognize you."

I don't recognize myself these days.

At least all the new, good parts.

Natalie nodded. "I thought as much." She gestured to her dusty jeans. "We've spent some time out working in the vineyard today, cultivating the soil. I ran to the store to grab some ingredients for dinner—more than enough for three. I assume you're on your way to see August?"

"I am. Have to keep a soldier on his toes." He accepted the bouquet from the vendor, hesitated, then handed them to her with a slight blush, making her laugh.

"They're beautiful. Thank you. And you're right, I'm definitely the roses type."

"Excellent." He handed the man behind the counter a twenty and told him to keep the change. "I suppose I'll see you in a few minutes at Zelnick Cellar. I'm interested to see how August has taken advantage of my investment. Maybe some new equipment, or . . ."

He trailed off, expecting Natalie to jump in with an answer. She didn't have one.

Investment?

Obviously not picking up on the fact that she was stunned, the man continued on while unearthing his car keys from the pocket of his slacks. "I know it has been only a few weeks, but I'm eager to see what improvements have been made."

A few weeks.

The commander had given August money? For the vineyard?

They'd been in such a happiness haze since returning from New York, they hadn't really spoken about the missed appointment with Ingram at the bank. They'd made no move to reschedule. August hadn't even brought it up. If his commanding officer had given August an investment weeks ago, had he ever needed a bank loan in the first place?

Had he been keeping a secret, too?

Had he even *needed* to marry her?

"What investment?" she croaked.

AUGUST TOOK THE rag out of his back pocket and swiped it across his sweaty brow, a smile curving his lips when he heard a car pull up in front of the house. *Honey, I'm home.* He'd been begging Natalie to utter that phrase just once and she'd refused, but he'd get it out of her eventually. Maybe tonight. Maybe *now*.

He stripped off his shirt.

Went to the back door and did a few pull-ups on the doorframe, hoping it would make his muscles pop. His wife was a sucker for these pecs, which was only fair, because he was a sucker for her. The week since returning from New York was not just the happiest of his life, it was the happiest of *anyone's* life, and he'd fight whoever disagreed.

As if he could even locate enough irritation inside himself to throw a punch. He was all sunshine and doves below the neck these days. His wife was really his wife. She was happy with him. She actually fucking *loved* him back, this human work of art. With every passing day, he discovered more about her, too.

Her ticklish spots, her very precise routine in the shower that involved around nine different products, all of which smelled like goddamn heaven, the silly voice she used to speak to the cat when she thought he couldn't hear.

The hopeful way she talked about her family as they continued to reconnect, the intent way she listened, like she couldn't wait to be his confidant, the way she sometimes just needed a rubber band for her hair. Seriously, he'd started keeping a collection of the little black bands on his wrist, because she could never seem to find one, despite the fact that they were *everywhere* in the house. Sometimes all he had to do to make her smile was hand her a rubber band so she could put her hair up in one of those crazy knots. The first time it happened, she'd looked at him like he'd just turned his chair around for her on *The Voice*.

They fought over control of the television remote.

They fought over *a lot* of things.

She couldn't cook for shit.

And he loved her with the fire of a thousand suns.

Which made those fights end pretty damn quickly, because his chest started to sting and all he wanted was to make her happy again. It helped that she didn't like fighting with him anymore, either. She'd grumped at him this morning before her coffee and two minutes later, she'd been crawling onto his lap at the dining room table with apology kisses. Leading to apology sex. His nuts were back in a knot right now, just thinking about how she'd pouted the word *sorry* against his mouth, straddling him.

Rocking just once on his lap and liquefying his brain.

Was it possible to marry her again? Or did he have to wait a certain number of years to renew their vows?

This phenomenal woman had snuck over barriers he didn't even know existed inside him. She'd started helping him bring Sam's dream to life . . . and slowly it was becoming their dream, too. Yeah, it was becoming *theirs,* and that was more than okay. It was his life now and he desperately wanted to go on living it forever.

August dropped down from the doorframe after a few more pull-ups, his brow knitting over the arrival of a second car. Who was that?

When he walked out of the barn, the person he needed to see was Natalie—and he did. Briefly. She glanced at him with a strange look on her face as she slipped into the house with a bunch of roses in her arms, shutting the door behind her. What the hell was that?

He started after her, stopping short when his CO climbed out of the second car.

"Cates."

As always, his spine snapped straight at the sound of his commanding officer's voice, but his mind didn't follow. Not this time. Something was up with his wife. Why was his neck tingling like danger was imminent?

Commander Zelnick approached with his hands clasped behind his back. "I don't mean to keep surprising you like this, Cates, but I never know when I'm going to get enough free time to drive up from Coronado." He nodded at the barn. "I trust things are on their way to improving."

"Yes, sir," he said automatically—and it was the truth—but a hundred-pound weight had dropped in his stomach and something was prodding the edges of his consciousness. "Sir, would you mind waiting here a moment while I figure out my wife?"

He didn't mean it to sound ridiculous, but his mouth wasn't connecting with his brain. She'd stopped to buy flowers? For their house? Why did that make him feel like there was a potato sack race happening inside his chest? And why hadn't she smiled at him?

Was something wrong?

Yes. Something is wrong.

He'd been avoiding thinking about it during their week of bliss, but with the appearance of his commanding officer, the monumental thing he'd been keeping from Natalie jumped up and dug its teeth into his jugular. Every time he thought he had gathered enough courage to tell her about the investment, he recalled the way her father and ex-fiancé had manipulated her with the contents of their bank accounts. Or her trust fund. Not to mention, the investor she'd met with in New York. How she resented their refusal to be straightforward about money.

A little longer, he kept thinking. *I'll tell her about the investment once some time has passed since my last fuckup.* Really, it had been just over a week since he'd sent her running to the other side of the country. They were so happy. He'd just wanted more things about their marriage in the pro column before he added *deceptive about money* to the con side.

"Of course, go greet your wife," the CO answered, laughing. "Didn't recognize her at the flower stand. She looks different. Good different. Happier."

"Thank you," August managed, pulse rollicking. "Did you . . . you didn't mention the investment, did you? I haven't told her yet."

The man only looked confused. "Why not?"

"It's complicated." August sort of just doubled over, catching himself with hands on his knees, releasing an unsteady exhale. "You did tell her. She knows."

"It came up, yes."

"Oh fuck."

"Cates?"

"Sorry. Oh fuck, sir."

This was bad. This was very bad.

His spleen was seconds from erupting, and he didn't even know where his spleen was located. Or its function.

Fix it. Fix it now.

"I need some time with Natalie, sir," he said, winded. "If you hear glass breaking or doors slamming, don't worry, that's normal around here."

"Should I come back later?"

August took a deep breath on his journey toward the house. "That's probably a good idea, sir."

With a brisk nod, the commanding officer strode to his car, as if a battle awaited.

And it did. The big one.

Why the hell had August kept this from her for so long? Didn't he know better by now?

August paused with his hand on the doorknob, then opened the door carefully, waiting a beat, just in case a plate or frying pan came flying at his head. "Princess?"

No answer.

Shit. I'm screwed.

Silent treatment from Natalie was so much worse than arguing, because he didn't get to hear her voice and it meant her feelings were injured. Utter torture.

"Natalie," he said, easing himself inside the house, "I'm sorry. I was going to . . ."

August stopped short just inside the door, because a sight greeted him that he wasn't expecting. Natalie was standing in the middle of the kitchen, wringing her hands. She appeared to be . . . nervous? Why?

Did people get nervous before they asked for a divorce?

Probably.

Acid flooded his organs, so thick he could taste it in his mouth.

"I'm sorry," he said again, his voice in tatters. "I was going to tell you, but we're so happy and I didn't want you to lump me in with your father and Morrison and Savage. Listen to me, it's not what you think. Yes, I accepted an investment from Sam's father. But it wasn't because I didn't want your help with the bank loan. I wasn't rejecting you, the way I did with making our wine. That wasn't it at all, Natalie. I just wanted . . ." He strode forward and took her shoulders, stooping down enough to put them at eye level, alarmed beyond words to find hers full of tears. *Christ oh Christ. I swore I would never make her cry again.* "I wanted you to get your trust fund. Because you needed it and I love you. I wasn't sure you would marry me if the deal was one-sided. I married you because the first time we met, you took my heart home with you in a doggy bag and never gave it back. I never *want* it back." He was talking in circles. *Get it together.* "Keeping this secret wasn't about pride. Or about making the winery a success on my own. I just wanted to do something important for the woman who is my reason for getting out of bed in the morning. It was all out of love. Nothing else."

Several seconds passed in silence.

Then, to his surprise, she nodded.

"I have to tell you something, too," she whispered, trembling in his hands in a way that was causing him acute distress. "Oh God, August . . ."

"What is it? We can handle anything."

She sucked in a breath and let it out slowly. "The day of the wedding, my father called and offered to release my trust fund." She searched his eyes as the tears began to drip from her own. "I said no. Not because of my pride, either, but . . . because I *wanted* to marry you. I couldn't put a name to how I felt about you at the time, but . . ." She swiped at her eyes, a sob sneaking out. "I loved you—I know that now. I know it so deeply."

A rush of unimaginable happiness blew in and knocked him off his feet.

"Sorry, hold on." August fell sideways into one of the dining room chairs, the piece of furniture skidding loudly under the sudden influx of weight. "I can't breathe."

Natalie knelt down in front of him, fingers rushing over him, as if to check for an injury. When she didn't find one, she clasped his face in her hands. "August."

"I'm here. I just can't tell if I want to cry or throw up."

"Don't do either of those things."

"Gotcha." He took her face in his hands, too, marveling. Fucking marveling over this woman. He probably would still be reeling from the unexpected gift of her confession a hundred years from now. And as long as she was there to hold him, that would be quite all right.

Appearing dazed, she shook her head. "So, technically, we didn't have to get married. We just . . . wanted to?"

"Incorrect. I *had* to marry you."

"You know what I mean."

"I know that I love you," he rasped, kissing her hard, memorizing his wife's tear-stained face and the affection radiating from her. "I know that no matter how it happened, it was right. I can't breathe for loving you and loving you is the only way I can breathe."

She shot off the floor into his lap, where she belonged, planting kisses all over his face, which he was all too happy to sit back and receive, his mind still struggling to play catch-up. *God, if you're listening, please, please give me a century just like this.* "I love you just as much, August Cates," she said, finally, against his lips. "Despite the fights. Maybe even because of them. Because there is no one more worthy of battling for."

His wife, the love of his life, kissed him with tears in her eyes.

And at last the world made sense.

Epilogue

Eight years later

Over the course of eight years of marriage, Natalie had seen August mad plenty of times. They'd always been, and continued to be, hot-tempered individuals and they ran a successful winery together. Of course they argued. The beauty was in the forgiveness—and they did forgiveness *really* well. Whether they fought over temperature management of the wine or planting strategy, they didn't stay mad long. One of them usually caved after five minutes of silent treatment. And she meant "caved" in the literal sense, because the wine cave was usually where they ended up engaging in frenzied apologies out of earshot of their employees.

Yes, she'd seen August plenty mad. But never so mad as today, when he found out their daughter's dance partner hadn't shown up for a recital.

"They've been practicing for five months and he doesn't show up for the *recital*?" August started to pace, a handful of fingers shoving through his wind-blown hair, which now contained a dusting of gray at the temples. "How is she? Is she . . ." He waved his hands in a giant X. "Princess, don't tell me she's crying."

They were outside the school auditorium in a huge group. Natalie, August, Hallie, Julian, Corinne, and her new husband. August's parents were there, too, having flown in from Kansas for the big night. Truth be told, it was hard to keep August's parents *out* of Napa. They'd discovered a late-in-life passion for Cabernet and were now the proud owners of summer linens and straw hats, fitting in seamlessly with the locals. August's mother referred to her stylish new attire as her "wine pants," and Natalie adored the woman to no end. After all, she'd raised the love of Natalie's life. A man who'd taken to parenting like he was born to be a girl dad.

Which was a very good thing, because they had three.

Parker, the oldest at seven. Parks for short.

Elle, the youngest, at two.

Both were currently home with a babysitter—the same home where August had carried Natalie over the threshold. They'd simply kept adding on rooms.

The cat was still punishing them.

Samantha, their middle girl, was a very serious five and a half—and tonight was her jazz recital. Her older sister, Parker, played sports. August dedicated a lot of time to coaching her teams. When Samantha had expressed an interest in dance, he was very adamant that he give the same level of attention to his middle daughter's interests, so she wouldn't feel slighted. He might have stopped shy of teaching the dance class, but he'd asked so many questions at rehearsals that the teacher eventually started ignoring his raised hand.

"Naturally, she is a little upset, but we had some cookies and juice with the instructor, so she's gotten her courage back," Natalie said, laying a hand on August's arm and drawing him close.

"She's okay. It's not ideal, but she can still do the dance without her partner."

"There's a dip during the second transition, Natalie." August looked at her long and hard. "She can't dip herself."

Her heart crawled up into her throat. "You know, she's going to get through this. It's going to be a good lesson. Life gives us lemons sometimes—"

"No one gives my girls lemons," he said, visibly offended. "That goes double for my wife," he said, leaning down to kiss her. "No one better be giving you any lemons."

"No one is giving me lemons."

Her mouth seemed to be distracting him from the problem at hand. "You look insane tonight, you know that, right?" he said in a lowered voice, his gaze traveling down the front of her burgundy silk wrap dress, his right hand lifting to squeeze her hip. "I was going to tell you when we arrived, but you sprung this whole missing partner on me. Damn, look at your legs. I could literally eat you alive."

"Seeing as though our entire families are here," she whispered, gesturing for him to keep his own voice down, "... that might have to wait until later."

"You read my mind. Cave date tonight?"

"We might as well put a bed down there at this point."

"Smart *and* hot." He pressed his lips to the center of her forehead, his arms wrapping around her in a bear hug. "How'd I get this lucky?"

She took a deep inhale of his grapefruit scent and for a moment, there was nothing and no one but the two of them. This man whom she'd married under the guise of a marriage of convenience, but whom she'd been in love with all along. This man who'd become her best friend, business partner, biggest supporter, and co-parent. They were the best thing to ever happen to each other and neither one of them took it for granted.

Looking back, eight years had gone by at the speed of sound, and yet every moment was so vivid that she could replay them in slow motion. It was almost like living through those cherished memories twice. The evening they'd opened a bottle of their first vintage and it actually tasted decent? August had put Natalie on his back and run through the vineyard while she was still holding the open container. They were covered in wine by the time they collapsed and made love under the moon, the scent of grapes and earth filling her nose. Two years of hard work later, their wine had started pouring better than decent, and it was good timing, because she'd just found out she was pregnant with Samantha.

Funny, she'd never envisioned herself as a mother. Not until she met someone who reminded her she was fearless. Someone who imbued her with twice her strength, because they were a team. In everything. Made Natalie feel like such a vital part of a family that she started dreaming of expanding it. August's response to her broaching the subject of having kids?

Princess, I thought you'd never ask.

They didn't come out of their bedroom for a solid forty-eight hours.

Ten months later, August had passed out from sympathy pains in the delivery room and hit his head on a metal cart, resulting in nineteen stitches.

He still had the scar and claimed it made him even more attractive.

Natalie couldn't exactly disagree. Who didn't like a reminder that their husband had enough empathy and love in his heart that he could lose consciousness over it?

That was August. Empathy, love . . . and unconditional support. When she wanted to use her trust fund to buy shares in VineWatch, he'd supported her without question and watched proudly at her side as that investment quadrupled in the space of a year. She'd managed to convince Corinne and Julian to do the same, their faith in her healing a deep-down wound that had been lurking since childhood. The Vos family had definitely grown closer since then. Family dinners were messier, thanks to their girls. Julian and Hallie were also parents to a beautiful set of five-year-old twin boys. One of them was very serious and had a deep obsession with sharks. The other was wild to the bone and had once been found hanging from the dining room chandelier at Corinne's.

One day in the not-too-distant future, these cousins were going to paint St. Helena red.

For now, they had a dance recital crisis.

"Do you think I should go talk to her?" August asked now as he smoothed Natalie's hair. "Or am I going to make it worse?"

"You only make everything better," she said automatically.

He dipped his head on a smile that was almost bashful. "You doing that thing where you rewind the past and get all sentimental on me?"

She pressed her lips together tightly and nodded. "Maybe."

Slowly, his smile gave way to a serious expression. "If I had one wish, it would be to slow down my time with you, Natalie. A hundred years won't be enough."

If they kept this up, she was either going to swoon or cry in front of their entire family. With a big inhale, she straightened the collar of his dress shirt. "Go talk to Samantha. She needs you."

He studied her face for a long moment, as if memorizing every feature, before striding away. Natalie didn't know what made her follow. Maybe she wanted to provide parental backup if the waterworks started again. Or maybe she just wanted to witness a moment between August and their middle daughter. But for whatever reason, she crept in his wake toward the stage entrance and peeked in through the crack of the door.

There was Samantha, the spitting image of Natalie at that age, sitting on August's knee in her emerald green sequined dress and matching mini top hat. As Natalie had feared, her lower lip was trembling again. As strong as her impulse was to enter the room and comfort her baby, Natalie remained in place. August had this.

"You know what?" Natalie's husband gave an exaggerated look over both shoulders. "That kid always had snot in his nose, anyway."

Samantha giggle-sniffed.

"They'll say he has chicken pox, but we know the truth. He couldn't keep up with you."

"No," said their daughter, always logical. "He could. It's prolly just chicken pox."

"If you say so," August said skeptically. "Here's what I know. I'm going to be sitting in the audience thinking about how brave you are. All of us will. You're *so* brave, Samantha. Just like your mom. Remember that story I told you about her winning over that meanie in a suit in New York?"

"Yeah."

"And the one about her marrying a big doofus so she could follow her dreams?"

Samantha gasped. "You're not a big doofus."

"I was. Still am sometimes. It's a good thing you girls love me anyway.

"Remember when we were cleaning out the wine cave and a bat flew out. I screamed, but your mom didn't even flinch. You get your bravery from her."

Their daughter was quiet for a long moment, her tiny throat muscles starting to strain. "Dad?"

"Yeah?"

"Do I have to be brave alone?"

"Hell no, you don't," said Natalie's husband, no hesitation.

And that's how August ended up dancing as Samantha's partner in the recital, with a miniature green, sequined top hat pinned to his head, every move executed flawlessly. Yet another memory that Natalie would replay again and again for the rest of their lives.

Don't forget to check out Julian and Hallie's story!
Secretly Yours is available now.

And keep an eye out for Tessa's new series . . .

Wreck the Halls

A fun, sexy Christmas romance coming Fall 2023

About the Author

#1 *New York Times* bestselling author Tessa Bailey can solve all problems except for her own, so she focuses those efforts on stubborn, fictional blue-collar men and loyal, lovable heroines. She lives on Long Island, avoiding the sun and social interactions, then wonders why no one has called. Dubbed the "Michelangelo of dirty talk" by *Entertainment Weekly*, Tessa writes with spice, spirit, swoon, and a guaranteed happily ever after. Catch her on TikTok @authortessabailey or check out tessabailey.com for a complete list of her books.

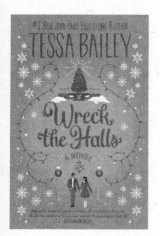